Dear Faye -
Enjoy the book and I
can't wait to attend

AN

UNCERTAIN

CURRENCY

a Crimewriter's meeting
at the Royal Norfolk!

Hope to see you soon,

Love,

January 2000
Brooklyn, NY

Dear Tony—

Enjoy the book and I
can't wait to attend

a Crimewriter's meeting
at the Royal Institute?

Hope to see you soon.
Cheers,

AN
UNCERTAIN
CURRENCY

by
Clyde Lynwood
Sawyer, Jr.
&
Frances Witlin

MEMENTO MORI MYSTERY

A Memento Mori Mystery
Published by
Avocet Press Inc
19 Paul Court
Chestnut Ridge, NY 10965
http://www.avocetpress.com

AVOCET PRESS

Library of Congress Cataloging-in-Publication Data

Witlin, Frances
    An uncertain currency / by Frances Witlin & Clyde Lynwood Sawyer, Jr. -- 1st ed.
    p. cm.
  ISBN 0-9661072-7-6 (alk. paper)
  I. Sawyer, Clyde Lynwood. II. Title

PS3573.I9153 U54 1999
813′ .54 — dc21   99-048075

Printed in the USA
First Edition

To:
Meher Baba and Adi S. Irani
Frey Faust
Poonam Srivastava
My long suffering parents and short suffering wife.

Mario Castigliani was twelve in 1948, a compact muscular boy dangling his legs into an archeological trench. *Il professore*, a bearded young scientist, Mario's new friend, was at work in the ditch, delicately probing the upper strata of exposed earth.

Excavation trenches crisscrossed the Umbrian hillside below Mario's home city, Perugia. The afternoon sky was immaculately blue. A breeze sparkled distant Lake Trastemino, stirred the poplars, and ruffled Mario's sun-bleached tangle of curls. The air smelled of wild anise and newly turned volcanic earth. He could hear cowbells made melodious by distance, the bronze tones of a monastery bell, and the soft *chunks* of the workmen's picks three trenches away.

Mario's sandalled feet, scratched by his truant scramble up the hill, hung level, he told himself, with the Middle Ages. The trench went down past the ancient Romans, deeper even than the Etruscans to whom Mario felt so powerfully drawn.

The professor laid his dental pick and brush on a stone near Mario. "Look what we found this morning," he said, handing the boy a tarnished octagonal coin. Mario could make out a lion's head and worn mysterious lettering.

And then, it happened. The undulant landscape and the earnest face of *il professore* dissolved into light. A shock stiffened Mario's spine. His eyes closed on luminous blankness. Energy flowed from the coin gripped in his hand. He exalted, throbbing with joy and vigor. Mario had discovered his muse. Or his muse had discovered him—a fickle, private miracle he would later name *la Lucia*.

I

A t six a.m. the August sun over Floraville, Georgia had burned
away the mist from the Flint River. The mill and the white frame
houses surrounding it lay exposed to the glare. Only in the hills to the
west, where the mansions of the millowners slumbered in the shade of
ancient oaks, was there any respite. On the state highway bypassing the
town there was little traffic—a bakery truck, another bringing newspapers from Columbus. Three farm pickups were parked outside the
Floraville Lunch, the sole establishment open on Main Street. Boxcars,
filled with five-hundred-pound bales of fiber, rumbled steadily out of
the freightyard on their way to the mill loading docks.

A few joggers panted along their customary routes. It was too early
for the stream of first-shift millhands to flow along the sidewalks. Several uniformed maids sauntered out of Blue Heaven, on their way to the
bus stop. They paused to stare at a solid red-haired woman, flushed and
out of breath, packed into jeans and a print blouse darkening with per-
spiration. She carried two lunchboxes, one old, one new, the new one
decorated with images of Barbie and Ken. A few tongues of pink paper
licked from inside it.

By ten a.m., Floraville was in the slow swing of its summer routine.
In the mills, workers guided yarn into the thundering looms; other crews
trundled the finished fabric into the stock rooms. In the park next to
Town Hall, two old men sat near the war memorial, warily eyeing the
formidable sun. A dozen laughing children, enjoying the last weeks of

vacation, played tag among the sprinklers. On the other side of Main Street, shoppers clustered under store awnings, complaining about the heat.

Except for the third-shift millworkers, only one man in town was still asleep. The shades were pulled down; a bedside fan stirred the stifling air. Mario Castigliani tossed on his lumpy hotel bed. He had arrived by bus, late in the night, but his exhaustion had deeper causes than his journey. Troubled dreams were driving him toward an obligatory wakefulness. He had much to do to prepare for his scheduled performance this weekend.

In a shock of light, his nightmare dissipated. He sat up, frowning at the open door and the lanky silhouette framed in it.

"Mr. Mario Castig-lioni? I'm real sorry to disturb you."

Mario pulled the sheet up over his chest.

"I'm the police chief here." The voice was low, polite but firm.

Ahi, a cop! Mario thought. And what have I done? I am a respected artist, guilty of nothing, *Signor* Policeman. Not yet fully awake, he tried to fathom the thoughts of the intruder. Mario smoothed his thinning mane of grey hair in a seemingly casual gesture. He yawned convincingly, massaging a spot between his eyebrows. This device usually helped to evoke his telepathic powers. But he received nothing from the man in the doorway. He must be one of those, Mario guessed, one of that two percent or so whose minds were closed to him.

"Saw your poster in the restaurant. I want to ask your help."

"*'Scuse*," Mario said, relieved. He waved noncommittally and got out of bed, using the sweaty sheet as a toga. In the bathroom he splashed himself with cold water and slipped into his maroon silk bathrobe.

The police chief had seated himself on the edge of the chair near the dresser. Mario rolled up the shade and offered his hand to his visitor.

"Tyler," the man said, rising. "Beaufort Tyler."

Mario gave the sinewy hand a precise, formal shake. He stepped to the noisy fan and clicked it off. "It does not help much," he apologized.

Tyler nodded. "Air conditioning still on the blink?"

"They promise it will be fixed this morning."

"Promises don't cost squat."

Daylight exposed the spartan economy of the room: the painted linoleum floor, the secondhand furniture. Mario's hand-tailored silk suit, worn at the cuffs, hung on the closet door. His silver hairbrushes lay on the dresser beside an open suitcase of finely crafted leather, scarred by countless journeys.

Mario's photograph gazed magnetically from a small stack of posters.

MARIO CASTIGLIANI
INTERNATIONALLY ACCLAIMED PSYCHIC
What Does The Future Hold For You?

Love? Money? Marriage?

Find Out Saturday, August 11, 8:00 PM
Pennington H.S. Auditorium
$10.00

Private Readings
Solved kidnap, murder and missing persons cases
Auspices: Rotary Club of Floraville: Youth Center Benefit

Two weeks ago his agent had sent a dozen posters to the editor of *The Floraville Weekly Clarion.* Mario had planned to tack up the rest the preceding night, but had arrived too late.

"How may I help you?" he asked Tyler, with an effort at patience.

Tyler pointed to the poster. "It says there you been on some police investigations."

Mario acknowledged this with a ghost of a bow. He had aged since the photo was taken; he was now in his fifties. Morning stubble blurred his handsome, leonine features. His grey eyes were veiled.

Tyler, fifteen years younger and a head taller than Mario, was ruddy and blond, his features irregular, high-cheekboned, with a prominent jaw. His keen blue eyes seemed to catalogue every detail of the room. He wore a badge and a service revolver. A police cap rested on his knee, above the sharp crease of his khaki trousers.

"Forgive me, Mr. Tyler. I've overslept. I must shave and dress and—"

"A man was found dead this morning," Tyler interrupted. "I think maybe he was murdered."

Mario's eyebrows went up. He did not look at the police chief. Money, he thought. *Che fortuna!* He studied the ornate cornice molding, disfigured by many coats of cheap paint. But what if *la Lucia* deserts me once again? His powers, to read thoughts directly; through hand-writing, or by holding objects, had flickered on and off throughout the past twenty-five years. "Are you requesting a private reading concerning this murder?"

Tyler shook his head. "I'm the only one thinks it's murder. The coroner, he's sure it's suicide."

"Who has died?"

"Old black man, name of Roy Washington. Sort of a local celeb-rity from the civil rights days. Look, Mr. Castig-lioni—"

"Casteel-yanee," Mario gently corrected him.

"Mr. Castigliani. You still interested in police work? I ought to warn you, the money won't be much. If you run over a couple thou-sand I have to clear it with the aldermen. But if you qualify…"

Mario raised his hand. "I do have a certain talent, Mr. Tyler. Yes. A clairvoyance, as it were. But to be frank, I cannot always depend on my gift. It has a will of its own."

His modesty, he knew, would protect him in case he drew a blank, and also gave the impression of scrupulous honesty.

"There is a problem of timing," Mario said. "Commitments. Book-ings. I must check with my agent." He gestured at the phone on the nightstand, detesting his lie.

Tyler's glance dropped to the fraying lapels of Mario's once el-egant bathrobe. "'Course I understand. Must be lots of demands on your time." He took out a pack of Marlboros and offered one to Mario.

"*Grazie, però no,*" Mario said, thinking, he sees through me. "I rarely smoke, and never in the morning." The mindreader's hand went to his forehead. No luck. A wall of steel. *Il diavolo nell' inferno!* How can I do this job if I cannot get into his head?

"Trying to kick the habit myself."

Mario thought, I like the man. He looks tired and worried, but still he is *gentile*. "You have made use of psychics before?"

"Never. All this ESP. Astrology. Crystal balls. Hope you don't mind me saying it, Mr. Castigliani, but I always thought it was a lot of…"

"Superstition and fraud," Mario said. "It may surprise you, Mr. Tyler, but I'm inclined to agree."

The police chief grinned uncertainly. "'Cept for you yourself, you mean?"

"My gift is a mystery, even to me. I cannot pretend to understand it. But it is genuine," Mario said with sincerity. "Perhaps somewhere there are others who possess it also. In all of my life, I have met only one. The rest were entertainers at best, charlatans at worst." He shrugged. "So. I honor your skepticism. But I find it puzzling that you consult me."

The police chief was silent. Mario reflected on the dead man. Elderly. Black. And mortal as am I. Is that something like grief on the policeman's face? And I, considering only my own advantage, he reflected with a twinge of shame.

"There is someone… who always wanted me to use a psychic on a murder investigation. But I've never had…" he faltered. He seemed about to say either 'psychic' or 'murder'.

"Someone…" Mario echoed.

His eyes went blank, as if sight had been sucked inward. The lids shut of their own accord. He swayed on the bed.

"Mr. Castigliani? You okay?"

Mario did not answer.

La Lucia had come back to him in all her radiant power. The trance, which opened minds and granted him visions where past became present, was upon him.

He heard a woman say, "One swallow doesn't make a summer." Her voice evoked the contralto tones of a violin. On his closed eyelids, Tyler's "someone" took form and face: a woman, dark, beautiful, troubled and troubling. How like she was to his own *amorosa,* dead more than twenty years! This vision was taller and slimmer, but had the same Etruscan look. Was she Tyler's beloved? His wife perhaps?

Tyler's love for her quickened in Mario's own blood. She drew closer, then so close he could see her richly fringed eyelids and a faint bluegreen vein on her forehead. Then she vanished.

Mario opened his eyes, now uncannily brilliant, and focussed point blank on the policeman. The impact pinned Tyler suddenly against the chairback.

"Jesus Almighty!" Tyler whispered.

Mario's gaze continued to the wall behind the police chief. Images flickered, some vague, some sharply delineated. Mario surrendered to them.

"The old man was hanged," he said hoarsely. "In a kitchen? I see a little old house. Books, many books."

Tyler's mouth was open. He nodded.

"A pink paper," Mario continued. "Crushed to a ball. On the floor of the kitchen."

A middle-aged woman in blue jeans. A framed news photo of an elderly black man, triumphant on the steps of a Federal Court House. A clock with a pendulum. Faces. Figures. All whirled before Mario, too fleeting to put into words. His heart pounded.

Then, *la Lucia* was gone. He saw no more: only the policeman transfixed on the edge of the chair and the blank wall behind him.

Mario covered his face with his large, aristocratic hands and bowed his head. He shuddered, then went limp. A tidal wave of gratitude washed over him. He felt Tyler's hand grip his shoulder.

"Whoa! Hold on there, buddy ro. Don't pass out on me."

Mario's breathing steadied. Tactfully disengaging Tyler's hand, he stood and shook his head to clear it. "*Grazie.* Thank you! Thank you so much. I am all right, *Signor* Tyler."

"All right?" the police chief exclaimed. "You're downright amazing."

"I was accurate then?"

"He was hanging." Tyler retrieved his cap from the floor and sat down again. "The flier was pink. Pretty damn scary. How would you know it was pink?"

Mario forced open the window. He leaned out, inhaling the thick humid air as though it were cool and refreshing. Then he smiled at Tyler. "A common color," he teased. "Perhaps a lucky guess."

"No!" Tyler insisted. "You saw it. I watched you seeing it."

"How do you know I wasn't there? In that house with the peeling white paint? Maybe it was I who did the murder."

Tyler laughed. "Looks like you got yourself one hell of a talent."

"Any skilled professional mindreader could have astonished you equally."

"I'm a hard man to astonish, Mr. Castigliani. If I'm right that Roy Washington was murdered—use your bag of tricks, if that's what they are. I don't give a nose-picking damn long as you help me find who did it. If you're interested in this job."

Mario nodded graciously. "If time will permit, I am willing to try."

Before they could shake hands, a beeper sounded in Tyler's hip pocket. He shut it off. "Mind if I use your phone?"

"By all means."

The pink shirt, Mario thought as he unpacked his suitcase, a lucky color. He took out a tarnished octagonal coin and tucked it into the shirt pocket. Then two books: a new paperback, *The Etruscan Language*; and the illustrated *Pottery and Sculpture of Ancient Italy*. He laid them on the lower shelf of the nightstand, noting that Tyler's eyes flicked to the titles.

Mario arranged his boxer shorts and T-shirts in a drawer. Though he seemed absorbed in his task, he caught every word of the phone conversation.

"Beau here. What's up, Ruthann? … They can take the body away. … Any luck finding Roy's daughter? … Try the Atlanta School Board, Candace Shapiro. … No. … No, the house stays sealed. The neighbors can carry their food on over to Cully Bates or somewheres. Let one of 'em offer his own house for the setting in. … Tell Bobby Lee I'm on my way."

Mario unrolled a pair of grey socks, the left one torn at the toe. He lobbed them into the wastebasket and took another pair. Now I can buy new ones, he thought, the hell with darning.

"Give Doc Osborne a call," Tyler was saying. "I want him at the hospital in half an hour. And don't let him give you any grief."

Is there a shoeshine stand nearby? Mario wondered, though his new calfskin loafers hardly needed polishing.

"How's Myrt doing, Ruthann? She get something to eat? … Take care of her, would you?" Tyler hung up and put on his cap. "I have to get moving, Mr. Castigliani. If you dress real quick, you could come along. I'd sure be obliged."

"I regret that I cannot. But if you wish, we can meet later." Mario glanced at his wrist, then remembered that his French watch was in New York, in an Eighth Avenue pawnshop, having financed this Floraville trip.

"Can you be in my office, say, four o'clock?" Tyler opened the door. "Right next to Town Hall."

"I will be there. *Arrivederci,* Mr. Tyler."

Mario shut the door and leaned against it. He felt like laughing, weeping. I need a celebration, he thought. Perhaps a festive brunch.

He remembered the violin tones of the dark magnetic woman. "One swallow doesn't make a summer." We say that in Italy, too, he told himself, except that our swallows arrive in the springtime. *"Una rondine non fa primavera."*

II

In the parking lot at the rear of the main building, two Floraville patrol cars and an ambulance baked in the sun. Swinging doors marked "Emergency" led into the hospital from the raised platform of the loading dock. Bobby Lee Petticord, a patrolman, and Andrew Abbot, a lieutenant, both under Beaufort Tyler's command, awaited his arrival. In spite of a conspicuous "Absolutely No Smoking" sign, they held lit cigarettes. The Lieutenant, black, in his thirties, a sardonic look on his sharp features, took slow, calculated drags and exhaled precise cones of smoke. Bobby Lee was pacing. His cigarette ash dropped unnoticed to the white concrete.

"Think he'll fire me, Andrew?" Bobby Lee was in his early twenties, his round face haloed by whiteblond hair through which the pink scalp was visible.

"Can't tell," Abbot replied. He leaned unrelaxed against the steel column with the No Smoking sign. The temperature had risen, but he was not sweating.

"Dammit all to hell, Andy—"

"Andrew."

"What's wrong with reading the Bible out loud? Is that a crime? Why'd he have to get so riled?" The patrolman stomped out his cigarette and wiped his brow with a blue bandanna.

"Quit bullshitting, Bobby Lee. You screwed up. Lost the place in the Bible. Smeared fingerprints from here to kingdom come."

"So I'm not perfect. What d'you expect at the crack of dawn after double shifts three days in a row?"

"Even the most raggedy-assed civilian knows you don't touch anything at a murder scene." Abbot made a grimace of distaste at his half-smoked cigarette and arced it into the parking lot.

"Hey. That weren't no murder. That old gasper strung hisself up as sure as you're standing here."

The lieutenant stiffened against the column. "Aren't we blessed we got a Sherlock like you on our team. Solved it already, did you." He took a step toward Bobby Lee. "Royal Washington was a giant in this town. And giants don't kill themselves."

"Doc Osborne says he did. And he's the coroner, right. And the boys on the ambulance—"

The roar of Tyler's souped-up cruiser interrupted Bobby Lee.

"That's him," Abbot said, as Tyler whipped the car into the ambulance bay. The chief braked to a stop, shut off the engine and mounted the stairs with a racehorse economy of motion. He and Abbot exchanged curt nods.

"Chief Tyler, listen." Bobby Lee tugged at Tyler's sleeve. "I remembered! You know that Bible?"

"Damn right I do."

"It was open way to the back. About fighting the good fight, marked with a pencil."

"One Timothy four. Verse six or seven," Abbot volunteered. "'I have fought a good fight, I have finished my course, I have kept the faith.'"

"For sure, Bobby Lee?" asked the chief. "Or you just covering your ass?"

"For sure."

Tyler scrutinized him, then turned to the lieutenant. "Duane show up?"

The lieutenant grunted, then said, "He did. We sealed the house, and I posted him on the porch."

"Who lives next door?"

"Cully Bates. The barber. And on the other side, Tonda Whitley and her grandkids."

"Cully see anything?"

Abbot shook his head. "Went to bed early. But Durrell—"

"The paper boy?"

"Only one Durrell Whitley in town, and he's the paper boy. He says he saw some tramp lurking around."

"Where?"

"Right there on Ruby Street. About ten p.m. Dirty clothes. Ragged beard."

"Okay, Andrew. Radio Duane and see can he get more description out of the boy. Then tell Ruthann to put out an APB on the tramp."

"10-4," said the lieutenant, starting down the steps.

"How about you, Bobby Lee. Find anything?"

"Couple of paint cans. Old cigarette butts. Rusty washing machine. Nothing in the garage shed, only some tools." A year ago Roy's illness had worsened and he had sold his car.

"What about the garden?"

"Gone all to ruin," Bobby Lee said, "'cepting the snap beans."

Tyler considered this. "Look like anybody been at 'em?"

Bobby Lee blushed. "Come to think of it, the vines were … sort of picked over."

Abbot, on the way to his patrol car, gave a short laugh. "You reported it, of course, Bobby Lee," he called.

"Well, no, I thought maybe Roy hisself—"

"Hell's bells, Bobby Lee," Tyler said. "Are you messing up again? Any footprints?"

"Ground's dry as a brick. I looked real careful."

A white, late-model Lincoln rolled into the parking lot and lurched to a stop. Doc Osborne heaved himself from the driver's seat, pulled out a briefcase, and slammed the door. His dyed black hair glinted dully metallic under the pitiless sunlight. Tall, paunchy, in his rumpled seersucker suit, he looked like a sack of laundry.

Abbot hung up the radio receiver on his dashboard and joined the coroner. "Pipe you aboard, Doc?"

Osborne grunted. He panted up the six steps to the platform, Abbot behind him.

"Appreciate you coming over." Tyler stretched out his hand.

The coroner brushed it aside. "Pain in the butt," he growled. "I already informed you it's suicide. I can't go running all over the county, because you get a wild hair up your ass."

Tyler steered him to the swinging doors leading to Emergency.

"They're holding the body in Pathology," he said as he maneuvered the coroner through the doors. A shock of chill, conditioned air struck them. "You know the way. I'll be with you in two shakes."

Tyler watched as Osborne waddled grumbling along the corridor. "Bobby Lee, you swing by the Floraville Lunch. See if anybody strange came in there last night or this morning. Put your ears on. If you hear anything at all, phone it in to Ruthann. Another thing. My crime scene photos should be back from Columbus in an hour or so. Have the drugstore deliver them right to the stationhouse. Then go get yourself some sleep."

"Type up my report first?"

"It can wait."

"Do I have to put in, like—" The patrolman hung his head. "—about the Bible? And Roy's garden."

"Write: Book of Timothy. Write: Somebody maybe picking the beans."

Bobby Lee beamed, mopped his scalp with his bandanna, and set his cap at a rakish angle. "I surely do want to thank you, Chief."

Tyler frowned. "No call for that, Officer. Get going. And act like you got the sense you were born with."

Bobby Lee went down the steps, saying, "Yessiree, yessiree." and crossed the parking lot.

Abbot and Tyler eyed each other. The rasp of the cicadas came to them from the scrub pines.

"Your instructions, Chief?" the lieutenant inquired evenly.

Tyler took an envelope from his hip pocket and removed from it the creased pink flier. "Bobby Lee tell you about this meeting tonight?"

"He did."

"Any idea what Roy and Myrt were cooking up?"

"Nary a glimmer." Abbot's large bright eyes, the whites very clear, stared at Tyler, who lowered his gaze. "You want the Blue Heaven scuttlebutt on that meeting?"

"Yes," said Tyler.

"Should I ask around the mill too?"

"I'll cover that."

"Yeah, figures," Abbot said bitterly.

"In Blue Heaven," Tyler told him, "we don't want just the mill stuff. We want everything. And check the backyards. The culverts and drainage ditches."

"Aye, aye, sir, as we used to say in the Navy." Abbot straightened. He was two inches taller than the chief. "Not my place to ask, I know, but who's minding the store?"

Tyler shifted his shoulders under the steady regard, and added, "Vernon Bond signs in at three o'clock."

The lieutenant said nothing.

"Crying out loud, Andrew," Tyler added. "That's plenty of manpower. Floraville isn't exactly in the middle of a crime wave."

"Kevin told me some perps unknown jacked up Huey Easton's MG and got his whitewalls." Abbot smiled, a slow dazzling smile. "The Baptist Ladies League is screaming that Tape & Disk is bootlegging filthy albums. And the plastic pigs in front of the Big Bad Wolf Barbecue got kidnapped again."

"Ruthann and Vernon can cope. We'd better get started, Andrew. They're waiting for me inside."

"Yes, sir. But don't you want me to try to get a current address for Roy's daughter?"

"Candy!" Tyler exclaimed. "'Course I want you to. I don't know how I forgot to tell you."

"By great good fortune," Andrew said, "I did not forget." His stare was implacable.

Tyler returned it unsteadily. "Andrew. Lieutenant Abbot. You've got to cut this out."

"It's not fair." Abbot said. He was referring to Beaufort Tyler's appointment as Chief of Police a year ago after the death of Chief Rutherford Kendall.

"No. It isn't fair," Tyler agreed.

"I earned it. I was in line for it. I'd have been a good chief."

Tyler tugged at his cap, setting it more firmly on his head. "So what could I do about it? If I turned it down, would they have given it to you?"

"I do my job," Andrew said sullenly.

"So do I. And right now our job is Roy Washington."

Outside the swinging doors, discreetly labelled Pathology, four people were waiting. Terry Hapgood, a male nurse, with golden hair and the tense grace of a classic statuette, stood guard to the left. He held a paperback, which he was nervously flexing. Margaret Flannery, the head nurse, in her fifties, corsetted and immaculate, was jotting notes on a clipboard.

"How do," Tyler said to the head nurse, and, "How do, Terry."

Doc Osborne leaned against a gurney, his briefcase on the floor beside him. He was talking with Reid Taliaferro, editor of *The Floraville Clarion*, a stubby impish man with a neatly trimmed beard. He scribbled in a reporter's notebook and chewed on an unlit stogie.

"According to statistics," Taliaferro was saying around the cigar, with a touch of provocation, "suicide is extremely rare in black men over sixty." A rumpled suit jacket was over his arm. He was wearing red suspenders.

The coroner pushed his bulk upright. The gurney slid a few feet along the wall. "You just listen here, Reid Taliferro" (which he, as everyone else in Floraville, pronounced as "Tolliver"). "If I say it's a suicide, you damn well better realize I know what I'm talking about."

"Hey, Beau," Taliaferro exclaimed, turning away from Osborne. "How did you find out, Reid? You got a nose six miles long."

"The proverbial little birdie." Reid flipped to a fresh sheet in his notebook. "I understand you don't support this suicide theory."

"It's not my job to speculate publicly about cases under investigation," Tyler said stiffly. He added with a shrug and a grin, "Hell, you know that, Reid."

"And it's my job as a journalist to get the whole story," Reid retorted lightly. "Relax, Beau, we got no quarrel here."

"You all and your little jobs," Terry Hapgood said. "Can't you think one minute about the man in there on the slab?"

"He was a patient here," said Margaret Flannery. "A real handful, but we all thought a lot of him."

Tyler gave each of the staff members a hard speculative look, and then turned to Taliaferro. "Do me a favor, Reid. Go on write your obit. This story's not ripe yet."

"I got to print more than an obit," protested the editor. "Roy's front page news."

"Soon as anything breaks, I'll let you know," Tyler put an arm around Taliaferro's shoulders. "Have I ever let you down?"

Osborne cleared his throat. "If I instruct my secretary to phone in my statement," he said to Taliaferro, "I assume you will give it the prominence it deserves. After all, I do represent the County." Osborne stood taller and crossed his arms over his belly.

Taliaferro took one last bite on his stogie, tossed it into the wastebasket and headed down the hall.

"Kindly explain to me," Osborne challenged Tyler, "why this *corpus delicti* was brought here instead of to the funeral home."

Nurse Flannery glanced at her clipboard. "Dr. Donlan offered to hold the body for twenty-four hours."

"At my request," Tyler added.

"You are not talking me into any autopsy," Osborne said. "Sick old dying widower. Put yourself in his shoes."

"Look, Doc, what harm could an autopsy do? If I'm wrong, that'll prove it. Two suicides by hanging," Tyler reminded him, "in less than a year. I don't buy it." He was referring to the death of his predecessor, Chief Rutherford Kendall. "Folks hereabouts mostly suck on their pistols. Or switch on the motor with the garage door down."

"Why don't you all just give him a decent burial," Terry said. "A guy has the right to put himself out of his misery."

"Listen here, son," said Osborne. "You're talking violating the law. The law of God and the sovereign State of Georgia. What good will it do to go cutting him up? Without even asking his kinfolk."

"We've been trying to reach his daughter," Tyler told him.

"She's not all that hard to find." said Margaret Flannery. "She's over in Macon."

"She was teaching school up in Atlanta the last I heard." Tyler said.

"You're out of date," said Nurse Flannery. "She's secretary at the Tabernacle now." The Tenfold Tabernacle was a small aggressive radio and television ministry. "Helping out Reverend Plenty. She married one of the deacons, Mr. Howard, three months ago."

Tyler's eyebrows shot up. He took his pad from his breast pocket and jotted a note. "What happened to Greg Shapiro?"

"They split up," Terry said.

"Humph," said Osborne, "I predicted that wouldn't last."

Tyler was already at the wall phone, saying, "Put me through to the police station." Osborne and the staff members avoided each others' eyes until he rejoined them. "Candace should be phoning us soon," he said.

"She's never gone give permission for anybody to go cutting up on her father," Nurse Flannery warned.

"Her permission is not required," Osborne said officiously. "If I authorize an autopsy, twenty daughters cannot veto it." To Tyler he said, "But as I have repeatedly informed you, I do *not* intend to authorize."

"It isn't like you, Doctor Osborne, to make such an error in judgement. If you'll pardon my saying so." The new voice was persuasive and charming. A.J. Donlan, M.D., Director of Warren Memorial, had joined them unobserved. He was fifty, but at first glance appeared no more than half that age.

His smile swept the staff members. There was a quality almost theatrical in his stance, as though he were enjoying their deference and their surprise at his sudden appearance. "Margaret. Terry." Between the two fair-haired men, Terry Hapgood and Dr. Donlan, there passed a questioning glance, quickly cut short. "Good to see you, Beau. It's been too long." He put his small, large-knuckled hand on Tyler's forearm. The director and Osborne had both used their influence in getting Tyler appointed police chief.

Donlan offered his hand to the coroner, who stood tall, and respectfully sucked in his paunch.

"Well, now," said Osborne, shaking hands. "Case like this doesn't require... 'Course, I always would be... uh... guided by your opinion."

"When in doubt, test it out, isn't that what you always tell me?" Donlan said lightly. "And the Chief, at least, seems to doubt this is a suicide."

"He was sure alive when he underwent strangulation," Osborne offered. "Pinpoint hemorrhages in the eyeballs."

"I'm sure you did your usual thorough preliminary," the director reassured him. "But we ought to go in.... This could be a landmark autopsy."

"How so?" asked Osborne.

"Chief Tyler..." Terry Hapgood said in an uncertain voice. He held his paperback close to his white-clad chest. It was titled *Let Me Die Before I Wake*. "I've got to go. Pressures and temps, on E wing." He was already moving along the corridor.

The wall phone rang, and Tyler stepped to it.

"Royal Washington was a keystone patient in our byssinosis research," Donlan told Osborne. "I would dearly love to take a look at the pulmonary area myself."

"I'll give Vergil a call," Osborne said. "So you can participate." Vergil Cox was the County Medical Examiner.

"Ah! Then you are going to authorize. Wise decision!"

"Seeing as how you advise it." Osborne picked up his briefcase and opened it on the gurney. He selected an authorization form. "Would you prefer the county morgue or a funeral home?" he asked, scribbling rapidly.

"Actually, I was thinking—" Donlan indicated the pathology lab. "We have ample equipment to do it here."

Osborne stopped writing, paused, then nodded. "The very latest, I imagine," he said.

"Margaret, could you assist?"

She consulted her schedule. "After three o'clock I could, Dr. Donlan."

Osborne was completing the form. "Wouldn't mind sitting in on this one myself."

Tyler joined them as they went into the lab.

"I just spoke to her," he said. "Candace. She took it hard."

"How does she feel about an autopsy?" Nurse Flannery asked.

"She wants it. Says this has to be murder."

Osborne grunted. "So who done it? Candy know?"

"She's driving right up, Doc," Tyler said off-handedly. "Let's ask her."

The pathology lab was ten degrees cooler than the corridor. The dimmed lights caught the gleam of the stainless steel table, the arched sink spigots, and the massive wall refrigerator. Nurse Flannery pressed a switch, flooding the room with fluorescence.

A woman in an aide's pink uniform was standing beside the

refrigerator. A waist-level drawer was pulled out half-way. On it lay the body, covered with a pale green sheet.

"Demetria, what on earth are you doing in here?" Nurse Flannery exclaimed.

Demetria Owens was broadhipped and narrow-shouldered, with the homely look of a backcountry woman. Her features, pendulous in her freckled face, expressed a sorrow incongruous in that chill impersonal laboratory.

"Somebody gotta stay here with him," she said, as the others drew near. She folded the sheet back to reveal Roy's staring, twisted face. "He look like old Satan hisself is after him."

"You knew him?" Tyler said to Demetria. He reached out as though to touch Roy's dead suffering face, then drew his hand back.

"'Deed I did," said Demetria.

"He was a good man," said Tyler. "I'm gonna miss him."

"Weren't no saint," sighed Demetria, "but Jesus already done forgive him."

Osborne cleared his throat ostentatiously.

"We sympathize with you, Ms. Owens," Dr. Donlan said, "but you really should not be in here."

Demetria bobbed her head respectfully, and then said to the nurse. "I'd be glad to fix his face peaceful, like I learned how from my grandmamma."

"We'll take care of that, Demetria," Nurse Flannery said with a glance at Dr. Donlan. "You go on now."

Demetria's sorrow-filled eyes regarded her, then Tyler, then the director. "You hear that?" she said softly to the dead man. "They're gone take care."

They watched her plod away through the swinging doors.

"She's quite right, you know," Donlan said. "We should indeed... ah... adjust his features."

"Before his daughter gets here," Tyler agreed.

"I'll give Vergil a ring," Osborne said. "Or, you know something, Doctor, you could do the autopsy yourself. Private arrangement, save the County some money. Since the next of kin is willing."

Tyler nodded.

III

The hotel HOT tap produced volcanic rumblings and a rusty trickle. Mario showered and shaved in the tepid flow from the cold tap, and dressed with the speed of a professional performer. In the mottled mirror backing the closet door, he saluted his image: I look ten years younger this morning, he told himself. Smart, yet tasteful. *La bella figura.*

He called the desk and asked to be put through to his agent.

"Leland and Katz," said Dawn Gilbert, the secretary, in her languid Olympian tones. Mario's clairvoyance did not function on telephones, but he had no difficulty imagining her: corn-rowed hair; earrings dangling against her long black neck; lounging at her desk, calmly doing her nails. In contrast, the office, papered with theatrical posters, had an air of almost frantic activity: loud phone calls, messengers coming and going.

Traffic sounds from Seventh Avenue and 45th Street, fifteen storeys below the office, reached Mario. A man's high-pitched whine in the background: "Hell, Solly, he's a total wimp. Kind a guy would stop for a red light."

"Hiyo, Romeo," Dawn sang out. "How you doing way down there in magnolia country?"

Under the breeziness, Mario heard something cold and wary. "Let me speak with Bernie," he said.

"Uhh, he's tied up just this minute, sweetie. Conference call."

"I gather no bookings have come in for me, *Aurora mia?*" Mario bounced gently on the lumpy unmade bed, enjoying himself.

"Well, you know how it is, Mario. Tough all over. Those East European circuses are filling all the slots."

"Never mind, *bellissima*. I'll leave it in your good hands... Green nails today?"

"No, Platinum Glitter, something new. He'll want to talk to you."

"I promise to get back to him later." He hung up and said to himself, much, much later.

Still smiling, he slid a half dozen posters into his briefcase, then took from it a slim folder of newspaper clippings. Which to show Tyler? "Clairvoyant Locates 'Kidnapped' Teenager." "Psychic Directs Police in Park Search." Not that one. That case had not worked out. He selected the four best stories and put the other four back in his briefcase.

There was a letter in the folder, too. It had been in his mailbox when he was leaving New York yesterday. He had stood in the foyer weighing it in his hand, averting his eyes from the hand-addressed envelope. Psychic insight from handwriting was one of *la Lucia's* gifts: off-and-on, undependable, sometimes unavoidable. Not always welcome.

The letter was from his daughter. The upper left corner of the envelope bore the feminine symbol as a logo and was engraved with her Madison Avenue address. On the plane to Atlanta, and the long bus ride to Floraville, he had been too down in spirit to read it.

Typed, he now noted gratefully; then shrank from the signature in Lauren's neat, careful handwriting. Her image was before him immediately, a squat woman of thirty-seven in a Norma Kamali suit which did nothing to alleviate her plainness. The cap of hennaed curls her hairdresser had provided, and her expert make-up, failed similarly. She strongly resembled her maternal grandmother, a servant woman of peasant origin who looked the role. Mario pressed his fist to his throat, against the sharp pang of pity his daughter always evoked in him. My poor Laura, *fanciulletta mia*, not everyone can be beautiful. Beautiful inside, like your Nonna, that's what counts. He squirmed at the canting hypocrisy of his own thought. *Certamente* it is what counts if scrubbing floors is your ambition, he told himself.

Her hard contemptuous thoughts now came at him like wasps: You trickster, you deadbeat, you sleazy Italian quack.

"Dear Father," said the letter. "Once again your check

failed to arrive as promised. How can you let me down like this?" Oh, my Laura. *Scusate!* They cancelled my booking, you see.

The letter went on, "This course in Corporate Dynamics may well be the key to all I have been striving for."

And for what are you striving, my daughter? Mario speculated.

Chairman of the board, her image retorted. **I mean Chairperson.** Of what? he asked silently. RJR-Nabisco? Time Warner?

Why not? he heard her reply coldly.

"As I informed you," the letter continued, "the classes are strictly limited to dedicated candidates. I count myself fortunate to have been recommended by one of my sisters at our WomanRap sessions who has already won promotions due to her CD training."

Mario thought of the seventy-thousand dollar salary his daughter was earning as a programmer, and her equally impressive income several years ago as an analyst on Wall Street.

Perchè non you pay the three thousand dollars, he thought, but immediately, apologetically, he withdrew the challenge. It was I who offered, after all, he rebuked himself. She is always without money, my Laura, *sempre* in debt. The big rent. The designer clothing.

"I ask you now to put the $1,000 advance in the mail the moment you receive this letter. Please, Father! I'm counting on you. *Your daughter, Lauren.*"

Tomorrow, *fanciulletta*, he promised silently, I will do just as you say. He tossed the letter into a bureau drawer and then shook himself as though shaking off the problems of his daughter.

"Lunch," he exclaimed aloud. The sign on the restaurant adjacent to the hotel had said 'Luigi's'. A *paglia,* or a *scaloppina*, or even just *spaghetti marinara al dente*. A big salad, a little *vino*.

He locked the door and started down the musty corridor. An ill-kempt tortoise tabby limped toward him, her tail held high. She meowed faintly and held out her left front paw.

Mario hunkered down and set his briefcase on the threadbare carpet runner. "Eh, little mamma cat, what's troubling you?" Many times in the course of the years he had wished he had the power to read the thoughts of animals. How pure and how honest they must be, as compared to humans!

The paw had an open cut and was hot to the touch. "And it is to me, Mario, you turn in your *dolore, eh, gattina mia,*" he murmured. "I am deeply honored."

He examined her gently, noting the slight swelling and tenderness of the mammaries. Then he tucked his briefcase under his arm and used both hands to carry the compliant cat down to the lobby desk.

The Gilmore had once been a fine hotel. Square pillars, one of them displaying Mario's poster, were of oak, glowing with varnish. The desk was carved rosewood. The wallpaper was peeling; the red leather couches patched with duct tape. But the general effect was still impressive.

Near the tall glass doors of the main entrance, a mop, pail and broom were leaning against one of the pillars. Mario saw a bald, skinny black man tending a potted palm which appeared to be dying. His thought came to Mario: **Tree perk up now. Otis gonna give you all the water you want.**

Through the open windows Mario could see two white-haired women on the veranda. They were seated on high-backed rocking chairs, one crocheting, one tuning a radio.

A hatchet-faced man in shirt-sleeves, wearing a grease-spotted tie, was behind the desk. He leaned forward, frowning at the doors, his clenched fists pressed to the counter. So where is the Hindu creep, Mario heard him thinking. **Why the hell can't he ever be on time.**

At the far end of the desk, a thin boy of about ten was polishing the brass of an old-fashioned lamp. **You mean son-of-a-bitch bastard,** he was thinking. **You know my friends are waiting on me.**

Mario slowed in his walk to the desk, nearly stumbling as the thoughts of all five persons rushed at him simultaneously:

Poor pitiful little old palm tree. You gotta be brave now. You gotta believe.

Leave that radio alone, Cora. You'll get us in trouble again.

I forget just where on the dial for Reverend Plenty—

Oh looka here who's coming. The Eyetalian con artist hisself.

I ain't gonna shine up all the brass in this whole hotel, you hear me, Daddy?

The cat trembled on Mario's hands and made a faint questioning sound deep in her throat. "*Non disturbate,*" Mario told her. He concentrated intensely, defending himself against the multiple invasion of his mind. He focussed on the man behind the desk, who was now sycophantically smiling at him, displaying tobacco-stained teeth.

'Kirby Garison, Prop.' said a crudely lettered sign above the panelled key rack behind him.

"Well, well, Mr. Castig-lian, I see you slept pretty good, didn't ya. That animal pestering you?" Mario heard him thinking **Beau Tyler's new sidekick, so I better watch my step.** Tyler had stopped by the desk on his way out, to demand in his quiet authoritative way the immediate repair of the air conditioning system: Mario envisioned a flash of that interchange.

"She seems to have injured her paw," he said.

The boy had stepped softly behind Garison, the can of brass polish in his hand. He stared eloquently at Mario. **He throwed her clean out the window yesterday. When she got underfoot. She hurt it then.**

You keep your blabbermouth shut, boy, Garison was thinking. "This here's my son Scott," he told Mario. "Pretty smart young squirt, if I say so myself. He'd sure admire to meet a real magician like you."

Mario nodded at the boy, noting the bruises on his cheekbone and arms. The cat, now on the desk, held her sore paw high and kept her bright yellow gaze on Mario.

"The cut is infected," Mario said to Garison. "If you will permit me… I have worked as a veterinarian, you see." He took his key from his pocket and held it out to Scott. "In my room, in the medicine cabinet, is a tube of antiseptic. Optopan Heilsalbe." He had bought it in Cologne three years ago when he was performing there. He found it more efficacious for shaving cuts and other small injuries than anything in the American drugstores.

The boy accepted the key and slipped away to the staircase.

"Mighty good of you to trouble yourself, mister," Garison said. "The air conditioning repairman's on his way. Everything else to your satisfaction? If you're wanting any extras…" **Maybe he'd like a nice piece of tail. Or some reefer. Nah. Happy dust's more his style.**

Mario, poker-faced, mentioned the lack of hot water and the uncomfortable mattress. His eyes were on the register, which he was skillfully reading upside down. William Friedrich, Chicago; Buster Culpepper, Sumter, S.C. A dozen other names of earlier dates, including two "Mr. & Mrs. Robert Smiths" in different handwritings. Mario's trick memory stored the information, while *la Lucia* helped him to receive insights: Friedrich was a salesman for an exterminating company, Culpepper a college football scout.

How good she is to me today, *la Lucia!* Mario thought. But he dared not bank on her help. He must go on stage prepared to perform without her.

From the veranda, the sonorous rhythms of black pulpit oratory blared and were quickly tuned down. "...and brethren, remember this lesson, that God wants you to prosper—"

"You shut that right off, Miz Cora!" Garison called loudly. The radio was silenced. To Mario he said, "Colored radio station. That's Miz Cora Danziger and her sister Hazel. They know good and well I don't allow it in this hotel." **That cheap nigger preacher,** he was thinking, **trying to get hold of Miz Cora's money.**

The proprietor was now reprimanding the man tending the palm. "Otis! Would you quit jawing at that tree? Boiler trap needs fixing. And I want you to tote the mattress out of the Governor Suite. Talks to plants all the time," Garison told Mario, lowering his voice. "He's missing a few spokes. But he's harmless."

He laid a finger against his nose and winked slowly as Otis picked up his mop and pail. Mario, aware of the oppression of the handyman, repressed a shudder.

Scott was back, shyly holding out the key and the tube of salve. But Mario was distracted, receiving a revelation from Garison. The cat stirred under Mario's automatically caressing hand, while he heard Garison silently say: **Bet Beau's paying you a pretty penny. What'll you do, conjure up Roy's spook?**

Mario thought *Roy.* Roy Washington, Tyler had said. The old man found dead this morning.

Will there be a reward?, Garison was thinking. **I could tell them a thing or two. Don't Tyler know old Earl was sprung Monday? How about that.**

"Won't hurt her, will it?" Scott was asking. "The medicine, I mean."

With an effort, Mario pulled himself free of Garison's dark inner monologue and smiled at the boy. "No. It does not smell good, but it will ease her pain."

"Is it magic?"

Mario laughed. "No, just a good antiseptic." He applied the salve carefully to the tremulous paw. The cat gazed at him, half fearful, half trusting.

"Critter sure took a shine to you, Mister," said Garison. "She ain't normally so friendly."

Mario sensed the wave of pure hatred that passed from the boy to his father. **Serve you right if this here cat scratched up your ugly face.** To Mario he said, "Should I fetch you a clean rag for a bandage?"

"No," Mario replied. "Let the air help to heal it. Can you make her a comfortable bed?"

Scott nodded. "In a box."

Mario gave him the tube of ointment. "Apply it tonight, and again tomorrow morning. Twice a day until she's well."

The cat stood up and rubbed her whiskers against Scott's hand. "Gosh, look at that," the boy said. "You sure it ain't magic?"

Garison said, "Guess we got to catch Mr. Castig-lian's show for that. Except who can afford ten bucks."

"Allow me," said Mario. He took his wallet from his breast pocket and produced three complimentary tickets. "One for Mrs. Garison," he said. The wispy gray woman who had signed him in last night was, he assumed, the downtrodden wife of the proprietor.

Mrs. Garison she ain't, he heard Kirby's thought. **Common law's good enough for that slut.** Aloud he said, "Yeah, well, she can't go, the missus. Somebody got to be on the desk here. But I'd sure like to invite Mr. William Friedrich. Traveling gentleman staying at the hotel."

"If Momma wants to go," Scott said, "I could mind the desk." He was cradling the cat who had fallen asleep in his arms.

"No, no," Mario told him. He took out a fourth ticket. "I'm depending on you to assist me. But don't expect rabbits from a hat. I am not a magician, I am a mindreader."

A short, rotund man of brown complexion had quietly come to the desk. "Mr. Garison," he said, extending his hand to the proprietor. "Now I am here as we arranged." He had a slight accent.

An hour late as usual, Garison was thinking as he gingerly shook the hand. "Afternoon, Mr. Patel."

Mario was made aware that the new arrival, originally from India, was eager to purchase the Hotel Gilmore, and that Kirby Garison was eager to sell it to him. Also that the two distrusted and despised each other heartily.

Mario tucked his briefcase under his arm while his forefinger massaged the spot between his brows. He made a swift search of Garrison's mind, hoping for some further reference to Roy Washington. But he found only sums of money and bargaining ploys.

"Gentlemen, I must take my leave of you," he said, nodding to Kirby and the Indian. To the boy he said, "She is a fine cat. Take good care of her."

"I will," Scott promised.

"How is she called?"

Garison interrupted his business conversation to laugh. "Mostly just Cat, or Damncat."

"Her name's She-Ra," Scott declared firmly.

As Mario left the desk, he bumped lightly into an innerspring mattress which Otis was carrying to the staircase. The pale blue satin ticking was mended, but in good condition. Mario could not see the man for the mattress; but he was arrested by what was going on in the handyman's mind. Otis was singing a silent song, a simple chant:

> "Old Royal danced on the air,
> Old Royal done gone from us,
> Gonna be a tree,
> Gonna be a peach tree,
> Flowerin' in springtime..."

How does he know about this death, and what does he know, Mario wondered. He was strongly tempted to talk to Otis, but he was hungry and feeling the press of time. Later, he told himself as he went through the main doors.

The full blast of the August day struck him in the face. The sun glared white in a pearl blue sky; only the roof of the wide veranda offered shade.

The thick air made Mario cough. He paused, aware of the Danziger sisters in their white wicker rocking chairs. They were deep in a low-voiced, impassioned argument. He could hear their words and their thoughts.

"It's every penny we have in the world," the elder sister was protesting. She was primly dressed in a dark print with a white collar, her hair in a neat silver bun. She wore bifocals and no makeup.

"Nothing ventured, nothing gained," retorted the sister Garison had called Cora. She wore a frilly yellow frock and large rhinestone earrings. Her makeup and curly hair-do were in the elaborate style of the 1930s.

"Cora, you're scaring the life out of me. Speculation, risk. Didn't we have enough of that with Papa?" Her thoughts were harsher. **A fool and his money... Headstrong reckless gambler just like him.**

"Poppycock. Reverend Plenty's a man of God, Hazel. What could be safer?" **You pokey old maid,** she added silently.

Mario, picking up pointers for possible use at his performance, stood very still, but Cora, who was impatiently tossing her head, underwent a transformation. Her cross expression gave way to a smile of dazzling dentures. She cocked her head archly and raised her plucked eyebrows.

"*Signor* Castigliani," she cried, with correct pronunciation. "*Benvenuto a* Floraville!" **Holy saints, would you look at him! He's gorgeous.**

Mario made his little bow and approached the rocking chairs. "*Parla Italiano, Signora?*"

"*Poco, poco...* I'm Cora Danziger, and this is my sister Hazel." The elder sister gave him a shy sweet smile and turned pink.

"We're looking forward to your show Saturday night," Cora continued.

"I am honored," said Mario, "to make the acquaintance of my fellow guests at this hotel."

"'Sakes, we live here," Hazel told him. "Ever since the war."

Mario made the formal gesture of kissing their liver-spotted hands, without actual contact. "I hope we will chat later," he told them and took his leave.

Main Street stretched before Mario, flat, a scene of one-storey structures and sparse trees. In the vacant lot opposite, a water tower displayed the slogan: FLORAVILLE—QUIETLY PROGRESSIVE, above a silhouette of a man in a rocking chair. Mario stepped off the curb, looking west along the dozen blocks to the hazy line of hills. *Piatto, squallido, lugubre.* A wave of homesickness struck him for the city of his boyhood, towered in mellow stone, cobbled and winding and graced with piazzas and fountains.

Mario crossed the parking lot to the restaurant, whose unlit neon sign featured a chianti bottle. Perhaps *coniglio* with truffles, he was thinking. He had heard that American Southerners ate a lot of rabbit. He entered, inhaling deeply the deliciously icy air. The place was small and drab, but the tablecloths of traditional red-checked linen heartened him.

"*Buongiorno, paisano!*" he called to the aproned man behind the counter, whose rugged face was surmounted by a shock of fair hair. Near him stood a muscular woman in a waitress's uniform, her face overpainted, her peroxided hair piled high in a net. A young waitress, blonde, pretty and also very much made up, was serving a table of three diners in blue jeans. Two of them wore caps with the word "Pennington" in script, and a stylized cotton boll as a logo.

Everybody is blond, Mario thought confusedly. Perhaps Luigi is a Milanese.

A beefy man in a wilted summer shirt, balancing his bulk on a stool at the counter, swiveled around to face Mario. His face was red and smiling. He wore a wide purple tie with an orange flower pattern.

"No use talking Eyetalian in here, Mr. Castig-lioni," he said, with a nod toward Mario's poster displayed near the cash register. "Everybody in this joint just talks good old American."

With a sinking feeling, Mario noted the tall plastic counter rack of unappetizing pies and cakes, and the neat rows of canned goods on shelves flanking the kitchen hatchway. The hatchway opened. A man's face appeared, gleaming with sweat and surmounted by a chef's cap.

Mario was receiving the silent reactions of those in the room, a mix of grudging admiration and xenophobic disapproval. The cook was thinking, **Now that's a suit, I'm telling you. Didn't buy that at no discount store.**

Mario automatically shook the outstretched hand of the man on the stool, and addressed the aproned man. "You are… Luigi?"

"Hell, Mister, ain't been no Luigi here since Hector was a pup." He too offered a hand, which Mario shook. "Gordon Wright's the name. And this here's the missus. And this'd be Mr. Buster Culpepper."

The thick red hand was offered again, and Mario suffered a bone-crushing handshake.

"We're neighbors," Culpepper told him. "I'm across the hall from

36

you at the Gilmore."

"Aha," Mario said. "You are the football scout. Would you care to join me at a table?"

Culpepper slid off the stool with surprising agility considering his bulk, and squeezed himself into a chair at a nearby table. He regarded Mario with a touch of wonder across the redchecked cloth. "Now how the dickens did you know I'm a scout?"

The pretty waitress handed Mario a menu, a blurry photocopy of an ill-typed original, listing Salisbury steak, fried catfish, and Virginia ham. Near the bottom, Mario read: Minastrone Soup. Spagetti with Meat Balls.

"I would like the minestrone," Mario said. "And the spaghetti. *Al dente,* please. And a large salad if I may."

"Coming up!" she sang, then called over her shoulder, "One minnie and a can of worms, Daddy." Mario winced.

"Something to drink?" Darlene asked Mario. "All this heat, you must be parched."

"A glass of red table wine?" he asked without much hope. "Chianti?"

Mrs. Wright put in, "We got no liquor license." She was thinking, **He could park his shoes under my bed any night of the week.**

"But your sign," Mario said, pointing through the plateglass window.

Everybody peered out at the sign with the chianti bottle.

Gordon Wright said, "Well, that bottle's purely for decoration."

"Cute, ain't it," Mrs. Wright added.

"Daddy could fix you a cherry coke," the waitress offered.

Mario sighed. "Very well, cherry coke."

"Shoot one and paint it red," the waitress called over her shoulder and sashayed to the kitchen.

"You ain't answered my question," Culpepper persisted. **Kirby told him. Or Miss Cora.**

"Concerning your profession?" Mario teased. "It was obvious."

Culpepper stared. **Do I got scout written all over me?**

"Your physique," Mario said, "is that of an athlete... after a certain age."

Culpepper said ruefully, "I'm out of shape, and that's the gospel."

"Many stars of the football field gain weight in later life," Mario soothed. "My own brother, a soccer star in Italy— That's our football. I know the enormous significance of this game in towns like yours and mine."

"So you reckon, what else would a fat old ex-linebacker be doing in Floraville."

"Could be a logical explanation," Mario said, deliberately lowering his eyes.

Only it ain't the truth, Culpepper was thinking. **You read it in my mind.**

The loud keening of a siren suddenly brought Mario trembling to his feet. His frequent exposure in New York to this frightful alarm had not inured him to the sound, which evoked nightmare memories of early childhood in wartime Italy.

"Noon on the dot," Gordon Wright remarked, with an approving nod at his accurate wallclock.

Culpepper, Mrs. Wright and the men at the nearby table were all checking their wristwatches. On the street the few passersby merely looked towards the west and then at their own timepieces.

Culpepper said, "That's just the mill si-reen, Mr. Castig-lioni. Blows every weekday twelve o'clock sharp."

Mario sat, only to half-rise again as a new ululation, less piercing, but even more blood-chilling, followed the siren.

"That's just them dogs," Mrs. Wright reassured him.

"Every day they yowl," said Wright, "when the si-reen goes off. Every damn mutt in town."

Mario laughed as the weird howling died away. The food arrived and for some moments neither man spoke. Mario took a sip of the scalding soup. It tasted of the can and was too salty. He stirred the mushy pasta and overcooked vegetables and pushed the bowl away.

The gluey spaghetti had the same metallic and chemical flavor. His salad was a pallid wedge of lettuce and a cottony tomato. He looked at the two limp slabs of refined white bread and the stone-hard rectangle of butter.

His appetite deserted him. He sipped his oversweet drink. If this is an example of Floraville cuisine, he was thinking, I will lose weight during my stay here.

Culpepper's concentration on his lunch was now giving way to thoughts of the morning's scouting. That junior team fullback. Pepsi York. What a powerhouse. Big kid. Couple of years he'll tip the scales at 240, I bet you. He speared a last mouthful of meat and chewed it lustily. Mite tough, but the flavor's perfect... Coach says Georgia Tech's already after him. Pokey little Peck College ain't got a prayer.

Mario also heard snatches of conversation and thoughts from the men two tables away. They were discussing in furtive tones rumors of the sale of the mill to a Japanese company. Mario gathered that two of the men were loading dock supervisors who feared they would lose their jobs.

He swiveled discreetly to look at them. At first they seemed identical: hunched forward over their food, redfaced. Then he noticed that one was smaller and darker than the others, and that the man facing him was wearing sunglasses.

"I hear tell they got these robots in Japan," the brownhaired man was saying.

"Wouldn't even need no loading crew," another confirmed.

The man in sunglasses took a folded pink paper from the pocket of his summer shirt and opened it on the table. Mario craned to see it, forgetting discretion in his excitement. The pink paper crumpled on the floor, in the kitchen, where the man had died. It is the same, he thought, murmuring, "*Dio mio.*"

"What say?" Culpepper asked rhetorically, reaching for Mario's bread. "Mind if I eat this up? Since you ain't using it."

"By all means, sir. Help yourself."

While Culpepper mopped up his gravy, Mario made out the wording of the flier in the mind of the brown-haired man: "...UPSET AND GETTING UPSETTER? ...WE DON'T WANT TO GET LAID OFF..."

"Meeting's tonight! Where'd you get holt of this?"

"Junior Collins, he give it to me this morning. Said as how he didn't know if supervisors was invited. But he reckoned since we're all gonna be up the same creek..."

The brown-haired man said, "Heck yeah, wages nor salary, it won't make no never mind if they sell—"

"Junior says Myrt and old Roy Washington are stirring things up. To fight back."

Guess you ain't heard the news, good buddy, the third man was thinking. **Roy's stirring up nothing, ain't that right, Cousin Earl, lessen he's doing it from the spirit world.** Mario trembled. The image of the dangling corpse flashed ghastly in the third man's mind.

"You and me better be there tonight, Ben," said the man in sunglasses.

Mario thought, So you saw him. You saw the dead man. A melange of commonplace thoughts from Culpepper and the Wright family inhibited his reception from the other table.

"Mind if I smoke?" Culpepper asked. He took a squashed pack of Salems from his pocket and offered it to Mario. "Care to join me?"

Mario accepted a cigarette and bent toward the butane-reeking flame of Culpepper's lighter.

"Wish I could give these things up," the football scout sighed, inhaling deeply.

Mario tried again to receive from the moustached man; and gave it up. "The young black... fullback," he said to Culpepper, assuaging his frustration by a display of powers, "*il ragazzo* you admired this mornin-—"

Culpepper sat bolt upright. The lighter clattered to the table.

"— will one day weigh one hundred and ten kilos," Mario went on, "that is to say two hundred and forty pounds." *Esibizionista*, showoff, he reproached himself. Lauren is right.

He glanced at the three men eating thick slices of watermelon. He was familiar with the way the denizens of this country used their hands to eat melon and corn on the cob. But he still reacted with distaste.

Culpepper was thinking **Mister, you're plumb magic.** Aloud, he said, "Bet you can't cook up a logical explanation for that."

Mario, suffering mild dyspepsia and annoyed by the babble of thoughts, laughed airily. "I do have a gift," he said, adding with a sigh, "though at times it seems more like a curse."

The words were no sooner out of his mouth than all psychic perception was abruptly cut off.

Mario's world suddenly seemed peaceful and empty. He heard only the hum of the air conditioner and the voices of Mr. and Mrs. Wright checking a supply list.

In vain, he pressed the spot between his eyes; then fumbled in his shirt pocket. He caressed the octagonal coin, his fingers tracing its worn lion's head and ancient lettering. On countless occasions, this talisman had evoked his powers.

But now it brought him nothing.

He stared ahead, silently crying in a passion of regret, No, no, I did not mean it, forgive me, come back! *Brutto, idiota, monster, cretino,* he scourged himself. How dared I offend thee! Adored one, *mia benefattrice,* canst thou ever forgive me?

"Who the hell you gawking at, doofus?" Ben, the brown-haired man challenged Mario. His companion took off his sunglasses. Mario found himself the focus of three pairs of cold blue eyes.

Mario half rose in his chair, his mouth open. The crushing blow of *la Lucia's* withdrawal left him helpless to defend himself.

"Foreigners and gooks," said Ben. "Everywhere you look. Can't crack a boiled egg without finding one inside."

"Buying up the hotel," said the third man.

"Buying up the mill," said Jimbo Hobby. "Randy here," he gestured at the moustached man, "he done his tour battling gooks over in Vi-etnam. Now they're overrunning us here. Ain't gonna call it Floraville no more. Gonna call it Gookville."

Culpepper laughed at this sally, but said immediately, "Now you hush up, Eyetalians ain't gooks."

"To my way of thinking, they pretty near qualify."

Mario stood, shrugging off his suit coat. "I am proud to be Italian," he announced. "And no Italian would ever be guilty of such rudeness to a stranger." They are three, I am one. Each of them larger than I. They will beat me senseless. Good. Let them. Then perhaps She will forgive me.

Two of the men were on their feet and moving toward Mario.

"Talks big, don't he," said Ben.

"Maybe he's got a knife," Jimbo cautioned.

Randy, still seated, said, "Nah, he's just mouthing off."
Gordon Wright interposed his lanky body. "Just pay your tab and get on back to work. This guy ain't done nothing to you."

"Three against one," Mrs. Wright chided. "If that ain't yellow, I don't know what is."

"Hell, I'll take him with a three-punch headstart," Ben said.

"Go fight with who's buying up the mill. Or who's selling. Don't take your aggravations out on him." Gordon Wright stood toe to toe with Jimbo, who gave a weak laugh and turned away.

"Okay, Gordon. He ain't worth the trouble. Come on, boys."

Mario said, "I will be happy to step outside with any one of you. Or all of you."

"Simmer down, mister. Kind of a misunderstanding, let's say," Jimbo said.

"No hard feelings," Culpepper assured Mario.

The three men had gone and Culpepper's eyes were on him, questioning.

"*Scusi,*" Mario said, "I must take my leave of you. We can conclude our conversation another time."

Culpepper, plainly disappointed, nodded slowly. "Anyhow, I sure plan to catch your act."

"We all gonna be there," Darlene promised.

Mrs. Wright offered her rough, manicured hand. "Proud to have you visiting Floraville."

Her husband shook hands, too. "On the house," he told Mario, indicating the uneaten lunch. "And when you're feeling better, you come on back for supper."

Mario managed a murmur of thanks.

For my insult to Her, he told himself, I deserve to eat ashes and gall.

IV

La Lucia had always been a will-o'-the-wisp, his elusive miracle, fickle and demanding. On an archaeological site in post-war Perugia, she had first overwhelmed the adolescent Mario, granting him a vision of an ancient tableau.

A man's voice sounded, a long outcry in a language unknown to Mario. He received the sense of it: Will the drought end soon? Will the rains come? The speaker flashed before him: a robed authoritative figure, black-bearded and balding. The fingers of his left hand touched his brow in a ritual gesture. His right hand was outstretched as in warning. A swallow fluttered upward; and the figure was gone.

Mario's eyes opened. He was dimly aware that *il professore* recoiled from his gaze; then heard the exclamation of concern. From the shadowed ditch images swirled towards Mario. He saw the lion coin gleaming and new. An old man in a chlamys was tucking it into his cloth shoe, which had an upcurving toe. He was seated on a carved stool before a semicircle of children, unrolling a scroll on his lap.

"He is the teacher," Mario said. "He writes with …ink?" The image vanished.

Mario sprang to his feet, himself again, resisting the helping hand of the archeologist. "I am all right, don't worry about me!" he cried. He was exalted, throbbing with vigor and joy. "Look! *Vieni qui!* Over this way! Your diggers have missed it." He raced to the adjoining trench and leapt over it. A dozen yards further he knelt by a young cedar and placed the coin on the grass. The professor came running, followed by students and workmen.

"*Bada qui,*" commanded Mario. "You have to dig here."

In later years, Mario's recollection of that brilliant afternoon became wispy and blurred. The details of *la Lucia*'s advent remained indelible, but he was not sure how he had overcome the professor's reluctance, nor when the men began digging by the cedar.

His father, he remembered, had come charging up the hill, shouting, and struck him hard with the side of his hand, sending him sprawling. "You, Mario! *Cattivo!* I take off your hide!"

The archeologist thrust himself between the boy and his father. "Don't hit him, he has done nothing wrong!"

"*Scusi, Professore.* He is *un birbante, disubbidiente.* He runs up here bothering your work." Salvatore Castigliani stood panting, scowling at Mario. He was short and thick, a strong man with dusty brown hair, in a white jacket soiled by his day's labor. He was a veterinarian, serving the farms near Perugia. He often brought Mario with him to learn the family calling. That day he had been overseeing the insemination of the cows of a dairy farm on the plain below. He had sent Mario to round up the last of the grazing herd; the boy had run off.

"He is interested in our work," the professor said soothingly. "He's very intelligent, *Signor.*" He pointed to the cedar. "And a genuine help to us."

"This is not the first time!" his father complained to the archeologist. "He does this all the time. *Vagabondo!*"

Mario tugged at the professor's sleeve. The wide-set grey eyes brimmed with pleading. Don't tell him! Mario was signalling. Don't tell.

"You are too kind, *Professore.*" Salvatore roughly seized Mario's arm. But the boy knew that anger had gone from the man and flashed him a grin. He winked at the archeologist. He was used to his father's blows, to his short-lived rages of histrionic righteousness.

Companionably, they made their way down the hill.

Mario contrived to be by himself during the next few days. His experience had shaken him to his core. He was alternately enthralled and incredulous. One moment he yearned for the return of the power, to re-enter that clarity and consummation. Was it holy, the thing which possessed me? he wondered. Oh, yes. The next moment he shook his head.

He sensed that the marvel arose from *I Perduti,* the Lost Ones, his private name for the Etruscans. He was wild with curiosity. The man and the bird... a priest? Then the coin and the schoolmaster. What did it say, the undecipherable scroll?

His Uncle Massimo worked as Assistant Curator in the Museo Archeologico near the railway station. The dusty provincial institution was a favorite haunt of Mario's. He was allowed to wander freely among the irreplaceable vases. Books and periodicals were at his disposal once he had shown Uncle Massimo that his hands were clean. If the museum were empty, his uncle might unlock the glass cases so Mario could handle the helmets and lamps, the axes and combs used two millennia ago.

Now in his fevered bewilderment, Mario bore to the museum his burden of unanswerable questions. He knocked urgently on the heavy oak doors.

"It is after hours, *ragazzo mio.*" Uncle Massimo was a mild-mannered recluse, thin and bald.

"Please, Uncle. Let me in!"

With a slow owlish stare, the man swung the doors open. He turned up the lights and noiselessly withdrew to his cubbyhole, where he was playing out a book game of chess. The boy had the place to himself. His footsteps echoed on the marble floor. He stood before a bas relief of women performing an unknown rite. How beautiful were *I Perduti!* Perfect lips, raptly smiling. Large tilted eyes. Their bodies graceful and strong, slender yet rounded.

An hour slipped past as he studied the works of long-dead artists and artisans. Had he seen these scenes, these faces, at the trench? No. Not the same. But like. Very like. She showed me truly, *la Lucia.*

Doubt overtook him again. How can I know that the visions did not come from my own head? Imaginings, based on what I have seen, here, and at the dig.

That night, he experimented. His bedroom overlooked the garden of the elegant, decaying villa built by his mother's ancestors. Sitting upright on his narrow bed in a shaft of moonlight, Mario tried to summon *la Lucia*. Empty the mind, Mario, he admonished himself. Concentrate on one thing only. He shut his hand as though the coin were in it, recalling precisely the shape of the lion's head, and its jaws open in a soundless roar.

And the vast light encompassed him. A voice chanted fervently. He saw a matron in a brown robe, richly embroidered. When she disappeared, he opened his eyes on a new throng of visions. A shield raised in battle. A girl looking into a silver handmirror. A loinclothed ploughman steering a team of oxen. A banquet. The pattern of a ceramic platter. He smelled, even tasted, the roasted boar's head.

Whether the trance lasted seconds or hours he had no way of knowing. When it had passed, he flung off his nightshirt and ran into the garden, naked as Pan. With all his might he embraced an almond tree, weeping and laughing, laughing and weeping.

A week after the first revelation, *il professore* sent a message to Mario to come to his room in the Pensione Arco-Etrusco. Mario ran through the cobbled streets, to the Corso Vannucci, past the cathedral, past the Maggiore Fountain and the cafes of the Piazza IV Novembre to the *pensione* perched on the city wall.

He found his friend in a high-ceilinged room with a chipped antique bed. A long table with neatly sorted shards, coins and other artifacts stood near the tall windows which opened out on the city.

The professor offered the boy a chair and a glass of orzata. His bearing was grave.

"I have told your secret to no one, Mario. But I must know what happened, there in the trench. Were you playing a game with me?"

Mario shook his head.

"Did you see something? Someone?"

"*Per favore, Professore.* Don't make me answer." He must not, could not talk about it. About *Her*, he told himself. His throat constricted. He set his untasted drink on the floor.

"Please, Mario. *Prego.* I cannot tell you how important it is that I know."

Haltingly, Mario described a few details of what he had seen in the trench. He selected them carefully, as though he were asking *la Lucia* if she would permit him to tell this, and this. He said nothing about the nighttime reprise of his experience.

"Amazingly accurate!" the archeologist exclaimed. "But all this could be from what you remember, and from imagination."

"I have told myself that," Mario said.

"Has this happened to you before?"

"Never, *Professore*. It was my first time."

"When you spoke of the teacher, and the ink, Mario. Did you see a vessel beside him?"

Mario nodded.

"Can you describe it?"

"Pottery, I think," Mario said. "Red and brown. About as tall as a candle." He measured with his hands. "Thin on top, fat below."

"Any decorations? Markings?"

Mario squeezed his eyes shut. "The old writing maybe."

The archeologist withdrew a wooden box from beneath his bed and took from it a cloth-covered bundle. He unwrapped it, revealing a piece of pottery broken in two.

"We found this," The professor skillfully fitted the two pieces together. "three meters below where you placed the coin."

Twenty-six centuries in the earth had darkened and mottled the vessel. Otherwise it was as Mario described it.

"*Bucchero*," the archeologist said. "Seventh century B.C. There is every reason to believe it was used as an inkwell."

Mario was at the dig that summer whenever he could slip away from his father. Occasionally, his clairvoyance led the archeology team to artifacts of interest, though none so spectacular as the inkwell.

Il professore wavered between disbelief and conviction. "Scientists have hunches, too, Mario. Some prove correct. Usually there turns out to be some natural explanation."

"*Ah, sì*, I agree. I don't know how I do it, either."

They were working with the students and local laborers, dismantling the sorting tables and covering the trenches against the impending rains of autumn.

"Will you help us when we come back next spring?"

"If I can run faster than my father."

The archeologist laughed. He pressed a parting gift into Mario's hand: the lion coin!

"Eh, *Professore!* And what of the law? This must be worth thousands of lire."

"*Non ti preoccupare.* I have official permission to give it to you."

Mario pressed the coin to his breast bone. "I will treasure it always," he promised.

His powers, he discovered, were not limited to archeology. He was playing bocce one afternoon with his brother Stefano, three years older than he. A dozen schoolmates cheered and catcalled from the sidelines. Stefano was winning as always. He was a broad-chested, exuberant redhead, adept at sports, hero of the school soccer team. As Mario positioned himself, the bocchia in hand, the noisy shouts gave way to a vibrant stillness, out of which he heard his brother's voice. **I hope you miss, Mario.**

His arm still drawn back, Mario turned his head to stare at Stefano, who was faking a smile of encouragement. **Go on, little brother, throw it and miss,** said the voice. Stefano had not spoken. Mario received a brief shimmering vision from his brother: Stefano carried in triumph on the shoulders of the soccer team.

Mario threw and missed. He played badly the rest of the game. When he accepted defeat and shook hands with his brother, the uncanny hush returned.

Eh, you, know-it-all, the silent Stefano was saying, **you, Mario, the family scholar, who cannot make one bocce ball kiss another as I can.**

Mario gritted his teeth, but managed a congratulatory smile. Arrogant ass, I'll get you later. But their ongoing rivalry seemed petty compared to his newfound power. I was reading his mind! *La Lucia's* gifts, then, did not always require a full-blown trance. Thank you, oh thank you! I can read peoples thoughts!

"Eh, Mario. You got to help me with this." Stefano barged into Mario's room, looking belligerent and sheepish at the same time.

Dinner was over. Each boy had homework to do.

"Well, well, well. So you can't do your English again, *campione*," Mario said, adding silently, damned if you get help from me.

Stefano thrust his homework under Mario's nose. "Who can understand that stupid language. Fix it for me."

"I'm awfully sorry, Stefano. How about tomorrow?" Vengeance was sweet. But the careless scrawl in Stefano's notebook was oddly alluring. Another new power? Mario wondered. The writing wavered into pulsing light.

He heard Stefano thinking, **Little rat. You know I got to hand it in tomorrow.** "Come on, punk."

Mario suppressed his dawning excitement. "*Va bene*. Put it down over there, I'll get to it later."

Stefano hung over him.

"Don't breathe down my neck," Mario said.

When he was alone, Mario held the open notebook close to his eyes, then further away. He read: "Yesterday I go in *ristorante* new. Good night, Mister to me say the waiter; you command the *bistecca*?"

Then the words dissolved into light. The twelve-year-old Mario glimpsed a scene of clumsy adolescent sex that made him redden in embarrassment. Paola! Who could imagine it. She was the daughter of a dairyman who lived near the city, a plump quiet girl of pristine reputation.

The image dissipated, and he was unable to recapture it. Stefano, you dog. Then he wondered, what if I held something of his? The way I hold onto the coin.

He corrected the exercise and took it to his brother's room.

"Thanks kid, you're okay," said Stefano.

"Mind if I borrow this?" Mario picked up Stefano's penknife.

"*Certo*, take it. Just bring it back clean."

When the household was sleeping, Mario perched on his bed in the moonlight, the folded knife clasped in his hand. *La Lucia* did not overwhelm him, yet sounds and images came haltingly from the vibrating penknife. Whispers, gasps, giggles. Dim daylight in a crude shed. Stefano and Paola. Struggle, awkward grappling. The comic obscenity of Stefano's trousers down around his ankles. Mario dropped the knife, ending the vision. I do not want to see this, he thought. He felt unclean and ashamed of himself.

For some weeks he sternly avoided occult eavesdropping. But temptation proved too strong. He tried next with an apron of Modesta's, the family servant. She had been with them for seven years, humble and hardworking, averting her face with its big purple birthmark. Neighbors sniggered at her, but in these straitened times, the Castiglianis were lucky to have her. Her bastard daughter, Oriana, a year older than Mario, shared the domestic work. Pale, thin, her eyes cast down, her braided black hair covered by a white kerchief, she emulated her self-effacing mother.

The apron brought him Modesta's voice. **Yes, it is true I am under the evil eye.** Then the murky dream she was dreaming: A gypsy holding out two slabs of meat, one white, one red. **This means one son will drown,** Modesta intoned, **the other will die by stabbing.** Next came scenes, aching with homesickness, of the childhood farm from which she was banished. Mario swallowed the lump in his throat. But as the visions continued, he knew that this pitiful victim was blessed with a generous heart. She emanated affection: for her severe mistress, for her ghostly daughter, for himself and Stefano who wolfed down the delectable products of her ungrudging hours at the stove. And she was in love. Incredibly, romantically, faithfully, fervently. Whom do you love, poor Modesta?

Salvatore, my darling, her voice said.

Papa jokes with her, slaps her on the bottom, Mario mused the next day. He doesn't treat her like the wallpaper, the way the rest of us do. But he can't be her *amore*, it's ridiculous.

Moved by the warmth and innocence which lay below her silence, Mario brought her a bouquet of asters from the fall garden. She was in the kitchen taking a loaf out of the big iron oven.

"These are for you, Modesta."

She nodded, averted her face, and set the loaf on a rack. One hand covering the birthmark, she accepted the flowers. **The lad's wanting a vase,** he heard her thinking.

"In appreciation," Mario improvised, "for that delicious *risotto con tartufi* last night."

Disbelief and delight battled on her broad face. "*Il Signor* your Papa," she stammered, "he brought me the truffles." Never in my life did anyone give me flowers, she thought. **Not even my kind Salvatore.** "*Grazie. Mille grazie, Signorino Mario.*"

Mildly scandalized by the concept of his father in Modesta's beefy arms, Mario tuned in on him throughout that autumn whenever he could. They were often together on weekends: doctoring pets in the dispensary at the front of the house; treating the infections of a sheared flock of sheep; driving along the steep rocky curves in the hardy Fiat. Like the city itself, the car had survived the war years with relatively little damage, and was getting through the threadbare present creditably enough.

If only he would shut up once, Mario said to himself, so I could hear what he's thinking.

"Politics stink to high heaven, my son," Salvatore would pontificate as he drove. "The windbags preach social *giustizia*, hah, the worker's paradise, but they practice bureaucracy and corruption. Keep clear of them, boy, learn from your father."

"That's no problem, *Papà,* I got no use for any of them."

"Can men live like brothers?" Salvatore would muse aloud, with an expansive gesture which brought the car close to the brink. "And why not? The men of the land, the factory workers who make all we need, we are brothers already."

He raised his clenched fists. Mario grabbed the steering wheel. "*Papà!* God's sake! Hands on the wheel!"

The car swerved to safety. Mario peered past his father, over the drop to the spread of the misty green plain far below. He received his father's inner voice: **I should have run off with a gun. Joined the Partisans. Brave lads! And so few.**

Mario's best chances came when his father fell silent, eyeing the road. Mario listened, Mario spied. He learned little he did not already know: such was the candor and volubility of the man. He discerned no trace of Modesta, and concluded with relief that her love was secret and unrequited. He was not shocked to discover the identities of five of the women of the city who were Salvatore's past and present lovers. The boy had known for a long time that his parents were bitterly estranged. Yet Mario found his mother in his father's thoughts more often than any other person. When he knitted his heavy brows and grunted, he was usually talking to her. Arguing. Wooing. Angry. Admiring. Sarcastic and scornful under the sting of her constant rejection. Eh, Signorina Eleanora della Rovere. Eh, Princess. The martyr. Too good for a Castigliani. Performing your marital duties, a woman of ice.

She had borne seven children. Basilio, their eldest, had been killed during the Allied invasion of Sicily. Giorgio, a deserter from the Italian army, had been shot by the Germans. Two stillborn daughters, and a third who had not survived infancy, lay in the cemetery next to the della Rovere plot. Eleanora, blackclad, prematurely white-haired, knelt there every day. Knelt there, and in the cathedral, a rosary draped around her aristocratic hands, her wide-set grey eyes on the great crucifix.

V

Northwest of the highway, the fields of the Piedmont rose gently to the Appalachians. Timothy and soybean made carpets of dark green against the sweep of dull stubble where cotton had sapped the vitality of the earth. Clay soil sculpted in hard-baked wheelruts bordered the asphalt under a faint haze of red dust.

There were few cars on the highway. On Beaufort Tyler's left as he drove, the Flint River, narrow and sluggish at this season, ran parallel to the road. An abandoned farmhouse; a clump of turkey oaks; a one-pump service station, and the steeple of the new Pentecostal Holiness Church flashed past the police car. A ramshackle stand with a scrawled sign: Water Mellins and Sqash. An ugly prefab discount mart, incongruously citified.

Passing the Big Bad Wolf Barbecue, Tyler slowed the car and rolled his window down, receiving a blast of hot air acrid with dust. The plastic pigs cavorted in their accustomed tableau, raw pink against the sunburnt lawn. He nodded, grinned, closed the window and picked up speed. Good routine police work. Duane Potts had known where to look: twice before, at initiation time, the high school Letter Club had pulled this kidnap stunt.

At the bend where the Flint flowed under the highway bridge, Tyler turned onto Old River Road. Above the dam, a family, fishing with canepoles, waved as he drove by. Six boys wading in the glittering water splashed each other and shouted: "Here come the law!" and "Run for your life!"

Here the houses of Floraville began, shabby, one-family, clapboard structures laid out barracks style: the minimal housing of the mill villages from which the town had grown. The millhands who lived here had electricity nowadays, and indoor plumbing. The streets were paved: a marked improvement over the recent past with its plagues of dust in the dry months, mud in the wet.

Pennington's was the only active mill. It lay just beyond the ruins of the old Kendall factory, whose redbrick foundations were visible from the road. Old Man Pennington had bought out his competitors in the 1950s, and converted their plants to warehouses.

Pennington smokestacks were now in sight, two giant fingers dark against the whitish sky. The long squat mill and its outbuildings were surrounded by a barbed wire fence erected during the bitter General Textile Strike of 1934, and never removed.

Tyler drove through the open gates to the rear. He found a spot in the worker's parking lot. The loading area was deserted. Bales of cotton stood motionless on the conveyor belt leading to the Picking Room.

Inside the mill, all was cool and uncannily quiet. The moist air was relatively free of lint—a far cry from conditions fifteen years ago when Tyler had worked here. He found no workers in the picking area, nor in the long Spinning Room where the spindles were mysteriously stilled.

He strode through to the Weave Room, with its thirty-foot-high Hoeffelstadt looms. Quiet, too: only the hum of the air scrubbers. And here they all were: some forty-odd hands gathered in the shelter of the machinery, and a dozen or so workers standing together in the middle of the aisle, confronting a section hand and a boss weaver. Here they were, the remnant of a work force decimated by high technology, the folk of the mill, called lintheads and trash by the rest of the town. More women than men. Middleaged, mostly.

Several were holding pink fliers. The boss weaver had one clutched in his hand, which he was waving as he called out: "Whoever's on lunch, go eat. The rest of you, back to work or get docked an hour."

"Don't mean you no disrespect," the spokesman said with stubborn emphasis. "But we all has to pay our respects to Royal, too."

Tyler stood unobtrusively near the entry. Many of the hands, formerly his fellow workers, gestured in greeting when they caught sight of him. But a woman, new here since his time, snapped: "You anyhow got no cause to go calling the police on us."

Junior Collins, Myrt's third husband, a small, bald rooster of a man, detached himself from the huddle of workers and came to Tyler. "Let's go in Spinning," he whispered.

When they stepped into the adjoining area, he pulled at Tyler's sleeve, frowning up at him.

"What you holding Myrt down at the station for?" he asked urgently.

"It's only... I got to ask her some questions," Tyler replied.

"You know gosh darn well she'd never harm a hair on Roy's head."

"'Course I know that."

"He was like a daddy to her. *And* she'll be out a day's pay. *And* the kids got to run to Bonnie's for dinner."

"Don't take on, Junior. She's a real important witness. We need a full statement from her." He freed himself and put a reassuring hand on Junior's shoulder. "I'll speak a word to Jeff Pennington about the day's pay if you want."

Junior nodded.

"When did the news hit the mill?" Tyler asked.

"'Bout an hour ago. Myrt phoned me and... 'fraid I let the cat out of the bag. She's hopping mad at me already, on account of I gave leaflets to some supervisors."

"What's all the commotion in Weaving?"

"Colored's think the mill ought to shut down. In honor of Roy being dead. White hands, some go along, some ain't so sure. And everybody's het up about the Japanese. We're meeting tonight."

"Let's go back. I got to talk to them," Tyler said. He returned to Weaving, went to stand before the spokesman and raised a hand for silence.

"Listen, folks," he said loudly, and then, in his customary tone, "didn't anybody send for me. I came on my own 'cause I have business here."

"Nothing to do with poor Roy strung up like a dog, I suppose," the new woman put in.

"Maybe so, maybe no. My business is nobody else's business. But nothing to do with you stopping work, I promise you that." He pointed to the leaflet in the woman's hand. "Now about this meeting. It's called off."

He raised his voice again over the dissenting responses. "Get it straight, there'll be no meeting tonight. Roy, he's passed on, y'all know that. And Myrt Collins can't be there neither."

He waited until they had swung towards acceptance of the inevitable, then added, "Royal Washington, he was a great big part of this mill. I figure it's only right and proper the C.E.O. ought to shut it down half a day. I'm heading up front now, and I plan to speak my mind to him."

They thought it over, clearly mollified, and nodded in agreement.

Between Quality Control and Administration, a massive sliding steel door yielded to Tyler's push. Behind him the crash and clatter of the looms had already resumed. When the door slid to, he was in another world, peaceful, pleasantly industrious, free of the factory humidity. Russet drapes of the famous Pennington Sculpted Blend hung ceiling to floor. At the four, blue, free-form desks, four pretty young women, looked up from the keyboards to smile flirtatiously.

"Afternoon, girls," he said. "The Chief in there?" He did not wait for a reply, but with a smile and a wave, walked through to the inner sanctum, where Vesta Delacorte sat guard at her desk near the Chief Executive Officer's door. She was an ancient woman with a corded neck, a pillar of righteous vigilance, smart and correct in her grey pants suit and her skillfully styled brunette wig. Nobody knew how old she was. She had worked here for Old Man Pennington and for his father before him.

She never smiled, but her expression was cordial enough as she said, "Go right on in, Mr. Beau. Mr. Pennington's expecting you."

He opened the leather door on a room carpeted in white, with white drapes framing the landscaping at the front entrance to the mill. Oil portraits in twin gold frames hung on the left wall: the square-built, white-moustached Old Man looking upright and indomitable; and his gaunt father, whose stern eyes seemed to follow the viewer.

Automatically, Tyler whipped off his cap. Then, squaring his shoulders, he clapped it back on his head.

Jeff Pennington was not in the room. From behind the closed door of his bathroom, running water could be heard.

Tyler stepped silently around the big blond Scandinavian desk and flipped through the pages of the calendar. Many entries, some clear, some cryptic. "NY-M" appeared twice in the past month, each time taking up two full days. "New York-Matsumoto?" Tyler muttered speculatively. Matsumoto was the trading company rumored to be bidding for the mill. Yesterday's appointments ended at three p.m., followed by "Drive time" written diagonally across the bottom of the page. He riffled the pages again, and found the same entry every other Wednesday, always at mid-afternoon. He left the calendar open at today's date as he had found it, and examined the polished desk. It was bare except for the phone and intercom, a letter awaiting signature and a four-inch bronze Greek statuette of a nude youth offering a tray.

"Well, Beau, sorry to have kept you waiting." Jeff Pennington put a pair of canvas shoes with thick white soles under a carved and polished mahogany bookcase. "Not even time enough for jogging today." He held out his perfectly manicured hand, brushed Tyler's fingers, and went immediately to enthrone himself in the white leather chair behind the barricade of the desk. He was impeccable in his dark conservative suit, maroon tie and snowy linen. Freshly shaven, every hair in place. But there were dark circles under his bright eyes, which were large and lustrous, of a blue almost colorless. They seemed to encompass rather than look at Tyler.

"I needed a shave and a change," he went on. "Had to drive down from Atlanta in the rosy light of dawn..." He affected an elaborate manner of speaking in imitation of his late father, who had fancied himself a Classics scholar.

"How did you know I was coming?" Tyler asked.

"A.J. gave me a ring." Dr. Donlan was Jeff's brother-in-law and a member of the board which owned and ran the mill.

Jeff shrugged. "Just what was it you wanted to see me about?"

"I advise you to shut down tomorrow."

"Come now, Beau, we didn't shut down for a whole day even when Father died."

"Half a day, then."

"Have you any notion of the enormous cost that would entail?"

"I figure it'll cost you more if you don't."

"I have a five-hundred bolt order of damask to fill tomorrow, over and above our regular output." Jeff pointed to the chair beside the desk. "Sit down, Beau, and be sensible. Your loyalties do you credit, but..."

Tyler remained standing and said stonily, "My loyalties are to my job. Which is keeping the peace."

"They will not strike, nor will they run amok and smash the machinery. Have you had your lunch?"

Tyler sat tall on the edge of the chair as though rejecting its comfort. "I can't stop to eat now. You're mighty cocksure, Jeff Pennington. Guess you figure you got them so scared shitless over this Japanese deal—"

"Oh, for heaven's sake!" Jeff gave a dry laugh and pressed the intercom button. "Coffee and sandwiches, Vesta," he said, "for myself and my guest. One tourist group comes through the mill," he said to Tyler, "with polite bowing and clicking cameras, and the town is engulfed in panic." A light flashed on the desk panel, and he pressed the button again. "Yes, Vesta?"

"Your wife and your sister are here, Mr. Pennington."

Jeff frowned. "Tell them to make themselves comfortable in Reception for a few minutes."

But the leather door had already opened, admitting two women of remarkable beauty. Anne-Marie Donlan, Dr. Donlan's wife and Pennington's sister, was honey-haired, with a tumble of gleaming curls over her left eyebrow and vivacious baby blue eyes artfully painted. She was wearing a mini-skirted red lace dress drawn tight at her tiny waist, and cut low.

Claudia Pennington was taller than her companion and even more slender. Her hair, drawn smooth to a dancer's knot at the top of her narrow head, was black, as were her long tilted eyes with their sweep of luxuriant lashes. Her olive pallor was emphasized by a black knee-length linen tunic, worn over black tights and relieved only by a dull gold necklace of antique design. She wore no makeup and needed none. The effect of her severe clothing was as dramatic as an exclamation mark.

"Hey there, Anne-Marie," Tyler said. "You're looking mighty lovely today." But his eyes were on Claudia.

"Beau Tyler, what are you doing in this holy of holies?" Anne-Marie asked with a display of dimples. "Come to arrest my brother?"

Claudia inclined her head and said, "Beau."

"To what do I owe the honor of this unannounced visit?" Jeff inquired testily. He turned to his sister. "Anne-Marie, I trust you'll have the good sense not to go prancing around town in that getup."

Anne-Marie stuck out her tongue at him. It seemed pale in contrast to her scarlet lips.

"At least stay in the car," Jeff scolded. "Has Mother seen what you're wearing?"

"Oh, yes. She's had her daily hissy fit."

"Has A.J. seen it?"

"Oh, poof. A.J.'s too busy playing doctor. Or jogging. Wouldn't notice if I ran around naked as a jaybird."

"Money. I want four hundred and thirty-seven dollars," Claudia announced calmly. Her voice was low in pitch, with a violin tone. "They're delivering the costumes today for our Labor Day concert." Claudia taught ballet to a group of Floraville children.

"It's beyond me how you spend it all." Over the intercom Jeff said, "Vesta, bring me five hundred from petty cash, please."

"Really and truly," Anne-Marie said to Tyler, "how come you're here?"

"Beau's trying to persuade me that the Bolsheviks will overwhelm Floraville if I don't shut down tomorrow," Jeff said.

"Whatever for?" his sister asked.

"Roy Washington is dead. You haven't heard?"

Claudia gasped. "*Roy's dead...?* Oh, no. Oh, no." She moved with her dancer's glide to Tyler and held out her slender palms. "How terrible. Oh, Beau! I'm so sorry."

Tyler gripped her hands. "Yes. Last night."

"How—" Anne-Marie began; but Claudia interrupted, releasing herself from Tyler and whirling to face Jeff.

"Of course you'll shut the mill." she commanded. Jeff started to protest, but she walked around to tweak his ear as though playfully, and went on with a cool smile. "Never let it be said that R. Jefferson Pennington failed to honor a town hero, hey? And, by the way, how did everything go in Atlanta yesterday?"

He said stiffly, "I concluded my business satisfactorily."

"Stayed over with John and Margie Middlebrook?"

Tyler asked in a casual tone, "Would that be the department store Middlebrooks?"

"Checking up on me, Beau?" Jeff snapped. "Do you think I need an alibi?"

"Roy was *murdered*?" Anne-Marie whispered, obviously thrilled.

"He was a suicide," Jeff stated.

"Oh, no," Claudia said again. Grief seemed at home on her lovely face.

"That's as may be," Tyler told Jeff. "Number of folks might need to tell their whereabouts last night." Jeff bridled and Tyler went on, "I'm sure you'll check out just fine. And now you ought to listen to your wife. It's only decent to shut down."

"Will they call a strike if he doesn't?" asked Anne-Marie, still thrilled.

"Some might walk out, seems to me," Tyler replied.

Jeff brushed Claudia's fingers from his ear and slapped the mirror-smooth desk. "Very well. You win. All of you win. I'll have to get permission from the Board."

"Get permission from the Board, then." Claudia narrowed her eyes and smiled at him.

There was a knock at the door. "Come in," Jeff called. A languid black youth in a white jacket entered wheeling a tray with a silver coffee set and a platter of dainty sandwiches.

"My, don't that look yummy," said Anne-Marie.

"Y'all are welcome to my share," Tyler said regretfully. "Got to get moving." But he remained until the waiter had left the room, and then said to Jeff, "Another thing. You know Myrtle Collins, she's a spinner? She's down at the station. Nothing against her, she's just a witness. I'd appreciate it if she didn't lose out on her day's wages."

"I know her indeed," Jeff told him. "All too well."

Claudia said, "Certainly she'll be paid. Won't she, Jeff."

Jeff met the flash of her dark eyes, then looked away. "She'll be paid," he said sullenly.

Claudia took a bankbook from her tunic pocket and tossed it to the desk. "Phone the bank, there's a dear, Jeff," she said, "and shore up my collapsing account."

The outside temperature had climbed to over a hundred. When Tyler opened his car door, the heat from inside was so intense that he muttered, "Jumping Jehosophat." He lowered himself gingerly behind the wheel and felt the vinyl seat cover burn him through his clothes. He did not switch on the air conditioning. He drove to the front of the mill, and found a relatively shady parking space among the cars of the executives.

Jeff's white Buick, reddened with the dust of his eighty-mile drive, was parked in the area reserved for Pennington vehicles. Beside it, in the family Cadillac, Cordene, the Pennington chauffeur-gardener, slumbered at the wheel. He was a large man of chocolate complexion, fat but strong-looking, overflowing his sweat-darkened uniform. Tyler walked over to him and tapped him on the arm. "You can go on home, Cordene," he said. "I'll be driving the ladies."

Cordene came awake with a sleepy smile. "That's right kindly of you, Mr. Beau," he said. "I sure 'preciate getting out of all this heat."

Tyler went back to his car and watched the Cadillac drive off.

He rolled the windows down and eased into the driver's seat, his keen blue eyes fixed on the glass entrance doors.

And waited.

It was nearly one-thirty when the two women emerged. He tapped the horn and they came to the car.

"Now where's that Cordene?" Anne-Marie asked.

"I sent him off home," Tyler told her. "Get in."

Claudia said, "You've got your nerve."

"Claudia, honey, I do believe we are being abducted," Anne-Marie said, dimpling, as Claudia slid in beside Tyler. Anne-Marie got in and slammed the door. "Gosh almighty, it's pure roasting in here! You must be baked clean through."

Tyler pulled out onto the drive, closed the windows, and clicked on the air conditioning.

"You surely got no need to go waylaying fair ladies," Anne-Marie said as they drove. "Why, half this town's been making eyes at you ever since grade school."

Tyler and Claudia remained silent, and Anne-Marie went on, "Don't know just what it is about that ugly face of yours."

"Handsome-ugly," said Claudia. "Like a blond Abraham Lincoln,

I always thought."

"Phew! Claudia. Now you are talking Yankee hideous," said Anne-Marie.

"Cut it out, will you, the two of you," Tyler muttered, brick-red. Then he said, "If we could get away from the subject of my beauty, where do you want me to drop you off?"

"Anne-Marie wants to do some shopping at Milady's. I've got to go home to pick up some toe shoes. Then I'm due at my studio."

"You said you'd come shopping with me," Anne-Marie complained.

"Well, there it is, no time. You would insist on eating Jeff's sandwiches."

"Claudia never eats lunch," Anne-Marie told Tyler. "That's how she keeps her fashionable famine-victim look."

They had already reached Main Street, now lined with diagonally parked cars. The dozen-odd pedestrians they passed stared at the two socialites in the police car and then quickly bobbed their heads.

Tyler parked in front of the Tape & Disk.

"Have fun, you two," Anne-Marie said to Claudia and Tyler as she got out of the car and pirouetted, her mini-skirt flaring high.

"One of these days," said Tyler admiringly, "someone's gonna put her over their knee and spank her."

Claudia gave him a faint smile. Neither spoke as he drove over the Main Street bridge and swung right, toward the hills. A belt of woodland separated Valhalla from the rest of the town. When they came to a clearing surrounded by loblolly pines, he drove into it and parked out of sight of the road.

His eyes half closed, his lips parted, he leaned toward Claudia. She averted her head and moved away, her shoulder pressed against the window.

She said, "Don't, Beau."

"Yesterday—" he began.

"Don't presume on it," she said firmly. "This is today."

Tyler held out his hand, palm up, but she did not clasp it. "Forget it, Beau," she said. "Don't you know I'm poison?"

"I can't forget it. Wish I could."

"Just a kiss," Claudia said. "A moment of weakness."

"Cut the bullshit. You felt it like I did. I saw it in your face."

She took his hand then, clutching it painfully, and murmured, "I was cruel to let it happen. Forgive me." She flung her head back and shut her eyes. The fans of her lashes lay black on her pale cheeks. A bluegreen vein pulsed in her forehead, another in the pillar of her throat.

"I hate my life," she said.

"Claudia. Leave him. Leave the whole phoney setup."

She pushed his hand away and opened her eyes, "And be Mrs. Top Cop?" She pointed her sandalled foot at the shotgun lock mounted on the floor. "Thank you, no."

"You know damn well I don't plan to stick with police work."

"Oh yes. Back to the land and all that. Come off it, Beau. Can you see me as a farmer's wife?" She looked away from the naked appeal in Tyler's eyes and said, "Marry Bonnie, why don't you. You owe it to her after—what is it? Five years?"

"Seven," he said. "Bonnie's a fine woman. We understand each other real well. Marriage was never in the picture."

"Is that a fact? Try asking her, you might be surprised."

Pine needles showered lightly on the hood of the car. Claudia tapped the dial of Tyler's wristwatch. "I have to be downtown in twenty minutes," she said. "And how come you've got all this time to waste? At the mill office, you couldn't even stop for coffee."

"Skipped lunch," he replied. She looked at him with raised brows, and he said, "Okay, you're right, it's stolen time. But in Jeff's office... it was more... I can't stand seeing you beat up on him."

"Masculine solidarity, is it," she said with a melancholy smile.

"Maybe a little. Not much. Me and Jeff, we were never friends. It's just... you've changed a lot, Claudia."

She winced, gave a shiver and said, "Steal five minutes more, and tell me about Roy."

"Not much I can tell you yet. Myrt found him this morning." He looked away from her into the green of the trees. Mosquitoes were dancing just beyond the windshield. "Hanging," he said.

"Oh, God. Poor Roy. Wonderful Roy. I can't believe it."

"I don't either. Whole thing smells funny."

"Can I help, Beau? I want to help."

"You maybe can... What's Jeff up to in Atlanta?"

Claudia stared at him, and laughed uncertainly.

"All right, I can pretty well guess," he told her. "Roy called a meeting. About this Matsumoto rumor."

"You mean, the least hint of labor trouble—"

"—would queer the deal," he finished for her. "If there is a deal."

"You think Jeff's capable of murder?" She laughed again, then said. "You know, I do believe he is... Candy coming down?"

He switched on the ignition and backed into the road. "She'll be here any minute."

"She and Roy weren't speaking, you know," Claudia said. "He cried when she broke up with Greg Shapiro. Hated her new marriage."

"Why's that?" Tyler asked.

"He said Reverend Plenty and his deacons are ruthless robbers of the poor."

They drove through wide shady streets, past the Hapgood Colonial-style mansion and Mayor Sondergard's in 1920s gingerbread style. Fountains and sprinklers played on velvet lawns.

"You know this mindreader giving a show Saturday?" Tyler said.

"I believe in them. It would be wonderful if you could hire him to work on..."

"I already have," said Tyler. "The problem is, money. Consultants come high."

"How much?" Claudia asked.

"I told him two thousand. Ought to be three. The budget can't stretch more than five hundred."

Claudia said, "I'll phone Jeff from home and tell him to put three thousand in the P.D. account."

They passed the Donlan house, long and low, its modern lines blending into the scenery, and the pool and tennis court beside it. Tyler pulled up before the Pennington mansion, of dressed stone, spacious and gracious.

Tyler asked, "Remember how we climbed up here, long time ago?"

"Peeking through the hedges," Claudia said. "In our draggletail overalls."

"When we came to this house," Tyler mused, "you said, 'This one's the best. Here's where I want to live'."

"And now I live here." Her tone was so desolate that Tyler unthinkingly reached to comfort her. She slipped out of the car, and said through the open door, "Behave yourself." She clicked the door to, and glided up the flagged path.

She was gone only a few minutes. When she came back, a shoe bag dangling from her arm, she was carrying two prescription slips in her left hand and a frosted beaker in her right. "Drink up. Can't have you starving to death."

"What is it?"

"Carrot and orange juice, with wheat germ."

Tyler made a face, but tasted the drink. "It's good," he said in surprise. He downed it in four gulps while she got back into the car.

"I reached Jeff. The money's on its way," she said. "Drop me at the drug store, Beau."

Tyler said as they drove, "That day, when we went down from here, you let me hug and kiss you."

"I don't recall."

"I do. We'd swiped some peaches from a garden. You tasted like the juice."

She touched his hand. "Stop torturing us, Beau."

He let her out at the drug store. "Want me to wait?"

"No, it's only a few blocks. Tell Candy to call me, would you."

She put two fingers to her lips, glanced up and down the empty street, then quickly brushed her fingers across his cheek.

VI

Diamond Jack's Pawnshop was a weathered wooden structure on Main Street, between the Kute Kurl Beauty Salon and a car wash. Guitars hung in the window above a hodgepodge of clocks, kitchen appliances and jewelry.

A bell on a string tinkled over his head when he entered. The pawnshop was long and narrow, dim after the dazzle of the street. Three ceiling fans stirred the musty air. On Mario's right were racks of shotguns and rifles above cases jammed with handguns. Then followed shelves displaying power tools and a miscellany of pledge items, each with its yellowing tag. Musical instruments were mounted behind the counter on the left.

Near the cash register, on a kitchen chair propped against the wall, a man sprawled, dozing, a crumpled plaid summer shirt on his knees. He had a thick mat of straw-colored hair and a scarlet face. His undershirt was gray with sweat.

"I beg your pardon," Mario said softly.

The heavy-lidded eyes opened, glazed and out of focus. The man reached for the open can of soda on the counter before him, and gulped from it loudly.

"I would like to look at some inexpensive watches," Mario told him.

The man pointed to the rear of the store and closed his eyes again.

Mario picked his way through a clutter of television sets and shaky overburdened tables. The back room was brighter. Dust-filled rays of sunlight came through tottering piles of speakers and amplifiers. Near the door, two oldsters were playing cribbage at a card table. Three middle-aged men in bib overalls, long-legged and potbellied, lounged on wooden chairs. One of them was rhythmically chewing. A sandy-haired man of similar build, wearing chinos and a checked shirt, was rewinding a fishing reel.

"I'm telling you, upstream of the mill," he was saying, "there's still bass to be caught. Fit to eat, too."

Mario cleared his throat delicately. All eyes swung to him. The hand of a cribbage player poised motionless above the pegboard. Conscious of his silk suit, pink shirt and calfskin loafers, Mario felt like an intruder from a far planet.

"Gentlemen," he said with his little bow.

The nearest man picked up an empty coffee can and spat into it a stream of tobacco juice.

"They ain't none here," said the man with the fishing rod.

This brought a wheeze of laughter from the card players. The others continued to stare straightfaced, though the corners of their mouths twitched.

"You have some watches in your display window," Mario began.

The man laid the rod carefully on a guitar amplifier and stepped over three pairs of booted feet to join Mario in the doorway. "You buying or selling?"

"Buying, if the price is low," said Mario. "Allow me to introduce myself. I am Mario Castigliani."

"Jackson Sprague," said the other, with a brief hard handshake. "Come on out front."

"Look out for him, Mister," the tobacco chewer said. "Last watch he sold didn't have no works inside."

"Known locally as Honest Jack," said another, with a slow wink.

Mario followed the proprietor past the sleeping guardian of the cash register.

"Man like you, I'd 'magine he'd be wanting a real snazzy time-piece," said Sprague when he had placed the tray on a front counter. "Now this Rolex here—"

"I would prefer the least expensive," Mario told him. "You see, I foolishly forgot mine when I left New York."

"From New York are ya," the pawnbroker said, with a look of

disgust which he quickly veiled. "Okay, thirty-five bucks for this Seiko."

"I am prepared to spend only in the range of ten dollars," said Mario, enjoying himself.

"Who you kidding?" asked Sprague.

They finally settled on twenty-two-fifty, with an expandable metal wristband from a costlier timepiece thrown in.

Sprague wound and set the watch. "What you doing in town?"

Mario took out a poster and held it up.

The pawnbroker studied it with interest. "Well, I'll be damned. What's that you are, a physic?"

"A psychic," said Mario. "I read minds."

"That so? No wonder you could jaw me down so good." Mario winced, and Sprague went on, "Read that twenty-two-fifty in my mind, did ya."

Mario replied with a cryptic smile, and then said, offering the poster, "Would you permit me...?"

"Sure thing, hand it over," Sprague told him. He stepped up into the window, replaced the tray of watches, and propped the poster against the grimy glass.

When he was back behind the counter, Mario paid him and said, "Thank you, you are most kind. Can you tell me perhaps where there is a public telephone?"

"A phone... if the call's local, you're welcome to use mine." He waved in the direction of a wall phone.

While Sprague busied himself with a ledger, Mario phoned the Rotary Club and arranged to meet with one of its officers after his Saturday performance. Then he called the high school custodian who said Mario could check the stage and sound system two hours before curtain time.

The bell over the shop door tinkled. A gray-haired man with a stubble of beard came in, giving a furtive glance behind him. He craned his scraggy neck to peer into the dim store, and approached the counter.

"Hello, Jack," he said quietly.

He wore a suit that looked cheap and new but was already deeply wrinkled and stained.

Sprague frowned as though puzzled. "What can I do you for," he said, and then with an intake of breath, "Holy shit! Earl. Earl Langford!"

Mario started. Is this then the Earl in the hotel proprietor's thoughts? he wondered. And in the mind of the man in the restaurant? He turned his face to the wall and kept the handset to his ear, though the custodian had already hung up.

"Keep it down, would you," the man pleaded. "I ain't s'posed to be in town."

"Hardly recognized you," Sprague said. "When d'you get out?"

"Monday. Listen, Jack, I gotta talk to you." His eyes scurried to Mario, then away. He added, "Private."

Sprague said, "Go on in back, Earl. I'll be with you in a minute."

"Anybody back there?"

"Just the boys."

Earl Langford slipped past Mario with face averted. Mario said into the silent phone, "Oh, very good then. At six." He hung up, racking his brains for an excuse to return to the back room. But nothing suggested itself.

"All finished?" the pawnbroker asked, closing the ledger.

Mario laid two quarters on the counter. "For the phone," he said.

"Nah, forget it. Local calls is unlimited."

"You are truly generous."

Sprague grinned. "First time ever anybody call me that," he said.

The Shop 'n' Save was crowded with long crude counters piled with remaindered merchandise. Wall-ghosts revealed where mirrors once stood. Mario was the only customer. He selected five pairs of solid-color socks from the unsorted heap on a table. He was shivering: the air conditioning was on full blast.

He took his selections to the cashier, a buxom pony-tailed young woman in a white blouse, who was dully eyeing the cover of a magazine titled *Modern Bride*. A half-written letter lay before her. When he approached, she covered it with the magazine.

"Will there be anything else, sir?" He could see that she had been crying.

"Thank you, no." He handed her the last twenty from his wallet, noting the surprisingly large diamond in the ring on her plump hand. When she turned to the cash register, he tilted the magazine upward.

Her letter, in a round schoolgirl hand, began, "Darlingest Lonnie, It's no use, I got to go through with it."

He replaced the magazine and was putting his parcel into his briefcase when she gave him his change. He took out a poster and introduced himself.

The young woman glanced from the photograph to his face and shook her head. "'Fraid I couldn't make it Saturday." Then with dawning interest, "Gee. Is that true? You can read the future and all?"

"At times I can," Mario lied.

"Maybe I'll try to get there."

"May I post this in the store?"

She took the poster hesitantly. "Mr. Erskine, he's the boss, he'll be back in a few minutes." But she leaned the poster against a display stand, and added, "I reckon he won't mind."

Mario found the newspaper office in the next block, just beyond the First United Methodist Church. "THE FLORAVILLE WEEKLY CLARION" was painted in gothic lettering on the window. Mario was gratified to see his poster in the corner.

Inside, the air was mildly cool, a relief after the sultry street. There was a smell of dust, glue and stale cigar smoke. A young man with fair hair worn long in the hippie style of the 1960s sat at an antiquated desk, typing rapidly with two fingers on a computer patinaed with ink and cigar ash. The front leg of the desk was missing, replaced by a chunk of raw wood.

He got up to shake Mario's hand, saying, "Well, well, you're the psychic. Glad to meet you, I'm Phil. Looking forward to your show."

"On the Clarion staff?"

"I *am* the staff," Phil said with a sigh. "Reid's upstairs. You could go right on up."

Mario made his way through stacked bundles of back copies to a steep cobwebby staircase. It led to a loft even more disorganized than the office below, except for the workspace around two electronic typesetters. From the street window, hot sun flooded in, competing successfully with the air conditioning, and highlighting the jumbles of layout sheets, notebooks, tape and pens. File cabinets, some with their drawers jammed open, stood against the wall.

Cigar smoke lay heavy in blue layers, emanating from a stubby bearded man wearing red suspenders. He stood at a slate-topped layout table, his sides heaving with silent laughter. He beckoned to Mario and pointed with his cigar at the item before him. Mario read:

> They tell me dogs don't go to Heaven.
> But I can't believe that's true.
> Because Jesus loves the loving-hearted,
> So he must love the doggies, too.
>
> Your dog is so faithful and loyal,
> And brings you your slippers and things.
> If anybody ever deserved it,
> He has earned his halo and wings.
>
> And I know in my heart, when my time comes,
> Old Snooker, he will be there,
> Wagging his tail and barking
> At the top of the golden stair.
> — Mary Jane Wilkins

Mario said, for the second time that day, "*Sacra innocenza,*" and then, "You will print this?"

"I'd print it," said the editor, "if I had to cut the lead story to get it in." He gave way to another paroxysm of noiseless laughter, and wiped his eyes with the back of the hand holding the cigar. "Every time I read it, it sends me," he said. He rested his cigar on an overflowing ashtray and offered a hand smudged with newsprint. "Welcome to the Bible Belt."

"You are Mr. Reid Taliaferro?" Mario said, shaking hands.

"Tolliver," said the other; and, to Mario's look of bewilderment, "We write it 'Taliaferro' but say 'Tolliver'. An old Southern pronunciation, Mr. Castig-lianee."

"Casteel-yanee," Mario told him, grinning, "An old Italian pronunciation."

"*Touché,*" said Taliaferro, returning the grin.

"But surely your people must have come from Italy?"

"Way way back in Colonial days. We don't advertise it. This town tends to be hostile to foreigners, by which they mean anybody whose grandad's grandad wasn't born in the Piedmont... Did you come to have a look at your ad and our story?" He picked out a current issue from a cluttered desk, opened it and handed it to Mario.

"Mainly I came to thank you in person for putting up my poster."

"No sweat," the editor said. "Durrell, that's our delivery boy, did the posting."

Mario glanced at the boxed ad, a replica of his poster, and scanned the five-paragraph story. It was about the Rotary Club and its planned youth center, which was intended to serve as a social antidote to the lure of drugs. Mario was mentioned in the final sentence.

Taliaferro had moved to another layout table, and was studying it with a thoughtful frown. "One of our local celebrities hanged himself last night," he said when Mario joined him. "Big news. The city papers will cover it, even *The New York Times*. I'm working out a photospread."

Mario concealed his excitement as the large-eyed high-cheekboned black face of his morning's vision, then ghastly in death, leapt out at him from a dozen or more photographs. Roy Washington bold and eager in youth, strong and challenging in maturity, frail but feisty in old age. He was shown on a platform with Coretta King; marching with Bayard Rustin; and shaking hands with Jesse Jackson. There were action shots of him addressing a rally, shepherding new voters into a polling booth, picketing the mill, gesturing in triumph on the steps of a courthouse. Mario recognized that picture: he had seen it framed on the wall of his vision.

"*Molto bravo*," he said. "A remarkable face."

"Remarkable man. One of a kind." The editor tapped a picture before him. It showed an earlier Floraville with fewer stores and an unpaved street. A line of National Guardsmen aimed their rifles at a huddled phalanx of gaunt millworkers, most of them women in shapeless cotton dresses. They shrank together in attitudes at once fearful and courageous. There were only three or four black faces, one of them that of small defiant boy.

"Before my time," Taliaferro said. "General Textile Strike, 1934. That's Roy in front, all of ten years old. Already in it up to his skinny neck. Was a courier for the union organizers."

"Did they get their union?"

"They got shot. Five people killed that day. Roy, he never gave up on the union. After the mill was integrated, in the sixties, he and a few other diehards nearly succeeded." The editor opened a folder of clippings and laid it before Mario. "But every attempt won them something. Wage hikes, cleaner air."

Mario flipped through the clippings, stopping with a wordless exclamation when he came to the headline: "Langford Sentenced in Gutmacher Case."

"But I know of this case!" he said. "I remember it on television." Barry Gutmacher, a civil rights attorney, had been forced from his car and beaten to death by Klansmen. The investigation and trial had dragged on for three years, resulting in a single conviction.

"It made headlines all over the country." Taliaferro said. "Plenty of witnesses, but only Roy had the guts to testify. Earl Langford, he was the fall guy. Thirty to life."

He pointed to a large cabinet photo in the middle of the table: Roy, looking distinguished in a tuxedo, with an arm around a young woman in a bridal veil, whose large eyes and high cheekbones echoed his own. His other arm embraced the groom, a beaming white youth with outstanding ears. A memo slip taped to the frame said, Not Run.

"That's Roy's daughter Candace, married Gutmacher's associate. Gregory Shapiro. Made quite a stir in these parts."

"But you did not print this picture," Mario said.

Taliaferro gave a bark of laughter. "The Clarion sticks its neck out from time to time," he said. "But there is a limit. I'm not looking for rocks through my window."

A phone half-concealed under the drift of papers on the desk was flashing a signal. Taliaferro shoved the papers aside, sat down and said into the phone, "I'm running out to Warren… Load the camera would you… Oh, and I can't find the Kendall file… Thanks, just put it on my desk."

He jumped to his feet and hurried to a rust-stained sink with a mirror above it.

"I have to go out," he told Mario. He washed his hands and combed his short beard, which seemed now to bristle with energy. "But you stay as long as you like. Make yourself at home."

He slipped a suit jacket over the garish suspenders, and took out a fresh cigar.

"Grazie," Mario said. "I would like to look through your current issue."

Taliaferro pointed to a table with brief items neatly laid out. He cleared his throat and said, "You might want to check these. Engagements. Births. Deaths. Social notes. Who's sick, who's on vacation, whose uncle is visiting where."

Mario stared, hardly believing his ears.

"We don't go to press until Tuesday," the editor said in a conspiratorial tone. He came to Mario and clapped him on the back, then went quickly to the head of the staircase. He turned, laid a finger to his nose, closed one eye, and spoke around the wagging cigar. "I won't breathe to a soul, Mr. Castig- oops, sorry. Mr. Casteel-yanee."

"Call me Mario."

"Mario it is. *Ciao.* Till Saturday."

The *Floraville Weekly Clarion,* circulation seventy-five hundred, covered local events only. The front page frequently headlined reports, always glowing, of revivals, of music evangelist rallies, church fund drives, and S.A.J. ("Sing Along With Jesus") picnics.

The general tone of upbeat piety and local patriotism was belied by stories here and there which hinted at the declining economy of the area and the stubborn ubiquity of traditional racism. In police news, moonshining loomed large on the docket. Fatal and near-fatal accidents due to D.U.I. ("Driving Under the Influence") were so common as to be merely listed. Automobile and firearm thefts were reported regularly, and battery and child abuse were not unknown. The rare homicides seemed to be domestic affairs.

Mario speedread and memorized the last four issues, including the classifieds and the store ads.

He wanted to return to the photospread on Royal Washington but felt impelled to take advantage first of Taliaferro's astonishing offer. He bent over the layout sheets of the coming issue's announcements, his lips unconsciously moving as he matched names to happenings to dates. He took a pad from his briefcase and jotted an occasional note: a rare practice for him, but justified by the extent of this treasure trove. One item elicited a grunt of gratification: "Mr. and Mrs. Hiram Collier announce the engagement of their daughter Christine to Victor Erskine, Vice President of the Floraville Merchants' Association."

A cheery whistling came from below, then the sound of light footsteps running up the stairs. In one tiptoed stride, Mario reached the desk chair and was seated, apparently concentrating on a back issue, when Phil ascended to the loft.

"I'll only be a minute," Phil said, heading toward the file cabinets. "Hope I'm not disturbing you."

"Not at all," Mario murmured, turning a page.

Whistling softly between his teeth, Phil searched the files. "Reid's got his own personal filing system," he said over his shoulder. "Elsewhere unknown in the archives of journalism."

He stacked four fat ragged folders marked "P.D." on a corner of the desk, and topped them with two labeled Kendall, Rutherford (Xfile Police). "These were right where they belonged, under K," he said. "That's why he couldn't find them."

"If you need anything," Phil told him, "give me a shout. Sink's over there. Toilet's behind the typesetter."

Phil, already halfway down the stairs, called back, "Reid said to give you run of the place."

Mario opened the top Kendall, Rutherford folder, thinking, Now why. Why this file at this time. An unmounted clipping fluttered to the floor. He picked it up and read:

CHIEF OF POLICE FOUND DEAD

The body of Floraville's Police Chief, Rutherford Kendall, was discovered Monday night, hanging in the attic of his home at 187 Pecan Street. Mrs. Kendall, returning from a two-week convalescence at Cherokee Springs, found him at 6:45 p.m.

"I never even knew he had cancer," sobbed the widow, who is the former Miss Veronica Webster. Terence Hapgood, R.N., who had attended Chief

Kendall at Warren Memorial Medical Center, affirmed that a diagnosis of colon cancer had been made only last week.

The body was taken to the Green Meadows Funeral Home. Funeral arrangements are incomplete.

In lieu of a note, Chief Kendall left an open Bible on a nearby table with Psalm 119:153 marked in pencil: "Consider mine affliction and deliver me: for I do not forget thy law."

The followup story took up two full pages, with pictures. Mario studied a late photo in which Kendall, thick-waisted, exceptionally tall, looked like a beardless balding Santa Claus.

Interviews and anecdotes gave highlights of a long and colorful career. Kendall obviously had been a prized and often-quoted town character. He had fulminated mightily against restrictions on search-and-seizure, and against the Miranda ruling. "'I'd give them their rights all right,' he had said. 'I'd press their pants where the sun don't shine.'"

The page ended tersely: "Lieutenant Andrew Abbot has been appointed Acting Chief of the Floraville Police Department."

Intrigued, Mario leafed through a "P.D." folder, stopping to read an item:

TYLER ASKED TO FILL KENDALL POST
Lieutenant Beaufort Tyler of the Americus police has been invited by the Floraville Board of Aldermen to return to his home town as Chief of Police...

Mario debated with himself whether to explore this rich vein now, or first to complete his perusal of next week's Social Notes. A picture in the uppermost issue on the desk diverted his thoughts: six little girls, beguiling in dance skirts and tights, awkwardly posed before their instructor, over the caption "Rehearsing for the Labor Day Recital." The camera was focussed on the children, with the teacher hardly more than a blur. But it was she who had caught his attention. Narrowing his eyes, he made out that she was tall, slim and brunette.

Is that you, my lady of the swallows? he wondered. His throat tightened. The text gave the names of the pupils and ended: "...under the tutelage of Mrs. Jeff Pennington at the Tremont Studio."

Finding the Pennington file was easy enough. It filled two cabinets and three drawers of a third. Daunted by its vastness, Mario tried to fathom Taliaferro's filing system, which was roughly by decade, starting 1900-10, and partly by first names: Abigail-Zebediah.

In 1970-80, he was distracted by a typed interview with an Alan Jesse Donlan, M.D., dated 1978 and tagged "Permission to publish withdrawn." Why was it in this file? he wondered, feeling cross with Taliaferro. *Guazzo,* sloppy! Then, scanning the introductory paragraph, he saw that Dr. Donlan's mother was a Pennington, and that he had married his Pennington cousin. The writer subtly implied the scandal occasioned in the town by this marriage.

Mario glanced through, stopping on the third page:

> "Enterprise! Have we forgotten the meaning of this proud word?" Dr. Donlan challenged. "The daring, the adventure it implies."
>
> He talked admiringly of the founders of Floraville's industry, the Warrens, Kendalls, Penningtons, Hapgoods and Yorks of the last century. "Grand old pioneers," he said. "They not only had the foresight to envision the potential of the region, but the guts to do something about it."

The interview contained no reference to the ballet teacher. Mario slid the pages back into their folder. A random search of the 1980-90 file contained nothing under "Jeff."

"Tremont Studio?" he murmured. He hunkered down before the cabinet at the end of the row and pulled out the R-U drawer. He found what he was looking for: Tremonte/Tremont (Xfile Rupert Jefferson Pennington). Mario opened it, nervously spilling half its contents to the floor. Her tilted dark eyes gazed up at him with poignant melancholy from a portrait photo. "Mr. and Mrs. Carmine Tremonte announce the engagement of their daughter Claudia to R. Jefferson Pennington..."

Una italiana. Tremonte was a Tuscan name, and also not uncommon in Umbria. He retrieved the fallen clippings and carried the folder, on his palms as though it were a living creature, to the nearest table. He went through it back to front, past to present.

CROSSROADS GENERAL STORE
BOUGHT BY LOCAL PEDDLER

Mr. Carmine Tremonte, whose brightly painted van filled with crisp snap beans, ripe tomatoes and farm-fresh eggs has long been a welcome sight on Floraville streets, will reopen the vacant Crossroads General Store at Carmel Avenue and Old River Road for the retail sale of local produce...

A mounted family snapshot was stapled to this over a scribbled list of names and the notation: "2/9/65. Not Run." Carmine and Maria Tremonte and seven children were grouped in front of their new greengrocery. Mario easily recognized Claudia among the children, leggy and with the look of a tomboy, clearly uncomfortable in her Sunday frock.

The glimpses of biography yielded by the folder were maddeningly incomplete. Claudia Tremonte at twelve, dancing in the school auditorium to Mendelssohn's *Spring Song*. At fourteen, costumed as the Sugarplum Fairy, in an Atlanta production of *The Nutcracker Suite*. Awarded a scholarship at eighteen to the New York School of Theatre Ballet. Briefly reported four times, in her twenties, as a member of a postmodern troupe, with favorable reviews quoted from New York papers. Then an accident on tour, a fall during rehearsal in an Amsterdam theatre. Multiple fractures of the right knee.

"*Poverina!*" Mario whispered. He had arrived again at the engagement photo. "*Cara. Bellissima. Perduta per sempre.*" He did not know whether he was addressing the woman in the picture or his long dead wife. His vision blurred with unshed tears. Half-blinded, he replaced the folder and closed the drawer.

He wandered to the window overlooking the vacant street, and stood there for uncounted moments, stirred and shaken.

Then he saw her.

She was walking away from him, halfway along the next block, a tall thin figure in black. There was no mistaking that swift dancer's glide, that graceful back.

Mario snatched up his briefcase and ran, nearly falling down the stairs. He recovered his balance, and was out the door, with a wild gesture at the startled Phil. He hurried along the scorching pavement.

Claudia Pennington was two blocks ahead of him now and moving almost as fast as he. The pitiless sun was in his eyes. Her figure seemed to flicker like the image cast by a slow magic lantern. Then she disappeared altogether, and he realized she had turned a corner.

"Reliable Feed Emporium" said the faded sign over the corner store. Mario stood panting under its awning and scanned the side street. A concrete row of stores with lofts above them faced a line of trees and one-family houses. The street was empty of people. He walked the short block on the far side, looked vainly up and down the cross street, and returned slowly, scrutinizing the storefronts.

The windows of the upper storeys were shuttered or curtained. Mario listened intently, hoping for the sound of a piano and the rhythmic thud of dancing feet. There was only the drowsy hush of the summer afternoon. He sighed profoundly, accepting defeat, and went back to the cross street. Without thought, his throat congested with emotion, he wandered through the town. He passed a uniformed maid wheeling a baby carriage and a woman in a sunhat weeding a garden. He came to a bridge under which the brown ribbon of the river meandered, and stood, heedless of time, gazing blankly down at the water. Leaves floated along its surface. A cloud of mosquitoes rose to sing in his ears and bite him.

The Town Hall clock struck three. Mario roused himself and looked at his newly purchased watch. Three minutes fast, or the clock might be three minutes slow. He ought to get back to the *Clarion* office and take full advantage of Taliaferro's impish generosity, then find a good spot for the last poster in his briefcase, then seek out a luncheonette and assuage hunger and thirst before his four o'clock appointment.

But he did none of these. He slapped at mosquitoes and gazed idly at the blood on his hand, then made his way back to Main Street and found the park. The heat of the day was at zenith. There was no one on the benches.

Mario sat fingering the insect bites on his neck. He breathed in fine spray from the sprinklers. He was lost in the past, remembering. Remembering how once long ago he had followed another blackclad woman, through other streets, past other shops. She too had been graceful and swift, and aristocratic of bearing.

VII

Communication between Mario and his mother had never been easy. She had an air of heroic self-control and a haughty accent that intimidated him. When he and Stefano were little, she had supervised their religious education. Now that they were growing toward manhood, she announced herself resigned to seeing them follow their anticlerical father.

"You are not to blame, my poor little sons," she told them. "Let it be on his head who has led you from Christ."

The boys heard the spite under the piety: their love for her suffered. Stefano protested that even *Papà* went to mass at Easter.

"One does not serve Our Lord only at Easter," she answered coldly.

Stefano avoided her. Mario could have done the same. With each passing year she kept more to herself. Only rarely did she call Mario to her spacious chamber.

She would say, "Read to me, *figlio mio*. My eyes are tired."

The lives of the saints. San Francesco's "Canticle of the Creatures." But she liked Petrarch as well, and the dramas of D'Annunzio.

"Your greataunt Rosamonda met him once. Have I told you?"

"*Sì, Mamma*, you told me."

"We wintered in Rome. On opening night I wore my violet satin with lace on the sleeves. The real Alençon, one can't find it nowadays."

"Yes, Mamma, I know. And an ivory fan."

This time-honored exchange was repeated one day soon after his fifteenth birthday. She surprised him by adding: "I was considered a beauty in those days."

"You are beautiful still," he said quickly.

She took her embroidery frame from the table by the sofa and contemplated the bright silks of the floral pattern. Mario shut the book of plays. Cautiously, he pressed a finger to his forehead. Her mute voice was saying **They called me a Titian. Before it turned white.** Then she started as though stung by a wasp, and glared at him.

"That will do, Mario! You have my permission to go."

She knows, Mario told himself as he left her. Somehow she knows. At the dinner table he tried again to enter her mind. Through the loud conversation of his father and brother, he received a few indistinct words from her. Then something like vocalized radio static. Deliberately produced interference, he felt. He lowered his head over his plate to escape her outraged stare.

He made several attempts that week, and found he could succeed only when she was unaware of his presence. He listened at the open door of her room while she sat nodding on the sofa.

He shivered at the gloom of her dream. Night and rain. Wind tossing the tops of a cypress grove. A grave gaped, a casket beside it. **Giorgio, Giorgio, child of my loins, oh, do not desert me!** Mario saw his mother's bony body nearly naked on top of the coffin. She embraced it with stifled moans. The rosewood lid became translucent, then transparent. The moldy corpse stared upward. **Papà, come back to me!** Another face, then another. **Zia Rosa! Basilio! Why have you forsaken me?** she whispered and sobbed.

Mario tiptoed away, his arms crawling with gooseflesh. Poor woman, poor Mamma! In love with the dead.

He cut school the next day to follow her to the piazza. She glided ahead of him like a black swan. He dared not walk closely behind her. Thoughts from strollers and shoppers intervened: he exerted himself to receive only from her. **Ha, Graziella! How dare you? The bracelet is mine.** An image, his aunt, dead for five years, as a fairhaired girl tossing her head. **You traitor, bugiarda, Zia promised it to me. And you know it, you sneak.**

Mario's mother entered a bookstore, and he ducked out of sight. When she emerged with a parcel, he followed again, tuning in on a different quarrel. *Porco.* The coarse word was doubly shocking in her fine Italian. **Filthy dog. Take your hands off me, you swine.** Mario saw his father's face, young, flushed with desire and wine, so close to his own that he stumbled against a cafe table.

After she completed her errands, she went into the cathedral. Mario waited, then entered discreetly. She was in the della Rovere chapel, in the hushed stained-glass glow beneath the soaring vault. He concealed himself in a nearby pew.

She was praying aloud. "…blessed art Thou, and blessed the fruit of Thy womb…" **Ohimè, bambina mia! My golden Angela! Why did you have to suffer like that?** Mario was made witness to the death agonies of his baby sister. "…Holy Mary, Mother of God…" **Our children died for your sins, Salvatore. Ahì, and for mine, that I allowed you to…** The sexual passage in her mind was so explicit that Mario could not suppress his loud gasp.

Eleanora did not turn her head. "…Pray for us sinners…" **But I will be with her in paradise, while you, assassin of innocence…** A huge wall of flames, and his father writhing in hell. **Burn, Salvatore. Va fan culo!** "…Now and at the hour of our death." **Burn, you son of a sow!**

Mario fled. Unseeing, unhearing he ran down through the city, flight after flight of stone stairways. Exhausted and panting, he came to a halt. He hung over a balustrade and vomited into a flowerbed. He clung there, in the chill rain, until the winter twilight fell. *Oh, Mamma, poor Mamma! It is you who are in hell.*

Maì più, never again! Mario vowed to himself. *I am finished with spying. Lucia mia, why didn't you warn me?* In that house of garrulous men, and of women who hardly spoke, he too became silent.

He felt old and thirsted for the healing purity of his miracle. The seasons rolled on, but he could not evoke her. The down on his lip grew thicker. His voice deepened. He was taller than his father. His innate cheerfulness, the bounce natural to his boyhood, did not reassert itself for more than a year. He plunged then into the rhythms of school and vacation, of work in the dispensary and at the dig. He tried not to touch the eye between his eyes. Looked quickly away from handwriting. When voices or visions came unbidden, he blotted them out.

Yet often at night he gripped the lion coin and pleaded for the pure, whole experience. *Have I offended her? She who gave me those powers?*

Mario was seventeen when *la Lucia* came back with the springtime. He had walked down from the city into the fields vivid with wildflowers, carrying books, and some bread, wine and cheese. He was behind in his studies: the scholarship exam in Milan was a scant two months away. A parasol pine by a brook was a fine place to study. Then he ate, drank and rested, his shoulders against the tree.

And the lovely light took him, exalting, dissolving. No clear revelations this time. Words and pictures so evanescent he hardly had time to absorb them. An old song of the countryside, the rough-clad goatherd who sang it. Picnicking lovers. A wreath of margheritinas, a fragrant sprig of green oregano, the poignant idyll of April. Two girls dancing with whirling ruffles of petticoats.

When it was over, his rush of joy carried him to the brook. How blue was the water, how clean! Mario drank from his cupped hands, and thanked her again and again. "Don't go, stay with me!" he called, smiling. He wanted to ask about those lesser clairvoyances. No palpable response. Only a growing conviction. "She does not care," Mario murmured. Her gifts are to use as I will. If they cost me pain, well, such is the price.

On the way home he gathered some *campanule* and *tromboncine* for Modesta. He had continued to bring her flowers from time to time. Because of that wonderful *tagliatelle,* he would tell her. Or the rabbit with *funghi;* the *zabaglione,* whatever. And her plain, good, marred face would beam.

He went back to reading minds: in the streets, the cafes, the sports fields. In the museums, on the farms, at the dig and at home. Not the mind of his mother, no, *basta!* But everyone else was fair game. I am the king of Perugia, he crowed to himself. He came across only one other person who, like his mother, could frustrate his attempts: her brother, Uncle Massimo. Three others were impenetrable: a surly farmer with a sick calf; Oriana, the illigitimate daughter of Modesta the family maid; and the fat placid widow at the newspaper kiosk. They do not block me on purpose like Mamma and Zio, Mario concluded; they just have a natural wall in their head. So thick and so hard even *la Lucia* cannot get through.

Va bene, one in fifty, who cares? He would press the spot on his brow and pick a new subject. He liked best to tune in on *le perugiane*. So many pretty ones, blonde, *brunette e rosse*. I am charmed by them all, he would chortle, and they are all charmed by me, Mario, *il bel giovane*. When I cannot see it in their eyes, I can read it in their heads.

Yet Mario found himself reluctant to fall in love. He was not a virgin. He had been only fifteen when he succumbed to the lively Signora Tresca, who had introduced a number of his friends to the garden of Eros. And last year he had dallied with Pippa Santini, the prettiest girl in the school.

Each of these brief adventures had been in its way delightful. But when the afterglow faded, Mario thought, Is that all? Is this what the poets have sung about down through the ages: an hour of tingling nerves and sweaty embraces, a spasm of pleasure? Well, good enough fun! But not to be compared to *la Lucia*. Besides, he had an uneasy conviction that *la Lucia* did not approve. Not that she could be jealous of mortal women. Certainly not! Simply that she preferred that he abstain.

One balmy evening early in May, Salvatore took Mario and Stefano to a political debate at the Palazzo Comunale.

"Don't you ever give up, *Papà*?" Stefano teased. They were in the throng inching toward the carved Gothic doors.

Mario was admiring, as he did every time he came to the Palazzo, the fanciful griffin, symbol of the city, and the bronze lion which stood near the entryway.

"—But in the question period," Salvatore continued, "there will be fireworks! From the audience! Every group on the left is sending a claque, anarchists, syndicalists, Trotskyists…"

Mario stopped listening to his father. In the press of the slowly moving queue, the excited chatter around him had given way to the eerie familiar hush preceding reception. Utter silence. And then: countless unspoken thoughts. All at once. Clamoring, whispering, muttering, calling, they attacked his head like a swarm of angry bees. Always until now he had been able more or less to focus on one mind alone. Always before he had the power to tune out if he wished. Now he stood helpless, his knees weak, his hands clapped over his ears.

Oh, what a nightmare swamp, what a stinking, writhing mass! Stupidity, malice, bald lust, cruelty, hypocrisy, apathy, brutal indifference, avarice, low cunning, hatred, ignorance, spite…

"Mario! Mario! What is it with you?" His father was hugging him, shaking him, when Mario came to himself.

"*Papà*, I am sick."

"I can see you are. Where does it hurt? Stefano, run, get the *dottore*."

"No, *Papà*. Just let me… go away, go home."

They moved out of the crowd into the piazza, near the fountain. Mario sat on the circular bench in the refreshing chill of the spray. His father and brother hung over him. "I'm taking you home," said his father.

"No, *Papà*, I'll take him," Stefano offered. "See, he looks better already. Stay for your *comizio*."

"Stay for the meeting," Mario echoed. "Both of you. I can get home by myself."

When he had persuaded them, he remained there in the fading daylight. Tears ran down his face, mingling with droplets from the fountain. Come on, Mario, he scolded himself. You more than anyone know people are bad.

The piazza was almost empty of people. They are all at the meeting, he thought. From the Palazzo Comunale, occasional waves of acclaim or of booing reached him. He gave a short laugh: the horror was fading. He grinned ruefully. No more will I vow to abstain. He knew he would go back to spying again. Like a lapsed alcoholic. I am an addict.

He jumped up and ran for home.

The villa was quiet. Mario rarely caught sight of Mamma these days. She was more than ever a recluse, undergoing sporadic attacks of mysterious disabling pain.

He entered the big kitchen, intent on leftover *chicces*.

"Modesta!"

She was not there. The stone floor was still damp from scrubbing. The tables were cleared, freshly washed. Mario peered through the strings of purple onions and the pale tubes of cheeses which dangled from the high beams. He saw Oriana in the scullery. She had paused in the act of scouring a laundry tub.

"My mamma's in bed, Master Mario, sir," she said softly as he approached her. "She wasn't feeling so good."

"She's sick?"

Oriana's gaze was lowered as usual. Yet tonight she looked different. A curling lock of black hair had escaped from her kerchief, and lay against her pale cheek. She is really very pretty, Mario thought. Even … beautiful. Why have I not noticed before?

"No, sir, only an *indisposizione.* Can I fetch you something?"

Mario stared at her, no longer hungry for food. He touched his finger to his forehead, though he knew she was one of the few he could not read. Her bodice, wet from her task, clung to her upper torso. Graceful and strong, slender yet rounded… She raised her head and opened large tilted eyes. Above perfect lips, raptly smiling. These eyes he read with no need of *la Lucia*'s help. *Ti amo,* they were saying, *ti adoro.*

He reached over the tub and touched her rough little hand. A thrill shot through him from crown to toe.

What new goddess was here, unseen in the scullery, striking him with such merciless ecstasy? Not *la Lucia!* Venera? His groin was tight with desire. His head reeled.

Oriana reeled, too, holding onto the laundry tub for support. He saw that the nipples of her high breasts had come erect against the wet cloth. Blows of passion struck like fists to his body and head.

"Oriana!" he whispered. "*Perduta mia!*"

She was backing from him, toward the room she shared with her mother. Her adoring eyes never left his face.

Then she was gone. He stood yearning, tumescent. Here is a power, he dizzily thought, as great as *la Lucia.*

In his room, a third goddess poured her gift through his window: *la luna.* Or are you three really one? he wondered as he undressed. He washed himself like a bridegroom. Put on his nightshirt. Took it off. Lay supine on his bed. Trembling and waiting.

The door creaked open, then shut. Oriana stood in the moonlight, barefoot, wearing only her shift. She undid her crown of braids as she came to him. Masses of silky black hair cascaded over him. He kissed her open mouth.

Later she said, "*Signorino Mario—*"

"Please. Not master, *bellissima.* Your servant forever."

"Mario. I'm afraid."

"I too am afraid."

"Will it hurt me…? *Non ti preoccupare.* I don't care if you hurt me, *amore.*"

Still later, as they lay afloat after their climax: "Will I get a baby, my Mario?"

He came down with a thump. "*In nome di Dio,* I hope not!" A shower of kisses on his chest banished reality.

"*Non ti preoccupare, carissimo.* I want you to give me your baby."

Mario propped himself on his elbow and spread Oriana's thick fragrant hair on the pillow. The better to see her. How brilliant the moon. Is such beauty possible then? Not sculpted in stone, nor painted on canvas? In warm bright living flesh.

She covered her face with her hands. "We have done a terrible sin."

He saw she was laughing, and laughed, too. "Let's do it again and go to confession together."

"And make love in the box. Now *silenzio,* or they'll hear us."

Dawn found them still caressing. They arose and stripped the bed. Not many years ago, Mario reflected, the mother of a bride would have hung such a crimsoned sheet from the balcony. "The proof of your maidenhead, Oriana."

She took up the bedclothes and noiselessly left the room.

Full daylight had come when she returned with clean sheets. She was in her long dress, kerchief and apron. He had put on his workclothes. They kissed in a new deluge of ardor.

"Tonight, *tesoro?*"

"Tonight, *amore mio.*"

And night after night after night. In the daytime, Mario thought of nothing but Oriana. Starved for sleep, wakeful with desire, he relived the moonlit hours. Her taut inner thigh, the curve from her breast to her shoulder, the pulse at the base of her throat. I ought to be studying. I'm due in the dispensary. I should climb up to the dig.

Instead he would steal to the kitchen or clothesline, seeking the headiness of a secret glance. Once, serving dinner, she brushed against the back of his head. Mario dropped his fork with a clatter.

"Eh, Mario, what are you mooning about?" Salvatore teased.

"He's in love," crowed Stefano. "Come on, who is she, eh, Mario?"

He asked his father's permission to teach Oriana reading and writing. "A fine thing," Salvatore approved, "I am proud that you have concern for the future of this poor white mouse. Help yourself to the books."

Oriana could recite the alphabet, sign her name, and read simple sentences, a finger under each word as she deciphered it. She learned with breathtaking speed, revelling in nursery rhymes and Pinocchio. And the lessons, of course, afforded opportunities to drown now and then in a kiss.

"This cat is well," Salvatore said one morning, lifting from a cage the Angora tabby of the mayor's wife. "You can take her home."

"I have to study, *Papà*." Mario stroked the cat's throat. She was purring. "Can't Stefano take her?"

"*Va bene*. Remember, at one o'clock we drive down to where the donkey was hit by a car."

Mario went through the house looking for Oriana. To his horror, he found her in his mother's dressing room, trying on clothes from a trunk. He smelled mothballs. She posed before a pier glass in a lowcut gown of emerald velvet. Pearls circled her ivory throat. Her wealth of black tresses was piled on the back of her head. Other garments lay on the bed, one of them violet satin with yellowing lace on the sleeves.

"Oriana, how dare you!"

She whirled to face him, flushed with guilt, unutterably lovely.

"My *m-mother*—" he stammered.

"At the *cimitero*. She won't come home for hours."

"—*your* mother."

"Out marketing."

"Still, what a risk, *pazza mia!*" Her laughter was merry as a child's.

She took up a plumed fan and paraded with mock hauteur. "And how do you like me?"

"No duchessa was ever more beautiful. How changed you are, Oriana." The downcast eyes and neat kerchief were now a disguise, a joke shared between them. When they were alone, she was as lively as an unbroken colt.

"It was you who released me from prison, my dearest." She took off the gown, revealing her mended *camicetta* and rough skirt. She folded away the finery, shut the trunk, and stretched her bare Etruscan arms to Mario. But however drunk with desire, however fevered with her contagious boldness, Mario drew the line. As they kissed, he moved her away from his mother's bed.

"We'll go to my room," he said firmly.

"*Avanti, popolo! alla riscossa—*" bellowed Salvatore as the car spiraled homeward. The injured donkey was making a strong recovery. The June sunset was a glory. "*Bandiera rossa, bandiera rossa...*"

"*Papà.* Eh, *Papà.* I got to talk to you," Mario said.

I don't like that tone, he heard his father thinking. **Am I about to be knifed in my guts?** "Well, go ahead, talk."

"I don't want to be a veterinarian. I am not all that crazy about cows."

"Who you kidding? Who is it sits up all night at calving time?"

"*Va bene,* I like the animals. But I want to be an archeologist."

Ahimè. Like il principe, her brother. "Like your uncle, eh?"

"What's so bad? He is a curator, assistant anyway."

Salvatore parked the car by the cliff at a wide stretch of highway. "Fancy name for a janitor. They gave him the job out of charity. After his failure."

"What failure?"

She doesn't boast about that, Donna Eleanora. "You don't know Massimo della Rovere was a *maestro di scacchi?* Almost won the national chess championship."

"I never dreamed."

"Afterwards, they cold-shouldered him out of the chess federation. On suspicion of cheating. Now he plays with himself only."

Mario brought himself back to his purpose. "Okay, *Papà*. Like *il professore* then. Why can't Stefano carry on the tradition?"

Your poor brother. He doesn't have the brains. Or the touch. "Stefano will make a big career in the soccer. Already he has good offers." Salvatore laid a finger to his large nose. "You afraid of the exam next week, eh, Mario?"

Mario blushed. "*Sì, Papà*, I haven't studied enough."

"*Ascolti*, I know you been tomcatting around somewhere. I'm not so dumb. If you fail, if you don't get a scholarship, I'll find the money for the college. Promise me you'll try a couple years anyway, working as a vet." **Please, figlio mio, please, my wonderful boy. Don't break my heart.**

"*Va bene, Papà*. I will try." I can not hurt him so much. I will ask him again another time.

Salvatore put the Fiat back on the upward road. "If you really don't take to it, *ti prometto*, you can study for archeology."

Fair enough, Mario consoled himself.

He had never been to Milan. As the train wound northwestward he gazed unseeing at the unfamiliar landscape, absorbed in thoughts of Oriana. Already our crazy rapture is dimming. The blinding iridescence of *la Dea Venere,* he decided, is like a skyrocket, not meant to endure. His love was now deeper but tamer. Her love was greater than his.

When he changed trains at Florence, he caught himself returning the flirtatious glances of a charming *turista* on the platform, and enjoying her salacious thoughts. Mario, pig and betrayer, he scolded without much conviction.

Bologna, Modena. The car was reserved for students bound for the national June scholarship examinations. His compartment was filling up with fellow applicants. Reggio, Parma. The young people talked of the impending exam, probing in hope of advance information. Mario listened to their thoughts. This Carlo, from Imola, he with the yellow cowlick, Mario told himself, is some kind of a genius. And really prepared, not like me.

For the first time it occurred to him that his clairvoyance might have opportunistic uses. I could read the answers in Carlo's mind. Could I not. Between him and me, Mario, who is not a bad scholar even when unprepared… Would you let me do that, *Lucia mia?* Sometimes so coolly permissive, sometimes my implacable moralist. He felt that she would not approve. But maybe, just maybe, she will let me get away with it.

Cremona. Milan. As he took his knapsack from the overhead shelf, a theatre poster on the platform arrested his eye.

WILHELM WINCKLER the WONDERWORKER

can read your future and your mind
Appearing Friday, July 10

Wonderworker is he? He could be another of Her proteges. I better come see him.

Mario jotted down the theatre address.

The train carried him homeward through the summer night. He knew he had scored brilliantly on the exam - with the unwitting help of one Carlo from Imola. Exhilaration, guilt and fear wrestled within him. He called silently on *la Lucia.* She did not respond. He tested his mindreading power on fellow passengers. It functioned, but feebly, it seemed to him.

At home Mario went to his room and undressed. No moon tonight, but the thick-clustered stars shone through his window. A fragrance of roses came from the garden.

Oriana came in on tiptoe, locked the door and flew to his arms.

"*Ah, cara,* you are hurting me!" Mario said. "Why are you troubled?"

"You came back," she said. "Hold me tight."

"*Amore,* I have not been gone for even a day. What will you do when I go off to school?"

"Yes, what will I do, oh, what will I do!"

He freed himself from her strong beautiful arms and seated her gently on the bed. "Look, dry your eyes, I have a present for you."

He took a parcel from his knapsack and watched while she opened it, already consoled. She unwrapped a jar, turned the lid and sniffed at the scent. "Like strawberries! Is it to eat?"

"*No, innamorata,* for the sore little hands."

"But there are two jars."

"One is for your *mamma.*"

Oriana spread some of the strawberry cream on her palm and stroked it into his thigh.

"Come to bed," Mario murmured, undoing her blouse.

When the examination results were published, Mario was an overnight celebrity. No other *perugino* had ever scored so high. His mark was the third highest in the history of the state program.

Guilty, embarrassed, he shrank from the congratulations. He locked himself in his room.

Stefano pounded on the door.

"Go away," called Mario. "I am trying to rest."

"Come on, open up. Uncle Berto has come. And the cousins. A committee is on its way here. They want to make you a big *festa.*"

Mario opened the door. His brother thrust the local paper at him. "Look, your picture's on the front page."

"I wish they would just leave me alone." Mario heard his brother's thoughts, a mix of sore envy and vicarious vanity. But there was generosity in him, too, admiration, genuine good wishes.

"Don't be such a modest *fiorellino,*" Stefano said. "*Papà* is *pazzo* with joy. Even Mamma is smiling."

"All right. I will come in a minute."

"And listen, *Zio* Massimo came by. He wants you to go to him tonight at the *Museo.*"

The lights of the museum were dimmed except in the glass-enclosed cubicle to which he followed Uncle Massimo. From the walls the Etruscans gazed with their great stone eyes and smiled their seraphic stone smiles. Mario felt their irresistible magnetism. He wanted only to plunge into their world and their time.

Two folding chairs and a table with a half-played chess game stood in the cone of light. Mario, his eyes on the board, seated himself across from his uncle.

"Look at me, *ragazzo*."

Mario flinched from the steady regard of Massimo's grave eyes. They were of the della Rovere gray, large, darkly circled in the sad, crumpled face, the irises so light as to seem almost colorless.

"You have been granted a great gift, *nipote mio*. Never abuse it. *Mai più*. Never again."

Mario stared. "How did you know, *Zio?* When did you know?"

"Since you were a *bambino* of twelve. I sensed it. You see, I too once had *la potenza*." Mario started to speak, but Massimo lifted his hand. "*Ascoltami*. Nothing, *niente*, in all of life can compare. She sets you alight like a flare in the darkness. Your very guts dissolve into radiance. Knowledge and insight, truth in its crystal purity, these she bestows. For their own sake. Not for *soldi* or gain. Not to win at chess nor to pass an exam by using the mind of another."

Mario stammered, "B... but she l... let me. I can still hear people's thoughts..."

"*Ah, sì*, she is patient. She gave me more than one chance. Withdrew, forgave, came back again... She let me win the match at Talinn. In Vienna, she allowed me a stalemate with Alekhine, *campione del mondo*. I scored higher in the Moscow Tournament than Tal. And again, *ancora*. But in Bologna... il Torneo Nazionale. In midgame she was gone. Never to return."

His hand wavered over the chessboard. "This game, with Roberto Calese. Queen's Gambit Declined. I play it over and over. I was winning until..." He stretched his soft dry hands to Mario, who clasped them across the table. "Without my gift, *capisci*, I was never of grandmaster calibre." He shook his head, then straightened his round shoulders and said in a stronger voice, "You are not a player, this must be a bore to you."

"I remember how you showed me the moves, *Zio*, when I was little," Mario said. "I could not sit still that long." He pressed his uncle's hands. "Maybe she will come back."

"It is more than ten years, *ragazzo*... Tell me, how do you call her?"

"*La Lucia*."

"Ah, a good name. *La Dea*. I called her *la Dea*."

From the dim rooms beyond, Mario felt again the presence, the pull of *I Perduti*. "But you have all this, Uncle. The beautiful ancients."

"When she went away, she took with her even my pleasure in them."

With linked hands, they sat in the quiet.

"There is a place between my eyes," Mario said. "If I press it…"

"Mine was at the back of my head."

"Have you known any others who…" Mario began.

"*Nessuno.* Only we two."

"*E mia mamma?*"

"She knew," said Massimo. "She had a way of blocking."

"So do you."

His uncle nodded. "You don't need my thoughts, *nipote*, all dark sorrow, or chess combinations… Does she show you the future?"

"Just the past and the present," replied Mario. "Were you able to talk with the dead?"

"In my trance I could hear them. Or in the *pensieri* from the mind of another. But it was not to me they spoke. Living or dead, they were unaware of me."

"For me it is the same," Mario affirmed. "Were there minds you could not enter?"

"A few. Even these, when *la Dea* would come in full power, were opened to me."

"*Zio,* do you know of a man Wilhelm Winckler? Reads minds on the stage?"

Massimo shook his head. "There are many *mariuoli* and tricksters of the theatre. I found none with *questa potenza*. Long ago I abandoned the search."

They stood, their hands still clasped.

"I want you to promise," Massimo said, "to be true to her always. To hold her above all others. Honor, obey her. Use her gifts only for good."

"Like marriage vows, Uncle!"

"No *matrimonio* was ever more sacred. Say the words! Not to me. But to her."

Mario bowed his head and closed his eyes. "I will be true to thee always. I will hold thee above all others. I promise to honor, obey thee, use thy gifts only for good."

His mood of solemn exaltation carried Mario through the festivities of the following week and was still with him when he got off the train in Milan. He arrived late at the theatre. The performance was already in progress.

Wilhelm Winckler the Wonderworker posed dramatically on the stage, pointing into the audience with an iridescent baton. A wheeled blackboard in a sequined frame stood beside him.

He was thin, all elbows and knees, constantly gesturing with high-tension energy. He wore a tight white suit of a shiny fabric. A white cloak with a scarlet lining lay over a chair. His hair, pointed beard and full moustache were platinum blond, but the thick slanting brows were black, like the visible hairs in the nostrils of his small hooked nose.

"One dear to you lies gravely ill," he was saying. His voice was harsh, resonant, projecting through the capacious, well-filled theatre to where Mario stood at the back. "But with proper appeals to…ah… the gods of good health… See me after the performance, sir, and I will help you petition them."

Mario heard the unspoken response of the man with the rucksack, who was standing in front of his seat in the third row. **I will do anything,** he was thinking, **I'll pay whatever it costs.**

Wilhelm Winckler was silently calculating. **Must be pretty well-heeled. Should be good for at least two thousand lire.**

Mario inhaled the electric atmosphere of the theatre. The rapt audience, the fascination of the performer, went to his head like strong wine. A conviction took him and shook him. It was swift, absolute as that born of *la Lucia*'s first advent, as that born of Oriana's first silent confession of love.

I should be up there, on the stage. This is for me. What I want to do. More even than delving for the ancient glories. Certainly more than doctoring donkeys.

He waited for a pause in the questions from the audience, and went down the aisle to find a seat in the front row. *Lucia, dea mia,* wilt thou allow me? Is it all right with thee? Her answer seemed clear. Yes, she would allow it. She even seemed pleased. As long as he used her gifts truthfully.

But what of *Papà*? And Oriana! I will hire a helper for him. I will send for her, together we will travel the world.

"For the next demonstration," Winckler was saying, "I require an assistant from the audience."

Mario raised his hand.

"*Ah, il bel signorino* in the first row. Will you come to the stage?"

Mario took the three steps in one bound, entered the spotlight, and bowed.

VIII

Bong, said the town hall clock. Bong. Bong. Bong. The loud muffled chimes floated down to the park through the heavy air, bringing Mario to his feet. His right leg was asleep from the pressure of the marble ledge.

He limped the few yards to the police station and entered, blinking in the chill, harshly lighted, little reception area. A lean woman with graying brown hair, perched rigidly erect behind a sliding glass window, was regarding him sourly. Her lips were tight, her eyes sharp and beady. Through an open door on his left he saw Tyler, long legs on a desk, a telephone to his ear. He waved at Mario and nodded.

Beyond the sliding window, Mario could see a switchboard and a computer.

Tyler laid the handset on the desk and came to Mario with his rapid stride. They shook hands.

"Mr. Mario Castigliani, Miz Ruthann Hubbard," he said.

Mario bowed to the unyielding Ruthann, who gave him a grudging nod.

Tyler exclaimed, "Hey, buddy ro, you look like what the cat drug in. The heat get to you? And the skeeters?"

Ruthann Hubbard said, "I been told its plenty hotter where he comes from."

"Yes, I am accustomed to high summer temperatures." Mario achieved a measure of suavity. "Though it is less humid in Italy."

"Ruthann don't mean Italy," Tyler said, straightfaced. "She thinks you're fresh out of Hell, in league with Satan."

Mario managed a polite laugh.

"Listen, I'm still on the phone," Tyler apologized. "I'll just be a minute. Ruthann'll tell you where you can wash up."

"In the back, on your right," Ruthann announced, not looking at him. "And I'll thank you to leave it as tidy as you found it."

At the foremost of the three desks in the back room, a tall young black officer, slender and fine-featured, was filling in a report form. He grinned dazzlingly and returned Mario's bow with a touch of mockery.

"I'm Lieutenant Abbot," he said. "If you're looking for the head, it's right over yonder." He pointed to a door in the right wall beyond a narrow table holding fingerprinting equipment. Above this was a bulletin board displaying clippings, memos, a duty roster and a police file card with a double photo, profile and full face, of a man with cropped dark hair and a long jaw. "Earl Langford," it said.

Through an open grill to his left, Mario could see into a bleak holding cell with a toilet and a high barred window. On the lower tier of a double bunk bed, a woman lay curled asleep. As he made his way to the washroom, Mario felt a twinge of excitement. Her tear-swollen face was partly obscured by an upflung arm, and her clothing was different. But he recognized her at once as the blue-jeaned woman from his hotel vision.

In the washroom mirror, he grimaced at his sun-reddened eyes and the smear of dried blood on his cheek and mosquito carcasses. As he made himself presentable, he faced up to a few facts and figures. A month's rent overdue. The imminent phone and utilities bills. The hotel. The thousand for Lauren, which was merely a downpayment. Thirty-seven dollars remaining in his checking account. And in his wallet...

He took it out and counted nine dollars in limp bills. Even a full house on Saturday, he told himself as he held his shirt under the handdryer, would not suffice to rescue me. I must not lose this opportunity.

He slipped the lion coin with a rueful caress back into his shirt pocket, and combed his unruly mane. I will give you true value, *Signor Capo* Tyler, he vowed to the mirror, using just my five good everyday senses.

"Exodus 22:18," Ruthann was saying as Mario came back to the front of the station house. "'Thou shall not suffer a witch to live.'" She had averted her face from Tyler.

"You think he flies around on a broomstick?" Tyler chided patiently.

Lieutenant Abbot, gracefully sprawled on a chair beside Tyler's desk, winked at him and said, "'Or *any one* that useth divination.' Deuteronomy 18:10."

"'They shall stone them with stones,'" chanted Ruthann, "'their blood shall be upon them.'"

"Leviticus 20:27," Abbot intoned.

Tyler laughed. "Enough Bible-thumping," he said; then to Mario, "It's a local disease." He waved Mario toward his office, where Abbot rose and offered his chair. Tyler asked the lieutenant, "Melanie still at the library?"

"Until five o'clock."

"Give her a ring, Ruthann," Tyler said. "Ask her what she can find out about a book named *Let Me Die Before I Wake.* Then hold my calls, would you."

"But I am familiar with this book," Mario said when he and Tyler were seated at the desk. The lieutenant sat on the window ledge, one long leg crossed over the other. "It is a publication of The Hemlock Society," Mario continued. He remembered how he had wrenched it from his daughter's hands on the sad occasion of her thirtieth birthday. "It's about euthanasia. And the right to choose suicide."

"Mercy killing," Abbot exclaimed. "Where'd you hear about it, Chief?"

"Terry Hapgood was carrying it this morning," Tyler said. He told Mario, "He's a nurse out at Warren Memorial, where Roy Washington was under treatment."

"And also the nurse of your former chief, *Signor* Rutherford Kendall," Mario said smoothly, "who died under strikingly similar circumstances."

Tyler studied him. "Terry Hapgood," he said thoughtfully. "I got the feeling this morning he wanted to tell me something. But he wouldn't hurt a deerfly, it's not in him."

"Black folks call him The Golden Angel," Abbot told Mario, and then to Tyler, "I don't know. Maybe we'd better check out Warren Memorial deaths over the last few years."

"Right," said Tyler. "Want to take care of it?"

"Will do," the lieutenant agreed. He turned to Mario. "How did you know about Kendall?"

Mario lowered his eyes, his expression sphinx-like.

"Aah, give us a break, would you," Abbot muttered. "Dozen ways he could have found out. I've got faith, in plain down-to-earth, competent and conscientious police work."

He stood up. "Want me for anything else, Chief?"

"Yes, if you'd stop by Tape & Disk before they close. Tell Nesbitt thumbs down on the X-rated home entertainment. He can send customers to their Kissimee branch. And thanks, Abbott, for the overtime."

"Just see I get time and a half," Abbott said as he went to the office door.

When the door closed behind Abbot, Tyler said, "Let's take care of money. Fifteen hundred up front, payable now. As much again in two weeks, or before that if we wrap up the case with your help. I expect you to work with me closely, even crazy hours. I told my staff, give you whatever you need. If we run over two weeks, if I feel good about your input, we'll work out something. Seem fair?"

"Generous," said Mario.

"If we solve it because of you," Tyler said, "you'd pretty sure get a bonus, couple thousand at least. "

Tyler took a checkbook from the middle drawer of his desk, and a four-page form headed "Consultant." "Red tape," he said. "I filled in my part." He slid the paper and a ballpoint pen to Mario.

Mario bent to his briefcase and produced the folder of newspaper clippings. "Some former cases," he said.

"Good." Tyler read them while Mario wrote the bald particulars of his life in his clear rapid script.

"This kidnap case," Tyler said, tapping one of the clippings. "Seems like you figured it out with just commonsense smarts. But this one..." He picked up an item headlined, "Mother Is Murderer, Psychic Announces." "No way you could have solved it without ESP."

"That's very astute of you." Mario accepted the check which Tyler held out to him and folded it into his wallet.

"Okay if I make copies of these clippings?" Tyler took the folder and the completed form and strode out of the room.

A dog-eared Bible with a bookmark lay on the corner of the desk, under two typed reports. Mario pulled them closer. P.O. Robert E. Lee Petticord. Lt. Abbott Abbot. He scanned the reports, then opened the Bible and read the passage lightly underlined in pencil. "For now I am ready to be offered, and the time of my departure is at hand. I have fought a good fight, I have finished my course, I have kept the faith."

"You don't mind?" he said when Tyler returned with the copies.

"No. Well. I wanted you to read the reports. The Bible... that's evidence. Found at the scene."

"Opened to this page on the kitchen table," Mario said.

"Yes. You already knew that this morning, I guess. But no sweat. It's been checked for fingerprints."

"And were there any?"

"Only Roy's and my patrolman's, who should've known better."

"Tell me about your staff," Mario said.

"Eight altogether, counting me and Ruthann. We're short a man this week, Floyd Bradshaw."

"He is ill?" Mario asked.

"Not exactly." Tyler looked down at the desktop, controlling his features with visible effort. "Suspended. His brother's into moonshining. Floyd's under suspicion of tipping his family off when a raid was due."

Mario raised his eyebrows.

"Running a still in the piney woods is a tradition 'round here," Tyler said, with an edge of defensiveness. "Kendall, the old chief, I reckon he sort of winked an eye."

"But you do not," Mario said.

"Not when the revenue agents are looking into it."

"Who was on duty last night and this morning?" asked Mario, returning this apparently embarrassing conversation to its purpose.

"Well, Abbott, Lieutenant Abbot, you met."

"*Molto intelligente*," Mario said.

Tyler nodded, "Navy. College grad."

"And believes you have taken his job."

Tyler's expression was troubled and stubborn. "When the old chief died, Abbott sure was the righteous choice. There was some behind-the-scenes stuff went on, among the people who really run this town. A.B.A. If you know what I mean. Anybody but Abbot."

"The wrong color?" Mario said.

"Yes. The New South's not always so new."

"This must make for a strain between you."

"I offered to transfer him. But he just bought a house, three years ago. Wife has a good job in the library. Couple of schoolage kids... Bobby Lee Petticord, now, he's still wet behind the ears. But he's gonna shape up. Had an accident musta been like two years ago. Kind of a town joke... He shot himself in the ass."

Mario laughed incredulously.

"He sat down on the toilet wearing his gun," Tyler said with a wry grin. "It slipped into the bowl and went off. Poor bastard'll never live it down. But Bobby Lee's gonna be a damn good cop one day. ... There's Duane, Duane Potts. He's out guarding Roy's house till the next of kin gets here. Duane's even younger than Bobby Lee, but he's got lots of savvy. Plays the banjo in the Barnstormers, that's a bluegrass band. You'll be hearing them at the Rotary reception after your show. You know about that?"

"Yes, they told me there will be some ceremony."

"Floraville's big wheels will be out in force. One other patrolman, Vernon Bond, he's out right now, finishing up the house-to-house where Abbott left off. About my age, used to have a drinking problem. Not long on imagination, but reliable.... Ruthann, Miz Hubbard. Don't judge her by today. Place would fall apart without her. Oh, and there's Kevin Petticord, Bobbie Lee's nephew. Just out of high school, helps out on the switchboard at night. A bug on electronics. He does his studying here."

"And that is your entire staff?" Mario asked.

"Enough's good as a feast. It's a law-abiding town."

"Drugs?" asked Mario.

"Marijuana, yes. High school kids. Harder stuff's beginning to sneak in."

"Prostitution?"

Tyler shook his head. "A fair share of hankypanky, but I don't know as any money changes hands. There's a grand old cathouse in Columbus. And Dollie's Massage, eleven miles north on Highway 27…

"What about Earl Langford?" Mario asked.

"You saw the card. On the bulletin board."

"A major suspect."

"I'm not asking how come you know so much," Tyler said, "It's no secret he made threats against Roy."

"He was in Floraville today," Mario said slowly, enjoying himself. The police chief's head went up; he stared at Mario with a puzzled frown. "And may be here still," Mario continued. "He no longer closely resembles your photographs."

"We knew he was getting out. Town's supposed to be off limits to him… Neighbor kid, out by Roy's, saw somebody last night. Gray hair. Stubble beard."

"That describes him," Mario affirmed. Should he part with further information, he wondered, or hoard it against the probably lean days ahead? He decided to plunge. "At two o'clock this afternoon," he announced, "Earl Langford was in the back room of Diamond Jack's Pawnshop on Main Street."

Tyler jumped to his feet and was reaching for his cap.

Mario held up a hand. "I will tell you here and now," he declared, "that this man is not the murderer of Roy Washington." C a r e f u l, Mario, he warned himself, *adagio!* What if he is the murderer? He well may be. In that event, the investigation will be over almost before it begins, with little profit to me. But his declaration had not sprung merely from the desire to make a dramatic effect.

Tyler opened the door and called to Ruthann, "Tell Vern to come in here, would you… Understand, Mr. Castigliani, I can't just take your word for it."

"No, *certamente* you cannot."

A short plump patrolman with a ruddy mustache, a report form in his hand, entered the office. He was sweat-stained and burned by the sun.

"Myrt's awake," he said.

Tyler went quickly through the door and toward the back.

"I am Mario Castigliani," Mario said, extending his hand across the desk. "You must be Officer Vernon Bond."

"The chief told us you could read minds, stuff like that. Never had one of them before," Bond said. He put the report form on the desk and shook hands.

Tyler came in and shut the door. "I put her in the I.R.," he said. "Listen, Vern, you know about Earl Langford?"

"Just we were keeping an eye peeled."

"He was seen today, over in Jack Sprague's. I want you to go there right away, see what you can find out. Don't barge in too direct, go easy. Jack plays it close to the chest."

Bond sighed. "What exactly do you need to know?"

"Is Langford still there? In town? In the vicinity? And where we can get hold of him."

"I'll do what I can," Bond said with a look of aggrieved reluctance. He moved slowly to the reception area.

"Hold on a minute," Tyler said. "I better send Abbott with you."

"Why can't he go by himself then?" Bond muttered.

"Now, Vern, you know you can get more out of those good ol' boys than a black cop. And snap it up, would you. I want both of you back here as soon as you can… "

Tyler re-entered his office. "Vern's been knocking on doors in the heat," he told Mario, with an apologetic shrug. "Thinks it's a lot of damnfool busywork anyway. He's sure Roy was a suicide." He glanced at his watch. "They're doing an autopsy right now, out at Warren. We'll get the preliminary results in a few hours."

"Tell me about Terence Hapgood," Mario said.

"In a while. I want you to see something." Tyler locked the door, then pressed a switch under the desk. A section of the wall on his left slid noiselessly open, revealing a six-foot-wide window of dark glass. Mario looked through it at the woman seated on a wooden bench facing the window. She was wearing a blue smock far too small for her, the buttons strained, the cloth gaping over her full breasts and belly, revealing a white slip also under great pressure. She looked freshly washed, her red hair combed back, darkened with water. Her eyes were swollen, her cheeks patchy from weeping.

"One-way glass," Tyler said. "You could talk, she can't hear us. That's Myrt Collins."

"Who found the body," Mario said. "This morning she wore jeans and a blouse."

"I told you about her? No. I didn't. Well, never mind," Tyler said. "I want you to listen in while I question her, see what you can pick up." He put a finger to his lips and slid open a small panel beside the window. Mario heard a heavy sigh from the woman on the bench.

Tyler closed the sound panel. "When that's open, you can hear everything. But in the I.R., Interrogation Room, they can hear you too." He pressed the desk switch to close the wall window. "Makes you feel funny, don't it, looking at people like that," he said with a grimace. "When they don't know you can see them."

Mario nodded. How much I like this man, he was thinking. We are *simpatici*.

"Surely such a room is standard equipment in all police stations."

"City stations," Tyler corrected him. "And not state-of-the-art like this. Old Chief Kendall, he wanted it here in the new quarters. Then he never got to use it ... Floraville's broke, like lots of towns in the region. We're on such a tight budget, I can't even get an intercom out of them. But at least we got this."

"How are you able to afford me?"

"We have ourselves a patroness." A fleeting smile softened the police chief's face. Mario reflected the smile on his own lips, thinking, Claudia. I am sure it is she.

There was a sharp rapping on the office door. Tyler opened it. Ruthann stepped into the room, closed the door and said in a stage whisper, "Deacon and Miz Howard are here."

"Damn it to hell," Tyler said, "don't these people use the phone?"

Ruthann frowned and held out her hand, palm up. "That'll be fifty cents for the swear jar."

Grumbling wordlessly, Tyler fished change from his pocket. Then he laughed with a touch of embarrassment, turning to Mario. "Anybody says one little cuss word or anything dirty around this stationhouse, Ruthann makes him put a quarter in her swear jar."

Mario said, controlling his impulse to grin, "For a good cause, I am sure."

"Tracts for unwed mothers, isn't it, Ruthann? Or yarn for the Missionary Knitting Circle?"

"Never mind," she said smugly. "And. I was under the impression you told me to hold your calls."

"Jesus almighty," Tyler expostulated. "You know damn well I didn't mean… Anybody else due to arrive?"

"That'll be fifty cents more," Ruthann snapped, holding out her hand again.

"Allow me," said Mario, springing to his feet. He took a dollar bill from his wallet and draped it across her palm. "For the unwed mothers," he said.

She gave him a curt nod and went out, Tyler following her. Mario saw a couple of heroic proportions. The woman, round-bodied, with a huge bosom, was clad in flowing striped robes, her head swathed in a kaffiyeh. The man, tall, handsome and powerfully built, was staring at Tyler with half-closed eyes, his lips curved in a secretive smile. He was dressed in a well-cut black suit and a black shirt with a white clerical collar. Both woman and man wore small gold crosses. Their bodies seemed to fill the entire reception area.

"Is that you, Candy," Tyler exclaimed, "in all those stripes?" He reached out, as though to embrace her, checked himself, and let his arms fall to his sides.

"It's me," she said stonily. "And this is my husband, Deacon Ira Howard."

"Yeah, I heard about that," Tyler said. Neither he nor Howard offered to shake hands. "You been… out to Warren?"

"I saw him," Candy said in a flat voice.

"Myrt's in there," Tyler said, indicating the Interrogation Room.

"Let me see her." It was an order rather than a request.

Tyler opened the I.R. door, but prevented Deacon Howard from following her. "Sorry," he said, "but you'll have to wait out here."

"That's all right, Candace," the deacon said. "The police chief and I have business to discuss." His speech sounded Northern and educated.

"Do we?"

"A little matter of two hundred and fifty thousand dollars. My wife is the sole surviving heiress to the money awarded Royal Washington by the Pennington Mills. I consider it your duty as the chief of this police department to see to it that my wife receives without delay every cent of it.."

"I don't know as I heard anything about any out-of-court settlement," Tyler said; then to Mario, "The lawsuit's been in and out of the courts for right near five years. Roy had brown lung, you know, the millworker's disease."

The police chief looked into the challenge of his visitor's eyes. "Understand, Deacon Howard, the way you tell it, for all we know the deal might not even be final yet." Howard started to speak, but Tyler raised a hand and went on, "'Course I'd do whatever I could anyway to see Candy gets her due. And that her dad's last wishes are respected. Do you know if he made a will?"

"Whether he made a will or not has no significance. Mrs. Howard's claim is beyond question. Her father was a very sick old man."

"Not senile yet by a country mile," Tyler told him. "Listen, sir, I got to ask you to put this on hold for a little. I'm under real time pressure. If you could maybe go get yourself a bite to eat." He stood up with such authority that Howard automatically followed suit, and Mario murmured inaudibly, "*Bravissimo.*"

"I'll wait out there," the deacon said, pointing to the reception area.

Ruthann's peremptory knock sounded on the door. The police chief opened it. She was wearing a straw hat and carrying her purse. "I'm leaving now," she announced. "Want the list of who called?"

Tyler pressed a knuckle against his forehead and sighed. "Go ahead."

"Collision out by the highway bridge." Ruthann frowned at the memo slips in her hand. "Two cars and a truck. Sounds like a D.U.I. Nobody hurt bad... Mayor Sondergard asks would you please see to it right away that all merchants are informed of his wife's, uh, little problem... Mr. Easton wants to know did you find his stolen tires yet... And Mr. Nesbitt over at that Tape & Disk says tell you he'll see you in you-know-where first."

Mario thought, Mr. Nesbitt owes her twenty-five cents.

Deacon Howard, with minimal courtesy, shouldered past the two in the doorway and sat ostentatiously upright on the foyer bench.

Tyler looked at his secretary with wordless appeal.

"Is there no one on the premises to help you?" Mario asked.

Ruthann snapped, "I've got a committee meeting half an hour

from now." Then, in a softer tone, she said, "I could call the church if you need me to work late."

"I'd sure appreciate it."

She took off her hat.

"What about Sprague?" Tyler asked them.

"He saw Langford all right," said Vernon Bond. "Tried to make out like he hadn't, but we got it out of him."

"Didn't get his dander up, I hope," said Tyler.

"No, we was real cagey. Jack says Langford come in needing money. Bus fare to his folks down in Stovall. A square meal."

Abbot added, "Sprague says Langford told him he hadn't eaten for twenty-four hours, except for some raw snap beans."

"Is that so," the police chief said; and again, "Is that so. Well, where is he? We got to bring him in."

"What grounds?" Bond asked.

"Violating parole, for starters," Tyler replied.

"Sprague claims Langford wasn't in the pawnshop more'n a few minutes," Bond went on. "Tried to get a hundred bucks. Jack give him twenty-five and sent out for a burger and fries."

"Who else was there?"

"The usual pirate crew," Abbot said. "Along with the geriatric cribbage fiends."

Mario cleared his throat. "I have reason to believe," he said quietly, "that Earl Langford has some connection with Mr. Kirby Garison, the hotel proprietor. A hotel with many vacant rooms."

Tyler gave him a look of surprise and gratitude. He said, "Can you check it out, Abbott?"

"Aye, aye," said Abbot. "10-4."

"Also," said Mario, "this may not be the appropriate time to investigate, but you should know that Mr. Garison may be a..." He squirmed on the windowsill, disliking the informer's role. But I should tell them, he thought, *immediatamente*. I must win their trust. And why should I spare that child-beater, that *ruffiano*.

The expectant eyes of the two policemen were on him. "He may be a conduit for illegal narcotics," he finished.

"There now," said Tyler. "You're already earning your keep."

Abbot said simultaneously, "We had an idea it might be Garison."

He went to the door. "I'll stop by and put out a few feelers. Shall I give Judge Polk a buzz? We might need a warrant."

"Yeah, do that," Tyler agreed.

When the door closed behind the two officers, Tyler locked it, and leaned against it, his hand to his eyes. Then he pressed the desk switch, opening the window in the wall. He and Mario stood side by side watching the two women, who sat holding hands, weeping without restraint. Myrtle Collins seemed almost slight in comparison with Candace, whose striped garment billowed over half the bench. Her face was a tragic mask raining down tears.

"Mrs. Howard has gained much weight over the years," Mario remarked, "but she is still a woman of great beauty."

The police chief made a sound deep in his throat, and Mario saw that the man was near to tears.

"*Scusi*," Mario said. "I am clumsy.... Royal Washington was a personal friend?"

Tyler said hoarsely, "Good friend. I feel bad that we were out of touch lately. You know how it happens." He turned his face away and stretched a hand toward the wall window. "I grew up with those two. We all hung out in Roy's kitchen. Candy, she was a peach."

He took a tape recorder from a desk drawer and slid a cassette into it. Then he said, his voice now clear and controlled, "The window switch is here, you see it?"

Mario nodded.

"The sound panel..." Tyler pointed to it.

"Yes," Mario said.

"Lock this door when I leave. Give me a chance to settle in there, then open the panel so you can hear."

When Tyler appeared in the interrogation room, Candace got to her feet, folded her arms and faced him majestically. Myrtle Collins shrank back against the wall and looked stubbornly into his face.

"Do we have to have that thing?" she said, indicating the tape recorder which Tyler was placing on a small table near her.

"Yes. We have to."

"Candy stays," Myrtle announced firmly.

"Right here," Candace said.

Mario drew the desk chair to the wall window, and sat down.

"Okay, I got no objection," Tyler said. "Long as you let us get through this fast."

"Faster the better," Candace retorted. "Deacon Howard has to be back at the Tabernacle, and I got to get out to the house."

"Not till I can go there with you. Or one of my men."

She stared at him, frowning.

Myrt said, "You can't keep her away from the house she was born in."

"'Fraid I have to, Candy, light of what your husband just told me. House stays sealed and guarded."

How will he manage that, Mario wondered, with his little handful of police?

"Goodness sakes, Beau," Candace protested. "I've got to go through Dad's stuff, take care of things for him. And there's funeral arrangements."

"I'm real sorry, Candy. Fact is, I want you and the deacon—and you, too, Myrt—staying clean out of the house the next few days."

"But I have to be in town, you know that!"

"Tell you what, give Claudia a call." He rapidly wrote two phone numbers on a memo pad on the table, tore off the top sheet and handed it to Candace.

Mario's lips moved as he committed the numbers to memory.

Tyler went on, "She wants to help out any way she can. She'll fix you up with a place... And now let's get this over so's I can drive Myrt home."

Myrtle said, "I don't need no chauffeuring around. Junior's picking me up in half an hour." Tyler adjusted and tested the tape recorder. "He says my kids is over at Bonnie's," she went on distractedly.

Tyler said, "Let's start at the beginning, Myrt. What was the last time you saw Roy alive?"

"I already done answered that this morning."

"She should have a lawyer present," Candace said. "Haven't you informed her of that?"

"She's not under arrest. Far as I'm concerned, she's not even under suspicion."

Candace grunted. "First one reports finding a body's always a suspect."

"That's what the book says," Tyler replied. "And so are the heirs, if any." He held up a hand to silence her. "But that don't mean I suspect either of you of anything." To Myrtle he said gently, "This morning you weren't in shape to answer a whole hell of a lot."

Candace tossed her head in annoyance. Mario jumped, sure for an instant that she had caught his eye. But she was plainly oblivious of him. He relaxed and pulled the chair closer.

Myrtle licked at a leftover tear and said, "Last night after supper I went over there."

"Why?" Tyler asked encouragingly.

"You know why."

"Come on, Myrt. You want us to spend the night here?"

"We was planning the meeting," she said sullenly.

"Anybody else there?"

"Two union brothers from the mill. And a woman hand. Do I have to say their names?"

"'Fraid so."

"Fred Whitley, he's on the boiler crew. Rusty Yates. Fixer. And Gladys Hedley."

"Go on," said Tyler.

"Otis was there. You know, the handyman at the ho-tel."

Tyler raised his eyebrows. "What was he doing there?"

"Came there a lot. Roy helped him with reading and writing. Said Otis was a real high-class poet, if he could get it writ down…

"Union office closed down, didn't it?"

"Nope, it's still going, three days a week. And I tell you straight off, plenty of hands getting mad enough now to sign up. You had no right calling off our meeting."

"What time did y'all get to Roy's house?"

"Eight o'clock p.m."

"How long did you stay?"

"Everybody but me and Otis went on over to Gladys's, must've been like nine o'clock. That's 'count of she got a good typewriter and a copy machine. Me and Roy was picked to make up the words for the leaflet. We was busy, so Otis, he didn't stay long."

Candy said, "What time did y'all get done?"

"Say, half after ten. Roy felt real good 'bout what we'd wrote. He hugged me good night."

Mario saw the shadow of grief pass across the faces of the women.

"You went home," Tyler said.

"No, to Gladys Hedley's. We run off the leaflets."

"How much did y'all know about this Matsumoto rumor?"

She shrugged.

"Jeff tells me there's nothing to it," Tyler said.

"'Course that's what he tells you. What d'you expect?"

Mario was thinking, Otis Feeney. I must not forget to speak with him.

Myrtle said, "Roy never killed hisself. Never. He was so fired up by what we was planning, why, he was lit up like a Christmas tree."

Candace put in, "And that's the gospel truth. I phoned him a few days ago. He was like a new man."

"If it happened last month, I could've believed he done it to hisself," Myrt said. "He was way down. Too sick to eat his lunch. But not how it happened, when it happened."

Tyler said nothing.

"That's how come I didn't think he was dead, hanging there." Myrtle's face screwed up, and tears fell from her eyes. "Well, like, 'course I knew he was. But I couldn't noways believe it."

Tyler gave her a tissue from a box on the table. "That's why you called the ambulance?"

"No. I called here," she said, blotting her tears. "But I told — what's his name— Kevin, I wasn't sure Roy was dead. I reckon Kevin, he called Warren Memorial."

There was an outburst of voices from the reception area, followed by pounding on the office door. Mario saw the three in Interrogation staring confusedly in his direction. He closed the sound panel. Moving swiftly, he replaced the desk chair, pressed the switch to restore the wall, and seated himself beside the desk as though studying Petticord's report. The furious knocking continued, though it was now on the I.R. door. It ceased. There was a babel of argument. Mario could not make out the words.

Then he heard Tyler calling, "Open up, Mr. Castigliani!"

Mario, the report in his hand, obeyed promptly. Tyler strode to his desk, pursued closely by a man flushed with anger, the coattails of his blue linen suit flapping behind him with the speed of his passage. He was more solidly built than the smiling youth in the wedding photo. His hairline had receded, but his ears still stuck out, and Mario knew this was Gregory Shapiro.

Candace Howard and Myrtle Collins, on his heels, almost tumbled into the suddenly crowded little office. In the lobby, the deacon had half-risen to a belligerent crouch, and was loudly insisting to the agitated Ruthann, who was waving her arms before him, "If he can go in there, well, by all that's holy, then so can I!"

Gregory Shapiro yelled simultaneously, "You're not letting them get away with this!"

Tyler, equally flushed, his jaw thrust forward, his clenched fists pressed to the desktop, shouted, "Get away with *what,* you crackbrain mule?"

Vernon Bond had come to the door, peering past Mario, vainly trying to catch the chief's eye.

"There'll be no repeat cover-up, like when they slaughtered Barry Gutmacher," Shapiro raged. "You know damn well they got off scot free, except for one dumb palooka, and he's already walking the streets a free man."

"Greg! Cut it out. This is Beau. Remember me?"

"The Beau I remember carried a picket sign. He and Claudia threw tear gas canisters back at the State Troopers." Shapiro's voice was lower, but still sharp with fury. "The Beau I remember didn't wear a gun on his hip and a badge on his tit."

Candace, her arms folded across the striped shelf of her bosom, gave a bitter laugh. "You're a fine one to talk. Nobody's found *you* on any picket lines lately."

"And how come I caught you interrogating Candy and Myrt," Shapiro accused the police chief, "with no attorney present?"

Tyler relaxed visibly and seemed to take control. "You can't have it both ways, Greg," he said. "Either you want me to carry out this investigation or you don't."

Mario felt a tug on his sleeve.

"Mr. Castilyan," said Vernon Bond. "Could I speak to you?"

He drew Mario through the lobby, where Ruthann, hopping like a sparrow, still held the towering Deacon Howard at bay. In her office,

Bond closed the door and the sliding glass window. "Didn't have no chance to finish writing up my report," he muttered to Mario. "Do me a favor, tell the chief... He—" He pointed through the window at the deacon. "He was in Blue Heaven. Stayed over all last night."

"Deacon Howard?" Mario exclaimed in a whisper.

"Yep. That's who. At the Owens's house, across the street from Roy's. Whole family's joined up with the Tenfold Tabernacle. Old lady Owens told me they fell behind in their tithes, and this deacon come to collect."

"I saw nothing about this in Lieutenant Abbot's report," Mario said.

"No, they wasn't to home when he knocked. He asked me to try 'em again."

"I will certainly inform the chief," said Mario. "Immediately." He returned to Tyler's office, wriggled skillfully between the quarreling couple, and spoke low into Tyler's ear.

Candace was saying, "How come you're so all of a sudden gung-ho for my Dad? After you let him down like that."

"You're the one let him down," Shapiro said, nodding toward the lobby, "when you married into that den of pious thieves."

"You talked him into settling out of court. He wanted to fight, wanted class action."

"Our friendship never wavered," he protested to Tyler, and then, turning back to his ex-wife, "I advised him for the best."

"The best for your precious Atlanta career," she retorted.

Deacon Howard, with Ruthann pulling at his sleeve, appeared in the doorway. "CANDACE!" he bellowed, then hissed at her, "Shame!"

Candace gasped, and lowered her eyes. She seemed to sag like a balloon losing air. "I'm sorry," she said humbly in a little-girl voice.

"I'm sorry what?"

"I'm sorry, Deacon Howard."

"And what else?"

"I'm sorry, dear Lord Jesus."

"You see that?" Shapiro said to Tyler. "If she got that money, she'd never smell a penny of it. But those Tenfold gonifs won't grab it either, I'll see to that."

"I might just sue you for slander," the deacon said.

Tyler asked Shapiro, "Does that mean Roy left a Will?"

The attorney shook his head. "Not yet. We were working on it. But he sent me a letter last week."

Junior Collins came to the office door, a shopping bag of clothing hanging from his arm. He went to Myrtle and looked up at her shyly. Mario thought, ah, this little man, he is in love.

"Still mad at me?" Junior asked anxiously.

She shook her head and embraced him. "No, it weren't real bright what you done. But you was too roused up to think straight." She freed herself and gave him a loud kiss. "Where's the kids?"

"Bonnie says they can stay over with her, if you want."

"The baby okay?"

"Still coughing a mite. Bonnie give her some soothing syrup..."

"Where are *our* children, Candy?" Shapiro asked, like a man coming back to himself.

Candace started to reply, but Deacon Howard glared at her. "Be silent." To Shapiro he said, "They are in good hands. The Sisters of the Tabernacle will give them the best of care."

"I'm picking them up and taking them to Atlanta," Shapiro announced.

"You'll do nothing of the sort," said the deacon.

Myrtle, at the same time, asked Tyler, "Could I go in back? Wash up and change?"

"Hold on a minute," Tyler began. "I got something—"

"Who the hell's that," Shapiro interrupted, pointing at Mario. "And why is he here?"

Mario introduced himself suavely. "Chief Tyler has appointed me as a consultant."

"Consultant on what? What's your expertise?"

Myrtle said, "He's that mindreader doing the Rotary show. I seen the poster."

Gregory Shapiro goggled, then began to laugh. "Old Beau," he gasped. "Old Beau. Who'd have thought it? What's next? Voodoo? Or horoscopes?"

Tyler brought his fist crashing down on the desk and said forcefully, "Now y'all shut your mouths. And listen up, every one."

He beckoned to Ruthann, who stood on one foot in the doorway.

When she came to him, he fished out a handful of change and poured it into her skirt pocket.

"You been cussing?" she said with a sigh.

"No. But I sure intend on it. Damn it to shit, piss, and frigging hell," he said quietly. "It's a zoo at dinnertime in here. And Roy not even resting yet in his grave. I tell you sure as you're born, Roy Washington was murdered." He paused for breath and looked around the room, searching the silent faces. Mario stood just behind him.

Tyler continued, "Nobody leaves this stationhouse before I get a full statement. Where you were and what you were doing every minute of the past forty-eight hours." He turned to Gregory Shapiro. "You got that letter?"

"I brought you down a copy."

"Give it here," said Tyler, his palm out.

Shapiro opened the letter on the desk before Tyler. Deacon Howard and Candace pushed in on either side of Mario, craning to read over Tyler's shoulders.

The letter was a photocopy of single-spaced block paragraphs typed in uneven lines without capitals. Royal Washington's address and phone number appeared over the date, 7/3/90.

```
to gregory f. shapiro, esquire, attorney-at-law
dear son greg,
here is what you asked me for on the phone yester-
day for making my will.  you know i was for court
all the way, not just for me but all us with brown
lung.  but you maybe right the bosses could weasel
out comes to a jury.  besides i know you got a big
practice now corporate law, not as much time for
me like in the old days.

speaking of candy, makes me mad enough to spit how
they got her bowing and scraping.  keep that
irreverend plenty and the sneakin deacon away from
the money.

now beau.   i purely despise seeing him in enemy
uniform.  ask him, hire on otis feeney.  no sense
leaving otis money, could not hold onto a sawbuck.
tell beau its not a condition, just only i asked.
```

okay, here goes. to my grandchildren, ella mae,
ralph abernathy, and harriet tubman shapiro i
leave and bequeath forty thousand dollars each
one, hold in trust for when time comes for college.
to the textile workers local in kissimee three
thousand to help out.
to myrtle collins two thousand to keep up the
organizing.
to beaufort tyler of floraville georgia, thirty
thousand, no strings.
all the rest to the medgar evers foundation in
harlem, n.y. they doing great teaching illiter-
ates reading and writing. they might think to
open a school here in the piedmont, but let them
decide.
i name you, gregory franklin shapiro of atlanta,
executor of my will. when you write this up
formal, put in whatever percent executors get and
dont shortchange yourself. one more thing, i sent
away for that living will. it came yesterday.
you was so busy you kept forgetting. oh, and i
leave and bequeath my books to durrell and fred
whitley of next door.

in brotherhood and solidarity

royal washington

p.s. hold in trust for candy whats in my checking
account when i pass on. right now 2743.96. i
know you would not let her want. and this house
of course is hers. only tell candy she cant sell
nor rent lessen she breaks free from the buzzards.

Candace Howard shoved Mario aside and bent over the desk, scanning the letter. The deacon shook his finger at it, and said to Shapiro,
"Can you possibly think this doddering libel will stand up in a court of
law?"

"It will stand," Shapiro assured him, "like a brick shithouse."

"We will see about that," the deacon said. "The Reverend Plenty does not lack for competent lawyers."

"And he keeps them *plenty* busy these days, doesn't he," Shapiro retorted.

Tyler's eyes were fixed unseeingly ahead of him. Candace brought her face close to his and said, "Well, well, well, Mr. Beaufort thirty-thousand-no-strings Tyler. What's that you were saying before, about heirs being suspects?"

IX

Night had fallen. A bloated red moon struggled free of its broken reflection in the black glinting river and cast pale shadows on the windowless walls of the pathology lab at Warren Memorial. It gazed down on the swingshift mill workers dangling their legs from the loading dock as they ate their suppers. When it cleared the park treetops, the moon turned orange, aureoled, lopsided, fitfully veiled by clouds, and shone intermittently through the tilted blinds of Tyler's office window.

Mario sat erect on the sill, so intrigued by the drama unfolding around him that he was scarcely aware of weariness, hunger and thirst. Tyler, at his desk, winding up his interrogation of Deacon Howard, also appeared fresh and keen despite the long demanding day.

Myrtle Collins, her preliminary statement completed, had left with her husband. Ruthann, after transcribing Candace's statement, had gone home. Bobby Lee was on guard until midnight at the Washington house in Blue Heaven. A truck driver, breath-tested, mug-shot and finger-printed, was sleeping it off in the holding cell. He had left his license at home. His brother was driving up with it from Calhoun Landing. On the foyer bench, Candace sat huddled, dabbing at her eyes with the fringe of her kaffiyeh.

Vernon Bond was manning the switchboard, talking at intervals in low tones to Duane Potts, a hollow-chested, stoop-shouldered young officer with a look of good-humored mischief. He stood nearby making crooked copies on the inefficient office machine.

"How much longer do you intend to detain me?" Deacon Howard

demanded of Tyler.

"We're about finished up," Tyler reassured him. "Just only how come you said first you slept over up around Cherokee Springs. Before I mentioned about old Miz Owens."

"The explanation is simple," the deacon replied smoothly. "I preferred that my wife should not know that I'd been in Floraville. As you are aware, there was considerable tension between her and her father."

"I don't exactly see the connection," the police chief said mildly. He flipped through the pages of a transcript, "Says here she told us you were collecting tithes in Americus."

"She was confused and in error. Understandably. See here, Chief Tyler. The Owenses will confirm that I did not leave their premises. I made no contact whatsoever with my father-in-law." Deacon Howard stood. "I have leaned over backwards to cooperate. I now insist my attorney be present before this inquisition continues."

"Like I told you," said Tyler, "that is your right."

Gregory Shapiro opened the door.

"Had your supper?" Tyler asked him, shutting off the tape recorder.

Shapiro wrinkled his nose. "The cuisine at the Floraville Lunch hasn't improved. You got any bicarb?"

"I think there's some Tums back in the can." Tyler got to his feet, yawning and stretching. "Be back here tomorrow," he told Deacon Howard. "With a lawyer if you want, that's up to you." He went to the door and said, "Vern. Call Bonnie and tell her I'm bringing a friend. Ask her, save us some eats."

Vernon Bond said, "Doc Osborne's on the phone."

Tyler strode back to his desk and clapped the handset to his ear. Mario came quickly to listen beside him.

Shapiro said, "Why don't you just read his mind, Mr. Castigliani? ...Nah, man, I'm just kidding. Sorry I laughed like that before."

Mario accepted the apology with a gesture and a smile.

"...No, sir, I'm not satisfied, not by a long shot. ...Yeah, I'll talk to Reid. "

Mario asked, "No indication of murder?"

Tyler affirmed this with a nod, and said into the phone, "Hey, Reid. Mighta known you'd be there... Will you climb down off my back? ...

Have to wait till tomorrow." He replaced the handset.

"Autopsy came up okay?" Shapiro asked.

"That's the way Osborne tells it." Tyler put on his cap and tightened his gunbelt. "Says the brown lung, the byssinosis, had got to the terminal phase."

"So it was suicide," Deacon Howard said, "and all this has simply been a waste of my valuable time."

"I don't buy suicide," said Shapiro.

"Me neither," Tyler told the deacon. "And you sure as shooting better show up tomorrow." To Mario he said, "Hungry, Mr. Castigliani?"

"Famished."

"Go on, wait for me out back, I'll be there in two shakes."

Mario went out the front way with a murmured "*Buona notte, Signora* Howard!" to Candace slumped on the bench, her veiled face averted.

Outside, moths, mosquitoes and flying beetles quivered and fluttered against the lighted glass panel of the door. On the nearest park bench, Duane Potts, a half-smoked cigarette dangling from his lips, a plastic cup on the bench beside him, twanged poignant chords on a banjo.

He seemed unaware of Mario, who walked quietly to the back of the shadowed building. Fireflies winked from the black clumps of shrubbery. Grass fragrance rose from the earth. A chorus of crickets provided a ground bass for the policeman's song, which followed Mario faintly to the parking lot in the rear. He stood in the shadows, gazing into the station's lighted back room. The blinds were raised high. I can see them, he thought, but they cannot see me.

The moon, now yellow as butter, was bright enough to gild the squad cars and illumine leafy treetops unmoving in the starless night.

"*Buona notte, mia luna,*" Mario saluted this old friend. The greeting was perfunctory. His mind was awhirl with the revelations of the day, jumping to improbable conclusions only to retreat to bafflement; and then leap off again. Concentrate, Mario, he told himself. Review everything, in orderly fashion. Who are the obvious *persone sospette*, who not so obvious? Earl Langford, to begin with. No doubt guilty of much, but innocent of this. Which of his Klansmen cohorts had similar motives of revenge? Who might have taken advantage of Langford's release date to commit a crime for which he would be blamed? The man,

Randy, who had seen the corpse. The hotel proprietor? Surely he would not then be so brash as to seek a reward.

The owners of the mill, the wealthy and powerful of the town? Royal Washington, newly intent on organizing the employees, would be a formidable threat. But if they engineered his death, why had they recently paid him a quarter of a million dollars? To avert suspicion, perhaps?

L'infermiere called The Golden Angel. He had been seen in Blue Heaven between ten and eleven last night by at least three neighbors. Angel of mercy, serial killer, in the pattern so much in the news in recent years? Had the former police chief fallen victim, too—or beneficiary—to such euthanasia? Then why were both bodies found hanging, why the suicide messages in the Bibles?

Mario sat on the hood of a police car. The singing had ceased, but the dry rhythmic chirping of the crickets was louder than before.

Royal Washington had sent for a Living Will, which indicated that he preferred death to a long, painful and expensive hospitalization. Mario knew all about Living Wills. He had completed one of his own, which lay in his desk drawer at home in his apartment, dated from the heartbreaking time of his wife's death. Had Royal Washington conspired with his nurse in his own death? At the very sound of a new trumpet call to battle?

A gleaming limousine turned into the parking lot, its tires crunching on gravel, the shafts of the headlights sweeping the shrubbery. A man in a chauffeur's uniform, almost as tall as Deacon Howard and considerably fatter, got out and entered the police station. Mario craned his neck to see past him, wondering why Tyler was taking so long to emerge.

Candace Howard came through the back door, followed by the chauffeur, two almost spherical figures. He held open the back door of the limousine for her. She slammed it shut and said with asperity, "I'm riding up front with you, Cordene."

Mario, unseen in the shadows, told himself, She has recovered her spirit, her anger, her bitterness.

"Miz Jeff say I should drive you like quality," the chauffeur told her.

She got into the front seat. "I haven't changed color yet, Cordene."

As they drove off, Mario made a half-conscious movement as if to follow them. Mrs. Jeff: Claudia… Then, with a sigh, he resumed his ruminations. Father and daughter. Most murders, he knew, spring from the hatreds coiled at the roots of many a family. Could Mario's own *fanciulletta*, his Lauren, commit patricide? Perhaps if the stakes were high enough. He brushed away this disquieting notion along with a singing mosquito which had alighted on his ear. Profit alone is also one of the commonest motives, he knew.

The Town Hall clock bonged a single half-hour stroke. Mario held his wrist high to catch the light from the stationhouse windows. Nine-thirty-five, said his watch. So it does indeed run fast. A visit to Mr. Jackson Sprague with the innocent purpose of having the watch adjusted might not be amiss.

The stationhouse door opened, releasing a carpet of yellow light. Mario heard arguing voices. Tyler came out, carrying a leather folder, and pulling after him first, Gregory Shapiro and then, Deacon Howard, who were speaking loudly at the same time.

"That's enough!" Tyler commanded. "Y'all just climb in your cars and get where you're getting to." He shut the door behind them with a bang. "Fight it out another day."

"I have telephoned the Tabernacle," the deacon said to Shapiro. "The eldresses will not grant you admission."

"I'm their father. I'll get a court order if necessary."

"Not before tomorrow at the earliest. And your visitation rights are twice monthly only, on weekends."

Tyler took hold of Shapiro's shoulders, propelling him almost at a run in the direction of a white BMW. They passed Mario without seeing him, Shapiro calling over his shoulder, "I'm not without influence, you know, I've made a few phone calls myself!"

When both men had driven away, Tyler walked slowly back toward the lighted window, laid the folder on the sill, and stood framed in silhouette. Mario sat quietly, waiting to be called.

"Mr. Castigliani?" Tyler said softly into the night. But he was looking upward at the moonlit sky. Suddenly he let out a whoop, a cowboy yodel, and flung his cap high in the air. "Yippie ki yi yai!" he yelled as he jumped to catch the cap, so loudly that the startled face of Patrolman Potts appeared at the window.

"Thirty long 'uns right out of the blue!" yelled the police chief, tossing his cap upward, performing a jig as he caught it.

The window opened. Potts called, "Hey, Chief, you in the high cotton tonight! Just only don't figger up the crop a'foren the weevils get at it!" He shut the window.

Mario approached the dancing silhouette.

"Well, bless your old black commie boots and whiskers!" Tyler was chortling. He gripped Mario's hands and waltzed him around like a circus bear. "You Roy! Crazy old stubborn old red!"

"Royal Washington was a Communist?" Mario inquired, releasing his hands, laughing in sympathy with the unalloyed joy of the police chief.

Tyler stopped jigging, and smoothed back his hair, which gleamed gold in the moonlight. His smiling face seemed as young as a boy's. "Excuse me, Mr. Castigliani, acting crazy as a bedbug." He put his cap on and retrieved the leather folder. "Had to let it out, you understand."

"I understand."

"Can't tell you how much this means to me. This money." Tyler steered Mario to his cruiser and opened the door for him. "No, Roy wasn't a Communist." He walked around the car and sat in the driver's seat. "Though lots of folks called him that."

He rolled down the windows and drove into the silent street. Streetlamps shed pools of pinkish light on the pavements and store-fronts, which gave back the fever of the day. "More like a liberal Mondays, Wednesdays and Fridays and some sort of lefty the rest of the week."

"A generous man," Mario said.

"All his life gave the shirt off his back."

It took Mario some moments to acclimate himself to riding in the outsize vehicle, which smelled new and clean.

"If you're not too starved hungry," Tyler said, "let's take a few minutes, drive out to my farm. Isn't far."

Mario assented, caught up in the police chief's high mood. They were passing a long, low, lighted building where workmen could be seen loading bolts of cloth into freight containers. "The mill," Mario said.

"Swing shift," Tyler told him. "Works until midnight. Maybe tomorrow you could stop by there." He gestured with his left hand toward rows of modest houses with lighted windows, some showing the blue glow of television. "This was the first mill village. Penningtons had a finger in everything. They weren't impersonal like the big manufacturers, you know, the Newcastles and suchlike."

"*Paternalistico.*"

"Used to be, every job, a house went along with it. Penningtons built the church yonder, set up the school and the baseball team. Brought in the district midwife, organized the burial club."

"Cradle to grave," Mario said.

The car crossed the highway and turned onto a bumpy country road.

"They felt *sicuri.*"

"They came off the land. Hard times on the land. Farming's a terrible gamble. Low stakes, high odds. Take like right now, this dry spell. Farmers all studying the sky, anxious and praying for a sign of rain."

"I do realize," Mario told him. "Small peasants in Italy go through this too."

"You come from country people?"

"No. I grew up in a mountain city. But I was often in the farms of the valley working with my father. He's a veterinarian."

Tyler nodded. "Then it could rain a flood," he went on. "Wash out the crop. And there's weevils and hoppers and cutworms and all. The mill paid cash money. Whole family could earn. And any roof over your head's better than none. My grandpa, my dad, though, they wouldn't give up on the land. Funny how farming can get in a man's blood."

"And it is in your blood, too," Mario said.

"Times I wonder am I right in the head," Tyler said. "They tell me the Piedmont's dying or doomed, so why can't I farm in the bottoms, or anywhere promising." He pulled to the side of the road and parked, the car tilted on a low embankment close to a ditch. "But here's where I got to hang on, like an old snapping turtle."

Mario gazed out over a harvested field under the moon. "Was this cotton?"

"Tobacco. Nobody's grown cotton in these parts past twenty years. Crop's moved west, into Texas. California. All mechanized, what they call agribusiness."

They got out of the car. Tyler jumped the ditch and walked a few strides into the field, Mario following him. Here in the open country-side the cricket chorus was louder and more musical than in the town. They heard the hoot of a mousing owl and saw its shadow flit by over-head. The light from above was so bright that Mario could read the insignia on Tyler's uniform. A moist warm breeze brought with it a whiff of manure and a perfume of hay. The police chief took cigarette papers from his pocket and a pouch which appeared empty. "Enough for one last cigarette," he said, folding a paper to receive the tobacco.

"Truly the last, or only until you buy more?"

"I'm hoping it's really the last. Don't trust myself." He rolled the cigarette with skill, lit up, and inhaled deeply. "At least I'm off tailormades." He pointed the lighted cigarette at the earth and said, "Rotten mean, cotton was. Back in the old days. My grandpa grew it on shares. Stoop labor, breaks a man's back nearly. Tears up your hands something awful."

"This is your land we are on?" Mario asked.

"Not yet, but it will be." Tyler made a wide sweep with his arm, a half-circle from north to south. "Seventy acres, two payments to go. My dad sharecropped thirty. The house I grew up in is over behind that rise. Baxter and Ivy Potts living in it now, that's Duane's parents."

"They are the owners?"

"Renters. Tenants still cultivate a lot of acreage." He pointed across the road. "Tobacco's meaner than cotton even. Worked my daddy until he was nothing but breath and britches. I wasn't more'n fourteen when he died. I was already in the mill." He turned his head away, and said into the night, "Still hurts bad, remembering how he hated the mill. He wanted me with him in the fields."

"I, too," Mario said, "wounded my father by choosing another pro-fession."

"Weeding and watering, suckering, pulling off cutworms, spread-ing cheesecloth, whatever, long as there was one bit of daylight. Did two men's work and couldn't keep food on the table. He died in the curing shed, putting up leaves, just keeled over."

"But surely these days," Mario said, "there are easier methods, ag-ricultural machinery…"

"Damn right," Tyler agreed. "For those can afford it. Me, I got no intention to get myself killed like my daddy. Tobacco? Forget it. I'm thinking of peaches. Pecans." He took off his cap. The dreamlike glow of the moon haloed his sweat-matted hair and softened his strong features. "Orchards'll be back there," he said, pointing. "And over that way. Sweet potatoes, maybe, through here, and a vegetable garden."

"Will this land support such crops?"

"I'll farm it organic, far as I can." He bent to knock off the glowing cigarette coal against the earth, then extinguished it with the toe of his boot. He opened the butt and gave the tobacco shreds to the breeze.

He took Mario's arm, leading him back to the car. "Come on, 'fore the skeeters eat us alive."

When they were driving again, Mario said, "What will happen to Mr. and Mrs. Potts?"

"They're welcome to stay on. I'll have me a new house anyway, build it myself." He turned at a crossroad. "Don't know what's got into me, rabbiting on and on."

"Happiness," Mario said. "Unexpected *buona fortuna* can be intoxicating."

They pulled into a small parking area near a white two-storey wooden building. Welcoming light flowed from all its windows, and from a wide front porch with tables covered by gaily colored cloths. A placard hanging from a post at the roadside said: "Bonnie's."

Mario glanced at the illumined street sign with its insect satellites: Carmel Ave. Old River Road. "Is this not the former grocery store run by an Italian family?" he asked in a casual tone.

"Now how in the world," Tyler said, staring at him, "could you possibly know that? ...Okay, never mind. I keep forgetting I got the conjure man here. Yes, it is. Name of Tremonte."

"Carmine Tremonte," Mario said. "Did he not have a daughter who married into the town aristocracy?"

Tyler gave a short incredulous laugh, and then nodded. "He's up in Columbus now, manager of a supermarket chain."

"Ah. His wealthy in-laws perhaps arranged this?" Mario suggested, thinking, No doubt they found their new family connection something of an embarrassment.

"That's just how it happened. Miz McRae, Bonnie," Tyler said, "she bought the place four years ago. Fixed it up, built on the porch there. Husband killed in the army, she used the insurance money." He switched off the ignition, but neither man moved to get out of the car. "But maybe you already knew that, too."

"No, I do not know everything," Mario teased. "Indeed I have questions to ask you."

"Ask away."

"Do you know of a man named Randy, a Vietnam veteran?"

"Randy Funderburk. His brother Ben's on the mill loading dock. Randy drives an ambulance at Warren Memorial. Why do you want to know?"

This explains how he saw the body hanging, Mario thought, oddly disappointed. But not why he kept the information from his luncheon companions.

A screen door slammed. A woman, rangy and big-boned, wearing a long denim apron over a T-shirt and jeans, called from the porch, "You, Beau! Will you for gosh sakes get your ass in here?" The entrance light shone on her wavy auburn hair. Even at this distance, she appeared vital and unusually attractive.

"Never could stand a foulmouth woman," Tyler called back to her. He got out and held the passenger door open for Mario.

"What you said before about happiness," the police chief remarked as they walked to the house. "You know, almost forgot what it feels like."

Mario experienced a brief, sharp yearning for the ecstasy of *la Lucia*. "It comes all too rarely in a lifetime," he agreed.

They went up the porch steps. Mario saw a carrot-haired toddler in a sunsuit asleep on the floor, slumped against the white wooden wall. From a shadowed table at the far end of the porch, the red glow of a cigar brightened and dimmed.

The woman stood with her hands on her hips, smiling and frowning at the same time. "'Bout time you showed your face," she told Tyler. "Me and Gwennie'll be washing dishes till midnight." She had a coltish grace similar to Tyler's. Her gold-brown eyes were lively, the bone structure of her face both strong and delicate under a sprinkling of pale freckles.

Mario bowed. She gave him a wide, warm smile.

"This is Mr. Mario Castigliani, Bonnie," Tyler said. "And you'd better watch out, he knows every single thing going on inside your head."

"Do not take that too seriously," Mario protested, shaking her hand. It was long-fingered and bony, the skin rough to his touch. "I am happy to make your acquaintance."

"Same here, I'm sure," she said with a touch of shyness. "Do we call you Mario or mister?"

"Mario, by all means."

Bonnie said to Tyler, "Isn't it dreadful about Roy. Just pitiful."

She pulled herself together with an obvious effort. "Where do y'all want to eat? Inside's nice and cool, but it's kind of a mess."

They looked through open green shutters into the dining room. Its tables were covered with bright solid-color cloths like those on the porch. Two redhaired children, a boy of about nine and a girl a year or so younger, were clearing away the remnants of meals, playing some sort of game as they worked.

"I saved you out some baked striper bass and cobbler."

"Couldn't do better than that," said Tyler. "I'd just as soon eat out here. Were they holding a meeting?"

"Meeting about a meeting, you might say. Informal," Bonnie replied.

Tyler laid his leather folder on the table and leaned his head back against Bonnie's bosom in a frank unselfconscious caress. He closed his eyes. "Gosh, you smell good."

"Go on. I smell like sweat, onions and dishwater," she said, drawing away from him. "Sit up and act decent. Know who's watching us right over there?" She pointed at the red cigar glow.

"I can guess," Tyler replied. "Your other beau. Don't he ever give up? Beats me why you lead him on this way."

"Quit teasing," Bonnie said, giving his head a light push. "You know I keep telling him he hasn't got a chance."

Mario looked up at the gibbous moon which was now riding high. A breeze had sprung up, bringing with it an overpowering scent of honeysuckle.

The toddler awakened with a low sleepy wail. Bonnie scooped her up skillfully, murmuring with matter-of-fact affection, "Want your bottle, Precious?" The toddler stopped crying and nestled against Bonnie, who gasped, "Sopping! Dripping!" She held the infant straddling her outthrust hip and went in through the screen door, proclaiming, "Now we both need a bath and a change."

"She has many children?" Mario asked.

"Those are Myrt's," Tyler told him. "Bonnie has a daughter, sixteen or thereabouts, Gwendolyn, she's helping out in the kitchen. Lonnie, her boy, he's already in college."

"She does not appear old enough."

"Farm girls used to marry young in these parts. Bonnie couldn't have been much more'n fifteen." He called to the far side of the porch, "Hey, Reid! Might's well come on over. I know you're there."

Taliaferro, in shirt sleeves, his coat over his arm, emerged from the darkness.

Tyler said, "Want you to meet Mr. Mario Castigliani.... *Clarion* editor, Reid Tolliver."

"It's a pleasure," the editor said. He slowly winked his right eye, which Tyler could not see, at Mario. He put his cigar stump on an ashtray and held forth his hand.

Mario thought, This *giornalista* knows how to keep a secret. "I was planning to come by your newspaper office, to thank you for the advance publicity," he murmered shaking hands.

Taliaferro turned to Tyler. "Autopsy findings must have been a blow."

"A setback anyways," Tyler replied. "Reid, I been thinking. You go ahead with the story, apparent suicide, the way you newspaper people say it."

"After talking to Candy," Taliaferro said slowly, "I think you're right it was murder. Just as well not to let the killers know. I'll phone in a story tonight, to the *Times* and the wire services. Give a big play to Doc Osborne."

Mario asked, "Was there an autopsy when your former chief, Mr. Kendall, was found?"

"No," said Taliaferro. "Plan to have him dug up?" he asked Tyler.

"This don't go in *The Clarion* yet, Reid," Tyler said, "but an exhumation is already in the works. "

Reid's eyebrows shot up. "How did you ever sweettalk Osborne into this?"

"No," said Tyler. "I asked Vergil himself." To Mario he said, "That's

Vergil Cox, the county medical examiner."

"*Apparentemente* we are all three thinking along the same lines," Mario remarked.

"A few things out at the medical center might also bear digging into," Taliaferro suggested.

"I'm considering on that," Tyler replied. "Listen, Reid. Do me a favor. Don't say anything about..." He gestured at Mario. "'Course it's more'n likely all over town already, but..."

The editor replied. "Fewer people know, the more Mr. Castigliani has a chance of finding out."

"I'll say goodnight, let you two enjoy your dinner. Tell Bonnie goodnight for me. See you tomorrow?"

"I'll do my damndest to fit you in. And I sure 'preciate your help."

He and Mario watched Taliaferro walk toward the darkness of the parking area. "I only know one other man," Tyler remarked, "with the nerve to wear those red suspenders." Mario looked at him questioningly. "Casey Pennington," Tyler told him. "You'll be meeting him Saturday night."

"I've been wanting to ask, would Terence Hapgood have reason to visit Roy Washington frequently?"

Tyler nodded. "Likely Terry and some other health workers made regular house calls. Anyways, when Roy couldn't make it out to the medical center. Why?"

"In your police reports, I noticed that several neighbors said Mr. Hapgood was there so often that they forgot to mention his visit last night." Mario opened Tyler's leather folder, which contained copies of the reports and transcripts. "Two affirmed they had seen him, or his car, but only when directly reminded."

The screen door opened and a girl wearing a white frilly apron over a pink dress carried a tray to their table.

"Hello there, Beau," she said with an arch smile. "Aren't you going to introduce me?"

"Gwen," Tyler said, closing the folder and putting it out of her way. "Mario Castigliani. Call him Mario."

"What a fantastic name." Gwen sighed. She placed the tray on the table and held out her hand. Mario rose, responding to her flirtatiousness. He bent over her hand to brush it with his lips. It smelled agreeably of food and some highly-scented lotion.

She gave a little gasp, giggled, and retreated into the business of serving their meal. Gwen was almost as tall as her mother, and of similar bone structure and coloring. Her freckles were larger and more thickly clustered, visible under a heavy layer of makeup awkwardly applied. Her hair was freshly curled in a style unbecoming to her. Mario thought with a pang of sympathy of his own Lauren, plain daughter of a beautiful mother.

Gwen said, "Momma'll be down directly, she just got the kids to bed. She's taking a shower."

"Mighty fancy apron you got there," Tyler complimented her.

"You like it? Kevin gave it to me."

Mario said, "And the fish looks *veramente delizioso.*"

The striper, with its accompanying vegetables, was garnished with sliced carrots and had a rich brown glaze. Gwen placed a wooden bowl of crisp salad next to each place, and a basket containing a freshly baked loaf in the center of the table.

Mario sampled the food. "But this is excellent!" he exclaimed.

"I did the limas myself," Gwen boasted. "Steamed 'em quick. Just like Momma."

Tyler was eating with appetite. "Bonnie grows her own vegetables out back," he told Mario. "Makes all her own bread. That's spoonbread there. Give it a try. And Gwen here can bake up a mean corn muffin."

"And rice bread," Gwen added.

Bonnie came out, carrying a tray with a tinkling pitcher and two tall glasses. "Iced herb tea," she said, serving them. "Specialty of the house." She had changed into a simple sleeveless dress of pale-striped cotton. Her wet hair, combed straight back, was already drying in the persistent heat into its natural waviness. She looked young and refreshed.

Mario sipped, drank deeply, and then murmured, "*Meraviglioso!* What is in it?"

"Rose hip and blackberry tea," Bonnie replied, "and some mint from the garden."

Mario helped himself to more spoonbread. "I cannot tell you what a welcome contrast this is to my lunch," he said as he ate. "Luigi's Restaurant made me despair of the local cuisine."

He was aware of a chill, a faint resentment in the glance between mother and daughter.

Bonnie said lightly, "Well, Luigi's is more a short order place, since the Wrights took it over."

"You have to know what to ask for," Gwen added. "They make a real good chicken pot pie."

"Nobody's better with ham," Bonnie said, "and their hush puppies put mine in the shade."

I have been clumsy, Mario told himself. "*Ma certo*, you are right," he apologized. "Forgive me." He gestured appreciatively at the table. "I could not dine better anywhere than I am dining tonight." He told Bonnie, "You must be famous as a restaurateur, and highly successful."

Bonnie laughed, pleased and mollified. "I make ends meet, is about all."

Tyler reached to embrace her hips with his left arm. "She's a lot better at cooking and canning than she is at business," he said fondly.

Mario wondered, Will he tell her about the thirty thousand dollars?

"Momma, can I go out?" Gwen asked.

"I don't know, Gwennie. It's way late."

"Just a walk by the river. I told Kevin I have to be home 'fore midnight."

Bonnie disengaged herself from Tyler's arm and shook her finger at Gwen. "You better be," she warned. "I won't have you hanging around that police station."

Gwen bobbed her head, grinning, and ran into the house.

Tyler said, "Most moral and uplifting police station in the whole county, thanks to Ruthann."

"Never you mind," Bonnie said.

No, he will not tell her about the money, Mario was thinking. Because despite the *benevolenza* between them, his heart is elsewhere.

The crying of the baby, interrupted by coughing, reached them from an upstairs window. "She has a summer cold," Bonnie told them, as she went through the screen door. "I'll give her some hot lemonade and honey."

"*Signora* McRae clearly has a gift for nurturing," Mario remarked, thinking, What a pity it is not she he wants on a permanent basis.

Tyler said, "Plants, animals or humans, she's got the touch. And she's the best nurse I know of, 'cept for Terry Hapgood." He opened the folder, frowning. "I got to talk to him, first thing in the morning."

There was a brief silence, except for the unremitting insect chorus. Mario asked, "What are your feelings about euthanasia?"

"Haven't thought about it much. I reckon it seems to make sense, like putting a horse or a dog out of its misery."

"I am strongly in favor," Mario told him. He closed his eyes, remembering the mute pleading on the face of his dying wife.

Tyler was saying, "Terry Hapgood, he told me once how much it means to him, being a nurse. He cares about sick folks a lot."

"So perhaps, if a patient wanted to die..." Mario prompted him.

"Yes, that could be. But I can't see him stringing 'em up. Don't know as he's big enough to handle a man the size of Rutherford Kendall."

"Nurses have special training in lifting people," Mario reminded him. He squeezed a lemon slice over his salad. "Why did Mr. Hapgood choose to be a nurse rather than a doctor?"

"I asked him that once," Tyler said, helping himself to more spoonbread. "Told me he didn't want all that responsibility. Said nursing seemed purer to him. Purer, that's what he said." Tyler put his empty plate aside, and reached for the napkin-covered dessert tray on the next table. "More herb tea?" he asked.

Mario nodded.

Tyler went on, "Could've been money, to tell the truth. Medical school costs an arm and a leg. Hapgoods are one of the richest families in town, but Terry and his momma are more like poor relations." Ice splashed in the tall glass as he tilted the pitcher. "A male nurse is a mighty peculiar creature in Floraville. Terry, I always liked him. He's about ten years younger'n me. Even way back when he was a kid, they used to call him sissy-boy and names like that. Not to his face, of course, seeing as how he's a Hapgood. And his mom was a Pennington."

"Is he homosexual?" Mario asked.

"Could be," Tyler said. "That's one thing this town won't stand for. Terry's got some kind of deep, dark secret, but I don't think it's..."

"Lifestyle?" Mario put in. "I believe that's the current euphemism."

"'Bout five years back there was a lot of mean talk and scandalmongering. He worked up north that summer, health aide, in New York, earning his nursing school tuition." Tyler held his frosty

135

glass suspended midway between the table and his lips.

"Why New York?" Mario asked. "Why so far away?"

"Anyways, his momma staged a heart attack, maybe real, maybe no. They tried to reach Terry. Only he wasn't working where he said he was. Lied to Miz Fanny, lied to his Cousin Eunice."

Mario said, "*Ma certo*, the secrets of these *aristocratici* would not be common knowledge?"

"Oh, no? That's what you think. They got a chauffeur, Cordene, sees all, tells all, innocent-like. Well, Terry tried suicide. Sleeping pills: they pumped him out. Note said: 'Mother, forgive me, I'm so ashamed.'"

"*Ma il mondo intero* was out of the closet by then!"

"Not in these parts," said the police chief. He imbibed a long draught. "Terry, I don't reckon he's a practicing gay, you might put it."

"Are there any in Floraville?" Mario asked.

"Sure there are," Tyler said, "but they mostly do their practicing out of town." He frowned at his dessert plate. "Keep this extra hush-hush," he said at length. "I'm damn sure and certain that one of the millowners, Jeff Pennington, is…"

Mario, a forkful of peach cobbler halfway to his lips, put it down untasted. Rupert Jefferson Pennington. Mrs. Jeff. Claudia. Mario experienced a brief whirlwind of ideas, surmises and hopes. Could this be a marriage in name only?

The police chief took a bite of his cobbler and sighed with pleasure. "Boy, wait'll you taste this. Bonnie outdid herself."

Mario ate the bit on his fork, enjoying the distraction from his disturbed feelings. "Perfect," he said.

Both ate dessert in silence. Then Mario asked, "Is it not very courageous of Terence Hapgood to work as a nurse here in his home village?"

"Fanny Hapgood, that's his momma, got him the job at Warren. She wanted him with her. Widow since Terry was knee high to a June bug…"

Tyler said, "If you'll excuse me, I'm gonna clear all this away for Bonnie. Hate to see her stuck doing dishes this time of night." He cleared a space on the table, wiped it with a paper napkin, and opened the folder. "Meantime you might want to look through this stuff. And here's your set of the crime scene photos."

Mario accepted the material, took his briefcase from the floor and put the papers and photographs into it. "But I will help you, of course. I'll examine all this later."

They assembled the dishes and cutlery on the trays, and carried them into the air-conditioned kitchen.

"Gracious sakes alive," said Bonnie's voice, "if the both of you aren't a sight for sore eyes." She leaned against the frame of the door, grinning. In the brightly lighted kitchen, her skin looked rosy and translucent under the pale sprinkling of freckles.

Tyler grinned back. "I figured Gwen cut out the back way, so we'd give you a hand."

Mario said, "As a modest expression of thanks for that superb dinner."

Bonnie gestured toward the window. Mario saw Gwen on the porch steps, standing very close to a thin, short youth with a shaved head, who was holding a Peugot bicycle with one hand and stroking Gwen's neck with the other.

"Kevin better look sharp," said Tyler, "or he'll be late to work."

"Chill out, Boss," Bonnie told him. "He's got his bike."

Tyler said, "A fancy apron, that's kind of a serious present, isn't it?"

Bonnie laughed. "Dinner's on the house, seeing y'all earned it."

"Don't you dare," Tyler said. "She gives away more food than she sells. Mr. Castigliani, I mean Mario, he's my guest here tonight."

"What we need is a stiff shot," Bonnie said, "the three of us." She opened the cabinet under the sink and produced a quart-sized Mason jar filled with clear liquid.

"Cherry brandy!" said Tyler with a sigh. "Ain't exactly legal, but it sure is prime. Wish I could join you."

Mario said, "A drink would indeed be most welcome."

"Come on, Beau," Bonnie exclaimed. "One little taste won't matter."

"Not even a smell," Tyler told her. "You know I'm driving."

"Yes, sir, Mr. Law 'n' Order," Bonnie grumbled, with a mock salute. Then she said, her voice carefully casual, "You'd be welcome to stay over, Beau, 'stead of driving."

"Nothing I'd like better," Tyler said, "but I got to get Mario back to the hotel."

"You could stay, too, Mario," Bonnie offered, "if you don't mind sleeping on a couch."

Mario bowed, "You are truly gracious," he said, "but I must go back to my room. Could I not walk from here? How far is it?"

"Seven-eight blocks," Tyler replied.

"But that is nothing," Mario said. "I would enjoy a walk."

Bonnie set out tumblers and a shotglass on the counter. "Three brandies coming up," she sang.

Mario followed Tyler to the porch. Gwen and Kevin were no longer in sight. "Down Carmel to Jefferson Avenue," the police chief said, pointing. "Then one block left to Franklin, and left again to Main Street. You'll see the Gilmore soon as you cross the tracks."

The sky was now thickly clouded, the atmosphere heavy and threatening. The moon was nowhere to be seen. "Smells like rain," Tyler said. "And we sure could use it."

Bonnie came out with the jar and glasses on a tray. They sat at a red-covered table. Mario sniffed his glass, inhaling the fragrance of cherries. The brandy, however, was not sweet to the taste. It was so powerful that Mario exclaimed, "*Dio mio!*"

"Now you know why they call it white lightning," Bonnie said. She added club soda to her own tumbler, sipped it and sighed happily. "Know how I got Myrt's hellions to go to sleep?"

"Told 'em I'd tan their hide good if they didn't settle down," Tyler suggested.

"Nope. Told 'em hush up or I wouldn't take 'em to the magic show."

"Ah! You are coming then," Mario said.

"A double mule team couldn't keep me away," Bonnie told him. "I'm closing the restaurant."

"I must take my leave, alas," Mario said when he had finished his brandy. "My head is already spinning." He stood up. "And my knees are turning to water. If I am to find my way to the hotel..."

"Phone you first thing in the morning," Tyler said. "Will you have time to come to the mill with me, and out to the medical center?"

"*Sì certo,*" Mario replied. "I am at your command." He repeated the directions to the hotel to Tyler's satisfaction, and bowed unsteadily

138

to Bonnie. "A thousand thanks, *Signora*."

"Careful!" she exclaimed with concern. "Don't go fallin' on your face! This stuff kicks like a mule."

Mario set off down Carmel Avenue with a wave to the couple sitting in the lamplit intimacy of the porch.

A sullen rumble came from the opaque sky.

They have repaired the air conditioning, he thought as he entered the lobby. He shivered. At the desk, the downtrodden consort of Kirby Garison was nodding over the register, her arms resting on the counter. Mario, feeling a twinge of guilt for having acted the informer, was relieved that it was she and not her lord and master.

"Good evening, *Signora*..." he began as he came toward her, hesitating as he recalled that she was not Mrs. Garison.

"Miz Hicks," she told him. "Miz Florence Hicks. Most everybody calls me Flossie."

"Ah. Flossie. I wanted to tell you that I will not be leaving on Sunday as I had planned. I will want the room a few days more."

She raised a work-reddened hand to conceal a bruise on her throat. He was vividly reminded of Modesta. "Won't make no never mind," she assured him. "You could settle up when you go." A smile came slowly to life in her colorless eyes with their drooping lids. "I like to tell you thank you, Mister Castilyan. My boy Scott..."

The smile made Mario realize that he had overestimated her age by at least ten years.

"He says you give 'im a free ticket for me to come to your show."

"My pleasure," Mario said. "I look forward to seeing you there."

"Well, no, I don't really do much gallivanting, you know. But sure was mighty kind and thoughtful. And what you done for his cat."

"*Prego!*" Mario said. "It was nothing. I also wish to inquire whether there is any office space available in the hotel, which I might rent for a few hours a day."

She shook her head. "I don't think Mr. Garison got nothing like that," she said. And then, "But he could maybe fix you up a corner in the dining room, with screens and things. A desk mebbe." She nodded toward the closed double doors at the far side of the lobby. "Mr. Garison, he uses it like for an office, but it's plenty big enough for two."

"That sounds as though it would do very well."

"'Course it's him you gotta ask," she said anxiously. "Best mebbe say it was your own idea."

"I will certainly do that," Mario replied. "I know the hour is late, and that Mr. Garison is probably sleeping. But I wonder if I might have a look at the dining room now, just to see…" He started toward the double doors, but she darted with a look of panic from behind the desk and blocked him.

"No! You musn't!" she whispered emphatically. "You can't go in there now!"

Mario backed off. "Forgive me," he said. "I did not mean to rush matters. Tomorrow will do very well."

She ducked her grey head and returned to her post. "But listen here, Mr. Castilyan. You need any washing done, or anything going to the drycleaners, me and Scott be proud to oblige."

"Thank you, *Signora* Flossie. And I will wish you good night." He bowed, and went up the stairs deep in thought. His room was pleasantly cool and appeared to have undergone a spring cleaning. He sat on the bed to test the firm, springy mattress now covered by fresh linen, a light wool blanket, and a green chenille bedspread, apparently new.

The bathroom, too, looked much cleaner, and the water was gratifyingly hot and clear. Mario showered, and washed out his socks and underwear. He put on his white pajamas and maroon robe, and arranged the papers Tyler had given him on the bureau top. Beside them he placed the notes he had jotted down in the *Clarion* office. But his eyes did not take in their content.

She must leave the desk sometime, he told himself. For a few minutes at least. If only to go to the *gabinetto*. He laid his silk suit on the bed and contemplated it. It did indeed need to go to the cleaners.

The suit draped over his arm, he went into the corridor. He bent low as he came noiselessly down the stairs. The hands of the clock stood at 1:45. The desk was unattended. He was in luck.

He saw no one in the lobby. As he approached the dining room doors, he heard a murmur of voices behind them. They sounded tense, conspiratorial, argumentative.

He leaned forward when suddenly a voice rose in his ear, "Mr. Castilyan!"

He whirled to see Flossie, studying him with pursed lips. "See you done changed your mind about the drycleaning."

"Why, yes, indeed." He awkwardly proffered the hanger, which she accepted. "Grazie. Will it be done by Thursday morning?"

"Of course."

Yawning, Mario said, "I guess should I get a good night's sleep then."

"Reckon I should, too."

In pajamas and robe, he trudged up to his room, paced for fifteen minutes, then crept down the back stairs and into the unkempt garden. Tendrils of kudzu massed at the edge in heart-shaped threats, outlined in the pure white of a moon at its zenith. Mario silently sent *la luna* his gratitude. He was accustomed to the night but not surreptitiousness and prayed that he would not step on tomato stakes or startle nocturnal creatures. A sliver of light diffused from a crack between the dining room curtain and the window frame. Even standing on tiptoes, Mario could not see in, nor could he distinguish the words of the low voices. His concentration fixed on the mysterious conference, he did not notice Cora Danzinger staring out from her darkened room.

When Mario circled around to the front of the Gilmore, the lobby was dark. He crept inside, easing the door shut, and glided towards the dining room door.

A voice beyond the door was suddenly raised over the scrape of chair legs on a wooden floor. "Damn your eyes, I ain't a-gonna do it! I ain't putting my ass on the line for y'all no more!"

Before Mario could retreat, the doors slid open with a bang. He found himself face to face with Earl Langford.

X

Half an hour after his self-contrived debut in Milan, Mario opened the door that had opened led into Willie Winckler's dressing room.

"Come in, come in, *mio caro Signorino!*" Willie was naked, hairy and unashamed. He had removed the false blond imperial and moustaches. His aquiline face still bore traces of greasepaint and seemed even more satanic than it had onstage.

Mario, respectfully averting his eyes, seated himself on a cracked wooden chair from which Willie scooped up an armful of costumes. Slowly now, Mario, *prudente*, the young man told himself. Let this remarkable mountebank do most of the talking.

"I trust you will forgive my state of nature," Willie was saying as he reached for a dirty dressing gown of topaz satin. "I assume from your talented assistance tonight that you are too sophisticated to be shocked by the undraped human body." **And tempting as a ripe plum**, Mario heard him thinking, **with the milk of innocence not yet dried upon your lips.**

"*Sta bene, ma...* I'm not used to seeing people naked. Except for my *innamorata*, that is."

"You are affianced?" Willie asked, zipping up a pair of tight black trousers. **So young and already entrapped by a female.**

"*Sì, Signor* Winckler. We plan to marry very soon."

"But I hoped you had come to inquire about an apprenticeship." Willie put on a flowing ivory shirt trimmed with lace, and sat on the dressing table stool, facing Mario.

"Yes. I would like to learn from you, and meanwhile to travel with you as your assistant."

Willie smiled widely, revealing yellowish teeth with unusually long canines. *Ach, Liebchen. "Ja,* we were a good team tonight, and will be far better once you are trained. But my arts cannot be taught in a week. They require months of study and practice, years perhaps."

"I learn quickly," Mario told him.

"But if you plan to marry and settle down, how then…?"

"Could not my bride accompany me? Not at first, *naturalmente,* but as soon as I prove my worth." Mario gazed at Willie with apparent candor and courtesy, trying not to grin as he read the progression of the man's thoughts: disgruntlement, disappointment, then resignation and a renewed determination to gain, if not a lover, at least a valuable stage partner. "If we are to work together, she must be with me," Mario said gently. "I'm afraid that would have to be a condition."

"Ach, so. I suppose it could be arranged. But tell me about yourself." **I don't even know his name.**

"Mario Castigliani."

"Excellent. It will look well in lights! With what mindreaders have you worked?"

"None, except with you, *questa sera."*

"But how did you know so much about those in the audience?"

Mario lowered his eyelids. "I read their minds."

Willie stared, and gave a short bark of laughter. *"Bitte, mio caro Mario.* We both know some preparations are needed. If I am to share my secrets with you, you must do the same for me."

"Mine cannot be shared, alas. I myself do not understand them. But I cannot always rely on them, which is why I need you as a maestro." Willie was silent, frowning a little, disbelieving, nonplussed. Mario continued, "I will answer whatever you like about myself. I am from Perugia, and until tonight had planned to study veterinary medicine at the university. I will be eighteen next March. I can also read and envision from handwriting sometimes, and sometimes by holding an object in my hand."

Does this callow provincial expect me, Willie the Wunderbar, to swallow this cock-and-bull story? But what if he really can do it. No matter how. Heilege Mutter! What a goldmine. Aloud he said, "Your parents, I assume, can afford to pay me for, let us say, six months tuition and your expenses?"

"Those are not precisely the terms I had contemplated," Mario said. "I would be willing to work for my expenses plus twenty-five per cent of the box office net. For six weeks. After that I would expect fifty per cent. If I prove valuable, *naturalmente.*"

"My dear young man!" Willie rose, took a cloak from a rack and flung it over his shoulders. "Such demands are unheard of in this profession. But come with me, we will discuss these matters at a cafe, over a glass of *barbagliata.*"

Mario rose too. "*Grazie*, but my train leaves in less than an hour."

"Stay the night as my guest, at my hotel. We can begin your instruction. The manager here has offered to hold the show over for three more nights."

"I must go home," Mario said. "And there seems little point in further discussion if you cannot meet my terms." Willie started to reply, but Mario held up his hand. "They are not negotiable," he said with a friendly smile.

Gott in Himmel. What a hardheaded little bastard. Somehow he knows that the manager's offer was contingent on his appearing with me. "I will be frank with you, Mario. Money is less important to me than the joy of educating so fine a pupil. I will escort you to the bus for the Stazione Centrale, we can talk as we go."

"*Va bene.* If you accept my proposal, I could be back here tomorrow in time for the performance."

Outside, the summer night was balmy. In the alleyway beyond the stage door, the theatre manager was speaking volubly to three well-dressed women holding autograph albums. Two appeared to be in their forties and one was sixty or more.

"...*Signor* Winckler will be out at any moment, I do assure you, *Signor.*" The manager was fat and bald, given to rapid gestures. The women caught sight of Winckler and Mario and came to them with fluttering hands and little cries. Willie bowed deeply, accepted a pen and signed with a flourish.

The eldest of the women told him, "I have left my name for a private reading."

"And what is your honored name, *gnädige Frau?*"

"Oh! I'm not German. Just plain American. I'm Mrs. Nelson Lovingood." Willie kissed her hand. "Beatrix Lovingood," she said.

Mario was not attending to the conversation. He was gazing across the piazza at La Scala Opera House, dark now in the summer months. I will see all the famous buildings, he told himself. All the great cities.

"A few questions, if I may," Willie said while they waited. "Since you are not of the theatre, how does it happen you are familiar with a concept such as box office net?"

Mario said with a sparkle of mischief, "I read it in your mind."

Willie laughed uncertainly.

"I am not making a jest, *Signor* Maestro. And while we're on the subject, I also read in your mind that you are attracted to me in a …shall we say, romantic? …sense. Allow me to make it plain from the outset that I am not and never will be interested in a relationship of that sort."

Mario puffed out his chest and rocked on his heels, reveling in the power granted him by *la Lucia*. To the now speechless Willie he continued, "Unlike my schoolfellows, I bear no ill will nor prejudice toward those who are lovers of their own sex. I have no quarrel with your way of life. But it is not my way."

What a waste, Willie was thinking.

"And I must add," said Mario, "that I will not help you to procure the sexual favors of anyone, *maschio o femmina.*"

He *has* been reading my mind! thought Willie. **Or am I that obvious?** "*D'accordo,*" he said aloud, unabashed. "You are unusually decisive and straightforward for one of such tender years." **You ride a high horse, mein fein Junge.**

Mario asked, "Will I have an opportunity to visit my home again when we finish here in Milan?"

"No. I am due in Strasburg next week. Then Amsterdam. I will not be in Italy again until the fall, when I appear in Rome."

"When *we* appear in Rome," Mario murmured.

Willie grinned. "I will arrange that you receive billing," he said. "And by the way, what other languages do you speak?"

"English, " Mario said. "Some French."

"In this work, you will need many more."

"When my gift is functioning," said Mario, "language doesn't matter. All thoughts come to me in Italian."

The bus rounded a corner and came to a stop before them. "*Arrivederci,* then, *Maestro!*" Mario mounted the bus.

"No later than seven tomorrow!" Willie told him. "*Arrivederci!*"

The parting from Perugia was hard, as hard as anything Mario had ever done in his life.

He arrived in the small hours, expecting to find the household asleep. *Will she be in my room, my Oriana, waiting in my bed? How will I tell her?*

When he closed the front door of the villa softly behind him, he saw that Salvatore was sitting vigil on the upholstered bench in the *vestibolo.*

"*Papà!* Why are you up at this hour?"

"Eh, Mario." **Here he is home. I was foolish to worry.** "I couldn't sleep." He followed Mario into the salon. "How was *lo spettacolo?*"

"Go to bed, *Papà. Domani* we'll talk," Mario said, heading for his room, flinching from the anxiety in his father's mind.

"*Sì, sì,* in a little while. If you're not too tired, we could have a talk?"

Mario's exhilaration evaporated. He swallowed hard, feeling something like a lump of metal in his throat. *Va bene,* he told himself, might as well get it over with.

"I do not want to press you, *figlio,* but I had a visit today. A student from the veterinary college, Enrico Ponti, he wants to be my apprentice."

"*Bene! Molto bene!*" Mario said. "Because I have decided..."

"*Sì, capisco.* You have chosen the archeology."

"Sit down, *Papà.*"

Salvatore sank into his lumpy armchair, looking up at his son. Mario took a deep breath and then told his news.

There was a silence so profound that he could hear the dripping of a tap from the kitchen. Then, rising to a menacing crouch, Salvatore bellowed without words at top volume. ***Scimonito! Fool! Betrayer! Traditore!*** Like blows Mario received the thoughts his father could not articulate.

In slow motion he came at Mario, who stood poised to duck and run, as in countless childhood confrontations.

"*Papà! Nelnome di Dio, Calmati!*"

Salvatore achieved an even higher decibel level. "*Imbecille!* Wastrel!" Mario danced backward as his father approached with hand raised to strike. Stand still, Mario commanded himself. Once he hits me a couple of times he will calm down, the way he used to.

Doors opened. He heard running bare feet. Modesta in her night-gown appeared in the shadowy passage leading to the kitchen. Behind her Mario glimpsed Oriana in her shift.

"Have I nurtured a *serpente* in my bosom?" Salvatore was shouting hoarsely. "Or a *cretino*? The best veterinary scholar in all of Italy! And you want to throw it away!" He kicked sideways at a small table inlaid with mosaic, which had once graced a della Rovere *palazzo*. The price-less flower-filled vase on the table tottered, spilling water, but Modesta darted to rescue it. Stefano, bare-chested, a towel wrapped around his loins, came to the doorway leading from his bedroom, frowning and blinking. *"Che cosa?"* he demanded sleepily.

"Your *fratello*, he has chosen a new career!" Salvatore yelled. "To follow his father and grandfather is not good enough for him."

"Papà! Prego!" Mario begged. "I meant no disrespect."

Stefano asked Mario, "Is it the archeology?"

"No!" Salvatore roared. "That I could endure. An honorable pro-fession." His hand still threatened, but he was no longer advancing on Mario.

"There's nothing dishonorable in going on the stage," Mario pleaded.

"On the stage?" Stefano echoed. **What the hell is this?**

"You, a Castigliani!" Salvatore sobbed. "Painted up like a *buffone, un pagliaccio!"*

"Silence!" commanded Eleanora's low, vibrant voice. She emerged from behind Stefano, her white hair streaming over the shoulders of her peignoir. Mario realized she had been listening for several minutes. Salvatore, deflated, muttered and scowled.

"I absolutely forbid it," Eleanora told Mario.

"Mamma, I am a man grown," Mario replied gently.

"And what will you be, an actor?" Stefano asked, and guffawed at the prospect. "A juggler? A dancer?"

"I have apprenticed myself to an internationally distinguished mindreader."

"Charlatans! Thieves!" Salvatore whispered. "And you deceived me, Mario. You never said a word."

Eleanora put her hand to her brow. "You have sold yourself to *il diavolo*," she told Mario solemnly. Stefano laughed again, then clapped his hand over his mouth. Eleanora turned her grey, sorrowful eyes to Salvatore and said bitterly, "And it is you who are to blame. Do you see now where your godlessness has led *nostro figlio?*"

"*Ascolti*, all of you," Mario entreated. "Last night I attended a performance of my new maestro. I went with no intention of taking up a life in the theatre. It was instead as though the theatre took me."

"You hear him? Bewitchment," said Eleanora. "The spells of the devil."

"I should chain you to *il letto*," Salvatore told Mario weakly. **Before I let you ruin yourself.**

Mario said, "Accept it, *Papà*. Mamma. I have given my word. Tomorrow I will pack a valise. My train leaves at noon. I will not return for at least eight weeks."

No one responded. The suffering mind of his father seemed blank. Stefano was thinking, **Bravo, fratellino! After all, you got a lot of guts.** Modesta was silently beseeching, **Don't leave us, dear little master. Your padre, he wants only that you should be a good man like himself.**

Salvatore said grimly, "And I suppose you expect me to give you *soldi?*"

He has capitulated, Mario thought. "*Al contrario,*" he replied. "I will be sending you money every week, to pay for an assistant."

Salvatore grimaced and spat into the vase.

Mario found himself looking into the eyes of Oriana, who had come out from behind her mother. As though magnetized, she walked a few steps into the salon.

Where had he seen that look before, that mute, impassioned prayer for respite, for rescue, for mercy? In the dispensary adjoining the salon. Yes. There he had seen such eyes, in the faces of animals mortally wounded.

He made a half-step toward her, forgetting discretion, his hands outstretched. She paled so swiftly that it frightened him. She lowered her eyelids, and was all at once transformed into the self-effacing, humble housemaid of his boyhood. She took Modesta's arm, and mother and daughter disappeared into the shadows of the passageway.

No one had noticed. Eleanora was addressing a stream of familiar reproaches at Salvatore who endured them stonily. Stefano's mouth gaped in an enormous yawn. "I'm for bed," he said, and to Mario, "I'll catch your act in Milano, tomorrow, *mio divo.*" **If I can raise the fare.**

Eleanora said, "Have you no pride, Mario? No sense of the noble blood that runs in your veins?"

Stefano yawned again and went back to his bedroom.

Salvatore was thinking wearily, **Already when he was a little boy he was a vagabondo. Disubbidiente.**

"I take pride, Mamma, in the challenging adventure on which I am about to embark."

"So I have sunk to this!" she said tragically. "One son who will make himself a public spectacle practicing the evil arts. Another who spends his time kicking a football. And their father who comes home smelling of the pigsty."

Mario steeled himself to silence, wanting only to go to his little room. She will be there, Oriana. I will take her in my arms, I will explain to her...

Salvatore said, "You won't change his mind, *Principessa,* by spitting venom on me and Stefano."

"You won't change my mind, Mamma."

She nodded slowly. "So be it then. I will say *addio* to you, Mario, here and now."

"Not farewell, but *arrivederla,*" Mario said. "May I kiss you?"

"You may not. If you go, you go without my blessing." She made a gesture of dismissal. But it was she who left the salon, her peignoir sweeping regally behind her.

"*Papà,* what an *imbroglio.*" Mario came toward Salvatore. He read in his father's mind that, thanks to Eleanora, he was already swinging to support and sympathy.

"*Domani, domani,*" Salvatore said gruffly. "Go to bed, *figlio.* Get some rest. You have much to do before your journey."

Oh, my lamb, *fiorellina mia,* my little one! But Oriana was not in Mario's room. The bed was neatly made. Mario undressed and went to bathe. She will be here when I return cleansed and ready for our embraces. But when he came back, in his pajama bottoms, toweling his curls, the room was still empty, austere as a monk's cell. He waited, hearkening to the silence of the house.

He went in search of her, to the kitchen, the scullery, the door of the servants' room. He heard only Modesta's rhythmic snoring and caught glimpses of her dream: himself, Mario, lying by the roadside, knifed by a *brigante.*

He went out into the garden. Oriana was sitting on a bench behind the *mandorlo.* She was fully dressed in her drab work skirt and apron, her hair covered by the nun-like kerchief.

She was paler than the moon above them.

Mario knelt to enfold her and kissed her dry shut eyes. "Come inside, *cara mia.* "

"*Sì, Signorino Mario*—I mean Mario."

When they were seated on his bed in the moonlight, he took her hands, kissed them and said, "In two months, perhaps sooner, amore, I will come for you. Or send for you."

"*Sì,* Mario," she replied obediently. "I will await your summons."

"We will be married. Wherever I go, you will be with me." He kissed her unresisting, unresponsive lips. "Oriana! *Che cosa?* You don't believe me."

She was silent.

"Have you no *confidenza* in your Mario?"

"*Io ti credo.* I believe you speak sincerely…"

"But?" he queried, stroking the exquisite declivity from her cheekbone to her chin.

"*Mio padre,*" she said, shrinking from his caress, "he, too, promised. To send for my mother, she told me that."

He tried to untie her kerchief, but she brushed his hand away. "*Per favore,* let us sleep apart tonight, Mario," she sighed. "The hour is late, you need to rest for your *viaggio.* "

"Oriana, *agnellina,* I will tell them. Tomorrow I will tell the world of our love. Tonight if you like. I will wake them and announce our *matrimonio.* "

"No, Mario. Let us keep our secret. When you send for me, we can tell them then."

"But *perchè?*"

"Mario, I beg you. I do not want them to know."

Mario felt an inexplicable relief. Then he held Oriana close and kissed her fervently, again and again until she responded. Trembling, she allowed him to undress her.

"I have brought you a gift, *mia bianca topolina.*"

He turned on the light, transfixed for a moment by her naked loveliness. Magic of anticipation surged in his veins. In *tutto il mondo*, he thought, I will not find a woman more beautiful. From his knapsack he took a small soft parcel and put it into her limp hand. "Open it, Oriana."

"*Sì, Mario.*" She took out a translucent silk scarf of deep violet-blue. "*Bellissima,*" she murmured, draping it over her hands. Tears gathered in her eyes. She held the scarf out to him. "Take it with you, Mario."

"No! It is for you to wear, my darling."

"Where would I wear it? It is… unsuitable. Take it, *caro*, as a memento. Of our nights together."

She turned out the lamp. They lay entwined in love and sorrow while the sky beyond the window paled into dawn.

As soon as the train started, Mario fell asleep. The journey was half over when he awoke from a dream of Oriana passive in his arms, a tear on her shut eyelashes.

Mai, never will I abandon you, my beloved, he thought. She doesn't believe me. Why should she believe me? How many servant girls have lavished their brief beauty on a few weeks of passion, only to spend the rest of their lives in the grey prison of servitude. Bearing their babies in shame. Mario reflected on the history of his own family. The della Rovere princes. Many a bastard had they begot. And the Castiglianis had fathered their share.

He laid his large shapely hand on the knapsack by his side. He had packed lightly, two changes of clothing. But her blue silk kerchief was folded on top. You will wear it at our wedding, Oriana. *Grazie al cielo,* she is not with child. What a complication if she were! *Certamente* I would make them welcome, my bride and my little one, keep them safe from harm; but just now…

La moneta! His line of thought switched abruptly. I forgot to pack the lion coin! How could I, at this very time when I need it most. His fingers flew to his breast pocket. There it was. He sighed in relief and fingered it, tracing the lion head and the octagonal rim. He would use it during the performance a few hours ahead. Should I tell *Signor* Winckler to get samples of handwriting from the audience? No, better save that for tomorrow night. And on the third night, I can ask to hold handkerchiefs, pens, small possessions.

He wondered if Winckler could provide him with a costume: something modest. Without sequins.

And I must sit in on one of his private readings, see how he handles that. Then I can work out a style for sessions of my own.

He felt keen and eager for the challenges ahead. For the gasps of the audience. And the applause.

And so began his journeys to the cities of Europe, to the theatres with grubby backstage passages and brilliant marquees. From Milan by Eurail to Strasburg; by hire car to Amsterdam. Heady stuff for one who had never before been beyond the borders of his own country, and only twice away from the city of his birth.

Mario loved everything and everyone, including his improbable, incredible mentor and partner. And Willie loved Mario, the young genie from an Aladdin's lamp, who was so quick a pupil, so flatteringly receptive to Willie's wealth of lore.

Performances, Mario soon learned, were not only in theatres. Willie preferred the great hotels of vacation resorts and spas, where he and Mario could luxuriate several days in first-class comfort, meanwhile amassing information for their evening appearances. Best of all, Willie rated private parties of the rich, from whom he exacted sumptuous fees, and then reaped a further harvest from private readings.

His engagements were scheduled from the home of a devoted middle-aged woman of Marseilles, one of his several wives. He avoided using the services of any established booking agent. "Leeches, all of them," he told Mario. "Cynical, lazy, and ruthless. Why should we give them our hard-earned gelt?"

Mario, reading Willie's mind, was aware of more compelling reasons: registry with an agent would simplify the task of pursuing police. Willie had left behind him a worldwide trail of unpaid debts, jilted women and corrupted minors. The police were not the only ones eager to lay hands on him. His bad luck at gambling, which he sometimes tried to redress by amateurish cheating, had turned more than one fleeced victim into an implacable enemy.

Mario, mindful of his vows to *la Lucia*, announced at the outset that he would play no role in shady dealings. He loftily reminded Willie that he, Mario, an *autentico* clairvoyant, had no need to cheat. Willie would respond with his uneasy laugh, torn between skepticism and credence. When will you tell me, my miraculous little Mario, how you do it?

In those first weeks, Mario also shied away from prophecy and prediction. "I cannot read the future," he said one day when they were together in a Vienna coffeehouse. "And if I pretend I can, I would feel...well, *disonesto.*"

Willie was dexterously floating heavy cream on his brandied coffee. A mournful stoop-shouldered waiter wearing a patched apron put two portions of sachertort on the chipped marble table.

"Mehr Schlag," Willie ordered. His appetite was prodigious, though he remained skeletally thin. "Predictions are a matter of science," he said grandly. *"Die Wissenschaften* of statistics and probabilities. If you do not neglect the necessary research, you will find it easy."

Mario ate the rich fragrant chocolate cake in small appreciative bites. Only soup for dinner, he promised himself. Unlike Willie, he already had a tendency to gain weight if he overindulged.

Willie was saying, "Bear in mind that accurate prophecies will be remembered, failures usually forgotten. Ask yourself what is most likely to happen. When you tell a cuckold that his wife will return to his arms if he forgives her, nine out of ten times you will be right. If you warn a shopkeeper against investing in larger premises, you can hardly miss. That is, given the current bankruptcy statistics."

He took a cigarette box, of iridescent pastels lettered in gold, from a pocket of his velvet cloak and offered it to Mario. Turkish tobacco, mentholated, gold-tipped paper tubes in a rich spectrum of color. "I order them from London," he said. "Only the English know how to make interesting cigarettes."

Mario shook his head. "I prefer the plainer sort." He smoked only occasionally, and only for reasons of sociability. Willie's cigarettes, he thought, are a good gauge of *nostre finanze*. Fancy ones when we're in the chips, like right now, but handrolled harsh tobacco when we're broke. Twice already he made me wait for my weekly percentage. Roulette. Baccarat.

"Some predictions are safer than others," Willie continued, smoke curling from the hairy nostrils of his hooked nose. "A pretty girl will receive a proposal of marriage. An aging man will lose someone dear to him. Almost everyone will go on a journey. Adjust your omniscience to circumstance and place. A marriage of peasants in Sicily will endure, a marriage of artists in Paris will end in divorce. During recession or depression, a speculator will suffer losses."

"And a roulette player," Mario said, "will also suffer losses, even in periods of general prosperity."

Willie laughed ruefully. "Do not tweak my tail, Mario. Many probabilities of future events can be deduced from character. An aggressive young athlete will get into a fight. A petulant mother will be neglected by her adult children." Willie rose and flung a handful of coins on the table. "And for character reading, you need no instruction from me. You are a genius at it."

"Instruct me anyway," Mario said as they went out. The street had a drab torn-up look, with patches of postwar rubble. The reconstruction of a building had been abandoned halfway. Several shops had wooden boards nailed across their windows.

"Alt Wien," Willie said with a sigh. *"Was für eine Tragödie.* I pity your generation, who will never know how charming this city was. Come. We are late. I will teach you character reading another time."

That later lesson dealt rather with the art of astonishing the credulous with what they wanted to hear. "Gaze deeply into their eyes, and say, *zum beispiel:* 'You have a serious character flaw: you are far too generous.' And the meanest man or woman will marvel, 'How true! How could he have known!'" Or tell them, 'I sense in you a certain creativity. You are sensitive, an artist.' And the dullest dolt will believe you."

When Mario announced that he wanted equal billing as a partner, Willie was quick to agree. On the subject of stage predictions, however, he was adamant. *"Mein lieber* Mario, that is the reason they attend. All the rest is froth and decoration." He presented Mario with a copy of the *I Ching,* and admonished him, "Study the classics. Also the astrology columns of the newspapers. There you will find many a universally applicable phrase, many a handy catchbasket."

Mario silently consulted *la Lucia,* who seemed not to object. I will use only harmless predictions, he promised her.

Life was a feast, not only of food, but of new clothes, new faces, new places. Or life was a fast, with one baguette shared for a whole day's food in Strasburg, and Willie picking up cigarette butts from the pavement. After a one-week stand in London, Mario was so flush he ordered a Saville Row suit; but when it arrived in Amsterdam, he had to hock it.

Most of all, life was a feast of women. Every night among the *ammiratrici* at the stage door, there were one or two, perfumed, seductively clad, whose bedroom fantasies shot through his veins like a forbidden stimulant.

He hesitated, lured yet shamefaced. During his first ten days as a performer, he resisted temptation. Then he surrendered and spent the night in the arms of a young Alsatian with violet eyes and an irresistible gamine look.

He emerged from her house at noon. *L'alsaziana* was uninhibited, creative, experienced. Hitherto he had flattered himself that he knew, from reading the swampy depths of a thousand minds, all the potentials of sex.

His performance that night was below standard, so distracted was he by flashes of erotic remembrance and anticipation. He hurried from the theatre to the woman's house without a word to Willie, and repeated and escalated the feverish experiments.

He woke the next day in her bed. *Lucia, mi perdoni!* he thought. Forgive me, my Oriana! *Scusi, Maestro, per favore!* In that order.

He had long been aware of *la Lucia*'s distaste for his sexual involvements. She tolerated such behavior, he felt, but would much prefer that he serve Her under voluntary vows of celibacy. Had he gone too far this time? Will She punish me?

He apologized later that day to Willie in their hotel room.

"*Bitte,* it is nothing. Anyone can have an off night. I know why, and I understand."

Mario blushed.

"*Ach, die Jugend! Giovanezza!*" Willie sighed, rolling his eyes. **If only!**

155

he was thinking. *How I yearn to be your teacher in this as in all else.*

Mario scowled.

"No woman, however expert, can cater to your desires as a man can."

Mario made a strangled sound, too scandalized for words.

He did not go back to the house of the Alsatian, putting her off with lame excuses. He resolved that henceforth he would save himself for Oriana alone. For an entire week he did not succumb to the ubiquitous allurements.

I do it for you, Oriana, he said to himself after his second fall from grace. To learn how to teach you, so our love can be amplified. When we are together, it is as though we are playing music on simple flutes. No melody is *così bella.* But now we can use an entire orchestra. He grimaced at this train of thought. Mario, you liar, he told himself. *Ipocrita!*

He had no way to get word to Oriana. Given her solemn stricture that he must keep their love a secret, he could not write to her. In vain he had racked his memory for a friendly third party who would smuggle a letter to her.

Early in August he had phoned the villa. He let the phone ring and ring, but there was no answer. *Papà* is off in the Fiat with his new assistant, Mario thought. *La madre,* she never answers the phone. Stefano may have left town already for the training camp. He tried again the following day, and got Modesta, who regarded telephones as supernatural and frightening phenomena.

"Yes! *Pronto!* Here I am!" she shouted into the mouthpiece. *"Casa Castigliani!"*

"Modesta, this *is* Mario. May I speak to Oriana?"

"Mario? *Perdonami, Signor,* but *Signorino* Mario is not at home."

"Ascolti, Modesta, this is Mario. I, Mario, am speaking to you right now."

"Il Signorino Mario has left the city, Signor."

"Modesta! Will you listen?"

"But if I ever see him again, I will tell him you phoned." She hung up without asking for a name or a message.

Mario was in Nice when a brief, scrawled letter from Stefano reached him by *fermo posta.* It had been following him around Europe, forwarded by the theatre manager in Milan.

Dear kid, Papa asks me to write and say, Thanks for the money.
He says you know he is not much good at writing letters, but he
is sorry he yelled at you and hopes you are doing okay. He
says he does not need the money, his apprentice Enrico is a whiz
and business is booming. Papa says he will save the money up
for when you need it. Tomorrow I am off for the Turin training
camp. Mamma is still mad at Papa. She has not even looked
at him since you went away. If she has to speak to him, she
does it through me and Modesta. I also hope you are doing
okay. It still gives me a charge to think of you strutting around
on a stage. Hope you get to be famous. Sorry I never made it
to Milan to see you. Your big brother, Stefano.

Mario folded the letter back into its envelope and went in search of Willie. He found him among the luncheon guests of the hotel restaurant, at a balcony table, sipping an aperitif.

"Maestro, I have to go home, you must appear tonight without me."

Willie glanced at the letter in Mario's hand. "Bad news?"

"No. *Mia fidanzata.* I have kept her waiting too long."

Ach so, she has found herself another bedmate, Willie was thinking. **Mercifully.** "*Caro ragazzo*, believe me, it is for the best. Please sit, you are blocking the sunlight."

Mario sat down but waved away the menu Willie proffered. "I do not have time for *la colazione.* I have to find out about planes. *Trenos.* Whatever is quickest. Do not argue about it, Maestro. I have to go."

"Frau Lovingood, Trixie, she went to considerable trouble to arrange things for tonight."

Mario knew that the widowed Mrs. Nelson Lovingood, whom they had first met in Milan and who had since become their devoted patroness, had some sort of influence in the New York world of theatre. On the board of something, he thought, trying to remember. Carnegie Hall? The Metropolitan Opera House?

"I believe Horowitz the American impresario comes to our performance tonight, he flies back to the States on Friday," Willie said.

"Come, Mario, it may be a slim chance, but we cannot let it slip through our fingers. Your fiancee will be happier married to a local admirer." **Dein Herz will ache a night or two, then you'll rest your head on another bosom.**

Beatrix Lovingood now came to their table, wearing an open terry beach robe over a conservative bathing suit. She had a pleasant, wrinkled face, deeply tanned. Her skinny legs were knotted with varicose veins.

Mario and Willie rose, bowing.

"Dear Willie. Mario. I'm on my way to change for lunch."

Willie kissed her hand, really kissed it, first the back and then the palm, pressing it to his lips a long moment. She gave a little gasp. When he released her hand, she said tremulously, "How are you, Mario? Fresh and rested, I hope." **I want you at your best tonight.**

"I am well, *Signora* Trixie."

He never got back to Perugia.

When he was changing that night in his dressing room after the performance, Willie, still in costume, burst in and swept him up against his hollow, sweaty, spangled chest.

"Pack! Mario! We are canceling everything! Herr Horowitz is enthralled with us. A private party at his penthouse tomorrow night." **A whole week of parties, Park Avenue, Long Island.** *"Ach, du lieber Horowitz!"* He lifted Mario from the floor and whirled around with him. The thrilling thoughts continued: **And he thinks he can book us into the Mermaid Grotto, they've had a cancellation. And perhaps, when his show closes next month, we will open at the Luke Ballinger on Broadway!**

XI

Earl Langford was as startled to see Mario as Mario was to see the fugitive. "What the—" He turned to his cronies, Kirby Garison and the pawnbroker, Jackson Sprague. Themselves as surprised and motionless as figures in a wax museum, they sat at the only uncovered table in the room. All the rest were eerily draped with sheets. A trail of footprints, resembling those left by a herd of animals, led through the thick layer of dust to the table. Mario glanced over his shoulder at the clock above the reception desk: 1:47.

"This son-of-a-bitch was eavesdropping!" Langford swung a wild roundhouse punch. Mario, his senses heightened by his moonlight creep, easily deflected the blow. He grabbed Langford's wrist and with his thumb, gouged a spot between his forearm bones. Langford grimaced but did not cry out and with his left fist, caught Mario in the solar plexus. Mario gasped, tightly maintaining his grip as Langford tried to brace himself for another punch.

"Stop it! Stop it!" shouted Flossie, inserting herself between the two combatants. Langford choked his punch just in time and seized the woman.

Garison and Sprague had eased themselves over, Sprague assessing the scene with rapid calculation, Garison's hatchet face a study in anger and cagey hypocrisy as he glared at the woman with cold, murderous regard.

"I didn't tell him," she pleaded with Garison. "Honest, I didn't tell him nothing." She covered her scrawny bosom and pointed helplessly at the suit over at the reception desk.

Sprague yanked Garison's arm, "Careful. He's been working with Beau Tyler. Come over this morning. We got to get Langford out of here."

"For our protection or his?" snapped Garison.

"Let me teach that New York physic a lesson," Earl lunged forward, but this time Sprague intervened.

"Please, Earl, leave him alone," begged Flossie.

"Forget it," said Sprague. "Come on." Outside a car was pulling up. From the porch came the sounds of rapid footsteps and an instant later, light from a powerful halogen flashlight swept through the lobby.

"Earl Langford!?" exclaimed Bobby Lee Petticord's voice.

Earl raced into the dining room. The flashlight bobbled as Pettticord shoved it under his armpit and hastily unholstered his pistol. Earl froze, one foot on the windowsill, when he heard the deputy retracting the slide to chamber a cartridge.

"Far enough," said Bobby Lee. "You know the drill."

Earl slowly lowered his foot; his shoulders sagged. "I ain't going back inside," he muttered.

"You two-bit bitch. Why in the hell you call the police?"

"Watch it," said Bobbie Lee cautioned Garison as he holstered his pistol and removed a set of handcuffs from his belt. "Or you're going down there with him."

Sprague stepped forward affably, "Jack and me's clean as a hound's tooth, ain't that right, Earl."

"I didn't phone the law," whined Flossie. "Didn't even consider it."

When Earl did not lift his wrists, Bobbie Lee yanked them to the front and cuffed them.

"Yeah," continued Garison. "Just damn coincidence he showed up when he did."

"It was I who phoned the police," came an imperious voice from the staircase." Bobby Lee swung his flashlight around. Cora Danziger, resplendent in an emerald green silk gown and white hair, heaped in a tiara-like coil, resembled nothing less than a diva in a Broadway spotlight. "I saw a burglar sneaking out in the back garden."

Mario put his hand on Langford's shoulder. "If it is only that you have broken the terms of your parole, I will speak a word on your behalf to the police chief." Langford's lips moved soundlessly. He smelled of fear. A tremor ran through him, and up Mario's arm. *Un misero esemplare*, Mario thought with aversion.

Silence reigned, broken only by Flossie, barely audible on the phone, and by a faraway grumble of thunder.

Garison cleared his throat. "Fixing to rain," he remarked conversationally.

"Nah," Sprague said in the same offhand tone. "Lay you twenty to one she'll blow over just like last week."

Outside at 2:45 a.m., *la luna*, who had traversed the sky, reappeared behind the thinning clouds. Like a harem dancer, Mario thought, peeping through her seven veils. He was still in his night clothes, in the passenger seat of Bobbie Lee Petticord's patrol car, with Sprague and Garison riding in the back. Tyler was driving the handcuffed Earl Langford.

"My watch reads 2:53," Mario said to Sprague, holding up his wrist over the back of the seat. "It runs fast."

"Just you stop by the store tomorrow," the pawnbroker said, "and I'll be happy to tighten her up."

The two cars arrived simultaneously at the parking lot behind the police station. Bobbie Lee, his pink young face blank and sleepy, scraped the fender of a parked Jeep as he pulled in. The rear rooms of the stationhouse were unlighted, but a glow came from the reception area. Tyler and his prisoner entered first, followed by Mario and the others. Bobbie Lee switched on the light, and for a moment the five stood, eyeing each other. Sprague and Garison looked alert, keen and secretive. Mario's head was swimming with fatigue. Langford and Tyler, who was uncharacteristically rumpled, appeared exhausted too.

Tyler strode to the front, the others trailing. "Where the hell is Kevin?" he demanded.

The switchboard was unattended. On the small table beside it lay an open magazine and a half-eaten sandwich of the type called a hero in New York. The sound of the toilet flushing answered Tyler's question. The slight, shaven-headed youth whom Mario had glimpsed on Bonnie's porch, came toward them, his hands pressed against his flat belly.

"That po' boy," Kevin told Tyler shamefacedly, nodding toward the sandwich, "it sure done me in."

"How bad are you?" Tyler asked.

"Got the gripes, got the runs. But I ain't a-gonna die." Kevin held out a hand to Mario. "Gwennie told me all about you. She says you're a Continental Cool."

"Ah! The attraction is mutual." The young man's hand felt clammy in Mario's, the palm feverish.

"Can you hang in there till morning?" Tyler asked Kevin.

"I think so. Only we're out of toilet paper."

Bobbie Lee yawned widely, and then asked, indicating Langford with his thumb, "Should I put 'im in your office for his phone call?"

"Yes," Tyler told him. "Then lock them all three in the I.R."

"Hold your horses, Chief," Garison said. "Me and Jack done nothing calling for no lock-up. We just come along to oblige you."

Jackson Sprague gave the hotel proprietor a furtive nudge. "The Chief knows that, Kirby," Sprague said. "And I don't mind waiting on him where he says."

"We got a goodly supply of tissues," Tyler told Kevin while Bobbie Lee carried out his orders. "But we sure as little green apples need help around here. Get on the horn, Kevin, call every living soul on the force. Anybody isn't falling asleep on his feet, ask him to report in for overtime."

"Floyd Bradshaw, too?"

"Yeah. We'll un-suspend him for the duration. Give Kissimee a holler, ask 'em can they spare a couple of warm bodies."

"Gosh, I'm sorry, Chief."

Tyler entered his office, beckoning to Mario. "Isn't your fault," he told Kevin from the door. "No wonder they call the Floraville Lunch the Vomelette."

Kevin grimaced, doubled over, then bolted toward the back. "Hey, Bobbie Lee," he gasped as he ran, "cover the switchboard, willya!"

Langford sat at Tyler's desk, his manacled hands on the telephone, which was in its cradle. "She hung up on me," he said. "My own sister."

"That call don't count," Tyler said. "Make another."

Langford shook his head. "Who to."

Tyler escorted him into the I.R. As soon as he returned and locked the door, Mario pressed the desk switch to open the one-way window; then slid back the sound panel. Tyler handed him a yellow-lined pad and a pencil, and took one for himself.

Langford was on the stool near the little table, slumped forward, his cuffed hands between his knees, the picture of dejection. Garison sat on the edge of the bench, shrewdly examining the walls, ceiling and fixtures. Sprague lighted a cigarette, and paced as he smoked.

"I'm gonna tell 'em," Langford was saying, in a low miserable tone as though speaking to himself. "Why shouldn't I tell 'em, if it keeps me Outside?"

Tyler pointed to a chair. Mario shook his head, and wrote quickly on his pad, "If I sit down, I will fall asleep."

"Me, too," Tyler wrote on his own pad.

"Now, Earl, you wouldn't do that," Sprague was saying with a hint of menace. "Even the lowest slime don't rat on his best friends."

Kirby Garison caught at Sprague's arm as he passed, and with his other hand shook Langford's shoulder. Then he frowned, put his finger to his lips, and pointed to the ceiling.

"Are you trying to tell us the joint is bugged?" Langford said with a dreary laugh. "Well, a-course it's bugged. Whole stationhouse prob'ly."

Sprague glared around the room quickly, stubbed out his barely smoked cigarette, and immediately lit another. "I got nothing to hide," he proclaimed loudly. "All me and Kirby done was try to help out an ol' buddy. How was we to know you was violating parole?"

"Y'all ain't no true buddies of mine," Langford said, his eyes on his handcuffs. "Reckon I found that out tonight. Reckon I been dumb as dirt, didn't figure it out in twenty years of hard time."

"'Course you got *real* buddies," Kirby said with heavy sarcasm, "like that mystery man was gonna make you rich and free."

Mario and Tyler exchanged a glance, and Tyler jotted *Mystery Man* on his pad.

"Okay, so he didn't show." Langford's head sank lower. "Don't rub it in. And anyways he ain't the only guy can help me."

Sprague rose, saying, "You talking 'bout them umpteenth cousins of yourn? Hell, to them you're no more'n spit in the fire."

Cousin Earl! With a sharp intake of breath, Mario recalled Randy Funderburk's thoughts in Luigi's.

Garison rose. He and Sprague stood close to the cringing Langford. "Y'all leave me alone, you hear?" he said doggedly. "I'm gonna tell what job you—"

Sprague clapped a hand over Langford's mouth. Garison hauled him up from the stool, and with Sprague, dragged him over against the window-wall. The pawnbroker said in an easy drawl directed to the ceiling, "Now, Earl, ain't no sin offering a man a job. Act of Christian charity."

The back of Langford's head was pressed hard against the wall. Mario could see the veins in his bald spot. Sprague's calloused hand still gripped the man's lips.

Garison brought his face so close that Mario and Tyler involuntarily shrank back. The hotel proprietor silently mouthed the words, "Just don't say nothing about no crank. You hear me?"

No lip reading skills were required to understand his words. Sprague's hands went to Langford's throat.

In two tiptoed strides Tyler was at the door. Mario relocked it, and was back at the one-way wall in time to see the police chief enter the Interrogation Room. "Sorry to keep you waiting, folks.... Hey. What goes on here?"

Langford, instantly released, sagged against the wall.

"Earl here was looking a mite peaked," Sprague said lamely. "We was propping him up."

"Needs a cup of coffee bad," Garison chimed in. "Ain't that so, Earl."

Langford massaged his wrinkle-scored throat, which bore the marks of Sprague's fingers. His bleary eyes scurried from face to face, as though weighing the relative threat from each. "I done took all I can take," he told Tyler. "I got my rights to a lawyer."

Tyler nodded. "We'll get you one. Some coffee, too, reckon we could all use a cup. Bobbie Lee!" Petticord ambled from the back room, rubbing his eyes. "Coffee all round," Tyler told him. "Then get the FBI and the State to run a records check."

Bobbie Lee waved Garison and Sprague toward the back room. Langford hesitated, as though reluctant to follow and reluctant to stay.

"Hang on a minute, Earl," Tyler said.

Mario stood at the open office door, leaning on the frame. Perhaps the coffee will save me, he was thinking, from collapsing where I stand. I am too old for nights

"Gosh almighty!" the police chief told Kevin. "You look sorrier'n a wet cat."

"I should've et at Gwennie's," said the white-faced youth; and then gamely, "Floyd's coming. Andrew's wife won't let him. Vern, he was so stoned sleepy he couldn't talk sense. Duane says he'll try to come in 6:30."

"Kissimee?"

"Working on it. They're shorthanded, too."

Tyler looked at him questioningly.

"One patrolman laid up with tick fever. Sergeant had a heart attack in some whorehouse in Columbus."

The police chief held up a hand. "Don't tell me the others," he said tiredly. "Go on, help Bobbie Lee. I'll be there in a jiff."

Kevin rose, groaned, and bent over, hugging his middle.

"Minute Floyd gets here," Tyler said with concern, his hand on Kevin's arm, "I'm having him drive you over to Warren. Or do you want an ambulance?"

Kevin shook his head and walked gingerly, still crouched over, toward the back.

As soon he was out of earshot, Tyler said, "I got a word to speak to you, Earl Langford. You can stand on your rights. Don't have to answer a thing. But the more up front you are with me now, probably the less time in the joint."

Langford opened his mouth, then closed it again. He looked at Mario, mutely asking the stranger in pajamas to intervene on his behalf.

"You were at Royal Washington's house in Blue Heaven last night," Tyler continued. "We can prove that. And we know why."

Mario took a deep breath, and plunged. "And we know about Randy." He caught Tyler's quick surprise, quickly controlled.

Langford's seamed face went ashen. "You're lying," he said. "It's a trick. Randy wouldn't blab on his own blood cousin." Mario and Tyler said nothing, letting their silence do its work. "All right, so what if I was there?" Langford blurted out. "I never laid a finger on him."

"But you saw who did," Tyler murmured.

"Mebbe so, mebbe no. I ain't saying. Everybody knows I had a score to settle."

"You went there to kill Roy Washington."

"Never. I never. Mebbe rough him up a little. Uppity old nigger sub-versive cost me half my natural lifetime." In spite of the chill of the stationhouse, beads of sweat stood out on his lined forehead. "I honest to Jesus never got me the chance to touch 'im. They can't sentence nobody just for intentions."

Silence again. Mario felt a wave of sleep beginning to engulf him, resistible only because of the intensity of the confrontation. *Ahì*, if only *la Lucia… così facile* this would be.

Langford was sniveling. "Jack Sprague and the boys, they let me down. Vowed they'd get Roy, then weaseled out on me. And you know like I know, Beau Tyler, a white man's obliged to defend his honor."

For an instant Tyler seemed unable to conceal his loathing and contempt. Then he said with his customary, calculated mildness, "You got five-to-seven yet to serve, now don't you, Earl. Seeing as how you made a monkey out of your parole. Tell me what you saw last night and… Can't promise, but I think I could have that cut down to maybe a year."

"A *year!*" Langford raised his joined wrists and wiped his brow with his forearm. "No. No. I swear a-fore God I druther be laying in my grave."

"That's a right good possibility," Tyler said coldly, "after you sit a spell in Ol' Sparky." He told Mario, "Electric chair."

Langford shuddered. "Who you trying to scare?" he said hoarsely. "I tell you they's worse things than dying."

Tyler swayed, shook his head hard, and propped his eyelids open with his fingers. "Okay, enough for tonight. Go on, get your coffee." To Mario he said, "If we don't catch us some shuteye, we'll drop in our tracks."

Mario watched Langford slip away, thinking, the ambulance driver may be the assassin. Or the Mystery Man. "Perhaps Langford hoped, still hopes, to blackmail the rescuer he was expecting. The Mystery Man. For immunity, or money? Or both."

"Is that from your crystal ball? Or are you speculating?"

Mario shrugged noncommittally and changed the subject. "What is crank?"

"Methamphetamines. We busted two operations when I was on the Americus force."

"So Jackson Sprague and the hotel *proprietario*…"

Tyler nodded. "I don't think they'd have the brass to cook it here in Floraville. But it's a real cheap set-up, do it in a barn, a garage. About five hundred bucks worth of glassware and chemicals."

"And Langford?"

"Maybe picked up some recipes in the pen, or distribution contacts. Right vicious stuff, can kill a user, but it beats moonshining all hollow comes to profits."

Which could explain, Mario thought as they went to the back room, why Garison is so in a hurry to sell the hotel.

Jackson Sprague rose, crushing his paper cup, and said, "Me and Kirby here gonna mosey along, Chief Tyler, if you give us the go ahead."

Langford was locked in the holding cell. He sat on the narrow bed, a folded clean sheet over his knee, sipping coffee and leafing through the Bible on the nightstand.

Bobbie Lee hung up the phone. "No outstanding warrants," he told Tyler.

The toilet in the washroom flushed.

Garison rose and joined Sprague. "We could answer anything you fixing on asking us come tomorrow."

"Sure, go ahead. Just keep yourselves handy for when I call." Tyler picked up two filled paper cups from the bench near the coffee machine. "Coffee's colder than a witch's tit," he grumbled, handing one cup to Mario and taking a sip from the other. "Holy shit, Bobbie Lee, we got nothing but decaf?"

Petticord rose, stretching. "We run out." He yawned.

Mario tasted the characterless fluid, grimaced, and put the cup on the windowsill.

"I got a fishing date tomorrow," said Sprague over his shoulder as he and Garison headed for the front exit.

"Break it," Tyler told him.

Faint moans could be heard from the lavatory, then the crunch of tires on gravel. Brakes squealed, a car door slammed, and a burly green-eyed man with lank hair came through the back door. He had large features and the look of a blond American Indian. His thickly muscled chest was bare, his uniform shirt over his arm.

"I come on the run," said the newcomer, "soon as I got your S.O.S." He looked inquiringly at Mario, who introduced himself.

"This here's Floyd Bradshaw," Tyler said. "Me and Bobbie Lee's so plumb tuckered out we're forgetting our manners." Bradshaw put on his shirt. "Kevin's real sick," Tyler went on, nodding toward the washroom. "I want you to drive him out to Warren."

"Floraville Lunch?" Bradshaw said.

"Tell me about it. Take a squad car. Then hightail it on back here, so's Bobbie Lee can get some rack time. Him in the cell, yes, it's Earl Langford." Bradshaw's eyebrows shot up. Tyler said, "We'll fill you in later."

"Can I have my gun?"

Tyler went to a small floor safe, which looked old enough for a Western movie, and hunkered down, turning dials. "Remember, Floyd, it's only for the emergency. You're still suspended." He handed Floyd a gun belt and weapon, and closed the safe.

4:30 a.m. The moon had set. The Town Hall clock struck the half hour, sounding remote and dreamlike in the hush that engulfed Floraville. Even the insect chorus had died to a droning hum that seemed a part of silence. The streetlamps shone iridescent with mist. The mill was lighted; and the police station, and the hotel lobby. All else was dark.

Mario was curled on his buoyant mattress under warm clean bedding, slumbering dreamlessly. Out at Warren Memorial, Kevin, pumped out and sedated, slept supine on a hospital bed. In her bedroom above the restaurant, Bonnie embraced a pillow with lonely fervor, and spoke to it in her dream. Beau Tyler, in his austere boarding house room two blocks from the stationhouse, sprawled face down, still fully clothed, with arms outflung on the counterpane.

Bobbie Lee Petticord was asleep, too, at his desk, his expression peaceful as a child's, his head pillowed on his arms beside the plastic bag containing his prisoner's possessions.

The overhead bulb in the holding cell had been turned off. A pool of light from the back office fell on the Bible, open on the nightstand, a stub of pencil between its inner margins.

In Psalm 146: verse 7, the words "The LORD looseth the prisoners..." were lightly underlined.

Against the bars, by a rope improvised from torn strips of bedsheet, Earl Langford was hanging. His cheap brogans, issued four days ago on his release from prison, and already cracked and travel-scarred, dangled near the overturned cell chair.

XII

Midway over the Atlantic, in Stan Horowitz's chartered plane, *la Lucia* deserted Mario.

When he became aware that he was no longer able to tune in on the thoughts of his fellow passengers, he turned sick with panic. Never before had *la Lucia* abandoned him entirely. She had denied him the full trance state for two years or more, but had left him the option of everyday clairvoyance.

Perchè? Why? he wondered, gripping the lion coin so tightly that it cut into his palm. So shaken was he that he was scarcely aware of their landing and the passage through customs. A taxi took them to the cheap hotel in the West Forties where Willie's Marseilles wife had reserved rooms.

He left Willie to cope with the unpacking, and slipped away to a dimly lighted bar down the street. There he sat with his head lowered over a beer and silently invoked his unresponding goddess.

If I can figure out *why*, he told himself, perhaps I can do penance and thus mollify Her. Have I embraced too many *lascive?* Gone too far on stage with phony prophecies? He felt no answering echoes. Gone, Thou art gone. *Sparita. Ahì, Zio Massimo!* Now I understand your desolation.

Il maestro must be told! Mario walked back to the hotel heavy in spirit.

At the small penthouse party that night the performance was not a total failure. Several of the guests had been on the plane, and Mario had read their thoughts before She left him. Willie, too, was not unprepared, having gleaned much information in Nice from the unsuspecting Trixie about Horowitz's circle of friends. But their appearance at a larger affair, the following evening in a Sutton Place duplex, fell flat.

Their socialite hostess was polite but disappointed. Stan Horowitz was angry. "What kind swindle you call this!" he chided. "Amateur night?"

He gave them one more chance that week, at an opening night party; then cancelled their other scheduled appearances. "A two-bit gypsy reads tea leaves couldn't do more mediocre," he growled to Trixie when she arrived in New York.

She was staunch and ardent in their defense. Mario knew that beneath her amiable manner there smoldered a self-righteous temper. Even so, Mario was amazed at the fury of the tongue-lashing she gave Horowitz on behalf of her darling Willie.

Il maestro was philosophical about Mario's loss of clairvoyance. Willie had never believed the gift was genuine, but neither did he completely disbelieve.

"Let us take two or three weeks off, *mein Knabe*," he advised. "Relax. Find ourselves. *Deine Kraft* will return."

At the parties arranged by Horowitz they had earned enough to carry them a few months. When Trixie offered a loan, Willie gazed at her with melting gratitude, but shook his head.

"To be her guest at dinner now and then, *ja*," he said to Mario later. "To accept a watch, a monogrammed wallet, *warum nicht?* But she must know that she can trust me never to exploit her loving *Freigebigkeit*." He rolled his eyes. "My old-fashioned mores and ethics forbid it."

Once at three in the morning, Willie was robbed and beaten by a sailor he had brought home. Mario, rushing to *il maestro's* rescue, was no match for the aggressor, who robbed him as well, and blacked his eye.

Willie put cold compresses on Mario's swollen face and stoically applied iodine to his own cuts. He would not let Mario call the police. *"Nein, nein, die Polizei ist nicht sympathisch.* We might suffer further blows and end up in *das Gefängnis*." He tenderly caressed a bruise on his arm. "The game of love," he sighed, "is full of risks and perils. That is one of its charms. I find it astonishing, *mein lieber* Mario, that in this, the world capital of amorous opportunity, you choose to live like a monk."

Mario had received only two letters from Italy. Stefano's was a detailed account of a soccer victory in Turin. Salvatore wrote illegibly to thank Mario for the money which no longer arrived so regularly; to scold him for sending it; and to report that he was prospering, and had taken on an additional apprentice. Neither letter mentioned Oriana.

He was becoming fond of New York. He rode the subway whenever he could spare the ten-cent fare. He liked to stand at the window of the front car, bracing himself as the train roared through the tunnel. Ruby, emerald, and amber lights, jewels in the darkness, cast bands of color on the arches overhead. Mario watched for the less frequent lights of a deep blue-violet, his favorite color, which blossomed into sapphires on the velvet blackness as the train approached them.

Gradually, as he explored the city, so vital and stimulating in its fall season, his sore heart eased, his alertness returned. Sugar Hill in Harlem, Flophouse Row on the Bowery, Central Park autumnal against its backdrop of skyline, the glitter of Fifth Avenue, the rich ethnicity of slums, the chess corner of Washington Square Park.

One Sunday he walked across the Manhattan Bridge when day was dawning rosy and gold, framing in pastels the soaring, noble, pointed arches of Brooklyn Bridge on his right. He picked up a small stone, leaned out, and dropped it into the river far below. How easy it would be to leap from here, he thought. They say you would be *morto* before you hit the water.

He did not wish to jump, but thought, If *la Lucia* never returns, it matters little to me if I am living or dead. His stage career without Her would never be more than second rate, a dreary succession of boring trips from theatre to half-empty theatre, a *lugubre* down-at-heel existence.

A coal barge passed under the bridge, then a white Coast Guard cutter. I will seek Her, he resolved suddenly, through all the world and time. It is not too late to go back to Italy, to take up archeology. I will delve for the lost cities and towns of the Etruscans, from whence She sprang. Or perhaps Her origins are even further back: Greece, Egypt, Sumer. The caves of prehistory. Wherever there is hope that I might find Thee. Such shall be my quest.

Now with the climbing sun the windows of the skyscrapers turned brilliant red-gold, blinding him. Or... was it another radiance, pure, unearthly, dizzying, that filled the curve of heaven even after his eyes had shut?

Shivering, shaken, he fell to his knees, his face pressed against the iron railing which he wet with his tears of thanksgiving.

Monday at ten a.m., Mario and Willie were at Stan Horowitz's office above the Fontaine Theatre on West 46th Street.

"He won't be in for another hour," said his girl-friday, Francine Tannenholz, turning to them from her typewriter. She was not much older than Mario, and pretty, her glossy brown hair cut in bangs, eyelashes beaded with blue mascara, and the healthy cornfed look of a Midwesterner.

"May we wait, *Fräulein* Francie?" Willie asked. "Such a pleasure to see you again," he told her. "We could await him in his office, so as not to distract you."

You can distract me any time, she was thinking. "He doesn't allow anybody in there," she said uncertainly. "And I doubt if he'll see you without an appointment." **He told me, if those two deadbeats show up, get rid of 'em.**

"Willie and I were saying only the other day," Mario told her, "why don't we invite that *incantevole Signorina Francie* to dinner?"

"*Ja, ja!*" affirmed Willie, ever quick on the uptake. **I follow your lead, mein geschickter Mario.** "To be our guest in our new quarters. I hope you like *Kartoffel Zuppe*."

"I love it," she replied, her eyes on Mario. **Whatever it is.**

Mario thought, If I can get her to wash off the *cosmetici*, she will be even prettier. And I need *una notte di amore*. To celebrate.

Francie rose, gathered three unsigned letters and carried them toward the inner office. "'Scuse me a minute, fellas," she murmured. She walked slowly and provocatively in her high heels and tight calf-length skirt, thinking, **Let him take a good look. You can never tell. Where there's life there's hope.**

Perhaps several *notti di amore,* Mario thought. Willie ambled after her, smiling his wolfish smile. Behind his back he signed to Mario to follow.

No, they can't go in. Stan'll fire me!

"Are you perchance free tomorrow night?" Mario asked, innocently, seating himself on a daybed covered by a Spanish shawl. Casting couch, he thought. I wonder if Horowitz and Francine... He searched through her mind, and found no such memory. Only the thought, **So let 'im fire me.**

Willie was standing, hands clasped behind his back, examining one of the theatrical posters with which the room was decorated.

"I'll check my calendar," Francine said. "But I think I'm free." Mario saw in her mind an earnest young man with a crewcut. **I break one more date with that creep, and he'll dump me.** "Should I bring white wine or red?" she asked demurely.

"OUT!" commanded Stan Horowitz from the doorway. He gestured with his thumb over his shoulder. "OUT! Before I call a cop to throw you out." His face beneath his silvery pompadour was scarlet. **Talk about *chutzpah!* Could you imagine such a thing?**

Mario said, "Talk about... nerve? Brass? Could you imagine such a thing?" Francine unobtrusively slipped away to her desk. Mario and Willie made no move to leave.

Horowitz, too angry as yet to react to the echo, was thinking, **A Kraut has-been, screaming queen, I betcha, and his Guinea punk. For lowlifes like this I had to quarrel with Beatrix Lovingood?"**

"A German... no longer potent? ...a blatant homosexual, I wager," said Mario, "and his Italian bedfellow. For human trash like this I had to quarrel with Beatrix Lovingood?"

Horowitz goggled, color draining from his face. **Who said that? What's he—reading my mind?**

"Who said that?" Mario repeated. "What's he—reading my mind?"

Willie, unable to contain his delight, was bent over making low chortling noises.

"Forgive me, *Signor* Horowitz," Mario said. "I would not ordinarily behave so rudely. But *Signor* Winckler and I must convince you that our powers have returned." He rose, his arm crooked to offer escort, and approached the speechless impresario. "Please be seated, *mio caro Signor.*" He led Horowitz to the swivel chair behind the desk.

In my own office, in my own chair he tells me sit down.

Mario did not bother to repeat this thought. He said, "I ask you now to think of an article, any *oggetto* about which you feel I could not possibly know. And I will tell you what it is."

"It has to be an object? How about... what Goldie said when I left the house this morning? The wife."

"Certamente. She said, 'Don't forget, bring home a dozen... onion rolls? And a bottle of schnapps.'"

"Bialys," whispered Horowitz; then added loudly, "You never heard of a bialy, it's a special kind roll? All right, Mister Smart Aleck, I got an object in mind."

Mario shut his eyes and pressed the spot between them. "Of metal, about two inches long. Nailed up next to an apartment door... the apartment of your late grandfather. Inside this small container, a tiny scroll. With Hebrew writing... *Una benedizione* for the household."

"We call it a mezuzzah," Horowitz marveled. "Okay, I give up. How do you do it?"

Willie put in, *"Natürlich, verstehen Sie,* we cannot tell you."

"As you know," said Mario, "we are psychic. Would you care to try with another object?"

Psychic, schmychic, so long as it gives Standing Room Only. "Okay. What I got in mind now you could never guess in a million years."

"The September school report card of your daughter's son."

"My Hilly," Horowitz said in an awed tone. "My little genius."

"Hillel Wagner," Mario continued. *"La sua pupilla dell'occhio,* the apple of your eye. Third grade. C+ in Geography, B- in Deportment, everything else A. Teacher's name—"

"Never mind. Enough already. You got me sold."

Willie was thinking, ***Ach, Mario! Liebchen! Ein hundert* kisses I could give you, all over your firm young *Gesäss.***

Horowitz's printers did a rush job on posters that very afternoon, heralding the appearance of the clairvoyants the following night at the

Mermaid Grotto. Willie, by his own request, was billed as His Excellency Ernst Eberhardt. Mario had heard him thinking, **Better be on the safe side. I have not yet used Eberhardt in America.**

The previous week during the New York debut of a Parisian chanteuse at the Grotto, an invasion of intrepid rats had emptied the famous nightclub in mid-ballade. The club closed for two days while exterminators took care of the problem; but the chanteuse was still under sedation at Roosevelt Hospital, thus providing a convenient slot for the sensational new mindreading team.

Their act was listed the following afternoon in the Entertainment Section of the *World-Telegram*, under "Not To Be Missed." Rave reviews appeared day after day: *The Herald-Tribune*; *The Times*; the *Daily Mirror*. For a while no gossip column was complete without an item mentioning them. *The New Yorker* sounded them out about a double profile. They were held over for three weeks at the Grotto, until they opened at the Bijou in Schubert Alley for a limited engagement which proved to be a smash hit.

Francine Tannenholz never got to taste Willie's potato soup, but she and Mario shared many a meal: after-show sandwiches at the Broadway Delicatessen; breakfast oranges, coffee and toast in bed at the 73rd Street apartment, or at her studio apartment on Pineapple Street in Brooklyn Heights.

"Mia dolce Francie," he said to her one night, reading her wistful thoughts as she rested her head against his shoulder, "I cannot let you cherish such hopes. Marriage is out of the question."

"Don't tell me, let me guess," came her muffled voice from lips against his overcoat. "You're married already."

"No, except perhaps in the eyes of heaven. *Probabilmente* she and I will never meet again. But I will wed no other."

The wind shifted, bringing a smell of snow. A foghorn sounded. Mario shivered. "Winter is here," he said. *"Andiamo,* we will keep each other warm."

Mario did a solo matinee Thanksgiving week. Willie was with Trixie at her attorney's office, working out legal details of their upcoming marriage. "I am taking her name," he had told Mario gravely. "William

Lovingood. Has a ring to it, *nicht wahr?* And no man can offer his bride a more profound tribute."

Nor himself a more *grande protezione* from the cops, Mario thought. Willie's offstage attire these days was richly conservative. He had his hair dyed its natural grey-black and had given away his wigs. "Beatrix prefers me this way," he said. *"Die Gestalt* of dignity." He had taken to lecturing Mario on the responsibilities of wealth and social position.

After the matinee, Mario found Stan Horowitz waiting for him in the flower-filled dressing room. "We got decisions to make, boychick. The Florida contract you could sign right now," Horowitz told him. The act was to appear in a Key West hotel over Christmas. "But after, how about on tour. Whatcha think?"

"I thought we were slated for the Booth."

"Could get the Booth, could get two-three other theatres. Lot of turkeys folding just now." **I should oughta strike while the iron is ripe,** he was thinking, **now I got him alone. Tell him to deep six the old fart.**

Mario went behind the screen to wash and change. "Where I go," he said, "Willie goes."

"Listen, Mario, I wouldn't steer you wrong. Willie's a monocle around your ankles. I'm thinking big, boychick. I'm thinking 1954. A world tour, then the West Coast. Broadway ain't what it used to be. I'm thinking television, that's where the future's going."

Mario came out from behind the screen. He was wearing his dove-gray London suit, long since retrieved from the Amsterdam pawnshop.

"Look at that, a regular Beau Gesture! I should only look so good. Me, I got the best tailor in New York. Costs me a fortune." Horowitz stood up and ruefully displayed his baggy tweeds. "And the minute I put on a suit, it's a *schmatta.*"

He took a contract from his briefcase. Mario scanned the paper with an expertise which would have made *il maestro* proud. He noted that Ernst Eberhardt's signature was optional.

"I cannot work on television, Stan." Mario refolded the Florida contract and put it into his attache case. "Willie and I will sign it to-night." **If he approves it.** I need him as much as he needs me. "If my powers should fail me again, we can still put on an impressive *spettacolo.*"

Sure, sure. Would maybe wow 'em in Peoria. "So what's the matter with television?"

"We tried it twice when we were in Paris. And radio. *Mia potenza* does not work at a distance."

"But I seen you—"

"*Solamente* when I have a sample of handwriting, or a personal possession. I am in a hurry, Stan." Mario put on his cashmere overcoat. "Have to pick up their wedding present."

The day after the show closed, William and Beatrix Lovingood married in Boca Raton, Florida. Mario was best man.

They succeeded in shaking off all but one dogged freelance photographer, whose intimate zoom-lens pictures of the honeymooners made a center-spread scoop for the *Daily News*.

"*Ein bedauernswerter* absence of respect for privacy," Willie muttered as he examined the newspaper a few days later in Horowitz's office. He and Mario were there to discuss the itinerary of their tour.

"Go on, you love it," Horowitz said. "And it don't hurt none at the box office."

Mario, lounging on the couch with the Spanish shawl over his legs, thought, *Certamente* he loves it, but with anxiety and *trepidazione*.

Francine knocked and opened the door without waiting for Horowitz's permission. She shut it behind her carefully, and put a finger to her lips. In her sweater set, dirndl and moccasins, her makeup subdued to please Mario, she looked wholesome and charming.

"There's a Madame Mignonette Augustine here to see you," she told her boss. **And I'm afraid she spells trouble.** To Willie she said, "I think it's really you she's after, Maestro."

Mario sat bolt upright, surmising, Madame from Marseilles!

Willie hastily thrust the newspaper under a couch cushion and looked around wildly. "*Ist kein* back exit from here?"

Stan Horowitz, followed by Mario, went to the outer office.

A stout, moustached woman in black was seated squarely on the bench. Her eyes were beady, her jaw grimly set. In one hand she held an envelope marked "*Documenti,*" and in the other a copy of the *Daily News*.

178

Il maestro was behind bars by nightfall. Beatrix Lovingood used her considerable clout to see to it that no bail was set. Mario made hasty arrangements with Horowitz's attorney, and hurried downtown to Centre Street, carrying five boxes of English cigarettes, a bunch of grapes and a bar of rose glycerin soap. He found Willie gray-faced with shock and fear, as shrunken and diminished as a plucked fowl.

Mario appeared alone that night, to a packed theatre, and surprised himself by the high quality of his performance. In the wings between curtain calls, he told Horowitz, "The tour's off, Stan. Schedule as many gigs as you can for me around town." He knew the legal costs would be enormous.

The expenditures in fact eventually added up to more than he could earn, plus all of his and Willie's combined savings. Madame Mignonette grudgingly agreed to accept a handsome lump sum and an annuity to drop her bigamy suit; but by that time, the fingerprint check had flushed four other wives. One of these was the victim of grand larceny: On the nuptial night in Niagara Falls, Maximilian the Marvelous had vanished along with her jewelry. Gravest of all, Wilhelm Winckler, a.k.a. William Lovingood, etc., etc., was wanted in Oregon, Texas and Illinois on three counts of statutory rape. The fact that he had served time in Lewisburg for income tax evasion was a black mark against him; and when his European crimes surfaced, Mario was in despair.

Trixie was implacable. She refused Mario admittance to her Village townhouse; would not speak with him on the phone, and returned his letters unopened. In the end, only her dread of the escalating public ridicule kept them from going to trial. She agreed to permit a plea bargain protecting Willie from extradition, and allowing two of his probable prison terms to run concurrently.

It wasn't much of a bargain. In mid-February, Willie, by then a piteous ghost of his former self, began serving thirty-eight years in the penitentiary in Ossining, New York.

March came in with bone-chilling winds threatening rain. Grimy slush filled the gutters. Mario, overworked and distraught, but functioning gamely, received a phone call from the police captain of his precinct. Would he be interested in helping to solve the Keith Higgins mystery?

Keith Higgins was a seven-year-old reported missing in December, by his mother Irene, a shapely platinum blonde cigarette girl at a 52nd Street nightclub. The child's pajama-clad body was discovered on a West End Avenue rooftop, with the back of the skull bludgeoned in. Suspicion fell on one of Irene Higgins's many boyfriends, a petty gangster who proved to have an ironclad alibi. The racy nature of the mother's lifestyle kept the story alive in the media for more the proverbial nine days.

Mario was definitely interested. The fee mentioned was substantial. He needed a rest from performing, but had to keep earning to pay off the balance of the lawyers' fees and his debt to Stan Horowitz. Also, he liked the idea of using his talents for detective work, and sensed that *la Lucia* approved.

He made an appointment for the following morning at the precinct house, and was pondering the little he knew about the case when he went home that evening. It was a Monday: the theatre was closed. Mario, watching every penny these days, picked up a loaf of pumpernickel and a wedge of cheese in the dairy store between the subway and his home. He was hoping Francine would be waiting for him, to share his frugal meal. Then he remembered that she had to work overtime.

There was still some daylight from the overcast sky. When he turned into his block, the wind from the river cut through his winter coat. Lightning flickered above the New Jersey shore. Thunder muttered.

He was halfway down the block when he noticed the woman sleeping on the stone steps leading to his apartment building. She was fat, scruffy-looking, huddled in a black shawl, her head resting against the stone curve of the baluster. A *sacco* of the sort common in Italy was at her feet.

Mario's first thought was, *Dio mio,* yet another Willie wife on my doorstep! As he came close to her he saw that she was not fat, but in the ultimate days of pregnancy. Not scruffy, only weary, cold and travel-stained. Drops of sleety rain stung his cheeks and struck silvery against her head. She woke and looked up at him.

It was Oriana.

XIII

The rainclouds burst over Cullowee County at 11:45 a.m. on Friday, August 10th, 1990. All morning the sun had burned with diminishing ferocity behind the darkening thunderheads. Now they obliterated it entirely, shrouding the countryside in a lurid halfglow punctuated by blinding sheet lightning and deafening claps of thunder.

The first drops, large as half-dollars, spun down through the dusty air and rebounded from the parched earth. On the farms, whole families ran out to greet the rain, tilting joyous faces upward to the warm, wet impact.

When the siren sounded, the shriek startled Mario awake, and precipitated him from the tangled sheets of the hotel bed. He stood naked in the middle of the room, looking around him in the panic always occasioned for him by the ominous sound. The hissing and rat-a-tat of rain brought him back to the present.

Mario pulled up the blind, and succeeded in raising the recalcitrant window. He thrust his head out, allowing the water, now descending in sheets, thoroughly to wake and refresh him.

"*Meraviglioso!* Splendid!" he cried. Through the marching walls of rain he could glimpse the water tower with the silhouette of the man in the rocking chair, and the train station which had been converted into the Women's Exchange. The rails of the roadbed were no longer visible beneath the roiling waters.

Then he recollected the purpose of the siren. *Mezzogiorno!* How could I have allowed myself to sleep until this hour! *Pigro* Mario, he reproached himself. He shaved sketchily and put on tan slacks, a matching summer shirt, new socks and shoes. He collected his papers and thrust them into his briefcase. Galoshes, he told himself, and fished a pair of plastic rainshoes from his briefcase. He snapped them on, and was out and down the stairs.

"Mr. Castig-lian!" called Kirby Garison, beckoning from the reception desk.

"*Signor* Castigliani!" cried Cora Danziger, who with her sister Hazel was seated by the plateglass window against the backdrop of the storm.

"Hey there, good buddy!" exclaimed the football scout Culpepper, rising from a chair beneath a potted palm.

"Wait up a minute!" said the boy, Scott, running toward Mario.

Mario, with hasty gestures, smiles and bows of apology in all directions, strode through the lobby. At the entrance, Otis Feeney, mopping up the water which had seeped under the streaming doors, regarded him dreamily.

Scott caught up with Mario on the terrace, and handed him a flapping black umbrella. "You gonna need it!"

"A thousand thanks, *ragazzo mio!*"

At the bank, a few shoppers sheltered under the columned portico; but inside, Mario found only the teller. He greeted Mario by name, pronouncing it carefully and correctly, even before Mario had shaken out the black umbrella. "Police Chief Tyler told us to expect you."

"I won't be more'n a minute, sir." The teller disappeared behind a door with a frosted glass window. Mario glanced at the nameplate before him: Edward York. The name Pepsi York surfaced in Mario's mind: the high school *calciatore* coveted by Culpepper.

"Check or cash, Mr. Castigliani?" said the teller as he returned to his post.

"Cash, please." Ah, *soldi! Bel soldi,* crisp and green, counted out by deft fingers. "Are you perchance a relative of the young, ah, fullback Pepsi York?" he asked as he slid the bills into his welcoming wallet.

The teller looked startled and pleased. "You heard tell of my boy?"

"He must be eager to play for a famous team," Mario suggested.

The teller considered this, then shook his neatly barbered head.

"He's a down home boy, Pepsi. Not like these cuttin'-up young'uns nowadays. 'Tends meeting regular and minds his momma."

"Ah! A rare treasure," Mario said as he took his leave.

On his way to the post office, Mario stopped at a small store to buy a Columbus newspaper. The store was dim on this dark day, and unattended. Dusty, old fashioned. *L'incanto dell'imminente* bankruptcy, Mario thought.

A stout, whitehaired woman leaning on a cane came from the back. She stumped her way on swollen, discolored legs to the far side of the counter, apologizing for having kept him waiting. Mario paid for the paper and purchased some three-by-five cards, a carton of Benson & Hedges cigarettes, and a tuxedo T-shirt in a large size.

The woman regarded him with friendly inquisitiveness. She exchanged the newspaper for another copy from a pile beside the cash register. "This one's dry," she told him. "Rain come up so sudden like, I..."

"Ah! I thank you. Can you perchance tell me where Peck College is?"

"I surely can. 'Bout thirty mile up the highway, turn left on Burnt Mill Road another fifteen-twenty mile. Can't miss it. Red brick, ivy, real old-timey school."

"A thousand thanks, *Signora.*"

In the street, the rain was so light that he did not raise the umbrella. A group of townspeople conferring excitedly under an awning fell silent as he approached.

The post office smelled of wet clothing and was full of people, perhaps waiting for the rain to stop. They, too, were in animated conversation, pointing and gesturing; they, too, fell silent when Mario entered.

A middle-aged woman in a loose print dress, her iron-grey hair severely confined in a net, stood behind the service window. Mario, approaching, could see that she was absorbed in reading the message sides of postcards from a batch of just-sorted mail.

He cleared his throat. The postmistress gave a little jump and covered the cards with her hand. Her eyes challenged him with shameless curiosity. She stared even harder when he asked for a thousand dollar money order. "And one for one hundred dollars," he added, "and another for one hundred and fifty." Lauren, Willie, and Mario's August rent. "And three stamped envelopes. Also a padded mailer for these," he said, indicating the carton of cigarettes.

Filling in forms and writing addresses at the counter, Mario was conscious of the eyes on his back. The uncomfortable silence was broken now and again by whispering.

"William Lovingood," he printed clearly on the mailer, along with Willie's prisoner number and that of his cellblock. He scribbled a note on the back of a post office form: *"Caro Maestro,* I will write you in a day or so, and visit as soon as I can." He slipped the note in with the hundred dollar money order.

At the window he asked, holding up the envelopes, "Shall I leave these with you or put them in the drop?"

"Give 'em here," the postmistress replied. She weighed the parcel. "It's gotta go priority."

Mario counted out the money.

"New York, En Wye," she read loudly from an envelope, "and Ossining. Ain't that Sing Sing, Mister?"

Whispers and murmurs increased behind him. He heard the words "Yankee" and "foreigner" and "magic show" and a man's voice muttered distinctly, "Person cain't sleep safe in his own bed."

Mario turned on the assembly. "And what may I do for you?" he asked sharply. "For any or all of you?"

Those nearest him retreated a step, and there was a general air of embarrassment. Mario saw that his vague impressions had been incorrect: they were only nine in all, and were not uniformly hostile. Nor were they united.

The tallest of the men wore a long grocer's apron. His prominent adam's apple bobbed several times before he said brassily, "Tell you what you can do for us: You can get on back to New York. Or Europe. Or Sing Sing."

"In all my born days I never heard tell of folks hereabouts hanging theirselves," one of the middleaged women said earnestly, "and now there's three."

"Two!" Mario protested, thinking, Royal Washington and Rutherford Kendall.

"Or somebody strung 'em up," said the tall man.

The postmistress put in, "Two since he got into town."

"Cain't blame him for the old Chief," the first woman said, nodding her rainhood toward Mario, "'cause he warn't here then."

"How do we know he warn't?" one of her companions rejoined; and then, to Mario, "Seems like anyways you brought trouble with you."

"Dear lordy!" said one of the women, coming forward and gesturing with a furled umbrella. "Where were you all raised? In a barn?" The woman following her was strong-looking, thickly built, in a transparent raincoat over a maid's uniform.

The young woman held out a slim, well-manicured hand. "I'm Melanie Abbot, Mr. Castigliani. Don't you pay any attention to this little display of our famous Southern hospitality." She indicated the three men, and then turned to her companions. "And this is Tonda Whitley, a friend and neighbor of Roy's; and her grandson, Durrell."

Mario saw the shadow that passed over all three faces at the mention of Roy's name. He shook hands, and said to Durrell, "I understand it is you I must thank for distributing my posters."

"It weren't no trouble," the boy said with a wide smile. "Scott Garison, he says he's helping out at your show tomorrow. Could I maybe come along?"

"I would be most grateful," Mario told him.

Melanie Abbott said, "We didn't plan to introduce ourselves when we saw you come in, because—"

"—we figured you'd be real anxious to get on back to the police station," Tonda Whitley finished for her.

"I haven't been there today," Mario said. "I am just on my way."

Melanie glanced nervously around the room. Mario's eyes followed hers, from the postmistress to the onlookers. They regarded him with that blank, inward gaze, masking fascination and fear, of those who witness disaster.

"Well," Melanie said with soft emphasis. "You better get right on over."

As he hastened along Main Street, a fork of lightning made livid the distant line of hills. There was a tremendous thunderclap. The rain returned with renewed power, driving into his eyes before a strong wind.

He fought the umbrella open as he reached the park corner and tried to steady it before his face.

"And now there's three." He remembered the words of the woman in the post office, and comprehended all at once who they meant.

A half-dozen people stood under a pin oak in the park, watching the police station through the driving rain. Mario, making his way to the rear entrance, saw faces staring through the windows of the Town Hall. The parking lot seemed too full. A big green Ford with Atlanta plates was parked on the graveled space outside the designated area. Mario also noticed an aging station wagon with *"The Floraville Clarion"* stenciled on its door; a new Lincoln with "CORONER" on its license plate; and a maroon car of a make unknown to him, bearing in gothic gold lettering the legend "God Is Love, God Is Peace, God Is Plenty."

In the back room of the stationhouse, a large man of about sixty, with dyed black hair, wearing a creased Palm Beach suit, lounged magisterially at the desk closest to the rear entrance. "…a matter for the County Board of Health…" he was saying in an oratorical tone. He broke off when Mario entered, and regarded him with a puzzled frown.

Lieutenant Abbot was at the front desk typewriter, an evidence bag beside him. Floyd Bradshaw sat eating from a paper plate, at the center desk, which bore an appetizing display of food.

"Grab a pew, Mr. — Mario okay?" said Bradshaw, indicating a few folding chairs against the wall.

"Mario is fine."

"Bonnie brung us all this," Bradshaw continued through a mouthful of sandwich. "Chicken 'n' lettuce on rice bread, apples 'n' oranges, squash pie. Bonnie warned, 'Steer clear of the Floraville Lunch.' You and Doc know each other?"

Mario held out his hand. "Mario Castigliani. I am working as a consultant for Chief Tyler."

"Doctor Horace Osborne. I am the coroner of Cullowee County."

"You know about Langford?" Bradshaw asked, nodding toward the empty holding cell.

"I have guessed," Mario said. *"Perdona, però* I must report to—is Chief Tyler in his office?"

Abbot rose and came to Mario, both hands outstretched, saying, "No hurry, Mr. Castigliani, he's tied up right now. Have some lunch."

Energy seemed to flow from his long fingers when Mario returned his grip.

You are *molto allegro* today, *Tenente*, Mario thought, all aglow as they say. "I am deeply sorry to arrive so late," he said. "I fear I overslept."

"The Chief said not to call you. We'd rather have you late than groggy." He nodded briskly and returned to his listing.

Mario settled down gratefully with a sandwich, fruit and coffee. "Tell me what occurred."

"I come back from driving Kevin 'bout five a.m." Bradshaw said. "There he was, strung up, and poor Bobbie Lee wetting his britches. Marked the Scriptures, Langford did, same like Roy Washington and old Chief Kendall." Bradshaw cut himself a wedge of pie. "Some verse where it tells how the good Lord sets the prisoners loose."

Mario exclaimed softly. "This seems beyond coincidence."

Doc Osborne gave a dissenting growl. "I swan!" he protested. "Y'all around here got murder on the brain. How in tarnation can you claim homicide when the *corpus delecti* is locked up alone in a cage? Suicide, copycat suicide, plain as the nose on your face."

Bradshaw went on, "Chief Tyler, 'thout no more'n an hour's sleep, he come right quick. Called Doc here to pronounce him. And Bear Sieburth. You know Bear, he made it from Atlanta lickety-split, musta set a new speed record."

"Bernard Sieburth," Osborne said in response to Mario's questioning look. "Georgia Bureau of Investigation, Senior Criminalist. Of considerable fame hereabouts."

Mario crunched a small juicy apple that had just the right *acidità*, while Bradshaw and Osborne extolled the talents of the apparently legendary Bear.

"Over five hundred autopsies."

"Does it all by his lonesome. Takes the pictures, collects the evidence."

"The teeniest hairs, the sorriest prints."

"Hear tell as he's fingered more'n a hundred killers."

"Claps a blue light top o' that Ford hog, and drives like Jehu," Bradshaw pointed to the puddle of rain water forming at Mario's feet. "Hey, good buddy. Ruthann'll have a conniption. The mop's in the can there."

"How is Kevin?" Mario asked as he mopped up the puddle.

"His old self. Ripsnortin' and rarin' to go," Bradshaw replied. "Hospital wants he should stick around overnight. Gwen McRae's out there keeping him company."

Abbot took the mop from Mario's hands and returned it to the lavatory, saying, "We can go up front now, Mr. Castigliani."

Ruthann Hubbard, coping with a busy switchboard, gave Mario a curt nod when he greeted her. In the foyer, Reid Taliaferro, writing on a pad balanced on his knee, sat on a folding chair. Beside him on the bench, Deacon Howard was eating a sandwich.

Another man of considerable girth, his loudly patterned expensive clothing bulging above and below a tight belt with a silver buckle, was pacing the tiny area.

Taliaferro rose, shook Mario's hand warmly, and gave him a slow wink. "Want you to meet Mr. Edwin Princeton, Deacon Howard's attorney."

The lawyer narrowed his heavy-lidded eyes and nodded, ignoring Mario's outstretched hand.

"This is that self-styled shaman I told you about," Howard said. "The powers he claims most assuredly do not come from God."

Princeton took a sandwich from a paper platter on the bench.

"They are excellent," Mario said smoothly. "I have just been enjoying one in the back room."

"I brought these with me," the deacon told him. "We of the Tabernacle do not eat the food of the blue-eyed gentile."

"Mr. Castigliani has grey eyes, and mine are brown, or didn't you notice," said Abbot, steering Mario to the door of Tyler's office. He knocked loudly.

"Your exterior is black, Lieutenant, but I fear your mind is white as leprosy," Deacon Howard said.

"Come on in," called Tyler's voice.

"I've been washed in the blood," Abbot said lightly, "of a few murders."

"Hah, and you need not look far for the murderer," Howard said loudly as Mario and the lieutenant entered the office.

"If, indeed, you want to find him," Princeton echoed.

"Reckon he means yours truly," Tyler said. He was sprawled in the chair beside the desk, still in yesterday's sweat-stained uniform. His eyes were glassy and bloodshot. In Tyler's own chair, a man with a round, jolly, face, russet-haired and lightly bearded, was rewinding a tape recorder. "Shake hands with Bear, Mario, old friend from Americus days."

The investigator rose and came to Mario in a single fluid motion, his hand outstretched. Built like *un orso*, Mario thought. Moves like *un orso*. *Madre di Dio!* Shakes hands like *un orso*.

"The Irene Higgins Case," said Sieburth. "The Kent Daumier Case."

"Ah! You have heard of these," Mario said, pleased and surprised.

"Classic studies when I was at the Academy," Sieburth said. "My instructor used to say you made a believer out of him."

Tyler stood up, swaying slightly. "I'll fetch us some folding chairs."

"Stay put, Chief, I'll get them," said Abbot.

Tyler sat down again, almost falling back into the chair.

Sieburth said, "I understand you were with Beau here when he was observing Langford, Sprague and Garison through the wall. Tell me what you saw and heard."

Mario gave a concise report, ending with Sprague's hands on Langford and Tyler's entry into the I.R. Abbot returned before Mario finished, and opened chairs.

Sieburth asked, "How much of a grip you figure Jack had on his throat?"

"*Sufficiente* to cause pain and breathlessness. Not *bastante* for permanent injury, Chief Tyler was too quick for that."

"Enough to leave bruises, fingermarks on the neck?"

"*Ah, sì,* they were clearly visible."

"About the methamphetamines," Tyler said. "I'd just as soon you'd hold off with that search warrant, Andrew."

"You mean," Abbot said, "if we find something, Garison and Sprague won't go ahead with the cooking?"

Tyler nodded. "Bound to be others involved. I'd like to catch 'em redhanded."

Abbot asked Mario, "When you mentioned drugs in connection with Garison, did you have anything specific in mind?"

"Pot, that's marijuana, of course. And happy dust. Cocaine, *credo?*"

Sieburth said, "Reefer's not all that serious compared to meth, but coke—that's penitentiary stuff, much longer sentences than speed."

"Maybe so," Tyler said, "but to my mind this local manufacturing is a worse social plague even than heroin or snort."

"Lot of moonshiners graduate into it," Sieburth said.

Sieburth turned on the tape recorder then said, "What about Langford's state of mind when he was in the cage?"

"He told us he would choose death rather than prison."

"Was he sincere?"

"Utterly. Intensely."

"In your opinion, was he suicidal?"

"Yes," said Mario, "and no. I would say he veered from total despondency to a desperate hope that someone would come to his rescue. Then despondency again."

"Do you think he was murdered?" Sieburth asked.

Mario did not answer at once. "Yes, I believe so."

"How?"

Tyler and Abbot both started to speak, but Sieburth put a finger to his lips and pointed to the tape recorder.

Mario said, "The assassin came in when Officer Petticord was perhaps in the *gabinetto* or attending to the switchboard. The key was on the center desk in the back room." He waited a beat, then added, "I further believe that Royal Washington and Rutherford Kendall died by the same hand." That's enough, Mario, he cautioned himself. Say no more at this point.

Sieburth gave him a grin. "How about a breathtaking revelation or two? From the great Mario Castigliani."

Abbot grinned too, and echoed, "Yeah, how 'bout that, Mr. Internationally Famed Psychic?"

"Like yesterday," said the police chief earnestly, "when you saw right into Roy's kitchen."

Remorse for his affront to *la Lucia* shook Mario. Guilt over his deception of Tyler made him squirm on the hard folding chair. "Forgive me..." he began.

Tyler said, "Would it help if you held onto Earl Langford's handkerchief?"

"It might," Mario replied, knowing it would not. While Abbot went to fetch the evidence bag, Mario concentrated on Willie's favorite lesson: Clairvoyance as the science of applied statistics.

By thumb and forefinger, Abbot proffered the unclean handkerchief. Mario accepted it gingerly and closed his eyes. *I must give them something that sounds concrete...* "I am not receiving well," he apologized, returning the object.

"Can you describe the killer?" Sieburth asked.

"My impressions are *indeterminati,*" Mario temporized, a hand to his brow. "Sketchy."

"Male? Female?" Abbot snapped. "Coloring? Age? Height? Weight?"

"Male. Not young," Mario gambled. "But not old either. Male. Coloring fair, that is to say, not brunette." Instantly he regretted these words. *What if the murderer is black?* "Eyes blue or hazel," he went on.

"You reckon he's a local man?" Tyler asked.

Mario nodded. *"Intelligente,"* he pronounced, thinking, *that is obvious enough.* "There is something not... *normale* about him. Sexually." *About him and all the rest of humanity, eh, Maestro!*

Even Abbot seemed impressed. Emboldened, Mario hurried on, "A smoker." *I have yet to meet anyone in this town who is not.* "I am not sure of this, but I feel he is trying to break the nicotine habit." He sighed, opened his eyes and removed his hand from his brow. "I wish I could give you more," he said, "but thus far..."

The investigator shut off the tape recorder. Abbot said, "I have a few insights of my own. Like, Bobby Lee was asleep, I assume."

"My fault entirely," Tyler told him. "I must've been out of my mind, leaving a green rookie alone on duty, tuckered out the way he was."

Abbot asked Sieburth, "How much trouble are they in? Bobbie Lee and the Chief here."

"Raking over the coals, of course. Inevitable. Beau shouldering the responsibility will likely keep Petticord from getting canned. When the dust settles, they might put him on administrative leave for a week... Y'all did try to get outside help, pulled a blank, I understand. I'm recommending for clemency."

"Sure 'preciate, Bear," Tyler said.

"'Course headquarters got to be satisfied there isn't any coverup," Sieburth said. "Losing a prisoner is a very big deal indeed these days. Main worry is the kinfolk. They go after you, could spell major trouble."

Mario said, "He has a sister in—"

"—Stovall," Tyler finished for him. "She hung up on him."

"Ruthann's checking with the joint about his family," Andrew told them.

Sieburth consulted the many-dialed watch on his two-inch leather wriststrap. "Nigh on two," he said. Rain-muffled chimes from the Town Hall clock affirmed the hour. Mario glanced at his own watch, which said 2:07.

"Got to get cracking," the investigator continued, "over at the funeral home. But first off, Mr. Castigliani, me and Beau want to double-check on Petticord. With your help."

"Where is he?"

All three men nodded toward the Interrogation Room.

Tyler rubbed his sore-looking eyes and slapped his cheeks gently. He said, as though to himself, "Then I got to tackle the deacon and his mouthpiece. Myrt. Candy. When in holy hell am I gonna go to Warren and the mill?"

"Where you're going," Abbot said firmly, rising to his feet, "is straight home to beddy-bye."

Mario suppressed a grin, thinking, *bene*, who is now giving *ordini* to whom?

Tyler frowned a little, and said mildly, "Sure wish I could do that, Lieutenant Abbot."

"Just you let me handle Howard and Ed Princeton," Abbot told Tyler. "One of those rare cases where I have a color advantage over you. Myrtle, she phoned in about eleven, wants to postpone coming here till tomorrow. Millworkers are holding a meeting, combination rally and memorial. Okay with you?"

"Yeah, okay."

"I thought you'd say that," said Abbot with a glint of a smile, "so I gave her your permission."

Tyler stiffened, then relaxed and laughed.

"Candace is up to her monumental ass in Blue Heaven friends and neighbors," Abbot continued. "Sent enough to feed an army over to the Church of Sweet Zion. She's kind of pissed off that there can't be a settin' in, just a visitation at River Jordan." He said to Sieburth, "River Jordan Funeral Home. Warren shipped the body there after they completed the autopsy."

"Not embalmed yet, I hope," Sieburth said.

Tyler told him, "'Fraid so. We called 'em too late."

"Candy's raising a ruckus 'cause she can't go to the house to get a burying suit for Roy," Abbot continued. "I thought maybe I could postpone the rest of her statement, and send her to Blue Heaven with Bradshaw."

And this *disposizione*, too, Mario thought, is already *per certo* an accomplished fact.

"Reid Tolliver says he'd be real happy to drive Mr. Castigliani to Warren and the mill. They can report to you later," Abbot concluded.

"Well," said Tyler. "Well. It's been a busy little bee."

"Vern ought to go off duty, don't you think? …Ruthann's out there phoning down the stand-by list."

"Did Doctor Donlan call?" Tyler asked.

"Yes, while you and Bear were in here. Says he found nothing suspicious with Roy. Offered his pathology lab for Bear to…"

"I'd rather do Langford in the Ethridge Funeral Home," Sieburth said. "And I'll call the River Jordan one, tell 'em don't set a date yet for the Washington burial."

"So. Go on home, Chief." Abbot rose and held the door open.

"No. I want to see this with Bobby Lee and Mario. Then I'll take you up on it, snatch me an hour or two."

"Or six or seven or eight," Abbot said as he returned to his folding chair. "Sleep yourself out, Chief."

Mario said diplomatically, "You would be leaving everything in good hands."

"The best," the police chief affirmed at length, and was rewarded by Abbot's dazzling smile.

Mario asked Sieburth and Tyler, "Would you permit that I tell Officer Petticord he will probably not lose his job?"

"Okay with me," Sieburth replied, "if you think it will help."

When they opened the wall window, the I.R. at first appeared empty. Then they saw Bobby Lee sitting on the floor, facing into a corner. His head was almost on his knees, which he was embracing. His baby-pink scalp glistened through the soft fair fuzz of his hair.

He did not stir when Mario entered. Mario touched his shoulder. The patrolman leapt to his feet and whirled to face Mario. Recognition and relief dawned together in his eyes.

"Ebbene!" said Mario gently. "Did you think I was about to take you to be decapitated?"

They sat together on the bench. "No more'n I deserve," said Bobby Lee mournfully. "Double shifts. I been pulling double shifts since Floyd got suspended. I'm no good when I get real sleepy. I oughta resign right now afore they boot me out."

"Tell me what happened," Mario said.

"I said to myself, Hang in there, Bobby Lee, keep moving, till Floyd gets back from Warren. Kept myself awake pacing like a zoo critter, from the desk to the switchboard and back again."

"Did you receive any calls?"

"Only the one from Floyd to say Kevin was okay."

"Did you talk to Earl Langford?"

Bobby Lee nodded. "He was setting on the bunk turning the pages of that there *Holy Book.* 'You believe in this stuff?' he asks me. 'Course I do,' I says. 'I used to,' he tells me, 'when I was a young'un.' And he says he about give up on Jesus and that." He took a tobacco tin from his pocket and contemplated it unseeingly.

"I believe it is permitted in here," Mario said, indicating the ashtray on the small table.

"My smokes are on the desk in back," Bobby Lee said. "I forgot 'em." He opened the tin. "This here's just an empty I carry around, collecting stuff for my daughter." He poured its contents onto his broad calloused palm. Bits of silver foil, flecks of mica, tiny tubes of gilt paper, and bright pebbles glittered on his hand. "My daughter Cindy, she asked me to pick her up any shiny bits I come across. For what her class is doing at school next term."

"I have a daughter also," Mario replied. "Not a child. She has been on her own for many years."

"Cindy's gonna be working on this project when school starts up next month, it's a map of the whole United States. Made out of clay and dirt and stuff from every state in the union. Cindy, she had this idea to make the borders out of shiny stuff." A look of pain came over the patrolman's round innocent face as he emptied his palm into the tobacco tin and snapped it shut. "Don't know how I can tell her I lost a job again," he said unevenly. "She's so proud of her daddy.... Don't know how to tell my wife, and her scrimping and saving, I ain't never gonna find me another job pays good as this."

Mario resisted the temptation to reassure him. Not yet. "Would you like me to fetch your cigarettes?"

"Nah, I'm better off without. Cindy, she's always at me to give 'em up." He heaved a sigh. "You was wanting me to tell about Earl Langford."

"Yes."

"Well, I knowed he was mean trash, worthless as old weasel snot. But I couldn't help feeling sorry for Earl. Seems like half the joint had it in for him. Specially two colored trusties beat up on him regular... He sat there with them clean sheets folded on his lap telling me his troubles and flipping through the Scriptures. 'Says here,' he says, 'a person only got to be honest-to-God sorry for what he done to get forgiven. You believe that?' he wants to know."

Mario maintained a receptive silence.

"So then we got talking about the different religions and all. How the Baptists claim you got to get your wetting. Catholics say you're 'bliged to tell it to a priest. 'And there's some religions say you have to 'fess up public-like, before the whole congregation,' I told him, 'but our preacher says, Just accepting Jesus as your Savior is enough.'"

"An interesting conversation," Mario said. "It must have helped to keep you awake."

"Did help some," Bobby Lee replied. "Then he begun singing, kind of off-key: 'If I had the wings of an angel, Over these prison walls I would fly...'" The patrolman sang tunefully, with deep feeling, his head thrown back, his eyes closed. "Old song," he told Mario. "And we sung together, 'Swing low, sweet chariot, Coming for to carry me home...' You know that one. Colored spiritual. Surprised me some, 'cause I knew he didn't have no use for the colored. But he sure liked that song."

"Then what happened?"

"He got real quiet, like he was thinking hard. After a while he laid down, hugging them sheets, and went to sleep. I was walking up and down again, almost asleep on my feet. Then afore I knowed it I was laying my head down on that desk. Never woke up till day was a-breaking and the birds was a-shouting... and I seen him hanging. And I seen the Bible. Funny thing. Right off I couldn't think of nothing but that bitty yaller pencil."

"Had you given it to him?"

"It was his'n. And I could of swore I put it in the bag with the rest of his stuff." He seemed close to tears. "I ain't nothing but a goof-up," he told Mario. "I always been a goof-up."

"Do you know what time you fell asleep?"

"Must a been like three-twenty-five, three-thirty." Bobby Lee looked into Mario's eyes with earnest appeal. "I reckon a person reads minds can tell what dreams mean."

"What did you dream?"

"I was home with my mamma, she's ten years dead. Cold winter time. She was tearing up rags to stuff in the chinks, keep the wind out. Me and my sisters was setting at the table, helping her."

Mario thought, The ripping of the sheets to make the murderer's rope, he heard it in his sleep.

"Then I dreamed an angel here in the cell. Like in the song. Goldie-hair angel all in white come down the cell bars. Lifted up Earl in his arms and carried him away."

Mario glanced involuntarily at the one-way wall, certain that the men watching and listening behind it were sharing his excitement. Had Bobby Lee Petticord been half awake? Was he a witness to the murder? "The angel," Mario said, "was wearing robes? Man or woman?"

The patrolman shook his head. "Don't rightly recollect. Bible says angels ain't neither men nor women. I ain't certain about the robes... You think it means I'm 'bout to die, dreaming I see an angel? Or that something good's gonna happen to me, spite of all?"

"I think you will not lose your job," Mario told him. "Nothing to do with the angel. Chief Tyler is taking the responsibility for what happened."

Bobby Lee's face showed a gleam of hope. "Mighty good of him," he said. "What will happen to *him*?"

"The state investigator, Mr. Sieburth, feels neither of you will receive much more than a reprimand. Provided Langford's relatives do not sue."

The door opened and Bear Sieburth shambled swiftly into the room.

Mario said, "I was just telling Officer Petticord that you—"

"Think I could maybe keep my job?" Bobby Lee finished pleadingly.

"Nobody's going to fire you," Bear told him. "I'm pretty sure. Might stick you behind a desk for a while, pending further investigation."

Bobby Lee's mouth opened, but no words came out. Again he seemed near to tears.

"I would like you to tell Chief Tyler and Mr. Sieburth about your dream last night," Mario said. "But first perhaps you should write it down. Try to remember more details, even if they seem insignificant."

Bobby Lee gave a sigh that was half a sob. "I sure want to thank y'all," he said fervently.

Mario said, "I have a packet of sequins in my hotel room that I won't be needing." The new tuxedo T-shirt would require no *lustrini*, he told himself. "I will bring them, for your little daughter." Bobby Lee looked uncomprehending, and Mario added, "Tiny brilliant discs in many colors, for costumes."

"Spangles!" the patrolman exclaimed. "For her map borders."

"Precisamente, spangles," Mario said.

XIV

The rain, now light and steady, spilled down the shut windows of the *Clarion* station wagon as Taliaferro drove bumpily through the town. The interior smelled strongly of stale tobacco and moldering paper. Mario sat in the passenger seat, his briefcase beside him on the torn upholstery, smoothing the damp cuffs of his slacks. The windshield wipers functioned imperfectly, with a squeaking rhythm. In the back, yellowed stacks of newspapers were topped by the borrowed black umbrella and a teetering camera.

Wide puddles fanned water from their wheels as they turned onto Old River Road. "The right admirable Andrew Abbott," Taliaferro said around his unlit cigar.

"Ah, sì!" Mario agreed. "I am most impressed." In less than fifteen minutes, the lieutenant had signed out Bobby Lee; dispatched the coroner with Sieburth to the funeral parlor; arranged for Floyd Bradshaw to take Candace and Shapiro to the Washington house in Blue Heaven, and to relieve Vernon Bond. He had diplomatically temporized in response to a phone call from the GBI, and had concisely instructed Mario and Taliaferro as to what to do at the medical center and the mill. They had left him sitting tall at the Chief's desk, with an air of command.

"And did you hear Ruthann!" Taliaferro exclaimed. "'Yes, Lieutenant Abbot!' 'Right away, sir!' Not one bit of sass out of her."

"Certamente he seems the man for the job," Mario said.

"Beau's good, too, damn good," the editor said, "but his heart's not in it. Well, nobody coulda done better." He wadded a tissue from a box on the dashboard ledge, and scrubbed desultorily at the fogged windshield.

Approaching the mill, they heard voices raised in song. Taliaferro drove around to the back of the main building, and slowed to a crawl. Mill hands had assembled in the yard. Some were bareheaded in the soaking rain, some wore rain hats. "Royal is our leader, We shall not be moved," they were singing. The loading dock was in use as a platform, with a row of chairs and a crate for a podium. Mario rolled his window down. Myrtle Collins, wearing a man's yellow slicker, her rain-darkened hair plastered in curly strands on her brow, stood at the front of the platform singing strongly and clearly.

"Just like a tree that's standing by the water, We shall not be moved…" A thin young woman stood near Myrtle, supporting her in *bel canto* with the descant of the old song.

The newspaper editor slowed to a stop.

Mario peered through the softly blurring rain. "Who is the well-dressed man?"

"Don't know, likely some pie-card down from Atlanta." Taliaferro said, "and that's Jeff Pennington himself just behind him."

Mario squinted, but could make out no more than a white triangle of face. He saw Durrell Whitley among the singers near the platform. The boy was holding the handlebars of a minibike with an empty rear basket from which a raccoon tail hung, heavy with rainwater. Taliaferro called to him, but Durrell was singing with such concentration that he did not hear.

The song came to an end. The union organizer stepped to the front of the platform, one arm raised against the rain. "Y'all know me," he said in a loud, gravelly voice. "Vince Shimansky from Kissimee."

He raised his voice over the swell of response. "What d'you say? We gonna lay down for it? Or we gonna make Pennington Mill honor the feelings of the swing and graveyard shifts?"

The crowd answered with the shrill, deafening whoops of the rebel yell. A worker called, "A-men!" and several hands shouted, "We ain't laying down for it!"

"We say the mill stays shut. Till day shift," Shimansky proclaimed. "Who's volunteering for a delegation?" He squatted, placed one hand on the loading dock, and jumped the five feet to the asphalt. A dozen millhands made their way toward him.

"Ecco!" Mario called over the swell of sound. "There is your *assistente,* there's Phil!"

"Victory or die-ie-ie-ie," sang the mill workers. Phil, his long blond hair in a plait, was standing on a box in a doorway, waving at the station wagon with his camera. Taliaferro waved back. "Good for him," he approved heartily. "Young Phil's acquiring the necessary nose."

"We cannot stay," Mario said regretfully. To find and speak with the Golden Angel, Terry Hapgood, in light of Petticord's dream, must take top priority.

"I know," the editor agreed with a sigh. The station wagon bucked and sputtered as they got into motion.

"Hold the fort! For we are coming…" The sound diminished. They were back on the road, the windshield wipers jerking and squeaking.

Taliaferro said, "I want to cue you in about Warren Memorial. Were you there yesterday?"

"I have never been there. Is it a government hospital?"

"Private enterprise, highly profitable, though they do get some public research grants. It was built a dozen years ago, as a model facility. Serving rich folks, mainly. Does a lot of cosmetic surgery, varicose vein removal, fountain of youth stuff."

"Are there other hospitals in the area?" Mario asked. Through his trickling window he saw mud-red water seeping onto the asphalt where a roadside culvert had backed up.

"Only the County hospital, about thirty miles north. Some of the aldermen thought Warren was a crazy gamble, but it's turned out to be a godsend for the town. We'd all have gone bust without it. A.J. Donlan, that's the Director, it's his brainchild." He veered again to the right to make room for an approaching Trailways bus. "You'll be meeting him in a few minutes."

Mario recalled the interview he had started to read in the *Clarion* office.

"Local wheel," Taliaferro said. "Born and reared right here in Floraville." The car trembled in the backwash from the bus as he regained the center of the lane. "His mother was a Pennington. She defied the Valhalla tribes, married a shanty Irish mill foreman."

"Valhalla is the neighborhood of the mill owners?" Mario asked.

The editor nodded. "A.J. grew up outside looking in, if you know what I mean. But he won the family's respect, even Old Man Pennington's."

"He has an interest in the mill, then?" Mario ventured.

"Some folks say he's the real brains behind Jeff Pennington… Had a big rep as a surgeon in San Diego before he came home. Officer of the Georgia A.M.A., finds time to teach a Bible class at St. Mark's Episcopal. Active in the Rotary."

Mario said, "Perhaps he can account for Terence Hapgood's movements last night."

"And the night before. And his own whereabouts. And those others on the staff. Tell you what, I'll introduce you around so you can start on all that, then I'll split and check on Kevin. They'll be less on guard with you than me."

"*Bene*. But don't go where I cannot find you if I need you."

"When I leave Kevin I'll be with Lisabeth Kendall in the nursing home. Friend of mine. She's a patient there."

"The widow of the old Chief of Police!" Mario exclaimed.

"No. His mother. His wife died three months after they cut Old Ruthless down. Lisabeth might have some leads for us. Ninety-four and often out to lunch. But other times, sharp as a tack." Taliaferro pointed ahead at the sign on a sprawling fast food restaurant: "Big Bad Wolf Barbecue." Three plastic pigs, wet and glistening, danced on the roof. "I'm a mite hungry, how about you. And we got more talking to do."

"I have lunched well," Mario replied, "thanks to *Signora* McRae. But, yes, I have questions for you. We should make notes, and we must decide how to proceed."

A greying, fleshy man in a long apron was wiping the counter.

"Quentin," Taliaferro said, nodding toward the poster. "Meet Mario, the man with the crystal ball."

"And what's the other one made of?"

At Taliaferro's and Mario's reproving look, the counterman asked hastily, "Want your regular, Reid?"

"Heavy on the sauce. And coffee."

"Coffee only for me, please," Mario said. He followed Taliaferro to a booth from which they could see the highway.

"Lisabeth Kendall," the editor said when they were seated. "Did Beau tell you about the law suit?"

"Royal Washington and the mill owners?" Mario asked, confused. "Had she any *relazione* with that?"

"No, no, this was her own case, against Jubilee Nursing Home. She was raising a ruckus, claimed they cheated her out of thirty thousand some dollars. This was back a couple years, never did get to court. The old Chief—"

He broke off as Quentin slid a platter before him. Sizzling slices of pork were piled thick on a bun, topped with reddish sauce and accompanied by cole slaw and fried onion rings. "Smell that! Ambrosia," he sighed.

Taliaferro said between mouthfuls, "*The Clarion* played her lawsuit low key at Chief Kendall's request. He was doing some kind of investigation."

"What were his findings?"

"As I recall, the nursing home came out with a clean bill of health. And there was some question as to the old lady's mental competence."

A red Porsche swerved to a halt before the restaurant. The car door slammed, and a woman in a hooded violet raincape ran in, calling, "A ham biscuit and some fries, Quent! Quick, 'fore I swoon clean away!" She tossed back her hood, releasing a tumble of honey-colored curls, rolled her big blue eyes and dimpled.

"Yes, Ma'am! You name it, you got it!" Quent said.

"Anne-Marie!" Taliaferro called, rising to his feet and hurrying toward her.

"Well, Reid Tolliver, bless us all!" She hugged him close and gave him a resounding kiss on the lips. He staggered slightly and made a gasping sound.

Mario approached them with his little bow.

"Mario, this is Anne-Marie," Taliaferro said, clearly shaken by the kiss. "Floraville's fairest flower."

She held out a slim hand, with gold-painted nails Her handshake included a subtle caress, and Mario felt a shock of electricity run up his arm. *"Molto piacere,"* he said with fervor.

"Eating it here?" Quent asked over his shoulder as he filled her order, wearing a broad smile of pleasure and sly amusement.

"I'd dearly love to," she sighed, "but I got to hurry on home." The raincape had fallen open revealing a gold embroidered mini-sheath.

Taliaferro's eyes swept down the tanned legs to the small rain-spattered satin slippers. "Evening dress?" he said. "You starting early, Anne-Marie, or finishing late?"

"You hush up, Reid. And don't you go writing about me in the *Clarion*," she admonished him with a mock pout, and then turned the full dark-blue power of her eyes on Mario. "The whole town's just languishing," she told him, "waiting for Saturday night."

"I, too, am eager and impatient," Mario rejoined, "particularly if you plan to attend."

When her food was ready, Quentin placed the paper sack in her hands as though it were a votive offering. She dimpled at each of the three men, pulled up her hood and ran outside.

"That's prime stuff, I'm telling you," Quentin said in a reverent tone. "It don't come any juicier."

"Hey, how about a little respect," Reid chided, grinning.

"Let's drink up," the editor said. "We're running late."

Quentin barely glanced at them when Taliaferro put money on the counter and waved goodbye.

"She's the director's wife," Taliaferro said when they were back in the station wagon. He took a cigar from a box on the dashboard.

Mario exclaimed in surprise, and then said, "The cousin! *Molto interessante.*"

"Jeff Pennington's sister." The unlit cigar wagged as they returned to the rainswept highway.

"Very interesting, indeed."

"Generally higher'n a kite, on liquor or sex or cocaine. Or on plain devilment. But I've seen her low a couple of times, and I do mean low. You wouldn't know it was the same woman… Rumor hath it she's head over ears about Terry Hapgood, who says he loves her like a sister."

"I am more than ever eager to meet this Golden Angel."

They had gone a mile up the highway when a horn sounded from a muddy sideroad dividing a stand of turkey oaks. Taliaferro slowed to a halt as an ambulance bearing the words "Warren Memorial Emergency Service" pulled out before them, bumping and splashing.

The editor spat his cigar into his lap. "Well, well, well! Can you believe this?" he exclaimed. He rolled his window down, and shouted, "Is that you, Randy?"

Mario stiffened. The driver opened his window and leaned out into the rain. "Hello, Mr. Taliaferro!" He had an air of mild embarrassment.

"Randy Funderburk," Taliaferro told Mario. "He—"

"We have met," Mario murmured, tense, craning to scrutinize the tall, moustached man who sprawled relaxed behind the wheel. His uniform was unbuttoned, revealing a curly-haired chest. Even through the raindrops, Mario thought he detected a heavy-lidded look of bemused afterglow.

The ambulance bumped in front of them into the lefthand lane, and drove off toward the town.

Mario said, "Do you think that he and *la signora, Signora* Donlan..."

Taliaferro laughed silently as they resumed their journey. "Yes, indeedy," he said. "I do so think. Madame Doctor Donlan herself, nee Anne-Marie Pennington, and randy old Randy getting in. Getting up in the world." He retrieved his cigar. "And it wouldn't be the first time that ambulance has done duty as a love nest."

Mario told himself, *Dunque, probabilmente* this prime suspect has an ironclad alibi. At least for last night. Though he may not wish to use it.

The yellow corridors of the hospital gave an impression of spring sunshine, and the atmosphere was dry and pleasantly cool.

A square-set, middle aged woman, immaculate in a nurse's uniform, rounded the corner, almost bumping into him.

"Scusi, Suora Infermiera!" he said.

"Pardon me!" she said simultaneously, and then, "Are you Mr. Castig-lian? I'm Margaret Flannery, the Head Nurse here."

"A pleasure to meet you. You were expecting me?"

"Yes, I understand you need information for Chief Tyler. Do you want to see Dr. Donlan first, or ...?"

"I was looking for his office," Mario said.

Nurse Flannery pointed to an Exit sign a few doors ahead. "I I saw him step outside a few minutes ago." She escorted him along the corridor, adding in a confidential tone, "Smoking, you know. Strictly forbidden here, but we have a few places where addicts can indulge."

"The director smokes?"

She laid a finger to her lips and winked at Mario. "Not very often," she said tolerantly.

When she pushed the heavy door open, Mario saw a short, slender, fair-haired man in a white uniform, a lighted cigarette between his fingers, leaning over a railing under the projecting glass roof. He started and turned quickly to face them.

"Terry!" exclaimed Nurse Flannery. "I thought you were Dr. Donlan. Why aren't you over at Jubilee?"

"Mrs. Kendall's expecting company. I don't have to be there till four." The light, pleasant voice sounded strained to Mario. *Una bellezza classica,* he thought. Beauty is not too strong a word for this man, not even in English. Willie would go *matto.*

Terry was gazing now at Mario as though resigned to an implacable doom. A deep, dark secret, Tyler had said. But this was not a face designed for concealment. Mario saw sorrow in the large dark-circled eyes, anxiety on the fine brow and clear-cut lips.

"Perhaps then, Mr. Hapgood, you are free to speak with me now?" Mario said. "I am here on behalf of Police Chief Tyler."

"I know," said Terry. "You're Mario Castigliani." He sighed and made a gesture of invitation to join him at the railing.

Nurse Flannery said, "Well, good, that will save some time. You'll probably find the Director in the Staff Room when you're through here. Straight back along the corridor, just by the water fountain."

The rain fell steady and light behind the motionless figure of Terry Hapgood and on the young trees of the well-kept grounds. Mario waited; he knew better than to speak first.

"Cigarette?" said the young man, holding out a pack of Carltons. Mario accepted one, and a light from a match unsteady in Terry's hand. "I saw you in New York, three years ago September. You did a dynamite show at NYU Medical Center."

"Ah, sì, a benefit." For the Cerebral Palsy Society, he remembered. I donated my fee, and *la Lucia, sempre la mia coscienza,* rewarded me generously. "You were living in New York then?"

"I worked there a couple of summers. To earn my tuition for nursing school."

"You worked in a New York hospital?"

"It pays a lot better there than here." A troubled look clouded Terry's eyes. "I wanted to raise my hand in your question period," he said shyly, "but I couldn't get up the nerve."

"And what would you have asked me?"

"Oh, love stuff, you know, the usual, will the one I love ever love me back. That kind of thing."

"*Ah, sì, i tormenti* of the heart." Mario sighed, exasperated by the ambiguity of English. In Italian "the one I love" would have to be either masculine or feminine. He brought himself to the business at hand. "Chief Tyler needs to know where you and other staff people were last night. And the night before. What you were doing." He puffed on his cigarette, and extinguished it in the ashtray balanced on the railing. "I have no official right to question you, *capisce,* but we thought you might like to tell me informally."

"Most of us were at a big party here Wednesday night," Terry said. "You heard of Gary Lansing?"

"A film director, is he not? Also television."

Terry nodded. "He was here for a hernia repair and the body-toning program. He's leaving this evening. The party was a kind of thank-you to all us Warren Memorial people."

"Do you recall what hours you were there?"

The last half-inch of Terry's cigarette apparently burned his fingers. He jumped, said, "Damn!" mildly, and immediately lighted another from the glowing butt. Then he said, "It started around eight, and went on to, oh, must have been midnight." He looked toward a rain-veiled poplar. "Of course, I was away for an hour or more. I drove over to Blue Heaven about nine-thirty to give Roy Washington his allergy shot."

Ah, Lucia mia! How I need you now! Mario cried inwardly. He had the distinct impression that Terry Hapgood was not telling the truth, or at least not the whole truth. Yet the timing accorded well with the reports of the patrolmen as to when his car was seen at the Washington house. Terry's hand, white-knuckled, gripped the railing, and he kept his face averted.

"You went regularly to Roy Washington's home for this purpose? Daily? Weekly? Monthly?" *Prudenta,* Mario, he warned himself. "With Terry Hapgood," Lieutenant Abbot had instructed him, "use your fine Italian hand. Get what info you can, but... We don't want him turning rabbit on us."

Terry's transparent face now showed disappointment and relief. He is aware, Mario thought, that *la Lucia* is not with me.

"A weekly shot. Sometimes he came here for it, a neighbor would drive him. But he wasn't always up to it. Roy lost a lot of ground in the past year."

"Tell me what you recall of Wednesday night. When you arrived at his house, when you left him. Your *conversazione,* his emotional state."

Terry swallowed hard.

"This is just preliminary, *naturalmente,* you need not be precise. You may be asked later to make a more formal statement."

"We'd got to be friends, like I was his nurse, he was my teacher. He had all those great books. I'm not much of a reader. That old man was. He'd put a book in my hands and tell me, 'Now you read this one real good, and come talk to me about it.'"

The rain was slacking. The sky midway between zenith and horizon brightened behind the cloud cover.

"Here at Warren," Terry said, "I don't do much real nursing anymore. I give massages, read to 'em, play casino, checkers. The pay is tops, and I get big tips. But I miss the real work. In Blue Heaven and the mill village, Roy got me helping the folks who were sick. Not for money. I liked doing it."

Through drifting clouds a pale disc of sun could now be glimpsed. Patches of pure delicate blue appeared on the opposite arc of the sky. "This last winter I thought sure he wouldn't make it. Could hardly talk, with the wheezing." Three large silver drops gathered on the roof's edge and fell sparkling behind Terry, barely missing his shoulder. "It's terrible," he said, his blue gaze full on Mario. "Watching people suffer."

The contagion of his earnest grief seized Mario. He was shaken by a spasm of rue and remembrance. *Ohimè,* Oriana, *mia!* Your black hair strewn on the pillow, your huge black eyes imploring, *Aiuto,* Mario, oh, deliver me, *lasciatemi morire!* Help me to die! He fought for control of himself. On a wave of intense empathy with the young man before him, he said, "*Ah, sì!* It is terrible, not to be borne."

The sun, still wan but brightening, already cast afternoon shadows. Terry said, *non sequitur,* as though to himself. "When you know you have to die, you want to talk. Never mind the card games and the cheery chitchat. You need to talk. About dying."

"We all know we must die," said Mario.

"But we don't believe it, not really, until we know there's only weeks left. Or days." His eyes searched Mario's, as though pleading for an answer. He tossed back a bright strand of hair, which had fallen over his brow, and said almost inaudibly, "Or hours."

It dawned on Mario that Terry was talking now not only about his patients, but about himself. Why should one so young, so evidently *vigoroso*... Yet he had tried before to kill himself. Mario thought, there is shame so profound, there are *circostanze* so dire that death is infinitely preferable. Floundering, searching for the right lead, he suggested, "And at times one might not wish to talk to an intimate, am I right? ...Rather to one's nurse?"

"Or to a stranger," Terry whispered. "The right stranger." He waited while Mario sought in vain for a response, then turned his face away and said, "There's never enough time for it, is there? And that's so sad. Dying, dying to talk. About what comes after, if anything does. About what you're sorry for, and what you're proud of. About, what's it all about, and does it all make any sense."

Angoscia, utter anguish, Mario thought with growing alarm. He put a comforting hand on the young man's shoulder, but Terry shrugged it off. "Nobody wants to hear it," he muttered, "except with one eye on their wristwatch, and their mind on their next appointment." He gestured toward a windowless building surrounded by flowering shrubs which could be glimpsed through the trees. "Terminal pavilion," he said. "They keep 'em alive, years sometimes, whether they want it or not. Even cryonics, a few."

Mario looked at him questioningly.

"Cryonics, the deep freeze, the minute someone dies. They hope a cure will be found, maybe fifty, a hundred years from now, and that they can be brought back to life. Dr. Donlan, the Director, he had refused to do it here. Called it a lot of malarky. But a couple years ago he gave in. He said we can use the money for pioneer research."

"You have a great admiration for the Director."

"Oh, yes! Dr. Donlan's a miracle man, everybody says so. You'll see." His face glowed in the strengthening sun, and then contorted swiftly.

Terry crushed his cigarette into the ashtray, gripped the railing and leapt over it to the grass three feet below. Grace and strength, come *un atleta, un ballerino!* His face, like that of a suffering child turned reckless, was tilted toward Mario, his palms upreaching. "Come on! Jump! I'll help you."

Mario hesitated.

"It's cleared up, see how lovely." Terry made a sweeping gesture which seemed to include the whole smiling day, the scent breathed forth by rainwashed grass and flowers, the flight in song of a red-winged blackbird.

Terry stretched his hands higher, and said, "We can talk while we walk. About when I got to Roy's, when I left, all that."

Mario leaned forward to grasp the hands, feeling secure that they would land him safely on his feet. Then he said, "No." He stood upright, thinking, I must phone the stationhouse immediately. If I am correct, there is not one minute to lose. *"Basta,"* he said. "I don't want to make you late for your patient. You can write all that out for me."

Terry's arms sank slowly to his sides. He averted his face again and said in a lifeless voice, "I've already done that. I handed it in to Mrs. Flannery."

Mario asked, "For Thursday too? Yesterday?"

"No, you need yesterday?"

Mario wondered, Does he not know about Earl Langford? Or does he indeed know more than any of us?

"Thursday's my day off," Terry was saying. "Can't give you much that's really exact. I drove around, walked around. Had some thinking to do."

"We would appreciate, put down whatever you remember... Meanwhile, let us talk more. I will look for you at the nursing home, just after four?"

"Yeah, sure," Terry said flatly.

"We will walk and talk, then? Later?"

"Sure. Later." He nodded, and walked slowly away, then stopped and turned. "You see what I mean," he said quietly, "there's never enough time."

Mario watched the slender, finely-proportioned figure, the head bent and shoulders sagging, until it was lost behind a row of poplars. He squinted at the naked sun in its circle of sulfurous clouds. Already the vault of the sky was misting over; already the freshness was gone from grass and leaves.

The heat was back.

Mario welcomed the cool of the interior. He remembered seeing a wall phone in the cross-corridor, and hurried to it. "I am trying to reach Mr. Reid Tolliver," he said. "I believe you will find him either with the patient Petticord, or at the nursing home with Mrs. James Kendall."

"Who is calling, please?" The switchboard operator seemed reluctant to put the call through.

"I am Mario Castigliani, assisting the police. It is quite urgent." He waited, pacing the short arc allowed him by the umbilicus of the phone, until the operator succeeded in making the connections.

"I'm real sorry," she said, "but Mr. Tolliver left the main building and hasn't got to the nursing home yet."

"Is it possible to get a message to him?"

"Sure thing."

"Say Mr. Hapgood will join him shortly, and I have something of importance to discuss with both of them. If Mr. Taliaferro could keep him there until I join them."

He hung up and made his way back to the lobby where there was a public phone. The receptionist was at the switchboard, her back to him. He fished a quarter from his pocket and dialed the police station. And what will I say to you, my skeptical Lieutenant Abbot, or to you, my trusting Chief Tyler? he asked himself while the phone rang and rang. That my powers today were no greater than those of any reasonably intelligent observer? That I could glimpse Terry's lies and evasions, but could not see through to the truth?

"Floraville Police," said Ruthann. "Sorry to keep you waiting." She apparently caught the exigency in Mario's voice.

A moment later, Abbot said, "What's up, Mario?"

"I have reason to believe that Terry Hapgood is contemplating suicide," said Mario, speaking low. "Immediately perhaps. Can you send someone? Should I telephone Chief Tyler?"

Abbot gave a long soft whistle. "I'll do that. Where's Terry right now?"

"He is due at the nursing home, with Mrs. Kendall, in five minutes."

"Did he mention a method?"

"Nothing precise. Just his *disposizione*. I think I have succeeded in getting a message to Mr. Taliaferro—"

"—not to let him get away? Good," said Abbot. "Good work. Me or the Chief will zip right over. Are you somewhere you can talk?"

"*Effettivamente, no.* I have not yet spoken with the Director. Shall I postpone that, and go at once to join Terry?"

"Let me think," the lieutenant said. "We absolutely have to cover Donlan. Can you make it quick with him?"

"I will do my best," Mario assured him.

He met no one as he hurried through the tiled hallways to the Staff Room. The door was open. A man with red-blond hair, fashionably styled, was standing at the head of a long table, holding a phone while shrugging into the jacket of an ivory silk summer suit. He appeared freshly shaven, with a faint scent, *sottile e distinto*. A white hospital coat lay over a chairback. At first glance, Mario thought him too young to be the Director.

"Make yourself comfortable, Mr. Castigliani, I'll be with you in one moment."

A radiant smile. Energy, charm and *autorità*. And not so very young at that. "*Grazie, Dottore* Donlan," Mario murmured, seating himself at a discreet distance and placing his briefcase beside him.

"Dear Violet, cross my heart," the doctor was saying, "I'll be at your side within the hour."

A scatter of pads, pens and half-empty water glasses bespoke a staff meeting just concluded. Chairs had been pushed back to various distances. A wheeled blackboard listed figures and hospital services under the heading: Rate Adjustments.

"Get your feet up, Violet. Compress on your eyes. Play a Bach partita, use the earphones."

Another remarkably goodlooking *essere umano,* Mario marveled. Three in a day: Anne-Marie, Terry... and now the Director.

"I must apologize," Donlan said as he hung up. "We'll have to make our session a very brief one." He gestured eloquently toward the phone.

"No, no, I understand perfectly. But I thought house calls were a thing of the past?"

"Private patient," Donlan said, "and my neighbor and friend." He opened a portfolio on the table and rapidly selected papers from it with the air of a magician producing stage miracles. "The wife, in fact, of our good mayor. She's subject to what our granddads called neurasthenia."

Mario watched the quick hands, enjoying the touch of showmanship not unlike his own. *"Nevrastenia,"* he said. "My mother suffered from it. *Formidabile."*

"Devastating pain," the doctor agreed. He slid the papers to Mario along the polished table top. "This is the autopsy report," he said, "and the statements of our staff people who were in contact with Royal Washington, or with his body, on Wednesday and Thursday."

Mario flipped through the alphabetized pages.

"Incomplete, I'm afraid," Donlan apologized, "in view of Earl Langford's death. Not everyone has had time to report on the past twenty-four hours."

Funderburk, Randy, Ambulance Driver. Mario paused. I must read these without delay, he told himself. But when?

"And one of our nursing home aides," the Director said, "a Ms. Demetria Owens, has not as yet handed in any statement at all."

"But this is excellent," Mario said, rising and placing the papers in his briefcase. *"Esattamente* what is needed for preliminary crosschecking. Any or all of you, *capite,* may later be asked to amplify these at the stationhouse."

"No question," Donlan agreed, glancing at his watch. "Whatever we can do. Anything you would like to ask me before I leave you?"

Mario hesitated. "Terence Hapgood, your nurse. I have just been with him."

"Ah, Terry. Everybody's favorite. Did he give you a satisfactory account of himself?"

"He seemed inordinately grief-stricken, disturbed."

"Ah, there's a boy wears his heart on his sleeve," Donlan said affectionately.

He is *un uomo simpatico,* Mario thought, this *dottore.* Why on earth is his wife not satisfied with so charming and sensitive a husband? Taliaferro's offhand voice saying, "She's head over ears about Terry Hapgood," echoed in Mario's memory.

"*Claramente* Royal Washington was far more than just a patient to him," Mario said as he and Donlan left the Staff Room. "But even so, his sorrow… one might even say despair."

Dr. Donlan halted, and faced Mario in the blandly tasteful corridor. "Despair! You're not overreacting?"

"I am not absolutely sure, but…" Slow down, Mario, he warned himself, *rallenta.* It is my task to elicit information from this *direttore,* not the other way around. Mario reminded himself that Donlan, too, ranked as a suspect and should be treated as such.

"Poor Terry!" the doctor exclaimed softly as they resumed their walk. "Wish I could go to him right this minute. Talk some sense, like a dutch uncle."

"He would listen to you, *Dottore,* of that I am certain." But how right you are, Terry! Mario thought: There's never enough time.

Donlan waved at the receptionist as they went out into the stifling air. "Where you heading?"

"The Jubilee Nursing Home."

"That way. You'll come to a rose-colored stucco building. A pleasure to have met you, Mr. Castigliani."

Mario bowed. He struck out along the path between bushes of white roses alternating with red. Their scent was almost overwhelming. He paused to adjust his watch from 4:16 to 4:05, in accordance with the clock he had glimpsed in the hospital lobby. Terry Hapgood will be there, he assured himself anxiously, with Taliaferro and old Mrs. Kendall. He cannot possibly have finished with her yet.

On the walkways of the nursing home, a few residents emerging after the rain took their afternoon constitutionals afoot or in wheelchairs. Four old women, one leaning on a quadrupedal cane, waited in attitudes of impatience. One of them waved a pack of cards at Mario, and called out, "Hello, Sonny, you play canasta?"

Under a striped umbrella just beyond the rose-colored building, Mario espied the group for which he was looking. Reid Taliaferro, standing, his suit coat over his arm, was immediately recognizable by his red suspenders. An aide was assisting a patient to maneuver her wheelchair to the table; and a white-clad man was seated in the shade.

Grazie a Dio! He was in time then. Mario's knees were suddenly weak. He swayed toward the nearest bench and sat, hard, on the wet slats. His temples throbbed from the burning sun, the floral and resinous odors, and a maelstrom of impressions. The hazel eyes of Otis Feeney, the starched cap of Nurse Flannery. The feet of the director, small and neat in canvas shoes, keeping pace with his own along the corridor. The prying eyes of the postmistress. The gleam of Officer Petticord's scalp though his halo of hair. The past four hours had exposed Mario to a glut of experience. If only I could have *un'ora di solitudine* to think it through!

"*Avanti,* Mario!" he said aloud, willing himself to his feet. As he hurried along the path, he saw that the man with Taliaferro was not wearing a uniform, but a white suit; was not blond and slim, but dark, balding, plump.

Gregory Shapiro! "Come join us, Mario," he called, waving at a lawn stool.

Taliaferro turned. "Where's Terry?"

"Where is Terence Hapgood?" Mario said simultaneously.

The tall *anziana* in the wheelchair, her blue lace cap askew over thin strands of silver hair, peered at him and said irritably, "You're not Terry! Where is the boy?"

"Did you receive my message?" Mario asked the editor.

"Yes, he didn't show yet." Taliaferro glanced at his watch. "Not to worry, he isn't real late… Mario, meet Lisabeth Kendall, my Jubilee sweetheart."

A clawlike hand wavered toward Mario's and then withdrew abruptly. "Dickie!" Mrs. Kendall scolded. "About time you got here. Keeping the lawyers waiting!"

The attendant at her side, a woman with a sad, freckled face, admonished gently, "Now, Miz Lisabeth, you know that ain't Mr. Richard."

Everyone spoke to Mario at once:

214

"And meet Demetria, Mrs. Owens, who's been lavishing TLC on the Kendalls since before the Year One."

Mario bowed before Lisabeth Kendall and kissed her hand. "I have indeed been eager to make your acquaintance."

He perched tentatively on the stool beside Shapiro.

"Greg's firm handles Kendall legal business," Taliaferro told Mario. The lawyer said, "Wouldn't miss a chance to visit with her."

Mario saw Demetria approaching the table with a tray of refreshments. He rose, beckoned Taliaferro aside, and confided his anxiety about Terry Hapgood. He did not mention suicide. "He seemed in a strange mood. I feel we should find him before…"

"You think he might cut and run?"

"Something like that."

"So you suspect he's our murderer. Euthanasia, of course."

Mario shrugged noncommittally.

Taliaferro put on his suit coat. "I'll go. Margaret Flannery will know his schedule. You see what you can get out of Lisabeth here. Won't be much, it's one of her battier days."

Mario saw Beaufort Tyler striding across the lawn and said, "*Un minuto.*" As the police chief came near, it was plain that he had not yet changed his uniform nor shaved. But his eyes were no longer bloodshot, and he looked alert and refreshed.

"Hey, Reid. Mario. Did you find Terry?"

Mario shook his head. "You came *molto rapido,* eh!"

"Had the pedal to the metal the whole way." Tyler quickly scanned the grounds and acknowledged Shapiro and Mrs. Kendall with an absent-minded salute. "Where'd you see him last?" he asked Mario.

"At about a quarter of four, walking from the hospital in this direction."

The editor said, "He might still show. Anyway, I'm about to track him down."

"No," said Tyler. "I'll handle this end."

It is I who should seek for Terry, Mario thought. "I feel some responsibility," he said. "I should have stayed with him, perhaps, instead of phoning the stationhouse."

"Hard to decide, sometimes, spur of the moment." Tyler was already backing toward the hospital. "Let me do it, Mario. I got more clout here than you." He stopped and beckoned them closer. "There's some rumpus out at the mill. Abbot's on his way, but can the two of you get right on over?"

"What rumpus?" Gregory Shapiro challenged, as he joined them. "Are you referring to the workers' rally?"

"Bunch of hands yelling, pounding on the loading dock shutters," Tyler replied. "Couldn't take time to check it out." He was on the move again. Over his shoulder he called, "I'll be back, Miz Kendall. Don't you go away now."

As his tall figure diminished along the path, Shapiro said, "I'm overdue at the mill myself. Let's go together."

Old Mrs. Kendall had half-risen, supporting herself with one hand on the table, and with the other holding forth a salver of sponge cakes. "Beaufort Tyler! Now where you running off to!" she called, sounding coy, hospitable, and perfectly lucid.

XV

By the time the rain stopped, the assemblage at the mill had more than tripled in size. Infants in arms or baby carriages and old people with gnarled walking sticks were among the newcomers. The decibel level was deafening.

At the rear of the yard, a row of folding tables had been set up, toward which a ragged queue bore paper plates to be filled with cold cuts, bread, crackers, cookies and potato chips. Bottles of soda pop were fished from tubs filled with rapidly melting ice. Behind the tables serving the guests were five young women and the dreamy youth who served Jeff Pennington's coffee and sandwiches.

Vesta Delacorte, Jeff's ageless private secretary, was supervising, her mouth tight with martyrdom. The impromptu team slapped food on the plates with reckless enthusiasm. "Enjoy it!" they called in response to the heads bobbing in thanks; and "Plenty more where that came from!"

Ms. Delacorte put her wrinkled, manicured hand to the foulard tie of her smart blouse, and frowned at three women who were waiting their turn. "I hope y'all realize," she said ringingly, "that it's Penningtons who put food into your mouth. All the union'll do is collect your dues."

"Yes'm, we sure thankful," one of the women replied; but other workers already devouring bologna sandwiches a few feet away reacted less humbly. A dye hand loudly scoffed, "This here junk food?" and another chimed in, "Ain't much skin off Penningtons' ass."

The secretary bridled, then with an obvious effort regained her ladylike manner.

A rich baritone sang: "Oh, I love my boss, He's a good friend of mine..." Over a roar of laughter, other singers joined in: "And that's why I'm marching, On this picket line..." Calloused palms clapped to the rhythm of the swelling chorus: "Hallelujah, I'm a bum..."

Vesta Delacorte, tight-lipped, glared at Vernon Bond who had posted himself at the open gate. He avoided her eyes as she made her way past him to the mill building. Sweat trickled from the band of his police cap. His plump, uniformed body was stiffly erect, and he was clearly striving to project a neutral official presence.

"Will y'all just hush now?" a man bellowed. "Miz Candace here, Roy's daughter, she willing to speak a few words."

A scatter of applause greeted the tall, stout woman in her flowing robes. "My daddy is gone," she told them, her powerful voice throaty with emotion, "and most of you here, you loved him." She lifted her hand to quell the calls of assent, and swept the crowd with her large liquid eyes. "He was a warrior," she said, "not a peacemaker. Some here were his enemies, and," she gestured toward the mill offices, "I don't mean only up front."

She had the full attention of the entire crowd. Even the food queue had stopped moving.

"Somebody killed my daddy. And maybe who killed him is standing in front of me right now."

The listeners answered inarticulately. Some stared around with a look of fear. Candace said, "Well. Welcome, friends, welcome, enemies. That was my daddy's way. Then, too, some here didn't care about him one way nor another, they just come for the free food. And that's okay, too. He'd have said, Welcome all. Roy Washington style. He loved to see folks eat."

Tears shone on her cheeks. Many scrubbed at their eyes with the backs of their hands. "A-men," said some; and "Tell it, sister."

Before she could continue, the overhead loudspeakers of the public address system gave forth squawking sounds. Then the genteel accents of Vesta Delacorte emerged larger than life: "May I have your attention, please. Our Chief Executive Officer, Mr. Jefferson Pennington, is about to address you."

Faint sounds as of muffled altercation gave way to a dramatic introductory silence. Then: "All who are gathered here today," said Jeff

Pennington's amplified voice, grave and sonorous, "must join me and the Board of Pennington Mill in mourning for Royal Washington."

"It is amply clear that word has already reached you of our decision to keep the mill closed until tomorrow morning," Jeff Pennington went on. "I am sure you realize that this unprecedented sacrifice of time and money is a measure of our deep—" The speech broke off. More muffled sounds of argument were heard. Myrtle said, "Vince, it's Claudia. Betcha anything." Shimansky eyes questioned her. "Claudia's his wife," she whispered. "It's her making him do it."

"...in this hour of grief..."

Mario and Taliaferro in the *Clarion* station wagon, following Gregory Shapiro's white BMW into the workers' parking lot, heard the words clearly.

The BMW inched into a scant space in the crowded lot, but there was no room for the station wagon. Taliaferro drove around to the front.

"We know you appreciate the bountiful refreshments we have provided, continuing our tradition..."

They parked near the glass doors of the main entrance.

"...of service to the entire community. We of Floraville need no outsiders..."

"Holy shit," Taliaferro commented.

"...to teach us how to pay our respects to one of our own." There was a crackle of static over a sharp, exasperated expostulation; then silence.

Phil, hugging his camera, his blond plait streaming behind him, rounded the corner of the building and loped to the station wagon. He poked his head through Mario's window and spoke excitedly across him to the editor. "I got everything, Reid. Can I do the story?"

"All yours. Fill us in."

More static was heard from the loudspeakers, then the voice of Vesta Delacorte: "Mr. Pennington thanks y'all for your attention, and invites you to continue the memorial meeting." The public address system went dead.

Phil said, "I was inside. Got great pictures from three-four windows, different angles. The delegation was refused admittance, see, and the hands got plenty mad."

"Mrs. Jeff came rapping on the front entrance here. Jimbo, he was up in Pennington's office when she sailed in snorting fire, and he found me and said, Spread the word quick, the boss just threw in the towel."

"You should have heard the cheering. Ain't she something, Mrs. Jeff!"

Mario felt his pulse quicken. Claudia. So she is here, my lady of the swallows! He sternly brought himself back to the business at hand. "Is Lieutenant Abbot in the building?" he inquired.

"No, he headed back to the stationhouse soon's he saw things were under control. He left Vern Bond back there at the gate, just in case."

A confusion of several songs could be heard from the yard, then Demetria Owen's piercing soprano: "I ain't gonna let Jeff Pennington turn me round!" The others joined in over a wave of applause.

"You cover it, Phil, until I can join you," the editor said.

"Really? Interviews and all?"

"Why not, you're doing great. Mario and I gotta figure out our priorities. Skip the front office, we'll get a better interview out of Jeff tomorrow when the smoke clears."

Phil ran toward the singing. "And before I'll be a slave, I'll be buried in my grave…"

"Should I get you back to Warren?" Taliaferro asked Mario. "Or to the police station?"

"I know Abbot said, Get statements here," the editor went on, "but this just isn't the moment."

Mario was not listening. Claudia Pennington was gliding rapidly toward them through the reception area. A trench coat and string bag were slung over her arm, and she was holding a ring of keys like a trophy. Her oval face was brilliant with anger.

He was out of the car even before she came through the glass doors. *"Aspettate!"* he cried, as she swept past him unheeding, to the executive parking lot. Taliaferro had opened the driver's door of the station wagon, and, one foot on the ground, was calling, "Hey, Claudia, wait!"

Mario hastened after her, Taliaferro following. But she had already opened the door of a white Buick, slid in behind the wheel, and started the engine. "Can't stop!" she cried to Taliaferro as she drove off. "Call me tonight, Reid!"

Irrationally, unthinkingly, Mario ran after the car for a few feet, then stopped himself in embarrassment.

"Well, well, well," Taliaferro said. "I had no idea you were acquainted."

"But yes. And no," Mario managed to say as he was steered firmly back to the station wagon.

"Where to?" Taliaferro asked as he backed toward the road. "Andrew or Beau? Wake up, Mario. Hate to press you, but I got to get back here quick as I can."

"The medical center," Mario said; then, "No, no, take me to *la stazione.*" The humidity had risen; his speech sounded thick in his own ears.

"Blushing like a schoolboy," Taliaferro teased him. "What is it? Worship from afar?" They drove along Calhoun Street toward the dull glare of the sun.

Mario, regaining a measure of poise, said lightly, "Ah, you have fathomed my secret sorrow."

"You knew her in New York?"

"Not *precisamente.*"

"You saw her dance there."

"*Sì,*" Mario lied.

"And you know the story, don't you. Beau told you? About her tragedy."

"I have heard about it," Mario said guardedly.

"One of these days I'll write an article on gang rape," Taliaferro said. "Or a whole book."

Mario stiffened, and faced away from the editor. *Violazione! Madre di Dio, poveretta!*

Mario recalled the dates in the Clarion "Tremont/Tremonte" file, and hazarded a guess. "She was sixteen years old."

"Fifteen. 1973. My dad was still alive, running the newspaper, breaking me in. 'Course we didn't print a word. Warrens and Yorks were implicated, Penningtons and Sondergards."

Taliaferro went on, "But the whole county knew. And sniggered. After that she was prey to every redblooded macho in town, the hot little Eye-Tye flashing her butt in a tutu."

"And beautiful even then," Mario said.

"Don't know about that," the editor rejoined, inching the station wagon forward. "'Course she was. But back then folks didn't appreciate her looks. Too exotic, you know. Peaches and cream was the standard, lily white."

Traffic had resumed its normal flow. They turned left on Mimosa. "Got to hand it to her," Taliaferro continued as they entered the stationhouse parking lot. "How she turned things around."

Mario said, "*Sì*, she achieved true *celebrità* and stature. If not for her accident…" He got out and came around to the open driver's window.

"Even then," Taliaferro mused, "look what she accomplished. She's Mrs. CEO Pennington and even Valhalla has to kowtow." He put the car in gear. "Okay, *arrivederci*, as we Eye-Tyes say."

XVI

"*Poverina! Miserella!* Forgive me, my Oriana!"

Mario and Oriana sat embraced, rocking back and forth, on the wet stone step of the entrance landing. Their tears mingled with the cold March rain. Oriana seemed incapable of uttering anything but his name.

When he had helped her upstairs and into the apartment, they wept again, locked together on the edge of Willie's bed; and again when she had bathed and he had dressed her in one of *il maestro's* long flannel nightshirts. Then he tucked her under the covers. She sat up, leaning her wet curly hair against the pillow, and lifted her face, rosy from the hot bath, to his kiss.

"How did you get here? Why didn't you tell me? Oh, my darling, *bellissima mia*, how you must have suffered!"

"Ah, it was *terribile*, the journey! And I was lost and nobody spoke Italian. Then *una signora, molto buona*, she read the address. West, I was east. She put me on a bus and spoke to the driver."

The fullness of her high breasts against the nightshirt made Mario weak with love and desire, with awe and guilt. Always before he had thought of pregnancy as disfiguring, comic, a touch repellent. But Oriana seemed to him magnificent, like a tree in blossom while heavy with fruit.

He caressed her cheek and shoulder, receiving the impact of their shared passion. With stern self-control, he withdrew his hand. "But the *bambino*, when did you know, why didn't you write me!"

"Your *padre*," Oriana was saying. "He gave me the money, and your address."

"Wait, *amore mia,* I should bring you some food, a hot drink, and then hear all about it."

She caught his hand and pressed it to her bosom. "I never told him. He guessed. Mario, *io ti giuro,* I told no one."

"Why? *Perchè?* Why did you not tell?" He counted the months in his mind, gasped, and said, "You knew already, when we parted."

"*La principessa,* she thought it was *il Signor,* your father. She has been ill with rage. My mamma thought so, too, she hasn't stopped crying yet. Your *padre* thought it was Stefano. Then he guessed. I never betrayed you, beloved." She placed his hand on her belly. He felt the living being turning and kicking within her, and backed away from the bed abruptly.

"We go to *l'ospedale* tomorrow. And to apply for our marriage license."

Tears brimmed in her black eyes. "You would marry me like this?" Her rough red little hands indicated the swell of her pregnancy.

"*Certo,* beloved, what did you think? Rest now, my Oriana, I will be back in a moment."

She half-rose, one leg thrusting from under the covers. "Where are you going? Take me with you."

"Only to the kitchen, dearest. Lie down."

Mario found a lone can of soup on his depleted shelves and set it to heating. The refrigerator yielded three stalks of celery, a few olives, a macintosh apple and half a bottle of milk. He made up two steaming cups of hot chocolate, then fetched the parcel of pumpernickel and cheese from the hallway where he had dropped it. He was arranging *la merenda* on a tray when he heard Francine's key in the door.

"Mario! I'm here!"

He heard her thoughts as she came through the arch to the kitchenette, her fresh candid good looks heightened by the chill rain. **Darling, darling, I love you, I love you.** Her raincoat was wet at the shoulders. **Food! Wonderful! You made us food!** She closed the rainbow-colored umbrella he had given her for her birthday.

"I smell soup!" she exclaimed gaily.

He stood stock still, the tray in his hands. Her eyes flew to the doorway of Willie's room, and to the pitiable lump of Oriana's luggage beside it. In three strides she was at the bedroom doorway, Mario a step behind her. Hot chocolate slopped from the cups into the saucers.

Oriana was asleep. She had flung back the covers. She lay on her side, one arm supporting her belly, the other over her head.

"Well, what a surprise," Francine said in a shaky voice. "Two for the price of one." The numbing shock and hurt in her mind left Mario speechless. He hated himself.

"Your lost Eurydice?" she asked. "The one and only?"

He nodded. **Women do die in childbirth, even nowadays,** he heard her thinking; and then, **Stop it, Francine, what kind of a monster are you?**

Mario put the tray on the end table near the doorway, and took the dripping umbrella from her. "Come, *mia* Francie, have some hot soup, you'll stay the night."

The hell I will. Let me out of here. "No, really. I just stopped by. I have to be home tonight."

"Francine, I'm so sorry. So terribly, truly sorry. I did not plan it this way."

"It happened," she agreed dully. She allowed him to help her off with her coat, and to carry the food to the living room coffee table.

She lifted a spoonful of soup to her lips and put it back. "It's no use. I can't swallow." She retrieved her coat and umbrella. "Mario! You're going to need money."

He hugged her close, and kissed the satiny brown hair on her temple. "Not from you, Francine. Stan will advance it."

But she freed herself and produced from various parts of her person what she called her "mad money": a ten-dollar bill from her stocking top and five from her skirt pocket.

"I'll repay you tomorrow," he promised as he saw her to the downstairs door. In truth, he thought, I can never repay you.

Lauren Bacall Castigliani was born in the Women's Infirmary on East 25th Street a week later.

The dark, hairy baby looked like an infantile blend of Salvatore and Modesta. A purple birthmark disfigured her left cheek.

Oriana wept. "It is *il nostro castigo,*" she said, "for our sin."

"*Macchè!* The doctors have already offered to remove it."

The tiny Lauren was still in the hospital recovering from plastic surgery when her parents were married in a small ceremony at the Church of Our Lady of Pompeii in the Village.

The birthmark was only a fading scar under a bandage when Mario brought his child home. Mrs. Chun, the building superintendent, invited the new parents to homecooked Moo Goo Gai Pan with the four little Chuns. Benny Palermo gave a them a Sicilian-style party, to which he invited his gambling clientele, and a number of fellow tenants.

Wheeling the infant to the shops of Broadway, Oriana by his side, Mario experienced the hubris of an eighteen-year-old *paterfamilias*. Oriana, astonished and thrilled by the abundance of sidewalk displays and tempting store windows, alternated niagaras of excited chatter with openmouthed silences. Her beauty was at its zenith. Heads turned, passersby exclaimed, as the brisk wind loosed her wavy black hair and whipped her cheeks pink.

Mario spent lavishly. "Plenty more if you need it," Stan Horowitz said, handing over yet another advance. "She should want for nothing, your Lollabrigida, and the *kleine kindele*." **You're good for it, boychick, never been more hot on the market.** He offered to pay for a nursemaid, a cleaning woman.

Oriana merrily rejected the idea of household help. The aging apartment with its giant windows and decrepit plumbing seemed to her, in contrast to the della Rovere villa, a miracle of modern convenience. "Like a doll's house," she said, as she scrubbed and tidied and rearranged.

They bathed Lauren together. "Babies change," Oriana would say hopefully. "Later she will be pretty, eh, Mario?"

"To me she is *bellisima* now."

Oriana sighed. "She has a nose like a potato. She looks like a potato."

But the young mother was attentive and devoted. "Little feet! Little ears," she would croon to the baby at her breast. "Drink, *bambina mia.*" For the midnight and four o'clock feedings, and on the rare occasions when the infant cried at night, Mario would rise sleepily from a warm embrace, soothe the baby and carry her to the outstretched arms of his lovely madonna.

The wordless imperatives of this scrap of humanity came to him clearly: **Milk! Diaper! Mamma! Cramp! Lonesome!** In the daylight hours, too, his tiny daughter's amorphous thoughts would come to him: her fears when a truck thundered by on the street below; her marveling pleasure in colors and shifting lights, in the spring smell of grass in Riverside Park, and in the tinkle of a music box.

To watch Oriana nurse the little one seemed to him a privilege almost holy. At night in the bed, by day on the peeling leather couch in front of the out-of-focus TV set, the tableau evoked for him Etruscan murals and sculptures.

Never before had he been so happy. A constant sense of reverent gratitude stirred in his throat and belly, even when he was on stage or giving private readings.

Oriana attended only one of his performances, escorted by *il professore*. In Perugia, he had been far above her socially; now he was an old friend from home.

The evening's entertainment left Oriana uneasy. Several times Mario had tried delicately to explain to her—without offending *la Lucia*—about his profession with and without his special gifts. She did not want to know. Her credulity was unquestioning, but to her these were powers eerie and threatening. Once she asked him, in bed, in the night, "And can you read my thoughts too, my Mario?"

"No, *carissima*. You are one of a very few."

The next morning in the playground while they were gently pushing the crowing Lauren back and forth in the baby swing, she said suddenly, "But you can read the thoughts of the little one." She caught the swing, and held it motionless, her large tilted eyes filled with distress.

"It is nothing to fear, Oriana. It helps me to be a good *papà*."

He had imparted to her a sketchy outline of Willie's saga. "But he is an evil man!" she exclaimed. "He deserves to be in prison."

"No, he is not, Oriana. And he is dear to me. Later on when you are more at ease in America, I will take you with me when I visit."

"And can he read my mind?"

"No. But he can make you believe he can."

She showed more curiosity about the professional tricks of the trade, and persuaded him to put on a private performance for her, complete with comic patter, decks of cards, folded slips of paper, and objects described through a blindfold affixed with her own hands.

"*Ma*, Mario, it is magic, *una stregoneria*. Tell me how you do it, please, tell me, am I not your wife?"

"*Kein Wort zu Niem*and, *il maestro* made me swear to it. Not a word to a soul. Unless one day—how would you like to assist me, on the stage? *In un vestito* all sparkling, and be famous like me?"

"Never, I could never!" she said, laughing and blushing in his embrace.

Letters from Stefano and Salvatore had long since ceased to arrive; and Mario, in light of Salvatore's prosperity, had stopped sending the unwanted money. He had reproached himself for neglecting to correspond, then allowed his old home to fade in his memory.

Belatedly he wrote to Perugia with news of the wedding and snapshots of tiny plump Lauren holding herself almost upright by the bars of her playpen. Weeks passed with no response from his father or brother. But a parcel arrived, clumsily tied, the address barely legible. It contained a baby blanket and a pair of pink booties, both much laundered and faded, and a packet of cream-filled pastry rolls, hopelessly crushed and soured.

From Modesta. Oriana pressed the blanket to her face and cried like a child for her mother.

"Why are you hiding her from us, your *shayna madel?*" Goldie Horowitz, Stan's wife, demanded of Mario.

"She does not like to go out so much. And the baby."

"I am sending my Hillel's own sitter," Goldie insisted. "The best, a free gift." She was fresh from the beautician, who had dyed her hair to match her name. **A wife is not a toy, a secret plaything.**

"Anyway, she will come to the party backstage on Saturday, she promised," Mario told them. He rose from the shawl-draped couch and pressed Goldie's thick scarlet-tipped hand. "Oriana is shy."

In the outer office, he waved absently at the mousy temporary secretary-receptionist. Francine was taking riding lessons on a dude ranch in Arizona, Stan having granted her an early vacation.

Do I miss her? Mario asked himself as he walked beneath the marquees of 45th Street. He shook his head. The honeymoon hothouse of love within him held room for his baby and his bride only.

Stan and Goldie are right, Mario thought as he went down the steps of the subway, it is high time for my lovely *colombina* to venture out of the nest.

Goldie swooped down on them the following morning in a chauffeur-driven limousine. "I'm taking you to Bonwit's, *teibele,* Saks," she told Oriana. "An outfit for tonight, another for the party. Mario can mind the *bubbie,* he's the papa." No wonder she's embarrassed to put a foot out of the house, look how he dresses her.

At home he played with Lauren, oddly disturbed by the vastness and naked candor of her innocent thoughts. After he fed her, they curled up on the bed while she napped. The house seemed empty and lonely. Later he took her to the playground.

When he let himself back into the apartment, he did not at once recognize the silver-sheathed woman with the blueblack shoulder-length curls, who might have stepped from the pages of Vogue. She stood before the full-length mirror on the hall closet door, a filmy evening wrap over her arm. One silver-sandaled high-heeled foot was elegantly pointed at a forward angle, as in the fashion ads. Crystal drop earrings sparkled, framing a beauty exquisitely enhanced by the arts of a professional cosmetician.

"Oriana!"

As on that earlier day when she had posed before the pierglass in his mother's dressing room, she jumped, whirled to face him, then gave a nervous laugh. "And how do you like me, my Mario?" The haughty mannequin look was replaced by a timid anxiety.

"No *celebrità* was ever more beautiful," he replied, paraphrasing his long-ago words. "But, oh, *cara mia!* Your hair."

The evening was a fiasco. In the restaurant, Oriana curtsied to the maitre d', tripped on the hem of her long gown, and then sat huddled, with downcast eyes, at the table. Her phrase-book English seemed to have deserted her.

At the theater Mario translated for her. She appeared dazzled by the set and costumes, deafened by the crash of the music and helplessly confused by the intricacies of the Elizabethan-cum-Broadway plot.

After the show, Mario hailed a cab, and over the strident objections of Stan and Goldie, took Oriana home.

"I have disgraced you," she said tragically when they were in bed. His reassurances were as balm to her bruised ego. When they had made love, she seemed restored. She sat up, lighted the bed lamp and demanded, "Mario, what means 'shrew'? 'Nudnick'? 'Charge account'? *Perchè* are numbers written on the walls of *il lavabo?* What means SRO?"

Until sunrise colored the windows, he answered her questions, at length and without allowing himself to laugh. Then it was time to feed the baby. Later all three slept cuddled in the big bed until the sun was high in the sky.

On Saturday at the closing-night party, Oriana acquitted herself admirably. She took her phrase book with her, and was soon the center of an admiring circle. With pride, Mario watched her from the far side of the Green Room. She is becoming aware of her *potenza,* as *della sua bellezza* and my wife, he told himself. She blushed at her own quaint mistakes and the delighted laughter they elicited. But she laughed, too, and basked in the attention.

From then on, as her courage and understanding increased, Oriana conscientiously took part in the society of Mario's New York, and shared in his recreations. It was more to please him than herself. Dining out continued to be a strain for her. At plays or at films of the art cinema circuit, Mario could see how she strove, for his sake, to grasp ideas for which nothing in her past had prepared her.

A trip to the museum, with *il professore* himself acting as guide, left Oriana silent and low-spirited. Mario walked homeward with her, wheeling the carriage along Central Park West. The May afternoon was summery, the park green and inviting beyond the stone wall.

"That small gold bowl," he said, still absorbed in the exhibit. "Did you notice *li animaletti* around its rim? The deer, and the lions?"

Oriana shook her head, and went to sit on a stone bench. "I am tired, my darling," she said when he joined her. She covered her face with her hands. *"Una stupida, una burina. Ignorante,* unworthy to be your wife."

"Macchè! You are *molto brava,* I am *il stupido."* He put his arms around her. Do I expect her to run before she can walk? he chided himself. And there is so much she could enjoy! The Bronx Zoo, the ferry. Radio City Music Hall. The boating and roller skating in the Park. Food shopping on Bleecker Street and in Little Italy.

At the ramshackle Amusement Palace, a caged chicken plucked a fortune card from a stack and presented it to Oriana in return for a nickel. "Your principles mean more to you than any money and success."

"Mario! That is true! How could *un pollo* know it? She is *psichica* like you!"

Television had fascinated Oriana from the time of her arrival. She watched situation comedies, talk shows, quiz shows, variety entertainment, cartoons, afternoon serials, old movies, news broadcasts, everything.

During the early weeks of her growing addiction, Mario, coming home after a performance or private party, felt an odd jealousy of Danny Thomas or Sid Caesar, of the flickering screen itself. Sometimes she would persuade him to watch with her on the old leather couch, but he was quickly bored.

In mid-June, Mario returned from a weekend hotel performance at Saratoga Springs to find a message from the captain of the police precinct. The captain wanted to know if Mario were still interested in working on the unsolved Keith Higgins case.

Mario solved the mystery in a single day.

At the precinct, he studied the case file and asked a few questions of the captain and two plainclothesmen. Then he requested a personal object currently in use by the grieving mother, Irene Higgins.

"She forgot to take this when she came in last week," the captain said, handing Mario a ruffled pink umbrella. Eyes closed, he sat with it pressed between his palms.

"She did the murder. The mother." His voice shook. He received her *angoscia* of guilt, her remorse more cruel than any imprisonment could be. She loved her little boy, though she had hated the burden he was to her. Her lust for a new *amante* who did not like children had tipped the balance; and it was he who had helped her dispose of the pajama-clad body. And now she was reliving her drunken rage: the hammer, heavy in her red-nailed hand, crashing down again and again

231

on the beloved head. Then the hysterical phone call to the boyfriend, and the horror of cleanup, the furtive trip through the wintry night to a nearby rooftop.

With shaking hand, Mario pushed the umbrella across the desk to the captain. He sat stoically through an hour of questioning, describing the hammer and the site where it had been thrown into the Hudson River; the location of the trashcan where the bloodied bedding had been concealed; the well-rehearsed phone call to the Missing Persons Bureau.

The Higgins trial received national prime time coverage, with frequent mentions of Mario and several interviews.

Mario went to Idlewild Airport to see off *il professore* who had courteously refused an offer to repeat for the fourth time his lecture series at the museum. He was joining an excavation team at Pompeii.

"I envy you," said Mario with a sigh. He wanted to say to this friend who had witnessed the birth of his mystery that he had not forgotten his vow. *Io ti giuro, Professore*, one day I too will dig. But the words stuck in his throat. *Io ti giuro, Lucia.* Outside the summer sun struck dazzling rays from the planes on the ground.

They walked together to the gate, to the point beyond which Mario could not go. He took the lion coin from his pocket and displayed it on his palm. "This is with me always," he said. "Do you remember?"

"I remember well."

They embraced and parted.

The next day a black-edged letter arrived from Perugia.

Mario knew before he opened it that it was *la madre* who had died. The della Rovere crypt among the tall cypresses flashed between his eyes and the writing. The funeral procession. Stefano and the gray-faced Uncle Massimo first among the bearers, *Papà* walking unsteadily behind.

"Your sainted mother has gone from us," Salvatore wrote. Mario saw her haloed in purity, and heard his father say, **I was never worthy of you, Princess. Ahì, these many years I sinned against you!** "She called your name at the last, my son, along with the names of our children already awaiting her in Paradise." Eleanora's third and fatal stroke sprang from the page. Mario saw her on her deathbed, her face askew in paralysis, white braids over her shoulders. Then Eleanora young, Titian-haired, smiling as Mario never had seen her smile in life.

Mario and Oriana decided against an immediate trip to Italy. The new demands on him arising from the Higgins case were crowding an already tight schedule. He sent their regrets in a lame note of condolence to Salvatore. To Stefano he wrote at more length, waiving his rights in his mother's estate. "I would like only two books, her St. Francesco and the d'Annunzio plays. A couple of photos of her, from the album. And her garnet bracelet, for Oriana, a keepsake." He wrote also to Massimo, though he knew that his uncle never answered personal letters.

Massimo did not long survive his sister. Word of his death from lung cancer reached Mario in September. He shed copious tears for the one human being whom he had known to be a sharer of his gift. Tears unshed for the death of Eleanora now streamed down his face as well, for these tragic siblings, last of the once-glorious della Roveres.

Lauren remained obdurately plain, to Oriana's increasing distress. Mario found the little potato-nosed face charming and good to look at, vivid with intelligence and wondering curiosity. But he had to admit to himself that she was not beautiful, nor even pretty, and was not likely to become so. *Non importa!* he told himself, hugging his Lauren protectively, trying to dismiss the insistent parade through her mind of blank and perfect TV faces.

His performance schedule in town and out deprived him of much of her childhood. During the autumn of her second year, he was on tour in Europe, performing to packed houses in London, Paris and West Berlin.

Oriana declined to accompany him. "We will be better here, *amore, la bambina* and I. We are not much for travel."

Oriana shopped in the Madison Avenue boutiques or the Fifth Avenue department stores only when the imperious Goldie Horowitz would not take No for an answer.

Some of her purchases seemed outlandish to Mario, such as a six-slice toaster and crocheted toilet seat covers; yet more frilly rompers and musical stuffed animals; and never-to-be-worn pajamas for him. These would then be proudly displayed amid a sea of boxes, tissue paper and other packing materials. Her sense of housewifely duty gave way on these occasions to intoxicated outbursts of passion. She would dance through the disorderly living room, embrace Mario tightly, and kiss him with irresistible fervor. Even her ingrained devotion to Lauren seemed in abeyance. "Come, my darling," she would whisper in his ear. *"La bambina* is well where she is, let us go to bed."

Sex between them continued to be powerful and poetic. On tour or in distant cities working on police cases, Mario would often go to his hotel bed tantalized and shaken by memories of their caresses. On a few occasions, his desire was such a torment that he spent the night in the arms of one or another of the eager charmers awaiting him at the stage door. Mornings after were clouded with disappointment and guilt. *Mai più, sposa mia,* none can compare to my darling, to my pure and ever-faithful one!

Mario's rare and distant extramarital amours were not the problem, especially as Oriana seemed blissfully unaware of them. The difficulty was that he required more from a lover than Oriana could provide. It took him years to admit this to himself, and to face the distressing truth that the bed and the cradle, however dear to him, were not enough. Nor were his social, intellectual and cultural needs satisfied by an occasional boating excursion on Central Park Lake or a family outing in Prospect Park Botanical Gardens.

Eventually he evolved a half-satisfactory compromise. Once a month, he attended lectures on archeology or related subjects, and claimed another evening to attend productions or functions of serious artistic nature. He always invited Oriana to accompany him, knowing in advance that she would choose to stay home in front of the TV set. The women he escorted on these occasions ranged from young to middleaged, from pretty to plain, but were all on a level of education higher than his own. Invariably, they were smitten with desire for him. He exercised strict self-control. At times he chided himself, eh, Mario, what *un opportunista,* picking the brains of this *femmina* or that, pretending not to be aware of her yearnings and her hopes. But any alternative course seemed to him even more reprehensible. He avoided even goodnight kisses, so as to return to Oriana clean of guilt.

XVII

The Kendall burial plot, fragrant in August with beds of ice-blue bergamot, was bordered with tall magnolia trees.

Rutherford Kendall's great-grandfather, Isaiah Brook Kendall, 1862-1935, was buried under the oldest slab in the family plot. He had arrived in Floraville shortly after its founding in 1882, and had been the first to recognize the potential of the Flint River's proximity to the cotton farms. He had manufactured a strong, cheap calico popular throughout the Piedmont.

Rutherford, the great-grandson of this pioneering individualist, was honored in death by a red granite headstone which dwarfed all others in the plot. Under his name and dates was a bas-relief enlargement of his badge, above a pair of crossed billy clubs; and, carved in Gothic letters:

"NOW HE KEEPS THE PEACE ETERNAL."

His wife, Veronica Webster Kendall, who had survived him by only three months, was buried in the adjoining grave with a pink marble marker which declared her faithful unto death.

On this humid night, these polished gravestones reflected the strong glare of a bank of floodlights and the headlights of a backhoe, which Kevin Petticord was operating with enthusiasm and considerable skill to excavate Rutherford Kendall's grave.

A barrel-chested groundskeeper stood muttering, signaling directions to Kevin. Toads croaked in rhythmic competition with the whine of the hydraulic mechanism, the clanking of steel and the growl of diesel. The toothed bucket bit into the earth, lifted grass and red clay and deposited it on a tarpaulin. There was a sharp smell of wet earth and, as the bucket bit deeper, a whiff of decay.

"Now if Typhoid Julie comes out of her grave looking for water," the groundskeeper shouted at Kevin, "you're gonna be the one to fetch it for her."

Moths and mosquitoes swarmed to the great lights, many immolating themselves against the sizzling bulbs. On the macadam roadway abutting the Kendall plot, Tyler's patrol car was parked, empty, its windows down and radio light glowing. Bear Sieburth's 387 Ford V8 was just behind it, blinkers flashing.

Bear was devouring a catfish sandwich from the Eat-and-Run Diner and shuffling through a folder of forms and reports.

On the back seat, Beau Tyler lay jackknifed. His face, softened by sleep, seemed almost childlike in the flood of incandescence. Clearly he had found time to shave, bathe and change to a fresh uniform. He stirred, then sat up, wide awake. Bear handed him a dripping can of Coke and a wrapped sandwich from the paper sack at his feet. Tyler nodded, gulped and munched, and said, "Hey, Bear. What the doctor ordered."

"Need some more shuteye?"

Tyler stared at his watch. "Ten-thirty! Holy shit." He got out of the car. "You should've woke me. Any word about Terry Hapgood?"

Bear shook his head, "Miz Hubbard called about nine, says no trace of Hapgood at Warren or anywheres else. Nor his car. Sheriff's men and the troopers—no response yet on your APB."

A flying creature with wide umbrella-tipped wings swooped into the vast circle of light, heading straight for their windshield, then zoomed upward, squeaking as it narrowly evaded collision. The two men jumped. "Dad-blamed bat," Bear commented absently. He indicated the backhoe. "That's Kevin Petticord up there."

"Fresh out of the hospital?"

"Fast-talked Abbot into letting him operate it, doing okay. Virgil's on his way here in the County worm-wagon." He flipped two documents from the uppermost folder and handed them to Tyler. "My autopsies, Langford and Royal Washington."

Tyler put the papers between them on the seat. "Terry," he said. "Got to find him. Any ideas?"

"How about we get Castigliani to take a crack at his handwriting? Like those other Missing Persons."

"Why not. 'Cept Mario's psychic nose seems out of joint just now."

"He'll come through," Bear predicted. "Done some super stuff."

"I know," said Tyler. "And he's an asset even without the hocuspocus. He said Doctor Donlan wants to help. Anybody reached him yet?"

"He's back at the medical center. Had a private emergency this afternoon. Mighty concerned about Hapgood." Bear drained his soda can and crushed it. "Ambulance driver thinks he saw Hapgood's car, 'bout four o'clock, leaving Warren. Heading south."

"Which ambulance driver?"

"Here, I wrote it down somewhere," said Bear, shuffling papers. "Andy something."

"Randy," Tyler said.

"Green compact, a mite chewed up."

"It never got to Valhalla, or to town, I'm right certain. We searched with a fine-tooth comb. What else did Ruthann report?"

Bear found his notes of the radio conversation. Tyler studied them in the harsh white light. Ruthann had not been able to locate Lisabeth Kendall's account, and the administrative records had not yielded anything concerning the aborted lawsuit. She had checked the hospital files and those of the nursing home for Terry's deceased patients and how they had died; and with characteristic conscientiousness had crosschecked against the patients of two other staff nurses. She had also reviewed Rutherford Kendall's brief colon-cancer history.

"Hapgood lost more patients," Bear pointed out, "than the other two nurses."

"Only three-four," Tyler said.

"Notice the dates. His died quicker."

"Serial pattern? Mercy stuff?" Tyler mused. "I thought of that. But hanging 'em up don't fit with the Terry I know."

"Maybe you know him too well," Bear said, grinning, "like in the Biblical sense."

"Go climb a rope," Tyler replied mildly. "He did want to tell me something yesterday. Do you know about that flap in '85?"

Bear shook his massive head.

"He swallowed a hundred Seconal. Rumor was he got caught in some fruit hanky-panky up in New York."

"Male nurses," Bear muttered. "Those angel-of-death killings, remember? Let's check on Hapgood's patients at Emory General where he trained, and at—"

The floodlights flickered, then went out. The highpitched rumble of the generator ceased abruptly. Darkness surged over them, alleviated only by Bear's blinkers and the headlights of the backhoe, which went dark after Kevin braked to a sudden halt.

"Hell and damnation," Tyler said resignedly.

Bear switched on the dome light. "Out of fucking gas." The melancholy cry of a whippoorwill sounded above the pulsing din of crickets, toads and cicadas. A flashlight beam blossomed at the graveside, wavered toward the generator, and then approached the car.

"Hey, Chief," said Kevin at the window. "I'll hop on my bike and head over to the service station."

The groundskeeper, behind him, said, "That there generator gauge, it done got stuck again. We needs ten-fifteen gallon."

Tyler reached toward his hip pocket. "Hell and damnation," he said again with a sigh. "Left my wallet on the dresser when I hightailed it to Warren. Got some money, Bear?"

"Blew my last cent at the Eat-and-Run," Sieburth told him. "Reckon they'd honor a Middlebrook's credit card?"

"Or how 'bout my Georgia credit card?" Kevin grinned. A Georgia credit card was a short length of hose used to siphon gas out of someone else's tank.

Kevin was turning out his pockets. "Two dollars and fifty-seven cents here," he offered.

"Ain't cashed my paycheck yet," the groundskeeper apologized.

"Richest country on earth," Bear was grumbling, "and here the bunch of us can't raise no more'n a shithouse rat."

"Tell you what," Tyler said, "Floraville has an account up at that truck stop. Where the highway crosses the Interstate. Kevin could—"

"Shh!" Kevin, peering through the darkness at the grounds beyond the roadway, pointed a wavering finger. "What's that?" A vague glimmering shape was moving among the graves.

"Typhoid Julie!" the groundskeeper exclaimed in an awed whisper. "Come looking for water!"

Bear reached into the paper sack at his feet. "Reckon she'd settle for a Coke?"

But the white shape was already bounding toward them, barking lustily. "Hey, Spot," said Kevin, receiving the tongue lapping affections of a pure white German shepherd.

Bear studied the creature and observed, "That animal doesn't have a single spot on him."

"It's short for Spotless," said Tyler.

"How come 'equivocal'?" Tyler said, tapping the Earl Langford autopsy report. The dim light from the dashboard and the dome gleamed on his blond hair and on Sieburth's dense, dark curls as they pored over the official form.

"Suicide nor homicide, ain't official yet which," Bear replied. "'Course, this is just a prelim. Toxicology, now, I'm not equipped for the real subtle analysis. We got to wait till all three stiffs are through in the County lab."

Tyler's finger moved to the section on stomach contents. "We knew he'd ate a hamburger," he said.

"Exactly. Nary a trace of booze nor narcotics. Which argues in favor of homicide."

Static sounded from Tyler's radio, followed by: "Home base to Chief, do you copy? Over." The police chief went to his patrol car. When he made contact, Abbot said, "Word of warning. Fanny Hapgood's on her way to the cemetery. Hysterical."

"Terry contacted her?"

"No such luck. She's worried out of her mind," Abbot said. "I wrapped up with the deacon. Told him, Stay in town. Mario here, sparing me Ed Princeton's torture by militant oratory."

"Terry could have dumped his car somewhere," Tyler said. "Did Duane check out bus pickups?"

"At the service station and all other stops along the route," Abbot replied. "Want me to report on the standard Friday night mayhem in Floraville?"

"Not now, no, lessen there's something might help finding Terry."

When he was back in Bear's car, Tyler asked, "You heard?"

"I heard," Bear replied, still studying the Langford autopsy. "Let's get back to this 'fore the mamma tiger descends on us... The contusions on Earl's throat, now, could be real important. 'Pears like Jack Sprague, all ten fingers; plus there's a focal quarter-inch hemorrhage over the hyoid bone. Sprague maybe grabbed him there, too?"

"Like he vanished into thin air," Tyler muttered. "Terry, I mean." He returned his attention to the document on the car seat. "Quarter-inch hemorrhage," he echoed. "Could that be the cause of death?"

"Sure could, but Langford would have croaked then and there."

"Could it be self-inflicted?"

"Never in this world."

The police chief rearranged the reports, placing Roy Washington's on top. "Is there any substance wouldn't show up in a routine tox screen? Which could kill a guy or knock him out cold?"

Bear nodded. "Curare, for one. And chloral hydrate. And even non-prescription palliatives like Sominex, Benadryl, Dramamine. I'll make sure we get a complete extended screen in Atlanta."

Tyler said, "Old Ruthless been a-mouldering all year long. And lost his liver and lights. Think there's enough left of him? For your extended screen?"

"Should be. Roy Washington, now, he's a lot fresher. Your Doctor Donlan, by the way, did a crackerjack job on the autopsy. I asked him to send the organs on up to the lab." He yawned, and scratched himself under the arms. He got out of the car and stretched, as though in ritual obeisance to the ghostly moon. He poked his head through the window. "Hey, Beau. Come clean. Who did it?"

"Wish I knew. Sometimes I think, Jeff Pennington, or any of them up there on high in Valhalla. Then I think, has to be one of Roy's heirs, maybe somebody in the Tabernacle gang, expecting to inherit. Even poor, crazy Otis Feeney, he would have known I'd give him that job."

"Even you," Bear said, grinning.

"Right, I even suspect myself time to time," Tyler said, returning the grin. "And I fit Mario's profile a lot better than Otis. But none of this explains Kendall. Langford, okay, he likely witnessed Roy's murder.

But how the hell does the old chief fit in?"

Bear got back in the car. "Kendall might be suicide for real," he suggested, "and the killer could have copied his M.O."

Sieburth scratched his head. "Who stood to profit by the old chief's death?"

"The whole criminal element of Floraville," Tyler replied. The floodlights came on. Kevin flashed thumbs-up from the backhoe. "And his next of kin," Tyler continued. "And Andrew Abbott. And me."

The racket of the exhumation resumed. Bear raised his voice. "Strange, ain't it, how your name keeps cropping up."

A grey 1979 Chrysler came meandering toward them along the roadway. It swerved slowly to avoid Tyler's cruiser and bumped to an uncertain stop. Fanny Hapgood, frail and unsteady, her greying blonde hair unkempt, got out and tottered toward Sieburth's car. She was wearing satin, highheeled mules and a long, flowered kimono.

Tyler was out of his car and hurrying to her when she tripped and fell on one knee to the macadam. "Help! Oh, help me!" she sobbed as he raised and supported her. "Oh, Beau! Help! Where's my boy?"

"Now, now, now," Tyler soothed. The kimono had parted at her knee, which was bloodied and dirty. "'Pears like you hurt yourself, Miz Hapgood."

"Never mind me," she said brokenly. Sieburth shambled up, keeping a discreet distance. "Where's Terry?" she continued. "Why aren't you out looking for him?"

"First aid kit under my driver's seat," Tyler told Bear, who nodded and went to fetch it. "Here, lean on me, Miz Hapgood, hold tight to my arm." He brought her to Sieburth's car, opened the rear door on the side away from the backhoe, and lowered her onto the seat. "You ought to be home in bed," he chided softly. Her slim bare legs hung through the open door, mules dangling.

"How can I lie in bed, and my son missing? And how can you loll around like this and Terry God-knows-where?"

"Does Miz Eunice know you're out driving around in your dressing gown?"

"A.J. gave me a sedative, but I woke up. I asked Eunice could Cordene drive me. She told me, Go on back to sleep, Fanny."

Bear brought the first aid kit. Tyler carefully cleaned the wound and applied bacitracin ointment and a bandage.

"Don't fuss over me," Fanny went on shakily. "Go on, hurry, Terry can't be far away."

"Duane Potts is searching hard's he can, and we got the troopers and the county force on the lookout." She opened her finely cut lips in protest, tears coursing from her large blue eyes down the prematurely crumpled skin of her face. He held up a hand to silence her. "I can't leave here yet, y'understand," he told her. "But I'll be out there tracking Terry down just soon's I can."

"Tracking him down!" she whispered on a fresh flow of tears. "Like some kind of criminal? Oh, my Terry, my lamb! Is that what people are saying!"

"Go on cry, Miz Hapgood," Tyler said tenderly. "Do you a power of good."

Bear, who had returned to the driver's seat, swiveled around and asked in a casual tone, "Where d'you think Terry might've got to, Miz Hapgood?"

"Yes, tell us, ponder hard," Tyler encouraged her. "This is Mr. Bernard Sieburth, Georgia Bureau of Investigation, down from Atlanta helping out."

Fanny took the handkerchief Bear proffered and pressed it to her face. The nerve-racking noise of metal scraping metal made Tyler and Bear grimace, as the toothed bucket, now deep in the grave, hit the protective cover of Rutherford Kendall's casket. Tyler saw the groundskeeper signal Kevin, with a wide throat-cutting gesture, to stop the backhoe; and a moment later, saw both men jump down into the grave.

Fanny seemed not to notice. "The library..." She faltered. "He said he was going to the library."

"Ma'am, it's nigh on eleven o'clock p.m.," Tyler said.

"But the librarian..."

Red dirt flung high by unseen shovels fountained from the open grave. "We checked," Tyler told Fanny. "She hasn't seen him."

"Did you go to the lake house too?"

"Yes, ma'am, we did."

"The mill villages?"

"Checked 'em out real thorough, 'specially Blue Heaven."

"How about that Mr. Gary Lansing? You know he wanted to take Terry with him back to California? And Jeff," she said in a frightened, muffled voice. "Where's Jeff?"

"Isn't he home in Valhalla?" Tyler asked.

"He never got home yet. Did he take off for Atlanta again?"

"You think your son might be with him?" said Bear.

Fanny nodded uncertainly, but said, "No, why on earth would Terry be with Jeff? Except... well, Jeff's always inviting the boy to come with him to Atlanta." She looked quickly, her brimming eyes wide, from Bear to Tyler. "Now don't you go talking about this, neither one of you, you hear? No reason why his cousin shouldn't treat him to a little trip. But you know Floraville, how they lie and gossip."

Tyler told her, "I reckon Jeff's still at the mill, he's got a full plate there. But we'll check."

"Coffin's coming up," Bear said. He got out of the car. Kevin was perched in the operator's seat again. The metal-clad casket, roped now to the backhoe, came rocking into view and was lifted to the graveside.

Fanny slipped to the ground and limped to peer over the car hood. "What's happening? Who's that?"

"Got to get you home, Miz Hapgood," Tyler told her. He held her shoulders lightly, turning her away from the exhumation scene. The sound of the backhoe ceased. "Kevin!" he shouted through cupped hands. "Come on over here!"

Kevin came on the run, jumping over intervening graves.

Tyler said, "I want you to carry Miz Fanny Hapgood here on home to Valhalla. You could put your bike in the trunk."

"How do, Miz Hapgood," Kevin said. "I'll be glad to oblige, soon's we open up the..."

"Right this minute," Tyler ordered.

Kevin, crestfallen, opened his mouth and then shut it again. He swallowed hard. "Gee, Chief, can't I..."

"No," said Tyler. "You can't."

"Where's your bike?" Bear asked. "I'll load 'er for you."

Kevin gave Tyler one brief, pleading look. "Down by the office building there," he said, and then. "Thanks, Mr. Sieburth."

Fanny said feebly, "Could he maybe take me home the back way?"

"Yes," Tyler told Kevin. "Drive in delicate as you can, and fetch Odessa. Try not to disturb Miz Pennington nor Uncle Casey."

"Odessa will take care of me," Fanny said. "Cordene will put away the car." Her face crumpled into tears again. "Oh! Terry! Find him, promise me you'll find him!"

"That's my top priority," Tyler assured her. "Tell you what, Miz Hapgood. Could you maybe give Kevin here something Terry wrote? Just anything in his handwriting." She nodded. To Kevin he said, "I want you back on the switchboard soon's you're through."

"Yes, sir, Chief Tyler," Kevin said sadly.

"Do me a favor, call Bonnie, tell her I'm heading her way. In an hour or so, when I'm done at the station. Tell Andrew I'm about finished up here; and if Mr. Castigliani's still there, ask him would he wait for me."

"We'd best get up there," Bear said, nodding toward the open grave. The groundskeeper had already removed the top half of the coffin's sheet metal sleeve, and was now drawing the long screws from the weathered mahogany.

Mosquitoes found Tyler and Bear, descending in a singing, stinging cloud at which they slapped abstractedly. "Shouldn't we better wait for Virgil?... Hell, Bear, I sure wish you could stick around tomorrow. Help find Terry."

"Wish I could, but the bodies come first, you know that. You got Mario Castigliani, Lieutenant Abbot. Taliaferro'd pitch in, too, betcha." He started slowly up the slope toward the Kendall plot. "How about that Jeff Pennington, what Fanny Hapgood said. Jesus, gays everywhere now, ain't they. Reckon the whole Piedmont'd collapse if folks knew."

Tyler trailed him. "If his mamma found out, it'd ruin him."

Tyler sidestepped deftly to avoid a hoptoad on the path. "I heard tell about Anne-Marie Donlan's hankering, but it's news to me if her brother fancies him, too."

"Think he's humping Terry?"

"Nah, I don't think so. That about Gary Lansing, that's news, too." They stepped around the earth-heaped tarpaulin beside the grave. "I can maybe put Mario on it, if Lansing's still at Warren. And on Lisabeth Kendall, too. But Mario's got his show to get ready for. Maybe

Reid. Reid's a good idea."

The groundskeeper awaited them respectfully, leaning on his shovel. "Want I should open 'er up?" He nodded toward the outsized casket.

"Hang on," said Bear, as the black Cullowee County Removal Vehicle drove onto the roadway below. "There's Virgil now."

The short slight figure of the medical examiner, with his crest of white hair, emerged from the hearse-like car. Virgil Cox waved, and came up the hill. He nodded at Bear, shook Tyler's hand, and said, "Hey, Gene."

"Open 'er up," said Bear. "And hold your noses."

XVIII

How would you like to fix up *l'appartamento?* Redecorate, new furniture, repair *el'impianto 'draulico,* whatever you like."

She embraced the project with enthusiasm. Mario opened a joint account, upon which she drew with increasing aplomb. Performances, private parties and other career-related appointments allowed him little time with her; she was equally preoccupied. Often he would come home after midnight to find her asleep in front of the TV, with shoppers guides and advertising pages from the *Daily Mirror* spread out around her. She would spring up, wide awake at his touch. She would kiss him soundly, and take him by the hand to see the progress in the painting and plastering of Lauren's room; or to admire the medicine cabinet with swans etched around its lighted frame, the new refrigerator, the plastic chandelier for the dining area.

His half-hearted efforts were not sufficient to prevent the ongoing deterioration of his marriage. The lush atmosphere of the overfurnished apartment made him uncomfortable. Sympathetic though he was to Oriana's needs, he could not always repress his reactions to certain of her purchases.

"Dolcezza mia, please don't buy towels with gold threads in them."

"But Mario, they are so *elegante,* do you not agree?"

"I do not agree. They are vulgar, and scratchy to the skin."

"Bene, vulgar, I will exchange them for plain."

He saw that he had hurt her, but could not stop himself. "And toilet paper should not be tinted, Oriana, nor *profumata.*"

Tears sprang to her eyes. He embraced her quickly, but she shoved him away. "Please tell me what else your vulgar ignorant wife has done to offend you," she said coldly.

One night he came home early to find her curled up on the couch with the telephone, rapt in giggling conversation with Gina Palermo. Lauren, still in her school clothing, sat crosslegged on the rug, doing her homework, a bowl of potato chips and a dish of candy beside her.

Mario shut the TV off and silently commanded Oriana to hang up. She obeyed quickly, replacing the phone beneath the fullskirted doll used as a decorative cover.

"Why isn't she undressed and in bed?" he demanded. "Ten-thirty at night is no hour for homework."

When he was alone with Oriana, Mario burst out, "And why are you letting her gorge on *merda,* when you're forever nagging she should lose weight? And that Gina, isn't it enough the time you waste with her, without hanging on the phone?"

"Mario! *Caro! Prego!*" She stood up and held her arms out to him. "What's come over you? Lauren - she's only *una ragazzina,* she needs a treat now and then, no? And Gina, she's inviting us to go this Sunday to Aqueduct, Benny would drive us... last time..." she faltered " you enjoyed... you said you enjoyed..."

"Well, I lied. I'm fed up," he said brutally.

Oriana flung a sofa cushion which fell short, upsetting Lauren's candy dish. Bonbons rolled in all directions. "Eh, listen to him, the egghead, my big *intelletuale! Che snobismo!*" She threw a copy of *Readers Digest*, which struck him on the head.

He threw it back with a wordless shout. She picked up a china planter shaped like a burro, with a cactus growing out of its back. She had acquired this object, which Mario detested, only the previous week. It was still so precious to her that she hesitated, put it down and seized a phone book instead.

Mario's anger gave way to laughter, guffaws shaking him as he leaned against the wall, pointing at the burro planter. The phone book slipped from Oriana's hands and fell in a flutter of yellow pages. Brilliant with fury, she came at Mario, her hands held like claws, hissing Italian and English insults in a barely comprehensible stream.

Mrs. Chun's anxious rapping silenced them. They glanced shame-faced at their frightened daughter, who peered at them from her bedroom door. Oriana reassured the neighbor with a lame tale about rehearsing a scene from a play, while Mario calmed Lauren and got her back to bed.

Oriana was under the covers, her back to him, when he entered their room. He undressed, turned off the lamp and slid in beside her. Tense silence lay between them. Already he was stirred by rue and regret. He murmured her name and touched her shoulder. She turned to him. Tears, yes, and kisses, stammered apologies, caresses, mutual promises, and then a passion keener than any they had shared in months.

When she slept in his arms, her head on his breast, he lay for a long while open-eyed in the darkness. *Ahi, mio dolce amore,* my darling, what is happening to us?

Mario's frequent obligatory absence from New York became the saving factor in the preservation of his little family. The hate and anguish that seethed in Lauren, the anger and resentment he and Oriana tried to conceal, were after all part and parcel of the deep mutual concern which bound the three together. *L'amore* is *preziosissimo,* he told no himself, however paradoxical the emotions with which it may coexist.

Love among them there was in plenty, especially fulsome when they were apart. *Che peccato* that love is not enough! Yet it was sufficient to make of each reunion a tender celebration, with unspoken vows to try harder.

During Lauren's primary school years, Mario arrived at a sort of plateau with Oriana. Their married life was amiable, fond, diplomatic, devoid of the earlier peaks of ecstasy and the plunges into open antagonism. Quarrels between them were mild and infrequent. Their kisses over the long-distance telephone were more fervent than those exchanged in bed. More and more, by tacit agreement, each pursued his and her separate interests.

Compared to most *coniugi*, Mario consoled himself, we do very well. If only we could do as well with *nostra figlia.* Though Lauren accepted the role of affectionate daughter, there was a widening gulf between her and her parents.

When she started fifth grade, Mario found a more suitable private school. It was small and expensive, with high standards of scholarship. Her marks were excellent, particularly in arithmetic and general science. She made friends, not with the pretty girls who were the objects of her crushes, but with less decorative, more studious classmates. Often she would stay the night or the weekend with one or another of these girl-friends.

"Why not invite your *amiche* here sometimes?" Oriana suggested. "How about a *festa* for them, a pajama party?"

"We would make them most welcome," said Mario, "and leave you to yourselves. You could be the hostess."

He knew beforehand that Lauren would decline the offer. She has not forgiven us, he told himself. Envy gnaws at her heart; scorn is her anodyne. So she tells herself we are not good enough for her friends. **Silly Mamma, with the dopey bargains and the boob tube. This 'diculous apartment. And Daddy some kind of show-off freak.**

Often Mario wished that his daughter's mind were closed to him.

STURDIVANT'S BALCONY
COLLAPSES - 9 INJURED

Eight customers and a construction worker have been hospitalized following the collapse of a balcony and a section of wall in Sturdivant's department store. Six people fell fifteen feet to the ground floor. Only one was seriously hurt, having been crushed by the wall which tore loose a few seconds later. Two shoppers were knocked down and trampled by the screaming crowd rushing backward out of harm's way.

"All dangerous areas were clearly demarcated and closed to the public," declared the Sturdivant manager. "The store cannot take responsibility."

"She was after that bathing suit, see," Gina jabbered distractedly while he paced in the hospital waiting room. **With the built-in bra.** "For Lauren, you know, for the summer camp." Gina's frosted black hair was mussed into witch locks. Mascara streaked down her aquiline face.

Lauren was curled under a hospital blanket on a bench nearby. Her eyes, sharp and black in her swollen face, were fixed on Mario.

Mario hardly heard the choked rambling words, so overwhelmed was he by the horrors in Gina's mind: Oriana, merry and high-spirited, then suddenly drained of color, her mouth wide in a silent shriek as the balcony dropped beneath her. The multi-voiced outcry of those who had followed her lead and fell with her. The shouts from the stampede below. Then the crash of the wall, blotting Oriana from Gina's view with huge chunks of masonry and billowing plaster dust.

I told her, don't go there, Oriana. Danger, it says.

Lauren said, "Daddy!" and sat up with her arms outstretched to him. He knelt on the rug, his head on her shoulder. She held him as though he were the child, she the parent. Her mind seemed calm, and surprisingly empty. **Dear darling Daddy, don't worry. Don't cry, I'm here, I'm not going to die. I will take care of you.**

He jumped to his feet. "She is still alive," he told his daughter, not knowing whether or not this was true. "We will not let her die." Whatever the cost, whatever has to be done, *mia carissima*, I will not let you die.

Oriana never spoke again after the accident, except with her anguished and eloquent eyes during the rare periods of consciousness.

He would come home from the hospital to share with Lauren the sketchy meal she had prepared for him. They spoke little, and only of commonplaces. He heard her constant, silent beseeching: **Let her go, Daddy. She's hurting so bad, she wants to die, and you know it.**

Oriana died that October.

Mario did what had to be done, moving like an automaton, arranging with the help of friends and neighbors for the funeral and the burial. Lauren remained calm and helpful throughout those difficult weeks. He was puzzled and a little hurt that the child seemed hardly to mourn.

Lauren continued to worry Mario. He had cherished some vague hopes that she might want to study archeology. But she had other ideas. She was determined to take business courses, to prepare for a career as an executive. Mario had laughed uneasily when she first announced these plans. What can a twelve-year-old *ragazzina* imagine the life of a business executive to be? He soon discovered that there was nothing whimsical nor childish about her ambition.

"Money," she had told him gravely that morning as she ironed her school uniform. "Money is what I want. I want to be at the top. That's where the power is, Daddy. All these science and arts courses, they don't interest me." At least she is honest about it, he thought, feeling chilled. He made no attempt to argue with her. I do not like my daughter, he realized. I love her, but I do not like her.

The Etruscans of ancient Tarquinia buried their dead in charming little necropoles, with square rooms cut into volcanic tufa. Steps led down into the tombs, decorated with murals and gaily painted ceilings. The deceased lay in terra cotta sarcophagi beneath their sculpted images, often of husband and wife in affectionate embrace.

In contrast, Briarwood Cemetery, near Maspeth, Long Island, stretched for a mile on either side of the highway: a seemingly endless city of the dead, with ranks and files of small markers, identically square in accordance with the regulations. The low stone administrative offices and the massive building which housed the ashes of the cremated offered the only relief to the monotonous grid.

Oriana Castigliani
b. April 16, 1934, d. October 9, 1965
Beloved Wife

Mario, greying now, heavy of body and spirit, sweated at the graveside in the blaze of the sun. In less than three hours he would be flying to Atlanta and then catching a bus, journeying to a land that seemed far more distant and exotic than his native Italy.

The hot wind shifted, bringing a smell of ocean salt. A young woman in black was kneeling three plots away, talking earnestly, inaudibly, to the grave. He felt the dreariness of life like a great weight on his shoulders. *Privare*, doubly bereft. Had Oriana always been his wife and *la Lucia* only his mistress? Or had it truly been the other way round, and now spurned, *la Lucia* admitted him only rarely to her marvelous embrace?

In his memory resonated the pure countertenor: "...that breast which was the nest of love crushed now by the hard grave..." Monteverdi: *Lachrime D'Amante*. *Il professore* had sent him the album soon after Oriana's death, with a note: "Do not play this yet, dear Mario, but later when your grief is not so raw."

"*Deserti i boschi, e correr fiume il pianto...*" The woods lie wasted, and the weeping streams... Mario had not visited her grave throughout the decades. It is not my *amorosa* who lies in the cemetery, he had told himself, only her pitiful broken remains. Memories of his mother haunting the tombs beneath the dark cypresses were sufficient to keep him away.

His fingers brushed the granite marker, tracing the carven name. "*A te dia pace il Ciel... honorata tomba e sacra terra.*" He heard again the pure melancholy of the madrigal, and was shaken by a bitter irony: May thou have the peace of Heaven... honored tomb and sacred earth.

Addio, my Oriana.

XIX

The sophistication of the lighting and sound systems of the Floraville High School auditorium came as a happy surprise to Mario. It provided a pleasant antidote to his melancholy reminisces and the frustration he shared with Tyler over Rutherford Kendall's role in recent events.

"The Drama Society, they put in the footlights," the custodian, a meaty man in a wrinkled blue uniform, told him. He walked with a slight limp, and smelled vaguely of whiskey and peppermints. "And Miz Claudia, she paid for the audio."

"*Signora* Jefferson Pennington, is she not?" Mario murmured, savoring her name in any of its forms.

Cheers and boos could be heard from a baseball game coming to an end.

"Yes, sir. First Lady of this here town, you might call her, next to Miz Eunice."

The conditioned air of the auditorium was chill and a trifle musty. Mario opened and closed the blue velvet curtain, pleased with its efficiency. He counted the four hundred and fifty seats. A multivoiced shout came from the ball field, followed by the jubilant chant: "We're the latest, we're the greatest."

"Can we moderate the air conditioning perhaps?" Mario asked.

"That's why all the others hate us," continued the chant.

"Well, sure, 'cepting folks like it good and cool."

Six-thirty, said the large round clock above the entrance; and Mario's watch concurred. He had found time to stop by the pawnshop, where

Jackson Sprague, elaborately polite and skillfully evasive, had adjusted the timepiece. Mario had not succeeded in eliciting any new information, nor in penetrating to the back room.

Fresh now from two hours of rest at the hotel, dramatic in his tuxedo T-shirt and black suit, he stood beside the steps leading to the stage, on which he had opened his briefcase. He took a packet of three-by-five cards and began to place them one by one on the front seats.

"Help you deal 'em out?" the custodian offered.

"*Molte grazie*, but my assistants will be here soon."

Alone in the cold empty auditorium, Mario sat down on the stage steps, still holding the three-by-five cards. He willed himself to concentrate on curtain time. But his thoughts, were on Terry Hapgood. How could I have let *l'inquieto* walk away from me yesterday! Last night at the stationhouse Tyler had produced a year-old letter written by Terry to his mother. Mario had gone through the farce of gazing at the handwriting, one finger pressed to his brow. "Sample too old?" Tyler had asked when Mario handed back the letter with a gesture of frustration.

This whole day had been fruitless, sterile, *vano, inutile*. Mario had dug into the files at both the police station and the newspaper office, but his concentration was poor and he had gleaned little. At the hotel, Flossie Hicks did not seem to know where her husband was, and Otis Feeney was nowhere to be found.

The one bright quarter-hour in his day had been his return to the newspaper store to purchase gifts for Durrell and Scott. They might prefer *soldi*, he had thought, but was somehow reluctant to put their voluntary service on a cash basis.

"What would you suggest, *Signora*," he had asked the friendly lame woman, "as presents for twelve-year-old boys?"

She limped along the counter to a display of toy cars. "Here's these, boys like 'em fine. Radio controlled. Nineteen-dollars ninety-five cents."

Under her guidance, he selected a red "Bigfoot" pickup for Scott, and for Durrell an "Ultra-Racer" glistening with chrome. The woman had gift-wrapped the boxes, fishing below the counter for rumpled pink paper that said: "Happy Easter."

"Hey, Mr. Castig-lian!"

"We ready to bust it out!"

Scott and Durrell, excited, well-scrubbed and in their Sunday-go-to-meeting best, stood before him in the high school auditorium.

"*Eh, ragazzi!* How good of you to come."

Their enthusiasm was contagious; their awed curiosity a balm to his sore ego. As they ran to place cards on the seats, Mario felt anticipation quicken in his veins. He himself set up the collapsible slotted boxes, with pads and pens, at each exit, and placed one prominently on the ticket-taker's table. "Requests for Private Readings" said the lettering on the boxes. "Please Print Your Name and Phone Number." A small rectangular container holding his business cards was affixed to each box, over the words "Fees By Arrangement."

By the time he had demonstrated for Scott the use of the cordless microphones, Mario's mood had swung high. He was all showman now, radiating energy. "Teach Durrell," he told Scott. "I want you to alternate, on stage, and within the audience."

He strode lightly down the aisle, took the four steps to the stage in two bounds, and inspected the props table which Durrell had arranged as instructed. "*Perfetto!*" he exclaimed.

Mario took his set of finger mirrors from their pocket in the lining of the briefcase. He stood with his back to the audience area, a few feet behind the podium, finding the precise position to mirror-read without detection from out front. He turned slowly. If I chalk mark just here… Durrell and Scott, practicing with the mikes, signalled to him happily. No, he told himself, returning the device to the briefcase. No mirror reading. It is not worth the risk of tampering with the innocence of these *giovanetti*. And in *ogni modo*, I do not need it. *Grazie a* Reid Taliaferro, I have material enough for two shows. If the turnout is good, that is.

At a quarter of eight every seat was filled. Durrell and Scott were setting up folding chairs between the last row and the exit doors. Surveying the audience through a peephole in the closed blue velvet curtain, Mario thought, It is good we did not turn down the air conditioning.

Mario rapped three times, and stood to his full height before the podium, relaxed and radiating charm. Durrell, behind the scenes, responded promptly: the curtain parted. On stage in the pink spotlight, Mario seemed tall. He bowed deeply then held up his large well-shaped hand to quiet the scattering of applause.

"*Benvenuti, Signor e signori* of Floraville," he began. "Welcome! Later your Mayor Sondergard will be here to greet you on behalf of the Rotary Club and the promised Youth Center." It was Mario's custom when he did benefits to request that the usually boring opening remarks be deferred until after the intermission. "Now you and I will together solve a few mysteries of the present; and we will ask our questions of the veiled future."

On this cue, Scott and Durrell entered from opposite sides of the stage and bowed awkwardly. "My assistants for the evening, Durrell Whitley and Scott Garison." Durrell was grinning sheepishly; Scott's face was scarlet. Scattered hoots and cheers came from their peers in the audience. "I trust you have all filled in the cards you found on the seats: your name and seat number clearly printed, then your question, if you have one."

The boys jumped down from the stage to collect the three-by-fives. "Meanwhile," Mario continued, "I want to ask the help of … the lady in the charming print frock in the third row?" He took his baton from the podium and pointed at an elderly woman who looked to him like a retired schoolteacher. She shook her head, laughing, protesting. "Now you get on up there, Momma!" said the woman beside her, almost pulling her from her seat. Mario smiled a dazzling invitation. "And this gentleman at the end of the row, and…" A few hands wavered up in the audience, making it easy for Mario to assemble five willing people on stage.

He handed each of them a two-by-three memo pad and a #3 pencil, and escorted them to the cleared end of the long table upstage. "Here, in view of all, I want each of you to write your name, and then a word, or a brief phrase—something you are certain I could not possibly know about. Let no one see what you write. It can be an object, a person, a place, a mere thought, whatever you wish."

With a flourish, he turned his back on them. He could see his briefcase in the wing, and on a sudden inspiration went to fetch a small packet from it. He returned immediately to the footlights. "And while they cogitate, I will ask *Signorina* Cindy Petticord to come up on the stage."

Bobby Lee, with a puzzled frown, brought his little daughter to stand before Mario. She clung to her father, her blue eyes round.

"*Signorina* Cindy," Mario said gravely, "I know there is something for which you are wishing." The child shrank closer to Bobby Lee, her lips parted. "Would it surprise you, Cindy, to discover that you already have that something?" Mario smiled slowly, irresistibly, until she smiled back. The silence was profound. "I want you to search, all over you, to find where it may be."

"In my pocket?" she ventured timidly.

He held the microphone close to her. "Yes, that is an excellent idea. But everywhere."

Bobby Lee said, "She got nothing in the pockets 'cause them jeans is brand spanking new from the Shop 'N' Save."

"In Daddy's pockets?"

He shook his head. The five at the table must be *preparati* now, he thought. He addressed them, but ostentatiously kept his face to the audience. "While *Signorina* Cindy looks for her treasure, I will ask each of you to tear off the sheet on which you have written. Fold it carefully. On the table you will find some small brown envelopes. Place your word or phrase in one and seal it." He waited in the hush while the little girl, having turned out her pockets, took off one of her sneakers and peered into it. "Hold the envelopes to the light. Can you see through them?"

"Nothing."

"Nary a glimmer."

"Completely opaque," Mario assured the audience. The woman in the print dress approached him, proffering her envelope, but he held up his hand. "No, you keep the envelopes. When you are back in your seats, put them somewhere safe but handy, until my Muse reveals to me what you have written down."

A rustling and stirring came from the audience as the five returned to their seats. Myrtle's boy said distinctly, "Gee willikers."

Mario hunkered down before Cindy. "Have you found it?" She shook her silky, fair head. "*Bene*, let us see. Open your mouth." She giggled, then opened wide. "Or perhaps..." he said, his fingers behind her ear. "Ah! *Ecco! Vedi!* What have we here?" He drew forth a glassine packet, held it high, and opened it while the audience gave forth a swelling reaction. "Hold out your hand." Utter silence. He shook out a little of the contents, which glittered brilliantly in the rosy spotlight. A white flash from Phil's camera captured the moment.

"Shiny stuff!" gasped Cindy.

"The spangles!" said Bobby Lee.

"Sequins," affirmed Mario. There was scattered applause, then a steady clapping.

"For the school map! Daddy, Daddy, look, all different colors!"

"Enough for the whole border," Bobby Lee said. "Now how'd you do that?"

Mario bowed. Sleight-of-hand was not his forte, but he could do a few simple tricks. And since they all seem to want magic, he told himself, why not? While Bobby Lee and Cindy made their way from the stage through the applauding assembly, he unobtrusively collected the pads on which his volunteers had written. He was careful to stack them in the already memorized sequence in which the writers had stood. Between the fourth and fifth pages of each pad was a sheet of white carbon paper. Willie had never needed carbon: he could read the message from the impression on the pad. But Mario preferred to take no chances. He stepped off the stage and put the pads in his open briefcase.

Then he returned to the podium, and flicked rapidly through about fifty three-by-five cards while he waited for quiet. Time for our little *giuoco*, he thought. But a man's voice from the middle of the auditorium called out: "Hey, Mister! Can you tell us are we 'bout to kick off World War Three?"

The audience reacted, talking all at once. Mario was unprepared, having given little thought to the latest crisis menacing the Middle East. He signalled Durrell and Scott, in the aisles, to switch on their microphones; and was surprised to learn how many here had a relative in the armed forces.

"There will be war," he pronounced solemnly. There was a hush. "But not a world war. A short one, though many will suffer."

"Will we win?" called a voice.

"Yes," he declared. "The United States will win."

"That's the gospel!" said Tonda Whitley, standing up. "What we wants to know is: *Who killed Roy Washington?*"

This bombshell effectively silenced everyone. Mario saw Tyler half-rise in his seat, his blue eyes sharp with warning. Reid Taliaferro was hurrying toward the stage, as though to the rescue. A tall, old man near the back, whom Mario recognized as one of the pawnshop cribbage players, yelled out, "Yeah, and poor old Earl!" A loud sputtering protest came from Doc Osborne. Ed Princeton got to his feet and called to Tonda, "You tell it, sister! You got a right to know!"

Hubbub ensued. Mario's right hand went up like a traffic signal. *"Amici, Signori, Signor! Prego! Fate piano!"* He waited until he had their attention. "As you must know, we cannot discuss these cases, since they are under investigation."

"Yeah, 'cepting you're the investigator," someone said.

Mario shook his head. "However, I can tell you this." He put his hand to his brow. *"Tonight, there is a killer in our midst!"*

A gasp ran through the audience. Mario waited: timing here was essential. He pointed to the eleventh row. "Will the man in the plaid jacket please stand up."

William Friedrich lumbered to his feet. The mystified shock on his round face slowly gave way to a broad smile. Tyler flashed Mario a look of gratitude, and sank back into his seat. Reid walked backward up the aisle.

"'Sakes, it's the termite man!"

"The bug killer!" A medley of voices affirmed it while the exterminator waved greetings. The gamble had paid off: the tension was defused. Laughter swept the auditorium. A number of men slapped their thighs.

Sacra innocenza, Mario thought. Never have I had an easier audience. "Please remain standing a moment, *Signor*. There is one among us tonight whose household is experiencing an influx of ants." He glanced at the three-by-five he had placed on top of the stack. *"Signorina* Eileen Schuster in Row 12, Seat 9A."

A woman with a long, horsy face got slowly to her feet. "That ain't so, Mister. We ain't pestered with no ants. We got the cock-a-roaches, same as everybody. Few wood rats out in the shed. But no ants."

"Your Aunt Emily, and her *sorella* Alice are staying with you now.

Your *Zia* Charity Enfield was there a fortnight ago, and next week you are entertaining Aunt Lavinia."

The pun in American English, for Mario a source of pride in his language skills, took a moment to sink in. On a new wave of appreciative merriment, he caught Reid Taliaferrro's eye. Poker-faced, they exchanged a fleeting conspiratorial glint. Then, smiling, Mario held out his arms in embrace of the audience.

They were his.

He took up a three-by-five card, and called out: *"Signorina* Christine Collier, Row 11, Seat 3A." The cashier of the Shop 'N' Save shrank back in her seat. She was wearing a limp nondescript dress; a dark kerchief framed her pale plump face. She had written: "Will I be happy married?" had crossed it out, and written: "Who should I marry?"

Scott hurried to Row 11, and stood ready with the microphone. Mario held the handwriting close, then far away, as though receiving revelations from it. Then he gazed a full minute into the tear-swollen eyes.

"Ah, Signorina, your dilemma is classic. Two suitors have asked for your hand. One is rich, one is poor."

She nodded. Speculative gossip buzzed through the auditorium.

"Are you sure you wish me to answer your question? Would you not prefer to ask me in private session?"

Scott held the microphone to her. "Go 'head," she said, barely audible.

"Your family and friends have advised you to marry the rich admirer; and you have consented. But in your heart, it is the poor one you love." She stood up at that, shoving the microphone away. Mario debated with himself whether or not to continue. Her frightened, pretty face was pleading for an answer. He went on, "My Muse tells me that marriage with your fiance will not be happy." He was tempted to add, mindful of Willie's science of statistics, And neither will marriage to the other be happy. He looked upward as though consulting some unseen entity. "The name of the *amante* you love begins with an L... Lorenzo? ...Leonard?"

"Don't say no more!" the young woman cried.

The buzz of conversation grew louder. Mario saw Bonnie McRae turn quickly to face Tyler. Her lips silently framed the word "Lonnie!"

Christine Collier, now in the aisle, gestured to Mario. "Thanks, Mr. Castig-ly," she said hoarsely, into the mike Scott held before her, "but that's enough!" She made her way unsteadily to the slotted box at the nearest exit.

"Cara Signorina," he called after her, "I will give your appointment the highest priority, and will help in any way I can." To the audience he said, "Any of you who prefer privacy, or who desire a full consultation, should leave your names and numbers in the boxes at the exit doors and on the lobby table."

"Costs plenty, I betcha," someone said glumly.

"My fees are scaled in accordance with income," he told them. Usually he would add: "No one is turned away." Thoughts of the money still owing for his daughter Lauren's course restrained him.

He took up another card and in a lighter vein congratulated an aging couple, who had not written any question, on their as yet unannounced golden wedding celebration to be held at Howard Johnson's. To the Floraville Wildcats coach he predicted victory for the coming football season. If they win, he told himself, they will remember. If they lose, they will doubtless forget.

He was surprised and touched to find cards from Scott and Durrell in the stack. Scott's asked: "Will She-Ra get better?"

"Your cat will not only recover fully," he announced, "she is due for a blessed event early in October." Scott, in the aisle, seemed not to understand, so Mario added. "Kittens." Chuckles greeted this, and a disparaging snort from Kirby Garison.

Durrell's question was: "What I'm going to be when I grow up?"

Mario looked into the bright, black eyes fixed on his own. *Lucia* help me! Such prophecies are all too often unhappily self-fulfilling. "You will be a journalist," he predicted, thinking, for this at least he has already shown affinity. "A distinguished foreign correspondent."

Durrell took a deep breath. There came clapping and a chorus of approbation.

Mario responded to three more cards, using his information from next week's *Clarion*. His method was simple. He replied only to questions to which he knew or could easily guess the answers. He handed the other cards to Durrell, who placed them on the props table. Scott, nimble and bright-eyed, ran about with his microphone, squirming his way to whatever seat Mario designated. The custodian, at the offstage panel, smoothly switched the spotlight to white or pink or yellow or blue in response to Mario's cues.

The tenth card he selected was scribbled on both sides, and read, "Buster Culpepper, remember in Luigis? How about that junior fullback, remember."

"*Signor* Edward York," Mario said. "Row 7, Seat 14B. And *Signorino* Pepsi York. Please rise. Also Mr. Buster Culpepper in Row 11." When the three were on their feet, Scott wavered uncertainly between the two halves of the auditorium. Mario said, "*Non disturbate,* Scott, there is no need for these gentlemen to speak. I have read in the mind of each a wish, a desire that they can fulfill for one another."

"Football scout," a voice said.

"Staying in the Gilmore, too," said another, in tones of skepticism.

"Those who know Mr. Culpepper may already have guessed," Mario said smoothly, "what may happen if the *signori* and the *signorino* confer during the intermission period." Father and son exchanged glances and then nodded at Culpepper, who clasped his thick hands over his head in an affirmative shake.

"Understand, dear ladies and gentlemen," Mario said when the three had sat down again, "I cannot answer everyone. Time will not permit. We will continue with your cards during the second half of the program. But now before our *intermezzo,* I wish to demonstrate a little more of the marvels of mind reading." Resign yourselves, he thought: Many credulous hopes must be deferred. I have a duty as well to those who have come to see *uno spettacolo.*

"May I have the help of four of you for this noble experiment?" Hands went up. A few people stood. Two even started toward the aisle in their eagernesss. Mario signalled to Durrell and Scott. "I leave it to my able assistants to usher four volunteers to the stage. Make certain that I am not acquainted with any of them." He stepped into the wing while the selection was in progress. From his briefcase lining he took a device known to professional magicians and spiritualist mediums as a Tom Thumb: a tiny pencil of a color matching human skin. Mario affixed it to his thumb with matte transparent tape. He took a three-by-six blue memo pad, and holding it high, returned the stage.

Durrell and Scott, clearly enjoying their first taste of the pleasures of patronage, had chosen four boys of their own age. Intimates, Mario thought, swimming and fishing *compagni*. I must instruct my *ragazzi* to choose next time a more representative cross section.

"*Benvenuti, Signorini!*" He had them introduce themselves and assure the audience that he had had no previous contact with them. "I want you to think of an object which you feel I cannot guess." He signalled for a green spotlight at center stage. "I will ask each of you in turn to empty his mind of all else. Concentrate, visualize your object there in the emerald light... *Amici* of the audience, I ask that you too focus full attention on the spotlit area, and try to envision what each *signorino* has in mind. Who knows, there may be clairvoyants among you who will discover their powers tonight."

He received their flattered sigh. One youth raised his hand.

"You are ready. *Bene.*" Mario held up the long yellow pencil he kept on the podium, and then, with a flourish, wrote on the blue pad:

You are thinking of—

"*Cari amici,* I have just written here the object in question. Continue, *prego,* to concentrate on the lighted area, in the hope of your own revelation." He waited a beat, and then said: "Tell them, *ragazzo,* slowly and into the microphone, what it is."

"My uncle's twelve-gauge shotgun."

In concert with the spoken words, Mario's thumb, concealed by his fingers and the tilt of the podium, moved unseen on the pad. Instantly he tore off the page and handed it to the boy. "Please read this aloud."

"'You are thinking of a 12-gauge shotgun,'" the boy read out in an unbelieving whisper.

"Louder, please," said Mario; and the boy obliged.

The audience reacted with wondering awe. A woman's voice rang out: "I seen it. Lordy, I seen that gun right there in the green light!"

Mario held up his hand to stem the applause.

The fat boy among the volunteers, blushing, asked in a low voice, "Do we have to say right out front of everybody what we got in mind?"

Mario smiled and shook a reproving finger. "*Vergogna, giovanetto,* shame on you! This is a family show for the decent people of Floraville." The boy grew redder and hung his head, grinning. "I will not embarrass them by reporting your naughty thought. Select another object! And keep it clean."

Sniggers came from the audience, and a few mildly pornographic surmises, followed by scandalized reproofs. Mario turned to another volunteer. "I feel you are ready, *ragazzo mio*. Wait, wait! Give me time to write it down." Again he wrote with the long yellow pencil:

You are thinking of—

"My Randy Travis gui-tar pick," the boy blurted.

"Slowly and clearly please, into the microphone."

The third volunteer had chosen a slingshot drag racer. Whatever that may be, Mario thought, as his Tom Thumb followed the spoken words.

"Okay, Mister, I got a new one," said the chubby boy when the applause died down. His object turned out to be: Dairy Queen double hot fudge icecream sundae, which the thumb-pencil wrote as "...fudge icecream sundae."

This elicited lip-smacking noises and moans of mock starvation. They are getting hungry, Mario thought. Corn chips and soda pop await them in the lobby. Mario thanked the four boys, dismissed them graciously, and announced the intermission. Hungry or not, he told himself, this applause is *bastante* for at least four curtain calls. He glanced at his watch, shook his head, and signalled to Durrell.

The velvet curtain swung closed. Mario made a beeline for the lavatory. There he relieved himself and then washed hastily without disturbing his stage make-up.

Voices and approaching footsteps could be heard. Mario locked himself in a stall. From the two-by-three pads he removed the carbon papers and crumpled them into the toilet. Then he sat down and rapidly memorized what was duplicated, matching it with names and faces.

"Chewing tobacco."

"Speck of dust gets in your eye."

Several men were now in the lavatory, talking about the evening's entertainment. *Bene, eccellente!* It is when they discuss where to go after the performance that one needs to worry. Toilets flushed, water splashed. Mario eavesdropped as always, although he would not use any information picked up here. Too *rischioso*. Someone might remember his black-clad legs visible under the door of the stall.

"How you figure he gets into your mind?"

"Some folks just got the Gift. You remember old Blind Luther Vaughn?"

The next pad read: Can't think of a blessed thing. The next: Trip to Vegas. The last: I will lift up mine eyes - Psalm 121.

The second voice continued, "Could tell you if the baby'd be a boy or a girl."

Mario tore the pages with the writing into small pieces and dropped them into the toilet. He turned his attention to the three-by-fives.

"Hell's bells," said a third voice. "That ain't nothing. The doctors can do that."

"Sure, now they could. I'm talking back then."

Not everyone had written a question, and not every question was legible. Approximately a tenth of the cards had been handed in completely blank. Mario did not weed them out. His young assistants, faithful to his instructions, had fairly well preserved the sequence of collection. This made it possible to match a seat and a face to a blank card, which might at some point be useful.

A clear majority of the questions had to do with money: Should we buy. Should I sell. Could we afford. How much do I get when Granddaddy kicks the bucket? What's the number will win the Florida lottery? How we going to make it through next winter?

Questions concerning love and sex came second in number: Should you ought to tell a friend his wife is cheating on him? Will a certain somebody let me have a date? Is he lying when he says he loves me? Eileen Schuster of the visiting aunts had written: How come I never got married? Gwen McRae: What's a good way to get rid of freckles?

A fourth voice from the sinks said, "How 'bout that Cooper boy, got his mind already in the gutter. Whoo-ee!"

"Wonder what he was thinking."

"That Eye-talian mindreader, he sure knew."

They laughed salaciously, repeating some of the shouted surmises.

"Old Quentin, he yelled out, 'Teacher's tits!'"

"I like to died."

Mario folded down a corner of each card which bore a question he planned to answer if time allowed. These did not include the many asking about the rumored sale of the mill and resultant job anxiety. Too hot to handle, like inquiries about loved ones in the Middle East. He shook his head also at questions asking the whereabouts of missing husbands, or of lost or stolen possessions.

Stall doors banged lightly, booted and sneakered feet went past him. He was suddenly unheeding, staring at a card:

Where is Jerry Hapgood?

The two piles of three-by-fives nearly slid off his knee to the tiled floor; he rescued them automatically.

Demetria Owens, R.N., said the card. Row 3, Seat 6B. The slender soprano at the mill rally, he remembered through the pounding of his heart. Terry, Terry, where indeed? And I, Mario, strutting like a *pavone*, forgetting all about you. Depression came down on him for a moment, and a sense of helplessness. He sighed, and put the card in his breast pocket. He recalled then that it was this nurse's family who had played host to Deacon Howard on the night of Roy's death. We must have a word with *Infermiera* Demetria Owens, Beau Tyler and I, he promised himself.

He continued through the stack, his showman's mood returning as he came across some frivolous cards: Bet you can't guess what I ate for dinner.

Cora Danziger asked: When am I going to get rich? Hazel had written: Where will me and my sister live?

Mario remained in the toilet stall, working swiftly but unhurriedly, long after the lavatory was empty of people. Plenty of time before I am due onstage. He estimated that the mayor's opening remarks and those of at least one other dignitary, plus sundry announcements, would consume fully a third of the remaining hour. When he had earmarked about twelve of one hundred and fifty cards, he decided to stop. *Sufficiente,* far more than I will need. I must allot time for another demonstration. The blindfold routine? Would they swallow that hoary chestnut? He smiled. *Certamente,* they would.

He stood up, flexing numbness from the backs of his thighs, and thoroughly flushed away the little carbon papers and the torn-up pages. He hurried through the wide, windowed corridor toward the backstage entrance. Midway, he came to an abrupt halt. A man was standing outside one of the windows, his face and hands pressed against the pane.

It was Otis Feeney. Mario went quickly to the door at the end of the hall and opened it.

Otis approached him slowly. "Miz Hicks at the hotel, she say you was looking for me." His hazel eyes in the half-light were luminous as a cat's. His smooth face, the color of coffee with cream, was candid and innocent.

Mario stepped out into the night, holding the handle of the open door. He looked back along the cross passage leading to the stage. He could hear the sonorous amplified words of Mayor Sondergard, punctuated by coughs from the restive audience. "...so that our wonderful young people need not be exposed to the corruptions of these terrible times..."

"*Sì*, Otis," Mario said hastily, "you have a song, about Royal, dancing. Can you..."

"You like that song?" Otis interrupted, clearly pleased. "Want me to sing it for you?"

"Go 'way, go 'way
Auto—
Mobile!
This ain't no place to hide.
Pine trees they don't want you here.
You fright'ning these here pines."

The chanted melody was high-pitched, weird, sending a shiver along Mario's spine. "*Molto bella,* Otis," he said. "Are you sure it was yesterday you made it up?"

"Was maybe the day before," Otis said uncertainly.

"And now in conclusion," the mayor was saying, "I wish to thank you all for the record attendance and—"

I absolutely have to go in, Mario thought desperately. But first I must ask... "A car in a pine wood? Did you see it?"

Otis nodded. "Come sneaking in, squelching the mud."

Mario heard the mayor introducing the high school principal. Reprieved! he sighed to himself. At least *cinque minuti* more.

Otis was saying, "It hid in them blackberry bushes, under the branches. Pines didn't like it, bushes was scared."

With immense relief, Mario saw Reid Taliaferro, fresh cigar and lighter in hand, ambling toward them along the corridor. "Reid! *Provvidenziale!*"

"How do, Mr. Taliaferro," said Otis.

"Hey, Otis." Reid gestured toward the stage. "I couldn't take one more pomposity."

"Otis sang me a song," said Mario, "about a concealed car."

"Sing it again, Otis," Taliaferro said, very alert.

"Y'all really wants to hear it?" His slow smile was warm and humble. He closed his eyes and chanted the eerie lyric.

Taliaferro said, "Beautiful, Otis. Just beautiful... Go on in, Mario."

"I'll stay and chat with Otis," the editor continued. "We're old friends... Where'd you make up that song, Otis?"

"Y'all know them woods. Nigh to Roy's, I stays there a lot." Reid bit his unlit cigar and nodded. "Made my song just on sundown," Otis told him, "'bout an hour after that car creeped away."

Mario, having started for the stage, turned back. "Who was driving?"

"The minute he gets back here on the stage," the principal said, "let's ask Mr. Castigliani if..."

Mario threw up his hands, shook his head and started reluctantly along the cross passage. He heard Otis say, "Couldn't rightly see who driving, where I was;" and Taliaferro's casual voice suggesting, "Little old green car?"

Mario stood still, unable to resist hearing the answer to this.

"'Twasn't green. Pines wouldn'a felt so bad was it green."

Mario, now in the wing, squaring his shoulders and smoothing his hair for his entrance, heard Otis say, "That car white, like dead bones picked clean.

The greeting from the audience as Mario came jauntily onstage drowned out all else. He bowed at the footlights, letting the audience clap themselves out. He needed the time, to discipline himself, to switch roles and recover his performance poise. He shook hands with the mayor and the principal and saluted the two women seated near the props table. The school clerk, he told himself, with announcements. The Rotary *segretaria* reporting the take. I could have stayed with Otis ten whole minutes more. Asked him to sing the Royal dancing *canto* for Reid Taliaferro.

The mayor clapped Mario on the back and invited him to repeat his performance the following Saturday.

"I would like nothing better," Mario declared. "I can give you a firm answer by Monday."

During the announcements he wrote a brief message to Tyler, suggesting that he join Taliaferro and Otis Feeney; and took Demetria Owens's card from his breast pocket. He folded it around his note. When Scott delivered these, the police chief glanced at them and nodded at Mario, then spoke quickly in Bonnie's ear. He strode softly up the side aisle, and out of the auditorium.

The evening's receipts were announced as more than five thousand dollars. The audience applauded dutifully. Mario clapped with sincere fervor: fifty per cent was his, minus, of course, his agent's fee and expenses.

When at last he was alone at center stage, with Scott standing by in the wing and Durrell in the aisle, Mario held out his arms again to the audience. They were venting their feelings at release from captive boredom by clapping, with whistling and stamping from the schoolboy element. Renewed rapport was a strong stimulant in his veins.

First, *quattro questioni* from the cards, he told himself, while he held up a hand for silence. Next, the messages in the sealed brown envelopes; after that the blindfold *scherzo*. Then more cards, if time permits.

He saw that Buster Culpepper had risen and was signalling to him. "I have a 'nouncement!" he called to Mario, taking the stage steps in a stumbling run. His full-fleshed body jiggled in his boldly patterned clothes.

"Would you like to come up on the stage?" Mario asked resignedly.

"Yeah, well, if it's okay." Culpepper wiped his crimson brow with a wad of tissue as he entered the spotlight.

Mario laid the mike on the podium and stepped quickly to the footlights at stage left, distancing himself from the oversized man. He wanted to preserve the illusion of height.

"Y'all be interested to know," Culpepper said into the microphone, "that Mr. York and Pepsi and me has shook hands on a agreement. Pepsi gonna sign up with my alma mater, that's Peck College, finest school in the whole State of Georgia. Gonna put little old Peck on the map."

The audience clapped sporadically. They are *impazienti,* Mario thought, to get back to the thrills of the evening.

"Stand up, Pepsi!" Culpepper said. The tall magnificent youth, smiling, head down in embarrassment, drew longer applause: a football star was always a matter of keen local interest. "I got to tell y'all Mr. Castig-lioni here, he just plain *saw* it, *read* it, in my mind yesterday," Culpepper went on. "Read I was thinking Peck College got no more chance to sign up this here miracle fullback than a snowball in y'all know where. Creepiest thing I ever see. Didn't anybody tell Mr. Castiglioni, 'counta I didn't breathe one single word to him, nor a living soul. I wouldn't tell you no lie. This man here's the genu-wine article."

And so I was, *Lucia mia*, Mario thought with rue. "*Grazie, amico mio,*" he said over the applause, willingly suffering the Culpepper handshake as a small price for so handsome a public testimonial.

"And now, *Signor e Signori,*" Mario said gaily, "what is your pleasure? Shall we answer more of your questions, or attempt a new occult experiment?" Culpepper and Friedrich had returned to Row 11 and Mario noticed that the seat between them was vacant. Had Kirby Garison been made uneasy by Culpepper's endorsement? Had he preferred not to remain in the same room with "the genu-wine article?"

"You seem about equally divided," he told the audience. "May I have a show of hands? All those who wish a demonstration? *Bene.* Now those who wish me to continue with the cards." He did not bother to count the hands. "*Ah, sì,* the cards have it." He maneuvered Hazel Danziger's to the top of stack, and called out her name and seat number.

"*Buona sera*, my gracious friend of the Gilmore!" he greeted her, when she accepted the cordless mike. "You fear you are about to lose your long-time tenancy at the hotel."

"That is what's on my mind," Hazel said tremulously. "Reckon there's no hiding it from you… Where can we lay our heads, me and Cora?"

Cora jumped up and took the microphone from her sister. "Y'all don't worry 'bout us," she said, with toss of her elaborately coiffed head. Her gold hoop earrings flashed. She gave her sister a quick glare, then resumed her forced smile. "We'll be just fine and dandy, Hazel and me. Rolling in clover."

Mario gazed at her in dramatic silence. He reviewed his considerable information from his Thursday reading of the minds of the sisters, buttressed by the *Clarion* files. The father whose gambling had reduced them to genteel poverty. Cora's *fidanzamento* to an auto parts drummer in 1938, who had jilted her that same year. *Che peccato* that I cannot use any of this here. Not for the world would I so humiliate them.

"*Mie care vicine,*" he said, "do not rely on your current investment. And wait at least six months before you consider putting more of your savings into—"

"Hold it right there, Mr. Castigliani!" Ed Princeton had stepped into the aisle, a hand raised in warning. He needed no microphone. "If you are about to slander and denigrate the Tenfold Tabernacle," he proclaimed, advancing toward the stage, "you damn well better keep in mind that absolutely nothing has ever been proven against the Reverend Plenty."

"Thank you, Mr. Princeton," Mario interrupted sweetly, "for your no doubt disinterested advice. I ask you now to return to your seat." He locked eyes with the attorney, who at length gave in, and went grumbling up the aisle. "*Signorina Cora,*" Mario said then, "we must explore this subject further, you and your sister and I, in private session. Miss Hazel, put your mind at rest. Whatever the future ownership of the Gilmore, you may continue to live there as long as you choose."

He saw Beaufort Tyler coming down the side aisle, and exchanged nods with him. You and I, Mario thought, together we will see to it.

Interflow with the audience was now full and harmonious. Mario basked in their concentration. "*Signora* Ivy Potts, Row 7, Seat 2A." She and her husband rose together, clasping hands. "Mr. and Mrs. Potts," Mario said, holding aloft their cards, "are also disturbed by fears that they are about to lose their home."

"Farmed there 'most twenty year," said Baxter Potts. "Renting," his wife told Mario. "The house ain't fancy, but we raised our young'uns there."

Mario's eyes consulted Tyler, who flashed him a swift thumbs-up. "You need not seek another dwelling," he told the anxious couple. "You will not have to move away. A new landlord may purchase the property, *sì*, but the house can remain your home."

"And not raising the rent?" asked Mrs. Potts; and her husband said at the same time, "And we just go on growing the t'bacca?"

"Whatever he elects to plant, you will be welcome to assist with it, on terms *certamente* no less generous than your present arrangement."

He noted Tyler's happy grin, quickly suppressed. The auditorium was alive with low-voiced curiosity.

Mario held up another card, thus tacitly telling the Pottses to resume their seats. "We sure thank you," said the man, "and we sure to gosh hope you're right." Mrs. Potts said, "It's a real marvel, you seeing so clear what's to come."

Mario bowed toward them, and then said, allowing no time for applause, "For the next three cards, I will not mention names. One seeks cosmetic advice, one wishes to know why she never married. T o the seeker I will say: Bleaches and creams exist in plenty, but I would advise that you leave your face alone. *La Natura's* endowments become you well: Do not mask nor diminish them." He did not look directly at Gwen McRae, but saw in peripheral vision how she wiggled in her seat, and Kevin's mock slap against her cheek.

"To the unmarried *signorina,*" Mario resumed, "a reminder that uncompromising selectivity exacts its price. Whether or not a suitor worthy of you should appear, you can be proud of your lofty standards." He kept his eyes on the ceiling at the rear of the auditorium, but was aware of the gratification on Eileen Schuster's long, equine face.

"To the third person…" He held up a blank card. "You will know I am addressing you. *Non disturbate.* Your secret is safe with me." Almost everyone in the audience, he knew, would assume he was speaking to him or her. "I sympathize," he continued compassionately, "and suggest a private consultation."

Many grateful eyes sought his own.

"But wait, *amici!*" he cried, stepping from the podium, hands clasped to his temples. *"Un minuto!* My Muse is speaking." He came to the edge of the stage, and said, very low: "The words in the brown envelopes."

The audience voiced their excitement, then were quiet in anticipation. Mario called the names of the five who had written on the pads, and asked them to stand. Durrell offered the microphone as the baton indicated.

Mario recited each sealed message exactly as worded. *"Allora* open your envelope and read aloud what you wrote." "Can't think of a blessed thing," drew a few laughs, but the mood of thrilled astonishment prevailed. When the last wondering, reverent voice had faltered away, silence gripped the assembly. Then the applause came at Mario, its impact pushing him back from the footlights.

"*Grazie!* Thank you!" he shouted as the clapping peaked. "But save your generous appreciation for later. We still have time for one demonstration, if that is your wish!"

"Ya-hoo!

"Whoo-ee!"

"Let's do it!"

"For this, I must be blindfolded, and once again I will need volunteers." A dozen hands shot up. "I leave it to Durrell to designate two people, neither of whom are known to me." He waited through the good-humored competitive flurry of the selection.

"Please stand, but remain at your seats," Mario instructed the chosen five. "*Ah. Bene.*" He waved his baton at a woman with curls of an improbable yellow, wearing a T-shirt which read, "Hug me, I'm Irish!" and then at the tall rotund Pennington chauffeur. He signalled them to come to the stage. "Please introduce yourselves."

"Nell McCourt. I work at the Dewey Dry Cleaning, reckon y'all know me."

"Huey Ogden, folks call me Cordene. I drive for Miz Pennington."

"Have I met or spoken with either of you before this moment?"

"No, sir, you ain't," said Cordene.

The woman shook her shining curls emphatically.

"Do you have a quarter? Each of you?" When they had given him the coins, he placed them firmly on his closed eyelids. "*Prego, Signor* Cordene, keep them there… Would you say I can open my eyes?"

"No, sir, not even a peek. Long's I holding these."

"*Signorina* McCourt, on the table behind me you will find a black blindfold. Please tie it firmly so that the quarters cannot move or shift." When they had satisfied themselves and the audience that he could not see, he asked them to remain onstage. "I would like you to monitor the demonstration," he said, "so there is no possibility of chicanery." He turned his back to the audience and spoke into the microphone. "Now, the three who are so graciously waiting: I ask that each of you bring to the stage an object, something you choose, from pocket or purse or from anywhere you wish. Select something truly difficult to guess… I have turned my back to make assurance doubly sure that I cannot be aware of your selections."

Low-pitched exchanges punctuated by ribald suggestions reached him from the fascinated audience. He raised and lowered his eyebrows vigorously, so that the blindfold moved imperceptibly higher. The weight of the coins falling forward against the cloth created narrow spaces, undetectable at a six-inch distance, through which he could clearly see.

"Durrell, *prego,* take the stool from the head of the table and place it near the footlights at the center of the stage... Jimmy, a white spotlight on the stool, please."

"We all ready, Mister Magic Man," said a boy's voice at his elbow.

"Ah, bene!" Mario turned, almost but not quite facing the speaker, in the manner of the blind. "Your name?"

"I'm Hoagy Petticord."

"Related to Officer Bobbie Lee Petticord of the Floraville police?"

"Naw."

"I am relieved to hear it," Mario said, "as I am acquainted with Officer Petticord, and would therefore have had to disqualify you... *Molto bene.* Please hold up your chosen object so the whole audience can see it." A rustle of laughter went through the auditorium. "Now place it on the stool in full view."

"Fresh Worms," read the legend on the cardboard container. "Mandy's Bait and Tackle, 19 Arrowhead Street."

"Concentrate, *Signorino* Hoagy. Clear your mind of all but what is before you on the stool." He paused in the whispering silence, then shook a reproving finger in the general direction of the boy. *"Prego,* do not attempt to distract me, *ragazzo!* Open your mind to me... Ah, that is better. You have chosen... something to eat."

Derisive laughter and crude comic sounds of disgust came from the audience.

"Naw, sir, wouldn't want to eat that."

"But fish would want to," Mario said. He waved toward the stool. "A container of worms."

He let the applause die away before he turned in the general direction of the next volunteer. He could see just enough of her to tell him that she was young and shapely. She had removed one sandal and was taking off her stocking. Muffled giggles came from the audience.

"Ahi, dear Madame!" Mario ventured boldly. "I would not dare reveal to these good folk what you are thinking!"

Loud laughter, in which she joined. A rebel yell. Mario milked every drop of innuendo from the situation. When he announced, "*Una calza di nailon,* sheer as gossamer, to grace a lovely limb," he groped for the stocking and pressed it to his lips.

The audience loved it. On the thunder of applause Mario whipped the blindfold from his eyes, and tossed the coins to their owners. Phil's camera flashed. Mario bowed, and signalled the custodian to black out the stage and house. When the lights came up again, the stool and podium had been pushed back, and Mario and the four volunteers stood in a row before the footlights. "Bow!" he told them. "You are stars, all of you!" I have time for one quick curtain call, Mario decided, glancing at his watch, with Durrell and Scott. Another one solo, then cut them off, and give them two more three-by-fives for an encore. *L'aristocrazia* will forgive me if I arrive at the reception a little late.

He never got to the encore. When the curtain parted for his solo bow, he saw Claudia Pennington at the rear of the auditorium, on the left side of the aisle, tall, and slender as a wand. A necklace of dull gold, antique-looking, perhaps Etruscan, defined her long ivory throat. Her fringed, tilted eyes gazed directly into his.

The curtain swung closed, then opened again to undiminished applause. He signed to Scott to leave it open, and raised a hand for silence. His eyes met and questioned hers, and it seemed to him that the room full of people ceased to exist, that nothing and no one lay between them. How to reach her, how to speak with her, he wondered. She will be at the reception, he told himself. But what if she is not? He looked quickly at Tyler, who now had one arm around Myrtle's boy, the other around his sister, and was evidently absorbed in answering the questions with which they were plying him.

"One moment, good friends!" Mario called. "There is a message, I have a messsage, for someone... whose name my Muse does not reveal." I dare not say it in English. Born here, will she know the adage in Italian? Will she remember her words of my vision, her words to Beaufort Tyler?

Mario waited until the room was still.

"Una rondine non fa primavera," he said, low and distinctly.

One swallow does not make springtime. Claudia's wide eyes widened, searching his own. She has understood, and remembered, Mario told himself. He was dimly cognizant of the stir in the audience, that people were craning, trying to locate the recipient of the mysterious message. Someone exclaimed goodnaturedly, "No fair! Speak American!" and another chided gently, "What's that mean?" Others, high-spirited and garrulous in reaction to the performance, were moving about, preparing to take their reluctant leave.

Mario, now on tiptoe, could not take his eyes from her. The masked oval of her face altered, became expressive. Disbelief was followed by wonderment; then deep respect; and then something more, so naked in its candor that it shot through to his very nerve ends.

Then with a swirl of skirt, Claudia turned and was gone.

XX

The gym had been decorated with multicolored paper streamers for the reception. The huge gold-fringed blue Rotary banner hung behind the platform. On stage, the Barnstormers, a bluegrass group, twanged lustily. Duane Potts, the band leader, flailed his banjo and sang, half slyly ironic, half deadly earnest.

A buffet, featuring dips, seafood salads, and biscuits in silver warmers, was laid out under a basketball hoop on a long table with a white linen cloth. Cordene, who had donned a white jacket, alternated between the great silver punchbowl and the coffee service.

Tyler and Taliaferro were at a table near the entrance, talking low with heads close together. The police chief, on the edge of his chair, downed a cup of coffee. One booted foot was out toward the door, at which he glanced frequently.

They were waiting for Mario.

Mario, stood behind the desk in the principal's office, his briefcase before him. He was still bewitched and bemused by his encounter with Claudia Pennington. Usually after performing he needed no more than ten minutes to remove his makeup, reorganize his props and devices, and glance through the contents of the slotted boxes. Tonight, taking grateful advantage of the offer of a place where he could be alone, he had remained for uncounted moments at the sink in the principal's bathroom, staring unseeingly into his own eyes.

Working hurriedly now, he emptied and collapsed the boxes. Over forty requests for private readings, which could add up to another five or six hundred dollars. *Un opulento* harvest for this unpromising little town. There were also a few cards praising the performance: Your show really kicked ass. Blew my mind.

He was about to toss the flattened boxes into the briefcase and hasten to the gymnasium when a knock sounded at the office door.

"Avanti!"

Durrell and Scott, plainly nervous, came up to him.

"The ticket lady, she say you want to see us," Durrell said.

Mario handed them the pink-wrapped gifts. *"Sì, ragazzi. Molte grazie* for your superb help tonight."

"Happy Easter?" Scott said with bewilderment. They unwrapped the presents and took out the toys. "The Bigfoot! Hey, Mr. Castig-lian! Did you read it in my mind?"

"You oughtn'ta done it," said the equally delighted Durrell. "Hey, Scott, looka mine. Ultra-Racer!"

"If I perform again next Saturday," Mario said, putting the slotted boxes into the briefcase, "would you be available to assist me?"

"Yo! We be there!" Durrell said; but Scott squirmed his shoulders and kicked at the floor. "If my daddy'll let me… Listen, Mr. Castig-lian." His eyes consulted Durrell, who nodded. "Some of them boys, they didn't pay no ten dollars."

"We snuck 'em in," Durrell added apologetically.

"Quite all right," Mario reassured them. The lobby box, he realized, was not empty. He felt the weight of a small object in it. His heart leapt with a wild sudden surmise. *"I giovannetti* were an invaluable addition to the audience," he went on unsteadily. *"E allora, scappate!* Shoo! I must join the Mayor and his guests."

"Race ya," Durrell challenged, as the boys left the office.

Mario waited until he could no longer hear the sounds of the radio-controlled race. Then he held the lobby box upside down and shook it. A business card with a key taped to its back clattered to the desk. Claudia Pennington, Tremont Studio, said the card. The address and phone number were printed on it. "After midnight," was written in ink in a small strong handwriting.

Mario, a hand to his pulsing throat, closed his eyes for a moment. He fancied that the card he was holding grew to playing-card size. *Tre Regine,* I had, that time *la Lucia* left me. She herself, the Queen of Diamonds. The Spade Queen, *mia madre.* Oriana of *Fiori,* Clubs in English. And now a quarter of a century after, the Queen of Hearts.

Tyler was waiting in the corridor when Mario at last came hurrying toward the gym. *"Scusi,* I am sorry to be late."

"I haven't got but a minute. I'm heading over to Blue Heaven to check for tire tracks in the pine woods."

"And you want me to accompany you." But I cannot, I must not, *a mezzanotte* I must — Mario broke off his own thought, remembering with a pang that his midnight tryst was with Tyler's beloved.

"No, we need you here, with your ears on. Pick up anything you can, 'specially from the Valhalla set. Appears to me you got all your powers back?"

Mario shrugged noncommittally.

"Certainly looked like you did, up on that stage." *Traditore,* Mario called himself, his thoughts still on Claudia; betrayer of friendship. Tyler was saying, "Never mind. You got good ears and a good nose."

From the gymnasium, applause for the Barnstormers could be heard, and a few shouted requests for favorite songs. "Do you have news of Terry Hapgood?" Mario asked.

"Nothing. Otis, he has a song about him, but it's way old. That one about Roy, though—"

"Ah, sì, has Otis told what it was he witnessed?"

"No, we need a lot more time questioning him. Slow and gentle. I got him in the holding cell." He held up a hand to quell Mario's protest. "He don't mind, he'd do any goddam thing for me. Can't have him meandering off.... Preliminary reports came in on the autopsies, Mario. Looks like Earl mighta died from strangling *before* he was strung up. Nothing much on the other two bodies until the extended tox screen."

Reid Taliaferro came out of the gymnasium. "Mario! Did you fall in? Will you haul your ass in there?"

"Okay," said Tyler. He took a few steps toward the exit, then turned and said, "If y'all aren't too wore out when this is over, join me if you can. Stationhouse'll tell you where."

Mario and Taliaferro entered to a white flash from Phil's camera. The musicians, striking up a new number, broke off and switched to "For He's a Jolly Good Fellow." Many joined in. Mario bowed. He quickly scanned the faces of the guests. She is not here, he thought. Will she come? Or has she gone to wait for me, to count *i minuti* until midnight?

Mario was seated between two empty chairs. Across the one on his left, he asked Dr. Donlan, "And your charming wife, is she not coming?"

"Ah! You have met. Charming she is, but punctuality is not one of her charms," Donlan said lightly. *Il dottore* looks even more *bello,* Mario thought, in his tuxedo and blue cummerbund. Donlan's hair under the ceiling cone light was a burnished gold. "Let's expect her when we see her."

The high school principal was droning on, with frequent references to the night's performance. Mario bowed mechanically each time he was mentioned, one eye on his watch. Ten-fifty. At eleven forty-five, I make my escape, even if I must stage an epileptic seizure to do so.

Dr. Donlan was speaking, pledging the support of the medical community for the Youth Center..

The mayor had resumed his seat. With a speculative frown, he was eyeing Violet Sondergard's cutlery. She smiled at him tremulously, talking with unconvincing animation too low for Mario to hear her words.

Mayor Sondergard reached to take his wife's beaded evening bag from her lap. She held on to it, with a little laugh, but he removed her hands. Mario saw him slip something from the bag under the table edge, and place it before him, covered by his hand.

Mayor Sondergard leaned forward and said to Mario heartily, "We're hoping you'll honor us with a few words after our musical interlude." He put his arm around Violet's shoulders. Her thin body contracted, but she did not resist the embrace. She turned her fixed smile on Mario. "Oh, yes!" she said. "We're right eager."

"A very few words then," Mario told them graciously, "since I am sure we are all rather tired."

The object from Violet's evening bag, now revealed on the table, was a silver butter knife.

In the school patio, deep shadow alternated with parallelograms of light from the corridor windows. The air, muggy and warm after the cool of the interior, smelled of tobacco smoke. Fireflies winked. Cigarette ends glowed from the dozen or more smokers who sat grouped by twos and threes at the trestle tables.

Mario and Taliaferro leaned against an unoccupied table at a corner of the patio. High on the outer wall, a screened cylinder gave forth a violet glow. "Bug zapper," Reid said, waving at it. He lit up, and said around his cigar, "Did you twig the mayor and the silverware?"

"*Sì*, what was that about?" Mario was tempted to ask, Do you know why Claudia Pennington is not here tonight? He had a need to speak her name, to hear Taliaferro talk about her. He swallowed hard, suppressing the impulse. *Questo uomo* is too clever, he may guess what is going on.

"She's a kleptomaniac, Vi Sondergard. Last reception, she stole the speaker's gavel."

"I want to fill you in," Reid was saying. "There's patches of pine woods all over Blue Heaven. Only one big enough to hide a car is right behind Roy's house."

"But the car could not have been Terry's, if Otis reports correctly."

"Certain as Satan, Otis always tells the truth. Pity Beau can't use him on the witness stand."

They could hear murmurs of conversation from the other smokers, and the *bzzt, bzzt* of insects electrocuted against the violet-lit mesh. Reid said, "Trouble is, like half the cars in this town are white."

"Ubiquitous hue," a voice said out of the shadows. "Or absence of hue, to be precise." Jeff Pennington had come up behind them unobserved, followed by Dr. Donlan. Jeff went on, "I drive a white car myself."

"And so do I," said Donlan.

"Although the manufacturers call it sand color."

"Question is," said Donlan jocularly, "why is it a trouble that cars are white…?"

Reid said, "*The Clarion's* way overdue for a new station wagon. I kinda fancy white, but —"

"I understand," said Donlan, lighting his pipe. "You don't want to get lost in the crowd."

"All cats are black in the dark." Dr. Pennington lit a brown cigarette and offered one to Mario. "That is your saying, no?"

"Grey," Donlan corrected him.

"Grey's not a bad idea," Taliaferro mused. "With red lettering."

"But you come out to smoke, and you are not smoking?" Pennington asked.

"Quite stupidly," Mario lied, "I left my cigarettes in my briefcase."

Pennington held out a silver cigarette case. "English Oval?" Donlan proffered an iridescent box filled with gold-tipped cigarettes in vivid colors.

"Sobranies!" Mario exclaimed. "A dear old friend of mine used to smoke these!"

"Help yourself," said Donlan. Mario lit up from Pennington's lighter, as a gesture in memory of Willie in Vienna, but only pretended to smoke.

"You should go back in," Donlan told Mario. "Have either of you found out where Terry Hapgood disappeared to? He's got the whole hospital in an uproar."

"Beau Tyler'll find him," Reid assured them. "He's got half the force on it."

Talliaferro and Mario slipped back to their tables.

Anne-Marie had arrived, and was sitting stiffly erect in the chair between Mario's and her husband's. Her blue linen evening gown, of uncharacteristically modest cut, was rumpled and creased. She stared straight ahead, glassy-eyed. Her honey-blonde curls were matted, her cheeks tear-stained. An untouched plate of seafood salad was before her.

Eunice Pennington, four seats away at the head of the table, seemed simultaneously to be smiling and glaring at the musicians. Her lips were compressed. Red spots had appeared on the pallor of her square face.

Mario saluted Anne-Marie as he sat down. She did not turn her head, nor did she respond to Donlan's connubial and sympathetic caress.

Anne-Marie smelled strongly of alcohol. *Sbronza, ubriaca,* Mario thought, drunk as a skunk. Immediately Terry Hapgood flashed to his mind. According to Taliaferro, she was in love with Terry. Was her sorry state *una riflessione* of anxiety? Of mourning?

Her large bloodshot blue eyes were now on him. He leaned closer into the fumes and heard her saying. "…stood you up. So awful sorry, sorry as I can be. Got stood up myself, y'all understand."

Anne-Marie was wagging a finger at the empty chair on the other side of Mario. She bent forward to talk across him. "Where the hell's Claudia?" she demanded of Pennington, loudly and clearly. Her brother's face was study in controlled exasperation. He frowned at her and put a finger to his lips.

Mario, with a rush of blood to his head, looked at his wrist: 12:02. Claudia stands at the window of her unlighted studio, he silently replied. She has twitched aside the curtain and is scanning *la strada*. Or she paces, barefoot.

Eunice Pennington had come quickly behind Anne-Marie and was hissing reprimands into her ear. "Momma! Please, Momma, don't yell at me, help me, Momma, I feel so rotten!" Anne-Marie sobbed. Donlan patted her hand.

Another stir disrupted the atmosphere. Kevin Petticord, his thin young face tense with urgency, was hurrying toward the speakers' table. "Dr. Donlan!" he said. The doctor jumped up. Kevin spoke to him low and rapidly. Mario overheard: Accident. Ambulance. Valhalla. Randy Funderburk.

Anne-Marie, slumping now, held upright by her mother's grip on her shoulders, had apparently heard the name, too. "Handy Thunderstruck," she was murmuring. "Candy Blunderbuck. Dandy Wonder—" Eunice clapped both hands over her daughter's mouth. Anne-Marie pulled the hands away and fell forward, her face landing in the plate of salad.

She does not yet realize, *poverina Signora* Donlan, Mario thought, that her amato has been in an accident. Accident? Or perhaps…

Taliaferro and Phil were already hastening in Donlan's wake toward the exit.

Mario got up, and went closer to them. "Burnt to a crisp," he heard Kevin say.

Duane said into the mike, "Folks, there's been a highway accident. I gotta go back on duty." He shook his head at the surge of questions. "That's all I could tell you right now."

Mayor Sondergard stepped up on the platform. "Let us hope no one was hurt," he began, as Duane and Kevin made their way to the exit.

Many of the guests were now on their feet, some coming towards the platform. Tonda and Cordene were rapidly clearing the buffet table. Odessa was supporting Anne-Marie, leading her through the maze of tables toward the door. Eunice had resumed her seat.

The big round clock on the gymnasium wall said 12:10. *Basta,* Mario resolved, I will keep her waiting no longer. He mounted the platform. "May I?" he asked Sondergard, taking the mike. The mayor nodded, plainly relieved.

The guests were still restive, some speculating aloud about the accident, others reacting with sly relish or righteous disapproval to the drunkenness of Anne-Marie. But most of them greeted Mario with applause.

"Cari Signori, amici," he called out to silence them. "The hour is late, I know you are eager to return to your homes. I have been asked to address you, and offer you now the kind of speech everyone most enjoys: That is, a very brief one."

He smiled and bowed in response to their approbation, then quickly went on, "Merely will I express my gratification and profound thanks, to you and all the people of Floraville, for the warm welcome you have given me. This is not *Addio,* but *Arrivederci,* not Goodbye but See you soon. For I hope next week to perform here again, in the service of so worthy a cause."

Mario bowed in all directions, then handed the mike back to Mayor Sondergard, and went quickly to the door. He turned to face them, politely fending off the inevitable petitioners descending on him. Mario firmly evaded their eyes as he backed out, bowing, into the hall.

E allora, Claudia, io vado, cara mia. Three strides to the office, to retrieve my briefcase, and I, Mario, am on my way.

XXI

The walk through the high school playing fields and the road that divided the cemetery took only a few minutes. There was an intoxicating scent from the bushes starred with trumpet-shaped blossoms, which Mario recognized as belladonna.

The town hall clock bonged the single stroke of the half hour. Across the street he could see the Reliable Feed Emporium with its sagging awning. Her block. The studio block. What am I doing? he asked himself, suddenly stock still under the street lamp. The shrilling, chirping, droning rhythms of the summer night encompassed him. He put his briefcase down, took off his jacket and absently flapped at the mosquitoes zeroing in on him. *Dove vado?* Where am I going? and, How dare I?

Beaufort Tyler will be at the scene of *l'accidente* now, expecting me, hoping I will come to help him. That is where I should be, my clear duty. But the recollection of Claudia, gliding rapidly, black-clad, around the opposite corner, was not to be denied.

He crossed, and in the side street found the number above a locked entrance between the yarn shop and Herman's Shoe Repair. The key turned easily. Stairs led up to a white door decorated with silhouettes of ballerinas. Unlocked. Inside all was cool and quiet, the stillness emphasized by the hum of air conditioners. Unlit, except for lamplight coming from a door ajar at the other side of the studio. A twin door on the far side was shut. As his eyes adjusted, Mario was startled to see a man in evening dress, a briefcase in hand, staring at him. In an instant he realized it was himself: the wall opposite was a mirror, with a barre running its length.

The loft was big, covering at least three of the small stores below, and bare except for a grand piano, a coat rack and two stacks of folding chairs. The floor was a satiny expanse of polished wood. Four outsized cartons were piled near the floor-to-ceiling curtains which covered the plate glass overlooking the street. The uppermost carton was open, spilling forth a froth of pale tutus. White soundproofing covered the other two walls, which bore larger-than-life photographs of dancers.

"Take off your shoes." The contralto voice with its violin tone thrilled through him, rekindling desire. "And lock the door." He obeyed, dizzy as he bent to place his evening pumps beside her silver sandals and his briefcase. He turned the lock and moved over the shining floor to the source of light.

Claudia was supine on the maroon coverlet of a narrow bed, in a room austere as a cell in a convent. A bracketed wall lamp shed indirect light on her slender body, and on a glass desk. A straight chair, a row of bookshelves. A silver-grey skirt was slung over the chairback. She wore only her leotard. Silken black hair lay in waves on the pillow; her arms were crossed over her chest. Like Giselle onstage, Mario thought. Like one who sleeps with eyes wide open. Or one laid out for burial.

He approached, his feet sinking into deep carpeting, and settled tentatively on the edge of the bed. Apologies for his tardiness rose to his lips, but she put her long fingers over his mouth and came upright, clutching him in a fierce embrace. "Don't talk," she commanded. "Hold me."

They kissed; or rather, it was Claudia who kissed him, long and hard. *"Dio mio,"* he exclaimed.

Claudia wriggled out of her leotard, and pulled at his T-shirt.

Her spare body gleamed in the lamp light. Diffidence and a rare humility cooled his blood when he stood naked before her. Shorter than thou, *panciuto,* greying hair on my chest, stubble on my chin, and *il sudore* of performing still on me. "Whatever do you see in me, *bellissima?"* he said. "I am old enough to be your father."

"You are splendid," Claudia said, pulling him down to her. "You are what I want, just what I want." She groped past him and switched off the lamp.

Claudia dominated, moaning and gasping, her articulate hands everywhere on him. Mario came too soon to his climax, and all his patient efforts could not bring her to hers. She turned from him, racked by dry sobs, fists beating the pillow.

"It's no goddam good," her muffled voice told him. "I'm no good, I can't."

He thought of her as she would have looked when she was fifteen, *violata* and in shock. And of the many who used her after that, before she was a woman grown. "How long has it been, *mia Regina* of Hearts, since you have lain with *un amato?*"

"Speak English," she said.

"I have a daughter, older than you, who still demands of me, Speak English."

"I used to say it all the time, to my parents and my *nonna*. Mamma, speak English! *Papà!* *In nome di Dio,* willya for God's sake talk English?... What's your daughter's name, where is she?"

"Laura," he replied. "Lauren, *davvero*. She's in New York."

"And who is Oriana?" He rose on one elbow, staring at her. "You said her name," Claudia told him.

"My wife," Mario said. "My first and only *vera amorosa*. She died."

"In one way," Claudia said after a silence, "it may be better that you lost her when you did."

"*Sì, sì,*" he concurred, "our marriage was headed for *il disastro*... But you have not answered *la mia domanda*: How long, without a lover?"

"Years. Six, seven. Not since New York."

"The affair broke up when you injured your knee?"

"The doctors said I'd never dance again. Funny how fast the lovers and friends vanished when they got the news."

"But you are dancing. You teach dancing."

"Not like before. Never again like before."

"And you are married. In name only, as the saying goes?"

"You know too much," Claudia said. She sat up and turned on the light. A strand of hair waved glistening down her brow and cheek. Her beauty was so absolute that he caught his breath, and reached for her. "How do you know?" asked her violin voice in his arms. "Are you a real clairvoyant?"

"Some of the time, *O Donna della Rondine*... That lone swallow, was it a kiss?"

"Yes," said Claudia, barely audible. "One kiss." The name of

Beaufort Tyler lay heavy and unspoken between them. She rose, went to slide open a closet door, and took out a short white terry bathrobe. "I'm going to shower," she said. "Care to join me?"

"I will wait." Mario was humble again, self-conscious. My middle-aged *corpo*, he thought. "I will shower after you."

"And shave." She came to run her fingers over his chin.

"Ah! I have reddened your exquisite skin."

While she was gone, he put on his boxer shorts and prowled the room. Three doors, he discovered: the one through which he had entered; the one from which shower sounds emanated, with a line of light at floor level; and another beyond it, which he opened. A kitchen-ette: efficient, shining clean, tidy as a ship's galley.

Turning back to the bedroom, he saw that there was a small window in the opposite wall, with tubular curtaining in grey damask as in the main studio. He pushed a fold of curtain back, and found himself looking down on a row of yards, some with vegetable gardens, dimly illumined by the street lamps on Main Street. He caught a glimpse of the Flint River two blocks away, black and gleaming as Claudia's hair.

He fetched his shoes and briefcase from the main door, and took out his shaving kit. When he went in his turn to the bright little bath-room, he saw that it connected to another room. He tried the door-knob. Not locked. The room was in sharp contrast to Claudia's: color-ful feminine clothing strewn everywhere, on the green satin sheets of an unmade king-sized bed; on the carpet and chairs; tumbling out of open drawers. A jumble of jewelry and cosmetics was strewn on the mirrored dressing table.

Mario returned to Claudia clean and smooth-chinned, his curls tight and wet from the shower. She was on the edge of the bed, bent forward, toweling her hair. A faint fresh odor of soap emanated from her, accenting her natural fragrance. Lamplight flowed over the ivory of her back and shoulders and reflected from her slim thighs. Long-muscled, sculpturesque, she was, *l'artonia* of her skeleton visible through the delicate veil of flesh. Not an ounce to spare, Mario thought. Yet there was *un accenno* of roundness, *sì,* the Etruscan look.

"Lie back," he commanded, taking the towel from her hand. He knelt to examine her right knee, and found the faded surgical stitches. He kissed the knee and held it briefly to his bosom. Then he stood to contemplate her, his large hands cupping her loins. "You have never borne children," he said.

"Can't," Claudia answered. "I'm no good that way either."

Lying on her back, with arms crossed above her on the rich scatter of hair, she was flat-chested as a boy. "One could wash clothes on your ribs," he teased her gravely. "We must feed you up, with *tortellini* and cream *pasticceria.*"

"No such thing as too thin, you know the saying."

"I am a European," he said. "I prefer curves and a touch of *dolcezza,* softness."

"Was she very beautiful, your Oriana?" she asked in a small voice.

"Not more beautiful than you. You are remarkably like her, an elongated she."

He got in beside her. When they came together in a kiss, he loosed the strong clutch of her hands and arms. "No, no," he murmured, "*rallenta, cara mia. Dolcemente*, gently, *teneramente*... There! Isn't that better?"

This time there was no mistaking Claudia's climax. Its intensity and duration were almost frightening. Mario rocked her, with wordless sounds of love. "I'm shattered," she said at last. "Gloriously shattered."

"Surely not for the first time?"

"There's been a few. Never like this."

"But you are starving," he exclaimed.

"Yes. I am starving. When do you go back to New York?"

"I think I will be here at least one more week."

"Take me with you."

Happiness, sudden as a blow, overcame him. *Mia perduta,* has she come back to me? In this Modigliani guise, now a woman of culture, sophistication. *Lucia, Venere, Luna*, do you offer me a second chance?

"I hate my life," Claudia was saying. "There's nothing here, nothing I wouldn't leave in a minute."

The surge of pure joy in his breast subsided and drained away. *"No, bella mia.* It is not to be," he said. "We have but this one night only."

"You are with someone, in New York?".

"*Sì,* I have *un' amata,*" he lied, thinking, That is the simplest way.

She rose, turned on the lamp, sat by him and ran her fingers through his hair. "At least I've had this," she said with a sigh. "I'm forever grateful." Tears suddenly overflowed the tilted dark eyes. "What will become of me?"

"You will escape from this evil marriage," he said lightly, stroking the tears from her face, "and marry another. One who loves you."

Her finger made circles down his chest, as though counting buttons. "Rich man, poor man, beggarman, thief; Doctor, lawyer…"

"None of these," he interrupted.

"Then tell me, O great Castigliani, who will it be?"

"You will marry a farmer. Six months of each *anno* you will live with him, close to *la terra*. Six months you will be in the cities of the world."

"Like Persephone," she mused. "I danced Eurydice, in 'Orpheus' at Jacob's Pillow."

"You will found the renowned Tremonte School of the Dance."

"Tremont. Oh, all right, Tremonte."

He slept in the light and woke in the dark to hear her saying, "…and I cried, Mario, do you realize I cried? Wet tears! I haven't been able to cry since…" She spoke haltingly, and then in a bitter spate of words, telling of the rape she had undergone. The masters, the young lords. "In their fine clothes and fast cars. And me, outside looking in, way down on the Floraville totem pole. Oh, how I'd admired them, before they did it to me." The scalding shame, her family silently blaming her. Her internal injuries, the abortion that left her barren. "They trashed me. When you get trashed, you turn into trash. I've never talked like this, Mario, never told anybody."

They had drifted into the kitchenette, and sat side by side, partially clothed, at the counter. They drank apple juice and crunched English biscuits spread with almond butter. He asked her, "Was Jefferson Pennington one of them?"

She laughed shortly. "Oh, he was there. They were all there, the Valhalla set. Jeff didn't make it with me. I thought then it was some kind of gallantry."

"And discovered later," Mario said, "that he was not responsive to women?"

"Marry me, I told him when I came back from New York, and I

290

won't tell your momma on you… Don't look at me like that, Mario."

"Blackmail," he said. *"Estorsione."*

"Roy used to say, Royal Washington, 'We all draw a line. Honor, integrity, self-respect, that's when you won't go below your line.' He was so wise, Mario, so wonderful and profound. I can't believe he's dead." She blew her nose on a paper napkin. "Roy said, 'The line's different, different times in your life. Goes higher, goes lower. Different, too, for different folks.'"

"And you went below your line, when you used Jeff Pennington," he said.

"Yes. But I had to. I had to get back at this town, or curl up and die… The kingpin of Cullowee County no less, and nobody knows he's just a turkey on a string." She furiously polished her knife on a napkin. "His mother runs him, A.J. runs him, I run him."

"Povero bastardo."

"Don't waste your compassion. Jeff's just as mean and scheming as I am… Mario, what about Roy? Do you think he was murdered?"

He told her a little, choosing his words, evasive while seemingly candid.

"But you can read minds," she demurred.

"Not always. Thus far, *la potenza* has not been of much help. Claudia. Do you know about Terry Hapgood?"

"That he's gay? That he's starving like I am? He lives where I live, he and his mother, in the cottage on the grounds. We're friends, but our paths don't cross often."

"That he's missing."

"Oh. I think it was just that he didn't show up for a patient, or something like that. Although the police came to the house." She kept her eyes down. Beau Tyler came there, Mario thought. She will not say his name. "I kept out of the way," she went on. "They upset Fanny, his mother, you know."

Mario shook himself, resisting the gnawing of concern. He switched subjects, reporting with charm and light irony the events of the reception. He said nothing concerning the accident or Randy Funderburk.

"Poor old Vi," Claudia said when he told her about the butter knife. "We used to be close. Anne-Marie and Violet and me. We thumbed our nose at this town, before she got so sick..." Claudia drew her index finger along his chest. "If, to quote you, we have this one night, hadn't we better make the most of it? Let's go back to bed."

Although he was surprised and gratified by the ready response of his body, Mario teased with mock regret, "You flatter me. I am no longer in the first flush of youth."

In her arms, the bed was *il mondo,* the room was the universe. Lamplight shed its pale gold. The desktop sparkled, a lake of glass beyond the curve of her shoulder. From the unlit bathroom with door ajar, gleams reflected from enamel as from sculpted limbs. Caresses and murmured talk, sleep and *conversazione* and embraces. Time flowed free of constrictions: hours stretched endless, or flew by like minutes.

When they heard the key turn the lock, they sat bolt upright, eyes wide on the half-open bedroom door. They clutched the sheet over their nakedness.

Claudia switched off the lamp. "Shush. Not to worry," she said in Mario's ear. "It's only Anne-Marie."

In darkness, he listened. She is removing her shoes, he thought, and fancied he could hear the muted progress of small unshod feet over the *lustro* floor. A light bloomed remotely as a door opened, and disappeared when it shut, leaving a line of brightness under the connecting door to the bathroom.

They heard the click of the bathroom lock, then another click further away. Claudia's lips brushed his ear. "She must have brought someone with her," she whispered. "She never locks herself in unless..."

"Who?" Mario breathed.

Claudia shrugged, muttering, "Jesus. Who can say?"

They listened to movements, vague stirrings and *suoni* undecipherable. Then Anne-Marie laughed, a sobbing laugh that made Mario shiver. "No!" cried her choked voice, and there followed a *cascata* of Noes, then a fragment of speech, with words not discernible.

Claudia said aloud, "Something's the matter." She got up and turned on the overhead track lighting. Mario blinked, then scrubbed at his eyes. Claudia belted her short robe. From the closet she tossed him a hooded, linen, beach poncho. He slipped it over his head and went to join her where she stood in *l bagno*, her ear to Anne-Marie's door.

Faint rustlings, then silence. Claudia drew Mario back to her bed where she sat on the tumbled sheets and coverlet, frowning at her bare feet beside his on the carpet. "No, she's alone," Claudia said. "She was talking to herself, I think."

"Still drunk, perhaps?" he hazarded. "Or high on *psicofarmaci?*"

"Could be. She may have fallen asleep now, in the light, with her clothes on."

Small thumping sounds reached them, as of furniture being moved. Then a louder thud, and a choking gasp quickly cut off. Claudia's dark eyes flashed into Mario's, and she was bounding high on her tiptoes, hair streaming behind her, to the kitchenette. He caught up with her and helped slide back the bolt of a door opening into the bedroom beyond.

Anne-Marie was hanging high above the floor, frantically struggling, arms flailing, legs kicking. Mario skirted the big bed. Claudia cleared it in an acrobat's tumble, and hugged Anne-Marie's knees, lifting her weight.

Mario righted the overturned dressing-table bench and hopped up in an instant, his swift fingers loosing *la corda* which bruised the frail neck. Anne-Marie's flower-fair face, angled awry, grief-stained and distorted by terror, was close to his own. Close enough to kiss, he thought inappropriately, scandalized at himself, as the thick cord dangled free. A blush glowed in her cheeks, then subsided. A gurgling sound came from her parted lips. Her eyes gazed, huge, blue as sapphires, past and beyond him.

Mario felt pounding fear yield to the first stirrings of thankful relief. Intent though he was on his task, he was yet oddly, sharply, aware of every detail. The trailing gilded cord, a belt from *una vesta di bagno,* no doubt, which echoed the gold of her curls, and was echoed again by the intricate brass of the lighting fixture from which it depended. A scent of talcum powder came from the tall, small-boned, soft-breasted body limp in his arms: the smell of *innocenza,* like a baby after a bath. Like Lauren *bambina*, after her bath.

So heightened were his senses that he could discern the very pattern of the brocade upholstery beneath his bare soles. When he and Claudia had lifted Anne-Marie to the bed, he saw that she was wearing a little girl's nightgown, of faded pink cotton printed with rabbits at play, too small in the shoulders, too short.

Claudia rocked her, murmuring comfort, with an undertone of passionate, empathetic, partisan indignation. The high-boned ivory cheek with its classic declivity pressed against the softer snowy one. Black waves of hair flowed over gold ringlets, in a tableau that stunned Mario with its sorrow and beauty.

Claudia's fingers touched the mark left by the cord, an angry red necklace already beginning to turn black and blue. Anne-Marie came to herself then and beat with her fists against her friend's shoulders and face. "Why can't you mind your own damn business?" she gasped. "Let me alone, oh, let me go, let me do it!"

"Anne-Marie, Anne-Marie! Don't do it, darling. Don't leave me alone."

They wept, embraced, and Mario felt tears on his own face as his arms encircled them both. Then Anne-Marie collapsed, eyes shut, lips parted, drooping on Claudia's shoulder.

"She has fainted," Mario whispered.

"No, I think only asleep. Here, hold her. Pet her. I have to make a call." He cradled Anne-Marie and kissed her temple, glistening now with a silvery sheen of sweat. Claudia's fingers played rapidly over the buttons of the bedside phone. She stood with her back to him, the handset to her ear.

"Answering machine," Mario said. She nodded. He contemplated the sleeping face which lay against the rough linen of his borrowed poncho. Pretty enough, he thought, to be a cover girl. Yet, seen close, with the fold at her ear that says, Over thirty. Blue hollows under the eyes and *zampe di gallina*. She must be as old as my Lauren, or *per caso* a year or two younger. *Ahì, mia* Laura! He had held her like this, seven years ago, when she too had tried... The white mound of pills I snatched from her palm, the spilled whiskey. Her poor plain face blotched with crying. Our only close moment since her childhood. "He promised to come, Daddy, no one ever comes, why should they, look at me." Mario's finger traced the contours of Anne-Marie's brow and chin. See, Laura, *la bellezza* you yearn for is not enough, *ancora* the heart can break.

Claudia said into the phone, "Ptolemy here. Call me. Urgent." She hung up.

"*Il dottore?* Her husband?"

"No way." Claudia walked slowly about the room, her face thoughtful. She picked up a man's raincoat from the floor, then a towel and a pair of nylons, and laid them over a chair. "A.J. hasn't twigged about this little hideaway, you see," she said, "and I plan to keep it that way. Or anyway I think he doesn't know. With him, you can never be sure."

"But he is so fond of her, *trova tanto simpatico.*"

She shook her head. "Keeps up a great front, doesn't he. I'm trying to reach Neal Mustafa, got to get her a doctor, he boards just a couple blocks away. But he must be on night duty at Warren."

"I have met him, at the reception," Mario told her. "'…Ptolemy?'"

"Code word. Anne-Marie and Neal, he used to come here all this past spring. He wouldn't spill the beans."

"And now she has someone else?"

Claudia shrugged and continued her haphazard abstracted tidying. "She's flesh and blood, after all. Not rigid and frigid like me."

Their eyes met. Claudia came swiftly to kiss him. He said, "We know better, do we not, you and I… Don't tell me she too has a white marriage." *Che ironia,* he thought, with every man lusting for her, excepting *lo sposo.*

"Not like my marriage, no, he isn't gay. But it's empty enough, I'd say at a guess, with A.J. in love with his work. Hell, Mario, don't look at me like that. The most sex-starved people are the married, you know that."

She went out of the room. Mario lowered Anne-Marie to the bed. She half woke with a quick intake of breath, her small hands tight on his arm. "*Dormi,* little one." He soothed her back to sleep, bemused and disturbed by her strongly sexual aura. He remembered reading somewhere that hanging was a uniquely erotic and euphoric experience. Even orgasmic. He shook his head, frowning, freeing himself of her magnetism. *Tu,* Claudia, it is thou I want, from this night on you flow in my veins forever.

Claudia returned with a ladder stool and a pair of shears. "Tell you what, Mario," she said as she ascended, seeming to float upward to the brass ceiling fixture, "you call Warren, I'm afraid the switchboard will recognize my voice." She snipped at the gilded cord, which fell in coils like a snake. She jumped down lightly as a cat, her long hair floating above her. "Ask for Dr. Mustafa, they'll page him. Say he should phone Ms. Ptolemy right away." She took his place at Anne-Marie's side and told him what numbers to tap out on the phone.

Mario kept his voice small and high in pitch, minimizing his accent. "P-t-o-l-e-m-y," he told the receptionist. She sounded distracted, as though under strain. Mario wondered, Have they brought *il corpo* there, the burned body of Randy Funderburk? "Yes," he said, "P as in popular." He made a conspiratorial face at Claudia.

She regarded him soberly. "I'm going to dress. She's all right now, I think, sleep's what she needs. But stay with her, in case." She shut the door to the kitchenette and unlocked the one to the bathroom. "There's Valium and some Nytol in the medicine chest. We won't give her anything until I speak to Ralph."

Her composure and energy impressed him deeply. *Eroica*, he thought, when she had disappeared through the bathroom. Mettle. This is the abused and rejected *ragazza* who picked herself up after they trampled her into the mud. This is she who defied the world when she lay crippled, who disciplined herself to dance again.

He heard the bolt slide to in the kitchenette, and the single ring of a phone there. He reached for the bedside phone, hesitated, then picked up the handset. Dr. Mustafa's deep arresting voice was saying, "No, you may speak, there is no one to hear. There's been some excitement here, a bad accident... How long was she suspended from—"

"—Just seconds, I got to her fast," Claudia's voice interrupted.

"I will come to you rapidly, I will find some colleague to cover my duties."

Mario was frowning at a sheet of stationery on the untidy dressing table. He hung up noiselessly, and went to gaze down at the square of heavy grey-blue paper covered with handwriting. It lay in a smear of face powder, surrounded by lipsticks and earrings. Anne-Marie's name and address were embossed in white at the top of the page. A slim gold pen lay near the note. The open box of stationery was on the floor at his feet.

"Though lovers be lost love shall not;
And death shall have no dominion. "

A schoolgirl script, painstaking, for the two lines of verse. After that the writing deteriorated, slanting up the page, almost illegible where it finished on the other side.

"Just to keep up the quoting tradition," Anne-Marie had written, *"like Roy and old Chief Kendall. No Good Book here, and anyhow I don't know is this from Shakespeare or the Bible. I didn't even know it had stuck with me.*

"Terry on my mind, Georgia On My Mind, 'sweet and clear as moonlight through the pines.' Dead, Terry is dead, Randy that dipshit he told me Terry is dead so what's the point of living. 'In the sweet bye-and-bye we shall meet on that —' something or other —'shore.' If you can believe the hymns, I can't."

A tear had blistered the paper here, blurring the words. Please, *no, prego,* don't let it be true he is dead, Mario prayed, one hand to his throat. He lifted the note to his eyes, then held it away. I beg you, *Lucia,* implore you, *aiutame,* come back to me now, tell me it is not true!

No voices or visions were vouchsafed to him. Mario automatically assumed that news of Randy's death had reached Anne-Marie and thus precipitated her suicide attempt. Unprepared for the revelation contained in the note, his knees weakened, his stomach whirled. He glanced to the softly breathing woman, tempted to wake her up and extract as much information as he could, but instead forced himself to read on.

"Got to forgive me, Momma," the letter continued. *"A. J., I'm so sorry, I know I didn't turn out to be the wife you wanted. This isn't my Will, the lawyers have it somewhere, but if this could be legal I'd like to change it. I leave all my money to Fanny. Fanny Hapgood. She's going to feel so awful, with Terry dead and gone and a murderer. Well, if he killed them, he did it out of love, you know that, to spare them the suffering.*

"That's enough, if I'm going to go through with it, it better be now," said the last scribbled line above her flamboyant signature. Near it another tear-blot swelled the notepaper.

Claudia came back, dressed in a dun-colored jump suit, a practice costume perhaps, with thick matching socks. She looked sad but determined. Her hair was sleek in an ebony roll crowning her high-held head. Through his numbed perturbation, Mario thought: Long-necked and graceful, you move like a swan. She was carrying a tray with a glass and a crystalline pitcher. A bulky blue polo shirt was slung over her arm.

She went to the bedside, checking on Anne-Marie. "Neal said she'd be thirsty when she woke, just give her water. Here, Mario, this is for you." She tossed him the polo shirt. "Get dressed now and out of here."

The garment fell at his feet unheeded. He handed Claudia the letter. Her eyes questioned him, and he pointed to the dressing table. She read with black brows knit. "Dylan Thomas," she murmured. "Imagine her remembering that." A few lines later, she held the letter to her cheek, and said, "No." Mario went to embrace her.

"Terry," Claudia said against his shoulder. "Terry."

"Do you think it is true?"

"No. Let's not believe it. Why should we believe it?" She withdrew from him, read the note through, folded it and weighed it on her palm. "Why, why, why," she said dully. "The suffering, Mario, the pain beyond bearing. Why's life so ugly damn cruel."

Thoughts of the wounded fleeing in wartime, of the hands of the starving outstretched in vain, and of the homeless in sleet and snow came to Mario. Nodding at the letter and then at Anne-Marie, he said, "And these are the favored, the elite who have never known hunger nor torture in prison. Whom all the world envies."

"There's no hierarchy," she replied in a somber tone, "of mortal misery."

"È vero," he agreed, adding doubtfully, "sometimes." He remembered the bloom of sexual triumph on Anne-Marie's rain-sparkled face in the barbecue restaurant; and the heavy-lidded glow of satisfaction on the face of Randy Funderburk at the ambulance window. She does not yet know he is morto, and neither does Claudia. Should I tell her?... No. Lascia stare.

Claudia spread the top sheet over Anne-Marie's legs. "That old bunny nightie. Security blanket. Odessa must have fetched it from the big house, my house next door."

"She has done this often before, the servant woman," Mario asked, "put her to bed?"

"Umpteen times. Odessa and Cordene, they coddle and cuddle her. Treat her like she was nine years old."

"Would she have walked here?"

"Never walk when you can ride, as we say in this neck of the woods. She'd have picked up that raincoat and some kind of shoes from the hall closet. When she tiptoed out."

After she woke to bleak desolazione, Mario thought. He contemplated the weathered man's raincoat folded on the chair.

"Which reminds me," Claudia went on, "I should go see do I need to move her car. Mario, hurry it up. We can leave her a little. I don't want you here when Neal comes." But she detained him a moment, one hand on his arm. "Do you think she saw you? Recognized you?" He shook his head. "Good. Discretion," she said, "isn't Anne-Marie's long suit."

As he hastily washed and dressed, Mario kept both bathroom doors open, his ears on the stretch in case the sleeper awoke. Claudia's bedroom was orderly and chaste, the bed neatly made. The polo shirt fitted him well, though a trifle short in the sleeves. He folded his suit coat and tuxedo T-shirt into a shopping bag. Shoes and briefcase in hand, he entered Anne-Marie's room.

"The car's fine, she tucked it away where it won't be spotted," Claudia told him. In his absence, she had spruced up the room. Clothing had been hung out of sight. The dressing table looked clean and organized. She contemplated him and said of the polo shirt, "Becomes you."

"Ample," he agreed. "Do you dance in this?"

"Wouldn't own anything I couldn't dance in."

"I will send it back to you," he told her.

"No, keep it," said Claudia. "I've plenty more like it. Let's not complicate things, darling, let's not leave traces." She came to lay her cheek on his shoulder against the thick cool blue cotton. "My present to you, souvenir of our trip to Alpha Centauri."

He put his arm around her and they stood a moment at the bedside, gazing down at Anne-Marie as fond parents might look at their slumbering child. I have *nesson* for Claudia, Mario was thinking. *Ohimè.* How I wish I could give her my most precious possession. What would it be? Not my lion coin, no, he thought, touching the crested pocket of *la camicia,* that stays with me even in my grave. He reviewed rapidly the few objects he owned which had value for him. *Mia madre's* garnet bracelet, which Oriana had treasured and Lauren despised.

"I have nothing to give you," he told her.

"You've given me plenty," Claudia said. They swayed together in a kiss. "I never can thank you enough."

"I will hold this night in my heart *per sempre*," Mario murmured. *"Grazie, grazie, mia carissima."*

Goodbye then, goodbye. He stepped into his shoes at the main door, one arm around Claudia's waist. *"Ecco,* look what she wore," he said, indicating with his toe a pair of tan canvas shoes.

"Little old feet must have been swimming in those," Claudia said, picking up the shoes. "They're closer to my size." She lifted her left leg, pointing her long narrow foot at him, in ballet style. He captured her ankle, and bent to kiss it through the fuzzy wool of the sock.

"One kiss more," he said, holding open the main door; and Claudia lifting her face to him murmured with lips close to his, *"Addio, Mario mio. Addio, mio amatissimo."*

Then he was out, down the stairs and into the street. The night had turned cooler. The pavement gleamed wet with dewfall. *La luna* rode high in the western sky, brilliant with the forecast of the morrow's heat. As he walked swiftly along deserted Main Street, the moon projected his shadow before him, vying with the street lamps. He paused at the *Clarion* office, admiring the new garment reflected in the plate glass. Expensive, handsome, well-made. *Un vero regalo,* he thought.

And I gave her only the gift of tears.

XXII

The August moon shone through the pines, patterning the sharp-scented little woods in green-tinted silver and black. Each tree stood on the dark shaft of its shadow.

"Let's recapitulate," Tyler said. So bright was the night that he turned off his flashlight. He and Abbot and Taliaferro had just returned from the scene of the crash, and were packing away the crime kit. "According to what we got out of Otis, the white car was here, say, from four-thirty p.m. in the afternoon to six-thirty p.m., maybe seven."

Otis stood near, his back to them. His hands lay caressingly against a pine with three branches torn from its rough trunk.

"Parked it right here," Abbot said, pacing a ten-foot clearing, "behind where the bushes are high." Pine branches were stacked at his feet. "Covered it with these, ripped off a few more."

"Like he done wrench off your arm," they heard Otis say.

"Maybe resin on his hands. Or on his gloves. Her gloves." Tyler squatted, and touched the earth strewn with pine needles. "Coming out, there'd still be plenty of light, even in here." He waved at a branch in a white-tagged transparent plastic bag. "Used that to sweep dirt and needles over the ground. After he'd kicked out the wheel ruts and footprints."

"And did a damn thorough job," Taliaferro said sourly, "even with the ground wet from the rain." He was dabbing insect repellent on his neck. "Anybody want more of this gunk?" Another tagged bag, this one containing a rectangular section of cut earth, lay near the first. "So what have we got, besides this itty-bitty hunk of car track from under the bushes."

"Not a lot," Tyler agreed. "Don't know as it'll be enough for the lab." He scowled at the tips of his boots and said. "Pee-yew." He wadded a handful of moist leaves and wiped the leather clean. "That Kevin. Threw up on my toes."

"I saw," Taliaferro said. "When they were putting the, ah, remains, charred remains, y'might call 'em, on the stretcher."

"I never cottoned to Funderburk," Abbot said softly. "But what a crummy, miserable way to go."

Tyler hunched his shoulders and muttered. "Hope the poor son-of-a-bitch was dead before the fire got to him."

"Delicate stomach, Kevin has."

Abbot passed the toe of his own boot speculatively over the ground. "Whoever stomped out those tracks, his shoes must be a sight to behold."

"Yes. If only we knew where they're at." Tyler stood upright and stretched. "Let's stow the kit in your trunk, Andrew. I'll tote the evidence in mine." He picked up one of the plastic bags, then put it down and said, "Did anybody get through to Bear Sieburth?"

"Switchboard reached him," Abbot reported. He balanced the long black leatherette case of the crime scene kit on Reid's outstretched forearms, and placed two pine branches atop it. "He's sending the county wagon for Randy."

"Hey, Otis," Taliaferro called softly. "You sure you don't got a song about dirty shoes? Didn't see a pair of dirty shoes?"

"Or a green compact with a dented fender," Tyler added with a sigh.

"Ain't seen no shoes," Otis said, joining them. "I'd sure admire to be of service, but there ain't no song about shoes. Little green automobile now. Did y'all think to look in the ga-rage?"

"What ga-rage?" Tyler asked quickly.

"Royal's ga-rage, that 'ere shed. He don't keep no car there no more, but I seen somebody's in it."

"When?" Taliaferro shouted.

"Don't know for sartin just when," Otis apologized. "Couldn't say 'zackly what color."

"Crying out loud," Abbot exclaimed. "Why didn't you tell us?"

"'Scuse me, Mister Beau. 'Scuse me, y'all. I didn't think on it."

"Never mind, Otis, not your fault we forgot to ask. You're helping just fine." Tyler picked up the evidence bags and said to the others, "*Let's go.*"

They gained the unpaved road where the two police cars were parked. Abbot radioed the police station.

Otis said, "If y'all don't need me no more, Mr. Beau, I should ought to get on back to the ho-tel."

"Stick with us a bit, Otis," Tyler told him. "We'd be grateful."

Abbot came to them. "Duane's back from telling Ben and the Funderburk family. Going off duty, but says holler if you need him." They started up the slope toward Royal Washington's back yard. "I told him about the shoes, everybody should keep a sharp lookout."

Taliaferro hastened after the long-legged policemen, Otis trailing. "Bobby Lee's 'round front," Abbot was saying. "Should we fetch him?" Tyler shook his head. The house looked like a child's cut-out, a rectangle topped by the low roof triangle, haloed in silhouette, backlit by the vigil lantern on the front porch. The darker shed sagged beside it.

When Taliaferro caught up, Tyler had already swung the shed door wide. The flashlights focussed on the pockmarked rear end of a green Honda. CXW-429, said the license plate.

Tyler ran to the house, skirting the yard, calling to the others, "Don't walk in the middle!" A square of warped cardboard was propped on the sill of the nearest window. He removed it, holding it gingerly by one corner, while his flashlight and Abbot's found the broken pane, shot through the dark bedroom to the kitchen beyond, and wavered to a stop on the slender, white-clad, golden-haired figure that dangled in the doorway.

A faint eerie keening came from Otis. He was shuddering visibly and swaying to the rise and fall of his ululation. His hazel eyes were aglow like a mountain cat's.

Terry Hapgood's suicide note was on the kitchen table beside the L.C. Smith manual typewriter.

```
i have sinned in that i have betrayed the inno-
cent blood. and he cast down the pieces of sil-
ver, and went and hanged himself.
```

do you remember that. the upper case isnt
working so i cant put a question mark. matthew
27, verse 4, i remember from bible class. i
should check it out but the police must have
taken roys bible. the class prize that year was
a bible with a white cover stamped with fancy
letters and gold leaf on the edges. it was the
most beautiful thing i had ever seen. except
you. later on i wrapped it in gift paper and
tried to give it to you on your birthday, but you
wouldnt take it. remember

i am writing this for you, only you. other
people will read it but i hope you will see it
eventually. i wont write your name, i promise,
but you will know who you are. i have never
loved anybody else, only you. i never told anybody, never told you, but you knew. and now that
i know the truth about you, i cant stand it. i
just want to be dead and never wake up again. i
always put you on a pedestal, i guess, and now
that i know your secret i just dont want to live.

re the pieces of silver, i did take money. i
sold myself like a worthless piece of sleaze. i
want you to know what i did when i worked as a
stripper in new york in the burlecue place. to
earn my tuition money. i havent any idea who
blew the whistle on me. i guess all valhalla
found out, and a lot of the town too. that isnt
the reason i felt bad. floraville always treated
me like some kind of freak, so i figured, if i
have the name might as well have the game. hospital work doesnt pay anywhere near as much. so
i learned to do the dancing, kind of silly stuff,
and the posing and all. the big money offers
came in the intermission and after the show.
quite a few rich guys came there to size up the
strippers. at first i only went with the ones
who didnt even want to put a hand on me. but
then i did go with somebody, we went all the way

as they call it. i wont say who, he is real famous and not out of the closet. but maybe you
will guess. he paid me enough so i was ready to
quit. but then the cat got out of the bag.

   i hated myself a long time after that. not for
the stripping and other stuff, but for taking
those thirty pieces of silver in trade. for what
should be only an act of love. i wanted to die
then too but they pumped the pills out of me. if
it hadnt been for you and roy and how i feel
about nursing, i wouldnt have got over it.

   this is getting too long, and i am wondering if
that is because i am maybe beginning to chicken
out. they say suicide is the cowards way, but
take my word for it, you got to have guts. this
time i am real determined.
about the innocent blood, about the old chief and
roy and earl langford. people will say i am a
murderer, but all three were more like assisted
suicide. they begged me to help them, all three.
roy was my friend and i loved him, he was the
hardest to do. but he was dying for sure, and
nothing ahead but more damn misery. torture. it
came a little easier for me because i had already
done it for rutherford kendall. he couldnt face
colon cancer and who is to say he didnt have the
right. the hanging part was to protect me, and
the bible verses was his idea. sort of poetic,
so i used it with the others, too. langford,
now,

                -- over --

                -page 2-

   i hardly knew him, and sure he wasnt a friend.
but he said he would rather be dead than in jail.

   thalidomide was very effective and i know it is
not detected in a routine autopsy. roy and the

305

```
chief were alive when i lifted them up.  i didnt
have any at the police station, so with earl
langford i used my hands and what i learned in
anatomy 2 and did what i had to do.  didnt hurt
him, he never even woke up and he was already
dead before i got him up on the cell bars.  roys
innards are still in pathology, in the jar la-
beled dudley.  i switched labels when they were
shipped off to the g.b.i.

    i took a risk for a good cause.  did what i
could to escape getting caught.  i dont regret
helping them.  that is not why i am calling it
quits.

        its you, only you.
        [signed] terence c. hapgood, r.n.
```

The signature was firm and meticulously legible, with a flourish crowning the T.

"Question is," said Taliaferro, "who is 'you'?" He was standing in his sock feet at the kitchen table re-reading the letter. The overhead circle of fluorescent light brought out blond gleams in his brown hair and beard. He was wearing the latex gloves Abbot had given him, and turning the page with tweezers.

The ruffled chintz curtains were closed, although sunlight glowed through them. From the gap at the top of the window frame, one long yellow ray shot through to deflect from the silvery bracelet of Terry's wristwatch. His body still hung in the doorway, turning back and forth almost imperceptibly. His blue eyes were half open, his clear-cut features hardly distorted in death.

"Who is 'you,'" Abbot echoed. "And what is your nasty little secret? 'Is you is or is you ain't my baby.'" His tone was straining to sound light. "Remember that song?" He was at the wall phone, holding the handset delicately by the earpiece between his gloved thumb and forefinger as he hung it up. A glistening black smear of fingerprint powder dirtied the latex. "'You' could be anybody. Even me or you."

"I grant you I'm a beautiful thing," Taliaferro replied in a similar tone, one hand on his beard, "but I never use aftershave."

Tyler and Bear Sieburth came in through the back door. "You don't need this," Tyler said, switching off the light. He opened the curtains admitting the green, blue and gold of the summer morning. "And why are you two doofusses still wearing gloves? We got all these prints hours ago." His red-rimmed eyes were glazed in the stone mask of his face.

Bear said, "We could cut him down now, you think?"

"Got all the cloth fibers you need?" Abbot asked.

Bear nodded. He was wearing jeans and a police academy sweatshirt, and carrying a thirty-five millimeter camera. His massive presence breathed eagerness: in contrast to the others, he looked wide-awake and ready for action. The big aluminum case of his crime scene kit lay open beside Tyler's smaller one just beyond the living room doorway.

Abbot said, peeling off his gloves, "I phoned the station, told them to get in touch with the troopers. Call off the search for Terry's car, we almost forgot."

"Good catch," Tyler said. Using the tweezers, he slid the suicide letter into a transparent folder.

Bear, taking equal precautions, put the typewriter into a plastic bag. "Though why we're being this nitpicking I wouldn't know," he mused, with a nod toward the letter. "Mystery's solved, the poor fruit snuffed 'em out and did away with himself. It's not like a homicide."

"Maybe so, maybe no." Tyler helped him put the typewriter in a box, which they sealed and labeled.

"Find anything more in the yard?" Taliaferro asked.

"Nary a print of foot nor finger," Bear replied, "and the wheel marks of Hapgood's Honda raked clean out of sight."

"Wonder why Terry made himself so hard to find," Taliaferro said. He and Abbot helped Tyler to clear the table of flashlights, notebooks, a sugar bowl and salt and pepper shakers. "He took as much pains as whoever drove that white car. And what was *that* all about, anyway?"

Bear righted the straight chair near the body, and stepped up. The wood creaked under his weight. "Parking and sparking, I'll bet." He slipped a plastic bag, slit to accommodate the extension cord which served as a noose, over the corpse.

Tyler handed him a pair of shears. "Otis get back to the hotel okay?"

Abbot and Taliaferro looked at each other. "Bobby Lee calmed him down some," Taliaferro said. "Dropped him off on his way to the stationhouse just after midnight. While you were casing the bedroom." To Abbot he said, very low, "Not now."

"Then when," muttered Abbot. Aloud he said, "About the white car, we may never know. Anyway, hiding a car isn't a crime... Listen, Chief. Got something to tell you. Bobby Lee phoned here, like one in the morning. When he got to the hotel, he stumbled on a whole bunch of stuff. Chemicals, lab equipment. Plus stolen goods, including Huey Easton's tires. Also a stash of reefer."

Tyler stared at him with a dazed look, his arms around Terry's body, helping Bear to support its weight. Bear stared, too, the shears in his hand. He asked, "Mario there?"

"No. Bobby Lee left him a note."

"And Garison?" Tyler said.

"Skipped."

"Jesus, Andrew. Now is when to tell me."

Taliaferro said, "There hasn't been one single minute to let you know about it. Without distracting you."

"Well, I sure as hell can't cope with it now."

"I already coped," Abbot said. "Told Bobby Lee, seal up the evidence, put out an All Points Bulletin. Everything else on hold till tomorrow."

"Good work," Tyler said. "You did right, Andrew. Thanks. Easy now, Bear." They lowered the body. Abbot regarded it with a look of angry grief. He reached out as though to touch it, then withdrew his hand. He said in a strained voice, "Should I check on Doc Osborne, Chief?"

"Yeah, do that." The dead man lay supine on the table. "Golden angel," Tyler said with a catch in his voice. "He looks like an angel." To Abbot, he said in a hard, brisk tone, "Doc's being his usual pain in the ass." He nodded toward the front porch. "Setting out there glowering."

"At least he's keeping the rubberneckers at bay," Sieburth said as Abbot went out.

Tyler mounted the chair and removed the electric cord from the overhead pipe. Taliaferro gazed down at the comely dead face. "Terry needn't have bothered that much, hiding his tracks. Blue Heaven was empty, they were all at the rally."

"Nobody on the porch," Tyler agreed. "We pulled Vern off to cover the mill commotion."

Abbot returned. "Doc's sure as hell irked," he reported. "And we got us more neighbors. Six-seven now huddling across the street. And Tonda's out there, Tonda Whitley. She yelled out that she phoned Candy, so—"

"Candy's all we need right now," Tyler said heavily. "Did you tell Doc he could mosey on home?"

"I told him with consummate tact and expressions of gratitude," Abbot said. "But he insists he will follow the ambulance when it leaves with the body."

"Speak of the devil," said Sieburth, bending to peer through the open venetian blinds of the living room. Deceptively comforting pink dawn light flooded the room, giving no hint of the sweltering intensity to come. The Cullowee County Hospital ambulance was pulling up in front of the house. He and Tyler went out on the porch to signal the paramedics as they unloaded a stretcher. Doc Osborne, frowning and muttering, heaved himself up from the porch rocker and thumped down the steps toward the ambulance. Three or four of the onlookers, Candace Howard among them, started to cross the street.

Tyler and Sieburth were quick to intercept Osborne on the path. Sieburth told him, "It's real good of you, sir, standing by like this, but—"

"Out of my way, *if* you please!" Osborne barked.

Tyler said, "A case like this, see, Doc, all we really needed was for you to pronounce him dead. We sure thank you for driving here so quick, but now—"

"Case like what?" Osborne snapped. "Suicide, not even a whisker of suspicion it could be murder, why can't you admit that? County got no business taking the body away."

"Well, now," said Tyler, "I figure you can't be too careful. Better safe than sorry, the way you always say."

Osborne shouldered between them, his belly bumping Sieburth's. "I do not require instruction in my duties," he proclaimed. "I will accompany the body, and make my protest known to the appropriate authorities." But he stopped and turned to confront Tyler. "And by the way, do I detect an I-told-you-so undertone, Beaufort Tyler? Very well, in one sense you were right about Washington and Langford. But I was not entirely wrong. Assisted suicide is still suicide."

"This way," said Sieburth to the ambulance team, leading them into the house. Osborne followed, but Tyler was detained by a strong, plump hand gripping his forearm.

"Would somebody kindly tell me," Candace Howard demanded with sarcasm, "just what is going on in my house?" Her billowing caftan, the one she had worn at the stationhouse on Thursday, had been laundered: its stripes shone clean in the lengthening rays of the sun.

"Morning, Candy. Wish I could tell about it. Soon as I can, you'll be the first, guarantee you that."

"Don't pamper me up, Beau Tyler. That's Terry Hapgood dead in there, isn't it? Durrell peeked through the back window hours ago. And Terry's car setting out in the yard plain as a church steeple."

"Candy, I got to go back in. Talk to you later, word of honor."

"Cop's honor. Not worth spit. I want to know right here and now, did Terry kill my father?" Her mouth worked strongly, and she rubbed at her large liquid eyes with the back of her hand.

Tyler squirmed, started to speak, and then shook his head. He took her shoulders gently in his hands. "Go on back to Andrew's, Candy." He indicated a red Ford Escort, Melanie Abbot's, parked up the street. "Did you come here alone?"

"Melanie offered to drive me. I don't need a nursemaid. Just a few straight answers is what I need."

"Deacon Howard still in town?" Tyler gazed past her at the house door, with Taliaferro's well-worn black loafers beside it.

"Now you know good and well the deacon had to hurry on back to the Tabernacle," Candace was saying. "Sunday morning!"

"What about Greg?"

"Stop changing the subject," she said sharply, her voice breaking. "Greg's in Atlanta, where else would he be." She took a tissue from a pocket and held it to her eyes. Then she swayed forward to burrow her face into his shoulder. "Oh, Beau! Oh, Beau! Poor Daddy, how could Terry? How dare he, without asking me?"

Tyler embraced her striped bulk, and said softly, "Candy girl."

"Just one more white man taking one more black man's life, that's how I see it," said her muted voice.

"Candy. You know that's not true." He put her from him and blotted her cheeks with the tissue.

"Yes. I know," she said with a sob and a sigh.

"You'll go back to Melanie? And wait for my call?" She nodded reluctantly. He indicated the neighbors across the street. "And tell all them go on home and get ready for church?" She nodded again. "What day's Roy's burying?" he asked her.

"Tuesday, one o'clock, Sweet Zion churchyard. You better be there." She started slowly toward the curb.

"'Course I will," Tyler said. He went into the house, picking up Taliaferro's shoes as he entered.

The body was already bagged and on the stretcher. Bear Sieburth was saying to the ambulance team, "I'll follow right behind you."

"And so will I," Osborne echoed grimly.

"Can you come back tonight?" Tyler asked Bear.

"What for, Beau? Why knock ourselves out? It's all over now 'cept a little red tape, we can pick up our marbles."

"Get us some rest," Abbot agreed.

"Open and shut case," Osborne stated. "And well you know it."

Taliaferro had stepped into his loafers and was leaning against the sink, slowly rolling a cigar between his palms. He exchanged a long look with Tyler. The police chief cleared his throat and said. "Please, Bear."

"Okay, you mule-headed jackass. I'll try to get back."

Osborne said, "And that's another matter I intend to report. Allowing the press on the premises. Unauthorized personnel, while the coroner himself cools his heels outside."

"He's not here for the newspaper," Tyler said reasonably. "Consultant. Helping me out."

"Strictly confidential, Doctor, I assure you," Taliaferro said.

"What happened to your other consultant," Osborne demanded rhetorically. "Your Italian sorcerer, the performing oracle. How come he isn't in here, too, contaminating the evidence."

The ambulance team exchanged amused glances. Abbot said, "Mr. Taliaferro came in *after* we finished in the kitchen, remember. You preferred to stay on the porch."

Taliaferro pointed the cigar at his own feet. "I took off my shoes. Wore gloves. Didn't touch a thing."

"Lift 'er up, one, two, three." The paramedics swung the stretcher so that it could pass through the doorway. "Ready when you are, Mr. Sieburth."

"Be consistent, sir," Sieburth chided Osborne, locking his crime kit. "With little or no likelihood it was murder, why not let 'em in?" He picked up the kit and followed the stretcher through the living room.

Osborne, at his heels, grumbled, "I'm gratified somebody other than me can recognize suicide. When it's staring you in the face." The others followed, carrying the camera and the evidence bags and boxes to Sieburth's car.

When the three vehicles had turned the corner, the police chief said, "You go on, too, Andrew. I want you to stop by the Gilmore, check out what happened."

The lieutenant said delicately, "The—ah—next of kin. You haven't forgotten?"

Tyler's grey face went a shade greyer. "Miz Fanny," he said through stiff lips. "No, I haven't forgotten."

"You could send somebody," Abbot suggested. "Not me, I know, somebody white. Ruthann, maybe, or Floyd."

"No," Tyler replied. "No. I'll do it. Soon's I leave here. Got to do it myself... Get going, Andrew. You can go on home after the hotel; your report can wait till tomorrow."

"Aye, aye, sir."

Tyler and Taliaferro watched Abbot's patrol car drive away. Tyler took from his pocket a tin of tobacco and rolled a cigarette.

Taliaferro lit his cigar, and offered the flame of his lighter. "Thought you'd quit."

"I thought so, too." Tyler inhaled deeply. Smoke flowed from his nostrils in two ghostly streams defined by the hot morning sunlight. Across the street, now cleared of people, the leafy treetops were busy with bird life. Through house windows here and there, faces peered at them.

"Come on out back," Tyler said. They walked to the yard and stood smoking, contemplating the little green car.

"Wonder how Bobby Lee found all the stuff at the Gilmore," the police chief mused. "Stroke of luck, that." Then, with a sudden gesture of decision, he announced, "I'm sealing it up."

"Terry's car. In the shed. Go get me my crime scene kit, would you, Reid."

Tyler drove the car into the shed. He was closing the door when Taliaferro came back with the kit. "Sealing tape," Tyler said. Together they applied the official yellow tape to the shed door and posted it.

"Bear's right," Taliaferro said. "You *are* treating this like a homicide scene."

"So what if I am."

"Can't you make up your mind?"

"Too many loose ends," Tyler muttered. "Too many questions. And coincidences." By tacit consent they went back to the front porch and entered the living room. It had a look of scrupulous preservation, like a parlor used only for formal visits. Strong daylight coming obliquely through the blinds laid slanted stripes across the wall of books and the chintz sofa with the framed photographs above it. The walnut clock ticked loudly. Its pendulum swung.

Tyler closed the blinds, and they went through the dimness to the bright kitchen. They sat at the table.

"I could make us some coffee," Taliaferro suggested.

"We'll get some at Bonnie's," said Tyler.

"Always a pleasure," Taliaferro said lightly, his eyes on the table. "I gather you'd just as soon not mess around in here." Tyler grunted. "You expect to be back with a high tech crew?"

"Let's say it's a possibility. Look, Reid. Overwhelmingly. Open and shut, like Doc puts it. I got to go along with that."

"Straightforward and simple," Taliaferro mused. "Too simple by half."

"I hear that. For instance, how would Terry know Langford was even in jail? Let alone how he felt about it. Okay, plenty plausible explanations, I could spin out a few myself. And what about Randy Funderburk? He keeps cropping up. This crash, was it really an accident?"

He got up and dialed the wall phone. "Tyler here. Morning, Ruthann! What you doing there on a Sunday?... Real good of you. Thanks! Floyd there?... No, just tell him, come on to Royal Washington's. We're setting up the vigil again... No, just a precaution. Till I decide if further investigation is indicated... Floyd come in? Ask

313

him to find out is Jackson Sprague still in town. Cautious like, 'thout getting the wind up." He replaced the handset and came back to the table, saying, "I keep telling myself I'm maybe not being objective. Feeling like I do about Roy and Terry. But ..."

Taliaferro said, "I am not satisfied, either, and I wasn't near so close to them. Look, everybody felt it. Why did Andrew hand me gloves? Why's Sieburth coming back?"

"And Terry's letter. Too perfect."

"Where is it?"

"Bear carried it up to the lab. He'll bring copies tonight, and we'll get the original back. Why?"

"An idea," Taliaferro said, taking his half-smoked cigar out of his pocket, "at the bottom of my mind. Just swam up to the surface. Couldn't swear to it, but I got the impression two people maybe wrote that letter."

"How so?"

"I'm not a qualified expert, but I know typewriters. Especially the ancient wrecks. The typing on side one is a lot more even than on side two."

"Meaning what?"

"Could be a touch typist began the letter, and a hunt-and-pecker finished it off. I'd like a closer look. With a magnifying glass."

XXIII

Through the streets of Floraville, churchgoers proceeded with stately decorum towards their places of worship. The bells of the First Methodist Church on Main Street rang out a solemn summons, reverberating into the hotel room where Mario lay sleeping.

He was naked, prone atop the green chenille bedspread. At four in the morning, he had been sitting by the telephone, so rapt in bittersweet re-evocation of his hours with Claudia that he could not bring himself to call the stationhouse. Under the lucent ripples of remembered passion and rue, in the murky depths of consciousness, the worry over Terry Hapgood had stirred like a sluggish sea-beast. What news of him: still missing; or found alive; or dead, as Anne-Marie believed. *I have only to dial* la polizia *to find out. And what would I do, what could I do, in any of those cases. What that could not wait an hour or so. Lascistare, let it be. Claudia* mia, *this time of aftermath is sacred to thee.*

A leaf from a memo pad lay beside him on the bed. The writing on it said: *"1 a.m. Dear Mario, I see you have not got back yet. When you do, Get your beauty sleep, Lt. Abbot says. Lots of news good and bad, but it can wait. Give us a call when you wake up."* The note was signed *"Bobby Lee,"* with *"P.O. Robert E. Lee Petticord"* block-printed below the signature. Then: *"P.S. Thanks again about Cindy."*

When Mario had returned in the small hours, the lobby was deserted, the desk unmanned. Relieved, he had stepped around it to take his room key from its hook, and had seen the note in his cubbyhole. Lights and low excited voices were coming from the half-open dining room doors, but Mario's need for solitude overcame his normally keen curiosity.

Now the powerful mellow voice of the Reverend Plenty penetrated the room. "...ten fold, my brethren and sisters in Christ, think what that means. A whole dollar for every thin dime you give, a hundred smackers for every sawbuck." The attendant at the gas station across the street had turned up the volume of his TV set. "And ten is only the minimum, my beloved friends ..."

Mario, without fully waking, groped under the bedspread for a pillow, and put it over his head.

"Now where else," the Reverend boomed, undiminished by the pillow, "y'all going to find an investment like that?"

Mario pushed the pillow away, sat up and pressed his knuckles against his eyes. He looked around, frowning, for the source of the voice. He stumbled to the bathroom door and reached around it for his dressing gown.

He tugged the window down in stages, shutting out the broadcast. He blinked, gazing around the room. His silk suit hung in a dry cleaner's bag outside the closet. His pink shirt, clean and mounted on a rectangle of cardboard, was on the dresser. He went to the phone.

Tyler said "I'll take it, Ruthann. Morning, Mario. " Mario listened to a terse account of Bobby Lee's midnight discovery, taking in the information without reacting to it. "They picked up Kirby Garison an hour ago, 'bout ten o'clock, just outside Mobile, Alabama. They're holding him there."

"And Terence Hapgood?"

A moment of silence, then: "Terry's dead, Mario."

Another moment of silence. "Dead," Mario echoed dully. "He has taken his life."

"We found him at Roy's. Hanging."

"He killed the others?"

"Said so, in his note. Look, I'll tell you about it when you get here."

He was not my son, Mario thought as he washed and dressed. Nor even my *amico*. We met only once.

He donned a white shirt and the silk suit. *Per domenica*. My concerns over him were *nevrotico*, exaggerated. I am in no way to blame for his death.

Mario felt abstracted, oddly uneasy. He pocketed the lion coin automatically, then folded and smoothed Claudia's blue polo shirt. When he laid it in the dresser drawer, his large hands lingered atop it for a moment. Then he took up his briefcase and walked with forced mechanical jauntiness along the corridor and down to the lobby.

The sun streamed in through the open doors and windows. The ceiling fans were turning. She-Ra the cat, looking sleek and contented, was lying outstretched on one of the red leather couches. Otis and Scott, washing down another couch, looked up and greeted Mario with a smile and a wave. The dining room doors stood wide open. The lobby looked clean and inviting. Even the palm trees seemed to have taken a new lease on life.

Flossie Hicks was at the reception desk. "Good morning, ain't it a beautiful morning!" she called to Mario as he approached her. She was wearing a yellowed white chiffon dress and a hat with a wide translucent brim. Its long ribbon was somewhat crumpled. Her thin lips were bright with rouge, her pale eyes enlarged by clumsily applied eye-liner and mascara.

"*Signora* Hicks! How well you are looking today!" Almost unrecognizable, Mario thought.

Flossie gestured deprecatingly at her finery. "Oh, this old thing. No sense letting good clothes just set there in the closet, I always say."

Mario nodded approvingly. "*Grazie* for cleaning my suit and my shirt."

"It don't make no nevermind. I'm expecting that Indian fella, that Mr. Patel? Didn't show up on time."

"Mr. Garison, I take it, is away?"

"Oh, yes. Yes, indeedy. And likely to be away for some time." She gave Mario her slow, radiant smile.

"At least three years," Scott said happily as he joined them at the desk. "Morning, Mr. Castig-lian. You shoulda been here last night. Was some doings!"

"Some po-lice was asking after you," Flossie said, "Officer Petticord, y'know. And the colored officer, he come by this morning."

"Thank you. I have been in touch with them. What happened last night?"

"It was that cat," Flossie told him. "Wherever she ain't supposed to go, she's bound and determined to find her a way in."

"She-Ra," Scott said proudly. "She must've snuck into that pantry room when Daddy unlocked it." He led Mario through the dining room. Flossie accompanied them. She pointed to a small door in the far wall. It was covered with the same wallpaper as the rest of the room, blue, patterned with silver fleurs-de-lys. It was sealed with yellow tape.

"He never knowed she was in there, I reckon," Flossie said, "when he locked it up. 'Bout 'leven o'clock, she started a-meowing. I looked for Kirby, Mr. Garison, y'know, he got the onliest key. Warn't nowheres to be found."

Scott said, "Then Buster and Mr. Friedrich, they come back from your show."

"A-meowing and carrying on fit to raise the dead," Flossie continued. "Scott come home right after, he 'bout threw a conniption."

"You broke down *la porta,*" Mario said.

"Mr. Culpepper, he busted it down," Flossie told him. "You shoulda seen the what-all Kirby had hid in there."

"Boxes and boxes," Scott said. "And stolen stuff, too, like guns and a VCR."

"G'wan, Scott, you didn't see nothing. Too busy hugging that cat."

"I did too see it. Was a whole coin collection, and I don't know what-all."

"And Officer Petticord arrived then?" Mario asked.

Flossie nodded. "Brung Otis home. We looked high and low for Kirby. Gone. The car gone."

"Shirts and socks, that's all he took," Scott said, "in a little old tote bag."

"Took every last cent of the cash," Flossie added.

"The lieutenant, he found more stuff this morning," said Scott. "Like a lot of white powder."

Flossie leaned toward Mario and whispered, "I 'spect it was am-pheta-mines."

"How do," Otis said from the doorway to Mario.

"*Buongiorno,* Otis."

"I done took out the trash, Miz Hicks. You wants me to vacuum the hallways?"

"You done did enough, Otis," Flossie said, clearly enjoying her generosity. "Lobby looks real nice. You could take off."

"Mr. Beau, he axed me step 'round to the po-lice station when I finish up here."

"*Prego,* Otis, tell him I will join you there soon," Mario said. "*Signora* Hicks, may I set up in here for my private interviews?"

"'Deed you could. Me and Scott'll fetch you what you need."

"Gentleman waiting to see you," Otis told Flossie as he left.

Mr. Patel was standing by the desk. He made a gesture of greeting toward Mario, and respectfully saluted Flossie. "Dear Madam, I trust you will forgive me my tardiness. I must speak with your husband."

"'Fraid that ain't possible," Flossie told him. "You could speak with me." To Mario she said, "The ho-tel's in my name, y'know." Mario and Patel murmured in surprise. "Kirby, he made me sign all them papers. Said it was only for taxes and stuff, I shouldn't take it serious."

Patel said, "But you are then the actual owner."

"I could sell 'er or keep 'er or what takes my fancy. Ain't made up my mind."

"But your husband and I have already agreed on the terms."

"Always had a notion I could run the place better'n Kirby," she said.

"Gee, Momma! Think we could swing 'er?"

"Hire me a manager, something like that," Flossie said languidly. "I plan to sleep on it."

"But Madam, I have brought the written agreement." Mr. Patel's black eyes were hard in his plump brown face. His full lips tightened with exasperation. "I am prepared to write your check today."

Mario said, "You should consult an attorney, *Signora.*"

"I'll do that," she told him. "That's what I'll do. You know of a smart one?"

Gregory Shapiro? Mario wondered. "I will inquire for someone competent and honest," he said. "And now, a*rrivederci, Signora.*" He bowed to Flossie and nodded at Mr. Patel.

The Danziger sisters waved greetings as Mario joined Scott at the couch. The radio had been turned down, but he could hear a shrill voice proclaiming fervently, "...he put a fiver in the collection, and the very same week the refund come. Fifty-two thirty-seven, outa the blue!"

On the couch She-Ra had rolled over, exposing her sumptuous white belly.

Mario delicately examined the wounded paw. "It seems almost healed."

"Should I stop putting the medicine?"

"One day more," Mario said. He went out on the porch, and pulled a chair up to the table. *"Buongiorno, care Signorine!"*

"Buongiorno, Signor!" Cora smiled, twirling her parasol.

Hazel clicked the radio off. "Good morning, sir! We sure want to thank you for last night!"

Cora asked, "You know what went on here last night?" Mario nodded. "Think Flossie'll sell?"

"Even if she does," Hazel told him, "she'd never let us be put out of here."

"So your prediction," her sister added, "has already come true. A wonderful talent, *Signor!*"

"Domani I will be offering private advice. Right here, in the dining room. I would like to schedule you first, *Signorina* Cora. Miss Hazel, you second. I will not charge for these sessions."

Cora said, "That's right kind of you, sir. I took it to heart, what you told us last night. But me and my sister can pay you, like anybody else."

"Call it a little gift to my gracious neighbors," said Mario, rising. *"E va bene,* we will argue it tomorrow."

The late morning sun hit him like a blow as he left the shade of the porch. He felt suddenly nauseated, dizzy. He swayed as he stood at the curb, thinking, *Non importa,* it is merely that I have had no food. He remembered the flavors of apple juice and biscuits with almond butter he shared with Claudia. Another wave of dizziness overtook him, this time mingled with yearning.

He looked along Main Street, with its seemly processions of Sunday worshippers coming from and going to church. Across the street to his left an old white Chevy convertible, its back seat overflowing with children, dogs and picnic baskets, had pulled up to the gas pumps.

Mario's temples throbbed. *Malato.* I am ill. I must find me *un gabinetto,* or I will vomit here in the public street. He turned back toward the hotel, but had no will to enter it. The Women's Exchange Thrift

Shop, grey clapboard with neat white trim, was just beyond Luigi's. He made his way there, with no other thought than that it would *certamente* be closed on a Sunday. Perhaps beyond it, out of sight, I can empty myself of whatever is poisoning me.

The shop was a few feet above street level, in what obviously had been a railroad station. Mario went up the wooden steps on unsteady legs. The reflection in the plateglass window seemed that of a distraught stranger. His sick eyes and mussed hair were superimposed on a display featuring a bentwood chair and a well-preserved bouffant petticoat very like one he had once bought for Oriana.

He saw now that only half of the station had been restored. The further end was of weathered and splintered wood fallen into decay. Through a misshapen doorframe he peered into the remnants of a waiting room. The ticket booth was still recognizable. Rows of metal supports showed where the benches had stood. Sections of the far wall were missing, admitting the blinding sunlight.

He went in, and found what had been the Men's Room. The toilet leaned askew, its tank top fallen beside it. He bent over it, and spewed forth a stream of burning bile. So did I vomit that day when I was a boy, when I ran down the stone stairs of my city, flight after flight, with the bitterness of *mia madre* burning my stomach and throat. And it came to him that now as then his physical distress was rooted in his mind and emotions. Guilt, Mario, and shame, he told himself. That is why I am ill.

Outside on the cracked sunbleached platform, in the broken shade of the ruined roof's overhang, a bench was still standing. He made his way to it, stepping wide over fissures in the concrete. He sat down on the three remaining slats and gazed blankly at the rank weeds of the disused roadbed.

You asked for my help, he told Terry Hapgood. *Solamente* to talk, to unburden your troubled *cuore*. I failed you and now you are dead. Whom have I not failed? *La madre* who bore me: Why did I not find time to make peace? *Il padre* who reared me, to whom I have never returned. Oriana, beloved, I failed thee again and again. And *Zio Massimo:* my solemn vows broken.

Thou, *mia Lucia.* Thou most of all.

His head in his hands, Mario hunched forward under the whiplash of self-castigation. *Ohimè, ohimè.* I have failed in my duty as well. I have gone below *la linea,* the line I set myself. Who said that, about the line. Royal Washington: Claudia quoted him. *Vecchio,* frustrated, suffering: yet he had clung to his honor.

I have taken the money, Beau Tyler, and what did I give in return? A few scraps of *informazione,* a handful of lies and tricks. Last night when you needed me, where was Mario then?

Confession and *penitenza,* he told himself. Nothing less will suffice. I cannot make amends to *i morti,* but I can to the living. The thought brought him relief. He rose and went waveringly to the thrift shop display window. *"Catarsi,"* he murmured to his transparent reflection. I will be purged, *purificato.* He wiped his brow with his handkerchief, then took out his pocket comb and tidied his hair.

Eh, *mia Lucia,* I must give back *i soldi,* the fifteen hundred. I must do that at once. Whether or not Thou wilt ever forgive me. He went back to the bench for his briefcase, then left the platform and walked behind Luigi's, avoiding Main Street. He moved in the general direction of the stationhouse through the Sabbath back streets of the town. Why should You forgive me? I do this for its own sake, *per onore e dignità.* And for Tyler, the good man who had faith in me.

Gardens poured forth their fragrance in the noonday sun. Baking odors mingled, and the savor of chicken dinners in progress. How *delizioso* it smells, Mario thought, but I am not hungry. A radio gave forth gospel music. A father and son were playing catch on a lawn. Mario crossed the street to avoid greeting them.

Chief Tyler, I will say to him, I have not merited your trust. *Io, Mario,* I led you to believe in *la mia potenza* when I had forfeited it.

A child sat on the porch steps two doors beyond, reading a Bible comic book. Mario recrossed the street, evading the gaze of two girls in Sunday dresses who sat in a porch swing.

I will pay back the money, Chief Tyler, one thousand tomorrow, the rest I will send from New York. Lauren must wait. Shall I tell him, Beau Tyler, why I did not join him last night? No. *Non é necessario.* No need to involve thee, Claudia *mia.*

He crossed the little bridge over the Flint River and turned right at the following corner. Main Street was just ahead. He saw no pedestrians. They are in *la chiesa* singing their hymns, he thought as he entered the Town Hall park, or have gone home to make dinner. He felt emptied and chastened, resolute and at peace.

"Hey, Mario!" Beau Tyler emerged from the stationhouse, hands outstretched in greeting. Mario gripped them, receiving a shock of energy. "I been watching for you."

"Bene. I must speak with you," Mario said. "Where can we be alone?"

"Come on over here," Tyler said, leading the way to a bench in the scant midday shade of a water oak. "Got a full house inside. Whole bunch of things you should know before you go in, like—"

Mario raised a hand to silence Tyler, thinking, *Alt!* First, *la mia confessione.* "Chief Tyler, I have cheated and tricked you. I resign from the case."

"How so? What are you, kidding?"

"For abusing your trust," Mario went on determinedly, "I beg your forgiveness. Which I do not deserve." How keen he is, Mario thought, how intent, scarcely seeming to take in my words. He does not appear weary, though he must have endured yet another white night. "I will repay the money, every cent."

"What in tarnation you talking about, buddy-ro? You solved it! Hadn't been for you, I'd never've figured it out."

"Figured what out?"

"Who killed them, of course. Terry. Roy, and Earl Langford." Tyler's excitement was highly contagious. "And Funderburk, yes. Old Ruthless too. I got him inside, can't nail him without your help."

Mario, deflated, bilked of his noble *mea culpa,* whirled through a bewildering mood change. *Meraviglioso! Ridicolo!* He was seized with a giddy impulse to laugh.

"Just wanted to tell you," Tyler was saying, "the others in there, we don't really need 'em. I called 'em all in for questioning, see, so's he wouldn't suspect." He jumped to his feet and pulled Mario upright. "Come on! You don't need me filling you in, you know it already." He propelled Mario to the front entrance. "Way ahead of me, aren't you. What the hell are you laughing at?"

The Town Hall clock was striking twelve. Each round stroke, it seemed to him, descended through the air outlined in light. Inside the police station the radiance was undiminished. Faces swam at him, respectful in greeting: Duane Potts at the switchboard. Floyd Bradshaw peering out from the back room with Otis beside him. In Tyler's office, Ruthann rose from beside the desk where she was taking a statement from Demetria Owens. The two women seemed to float past as he waved at them vaguely.

When he and Tyler were alone in the office, Mario gazed through the wall of the Interrogation Room. Lieutenant Abbot was in there, talking casually with Dr. Donlan. Nurse Flannery sat on a bench beside an athletic-looking young man wearing an ambulance driver's uniform. Lamar Cooke, Mario told himself. He did not know how he knew, but he knew.

"I hope it won't take too long," Nurse Flannery was saying.

Hopkins said, "I'm due back at Warren by two."

Mario sank onto the chair by the desk, and signaled to Tyler to turn off the sound.

"It isn't on," the police chief said.

Mario thought with sublime detachment, He has gone very pale. As from a distance, he heard Tyler whisper, "The wall window's not open."

Not the Interrogation Room, Mario saw in his onrush of vision, but *la cucina* in Royal Washington's house. Night, and the chintz curtains closed. His eyeballs pulsed in concert with his pounding heart. *La Lucia* had returned with all her sweetness, her clarity, her exaltation.

Terry Hapgood sat with his elbows on the table, his face in his hands. Dr. Donlan stood beside him, reading a letter which was still in the typewriter.

"Generous of you," Donlan was saying.

"How did you know I was here?"

"I knew. This was where you came, Terry lad. Where you always came."

Mario saw the chair beneath the noose.

"I can't do it," Terry groaned. "I thought I could. Haven't got what it takes."

"I'll help you." The doctor stripped off his surgical gloves, which were stained and torn. He took a fresh pair and a syringe from his pocket.

A few scattered images, and then *lo splendore* was gone. There was only the office, silent and prosaic, the wall blind, opaque, and Beaufort Tyler's awed blue gaze. Mario put his head on his arms on the desk, laughing and weeping.

"Mario! You okay?"

"*Ah, sì!* Oh, yes! I am well, very well!"

He jumped up, strode unseeing to the back and shut himself in the washroom. Again and again while he murmured thanksgivings, he plunged his face into his palms filled with cold water. He drank deeply, dried himself, and returned to Tyler.

He reported what he had witnessed in his trance. "There were odors as well. The smell of fear, of despair. And *una fragranza* as of a costly eau de cologne, which I have previously associated with this man."

"I think I smelled it, too," Tyler murmured as though to himself, "when I put Terry's car back in the shed." He was still very pale. His sober regard was a blend of disbelief and something approaching reverence. "You see anything else?"

"A pair of shoes. Laundered but stained. *Anche* torn gloves, the thin sort doctors use, spotted with some substance like tar. They were being cut into shreds with scissors."

"Pine tar," Tyler said. "Physical evidence, that's what I need. Something that'll stand up in court. D'you know where the shoes are?"

Mario sighed. "The shoes are with Mrs. Donlan."

"Anne-Marie!" Tyler shook his head uncomprehendingly.

"*Credo che* she borrowed them in all innocence."

"…And the shredded gloves?"

Mario shook his head. "We will locate them when we get his confession."

"You're ready to work," Tyler said. Mario nodded. "Did you see who-all's in there?"

Mario said their names. "I would prefer that he be alone. I may be distracted by the thoughts of the others."

"All right," Tyler said earnestly. "I'll send 'em off home... Arrest him? Hold on suspicion? What do you think? I don't have any evidence."

"*Non disturbate*. We will get more than we need."

"How should we do this?"

"You go in first. I will choose a good moment to join you."

Tyler went out, and returned immediately with a paper sack. "Coffee and ham biscuits. Ruthann sent Duane out for 'em."

"Floraville Lunch?" Mario lifted the lid of the styrofoam cup.

"Nothing else open on Sunday. But those should be safe. No, you go ahead, I had breakfast... Bear Sieburth called, Ruthann says he's on his way down."

"I am not hungry," Mario said. But the biscuit tasted surprisingly good, and the hot coffee was welcome.

"I talked to him earlier. They found Thalidomide in the bodies. All except Langford." Mario looked at him questioningly. "We got it from the suicide note, you'll see that soon's Bear gets here."

"Thalidomide!" Mario was astonished. "Isn't that a dangerous drug to have on hand?"

"Old Roy wasn't about to father any children. Nor, for that matter, was Terry Hapgood."

Tyler waved at the wall. "You need this open?"

Mario smiled. "Yes. At this point, it has to be open." He locked the door after Tyler. He did not immediately attend to the wall window, but sat eating and drinking. I must prepare to concentrate; wait until the others are gone. He finished both biscuits and looked in vain for a third.

He pressed the buttons to open the wall window and switch on the sound. Tyler was ushering Nurse Flannery out of the IR. Mario glimpsed Lamar Cooke and Dr. Hopkins just beyond her. "Sure want to thank y'all," Tyler was saying.

"And I?" Dr. Donlan asked mildly. **Why am I the only one not dismissed?**

He scents danger, Mario thought. Not alarmed yet, but uneasy. "I, too, have commitments, even on a Sunday."

"Just wanted to ask, Doctor, did Terry Hapgood have access to Thalidomide?"

A look of relief fleeted across Donlan's handsome florid face. **All's well,** he was thinking, **I covered it in the letter.** "Yes," he said. "It has some effects on the immune system. We use it in our brown lung studies." He sighed heavily. "Poor lad! Did the autopsy find it?"

All heart, are you not, Mario thought, *il virtuoso* carrying out your citizen's duty despite personal grief. I will go in now, he determined.

He closed the wall window and went into the reception area. Ruthann was not at her desk. *Bene,* he thought, as he knocked on the door of the Interrogation Room. This is not a moment for any thoughts except those of the charming *dottore.*

"Come on in, Mario," Tyler called. "Dr. Donlan and me, we were talking 'bout Thalidomide."

"Buongiorno, Dottore!"

"Good morning, Mr. Castigliani! An unexpected pleasure." Mario, shaking hands, was aware that Donlan was stifling an impulse to laugh. **If this is Beau's secret weapon,** he was thinking, **small's the need I have to worry.**

"Since you are a man of science," Mario said, smiling, "I forgive you your doubts of my psychic talents."

Donlan stared, disconcerted. **Did I say that aloud? Or did my face give me away?**

"No, *Signor Dottore.* I read it in your mind." Mario glanced at Tyler, who had put his hand over his mouth. He gave Mario a look of profound gratitude. "Thalidomide," Mario mused.

Tyler said quickly, "of course, it wouldn't show up in a regular tox screen. But it did in the extended. All four bodies."

"Four!" Donlan exclaimed. His ruddy skin had gone blotchy. A glaze masked his eyes.

"Rutherford Kendall, the old chief, remember him?" Tyler said. "Royal Washington. Poor Terry himself, of course." Dr. Donlan fumbled a box of cigarettes from his pocket. "Go 'head, Doctor, it's okay to smoke in here."

"…And the fourth?"

"Randy Funderburk," Tyler said gravely.

Saints preserve us! How could they know?

"I santi preserve us," Mario echoed. "How do they know?"

"This drug could serve to render a man unconscious? *Abbastanza* for purposes of mercy killing?"

Donlan gave his shoulders a little shake. His voice was unsteady: "Yes, if the correct amount were injected. It's hard to overdose on." *Careful here, Alan Jesse,* he was warning himself. *Don't fall for their tricks.*

"Be cautious," Mario said softly. "Do not be deceived by their chicanery."

Donlan seemed to shrivel. *He is shorter than I am,* Mario told himself. *He only appears tall, as I do on stage. By a conscious effort, which he cannot maintain now.* The dark blue eyes, eloquent, fascinated, were fixed on Mario's. *Rabbit and serpente,* Mario thought, with an irrational twinge of sympathy. *Questo uomo,* he reminded himself sternly, *had looked unmoved on the death agonies of Royal Washington.*

A rapid kaleidoscope of scenes came at him from Donlan's scurrying mind. Mario took the lion coin from his pocket, and shut it in his fist. His other hand went to his forehead, pressing the spot between his brows. The images swarmed even more swiftly. *I require an object to help me focus,* he thought, *una possesso personale.*

Tyler sat as though relaxed on the bench. Once again, Mario appreciated the police chief's talent for silence, for knowing when to wait.

"May I have one of your *Sobranies,* Doctor?" Mario reached for the iridescent box. Donlan stared at his cigarettes as though he had forgotten them. He handed a gold-tipped pink tube of tobacco to Mario, and placed a pale blue one between his own lips.

Mario closed his eyes. The Turkish tobacco was strong in his nostrils. He was in Donlan's mind, in the back of an ambulance, riding perched on the folded stretcher. Randy Funderburk pulled to a stop where the road overlooked a sharp drop.

"Brightcloud Leap," Mario said.

"Right close to Valhalla," said Tyler.

Now in the front seat. Donlan was saying, "Three hundred thousand, agreed. And you will leave town. You will never come back for more."

"A deal," Randy's voice said. "Drink on it." Mario saw his calloused hands take a Mason jar from the glove compartment.

He opened his eyes, and looked from Tyler to the hypnotized face of the doctor. "You contrived to put the drug into the whiskey," Mario told Donlan, "and only pretended to drink." The vision swam into new focus: the low distant mountains darker than the dark sky, the treetops below and the boulders illumined by the blazing ambulance. He asked, "How did you get home without your car?"

"Jogged home, I reckon," Tyler said. Mario caught a glimpse of Donlan in athletic underwear, a hospital uniform rolled in a strap on his back. "Valhalla was used to him jogging along, mornings and evenings. Laundry building's right there behind his house."

"May I have a light, sir?" Mario asked. The flame of the lighter wavered at the tip of Mario's cigarette, then moved shakily to Donlan's own.

"Stupid of me," said the doctor's almost unrecognizable voice. "I must have been wool-gathering."

Mario puffed but did not inhale. He was in a different vision now: inside a car moving through a carwash, the water sluicing down, the windshield and windows alive with rippling silvery light. Like being inside *una cascata,* he thought.

"White Mercedes Benz," he murmured to Tyler. "About eight o'clock, Friday night. The carwash on Main Street, near Diamond Jack's."

Tyler nodded. "We'll get Floyd to check it out."

Mario opened his eyes. The doctor had stubbed out his cigarette, and was nervously, thoughtlessly, emptying the remaining tobacco into the ashtray. He broke off the gold tip then, and rolled the paper into a tiny blue ball.

Mario appropriated the ashtray and put out his own cigarette. "Officer Bobby Lee has some identical gold tubes, *senza dubbio* with the filters still in them," he told Tyler. "In a tobacco tin."

"Picked 'em up outside Roy's back window, I reckon," Tyler said.

"*Sì.*" Mario envisioned the doctor in nurse's whites, as he parked the green Honda in front of the little old house. Then going to the yard, looking through the window at Roy Washington and Myrtle in the lighted kitchen, the grey head and the red one bent over the draft of the leaflet. "You had to wait, did you not," he told Donlan, "until *Signora* Collins had left." To Tyler he said, "He had to wait here also, in back of the stationhouse. He was smoking then, too."

"Thursday night," Tyler said. "Earl Langford. Wee hours Friday morning, really. We'll police the grounds, do some soil analyses."

329

Mario murmured, "*Credo che* I know *esattamente* where he stood."

"Might be some traces," Tyler said, "spite of the rain."

Dr. Donlan had risen. Out. Of. Here, he was thinking, I must get out of here. But he disciplined himself, and spoke with apparent composure: "Well, Beau, whatever this game is. Amusing! You play it remarkably well. One day you'll tell me no doubt how it's done. But now I must go." What can they prove, comes to that. Langford's dead, Randy's dead, no one else saw me.

"Not yet," Tyler said softly.

"Perhaps I can come back tomorrow. I'll look at my schedule." No Bible Belt jury'll convict on the word of a foreigner. A second-rate Italian showman.

Specialmente if you manipulate jury selection, eh, *Dottore*. "We are aware of your *potenza* and influence, Dr. Donlan. But do not count on it." It will not even be *necessario*, Mario thought, to put me on the stand.

"Got sufficient right now, A.J.," Tyler said, "to hold you. Suspicion of homicide. Want to get in touch with your lawyer?"

Panic, Mario read, quickly controlled. Then something gay and reckless rose in the doctor, evoking Terry's bright face as Mario had last seen it in the after-storm glow. A gambler, this doctor, Mario thought with unwilling admiration. He will try to bluff out his losing hand.

"Sure and I'll call him," Donlan said smoothly. "He's at Cherokee Springs. A pity to fetch him away from his Sunday golf, isn't it."

"Right this way," said Tyler. "You can use the phone in my office."

"The way I figure it," Tyler was saying, "Randy saw Donlan dressed like Terry, Wednesday night, driving the Honda away from Warren."

They were alone in the office. Mario's watch said two-fifteen. Donlan was now in the holding cell, having undergone almost two hours of sporadic questioning without breaking down.

"*Sì,* Funderburk recognized him. Then when the call came for *l'ambulanza*—"

"—he put two and two together. Or, look. Randy was Earl's cousin, y'know, or some kind of distant kinfolk."

"Earl witnessed Royal's murder," Mario speculated, "then ran away, looking for help."

"Yeah. Some food and a bed, and his bus fare. Funderburks, they'd have kicked him out."

"But not Randy."

"'Sit tight, I can get you off the hook,' he'd have said," Tyler improvised. "After Earl told what he'd seen. 'I could maybe promote you a chunk of cash, too.'"

"*Ah, sì,* Donlan is the Mystery Man."

Tyler block-printed "Wed. Aug. 8/90 *Roy*" on a yellow pad, and wrote under that "8-12 pm: Gary Lansing party." Mario rose and read over his shoulder. "8-9:30:" Tyler wrote, "Union meeting at Roy's." "Let's whup this into shape," he said. "We been working all over the map."

"*Molto bene,* write down what we know, then persuade the good doctor to fill in the gaps."

They exchanged a look of grim satisfaction. "Want some handwriting?" Tyler asked. He took a folder from his desk file. "Here's the original statements from Warren."

Mario selected those of Donlan, Terry and Randy. "I would like to see again *la lettera* Terry wrote to his mother."

Tyler produced it from the drawer, then left the room, returning almost immediately with a plastic bag containing Donlan's possessions. "Help yourself," he told Mario.

Mario took a grey silk tie with a faint pattern of coronets. "Countess Mara," he read aloud from the label. "This will do very well. Shall we construct our *cronologia* back there in the cell?"

"Why not," Tyler agreed, opening the door. "Save us some time."

Bear Sieburth had arrived when they returned to the office. "Hey, Beau," he said grinning. He got up from behind the desk and opened a folding chair. "Hey, Mario." **Knew you'd come through.**

The L.C. Smith typewriter was on the desk, Terry's suicide letter beside it. Evidence bags were piled near the window.

Tyler said, "Hey, Bear. Guess who we got in the lock-up."

"I already guessed." Tyler looked at him inquiringly. "That byssinosis research," Sieburth said. "Somehow it always stuck in my craw." **Just didn't fit in with Warren Memorial.**

"Incongruente," Mario said.

"Brown lung, that's stone blue collar," Sieburth went on. **Like a farmer grows orchids and turnips. Or a pet store sells peacocks and buzzards.** "Driving down today, I got to thinking: Man wears two hats. One high profile, one low."

"Sì, the medical director is also the mill owner," Mario said.

Tyler nodded. "Right handy for Pennington Mills to control a little brown lung research."

And *il direttore* is Pennington Mills, Mario thought. He remembered the violin voice in the kitchenette: Jeff. A turkey on a string. A.J. runs him.

"When you phoned about the letter," Sieburth said to Tyler, "we had a good look in the lab. Reid was right, two people typed it." **Signature's probably forged.** He went on, "So I got thinking, driving and thinking, whoever typed that page two—"

"—had to be the killer," Tyler finished for him. "I picked up on that too." He handed the letter to Mario who read it rapidly and said, tapping the signature, *"Sì,* Donlan wrote this. And *evidentemente* it was he with whom Terry was in love."

"That Bible class," Tyler said. "I had a mind to check out who'd been in it. Then I remembered, A.J. was the teacher."

Sieburth's eyes were on the letter in Mario's hands. **I'd sure give a lot to know how Hapgood himself would've finished it.**

Can I do this, *mia Lucia?* Mario wondered. He felt the affirming glow, and murmured. *"Grazie, mia bene fattrice, mia dea."* To Sieburth, he said, "Would you like me to type it out for you? The end of the suicide letter?"

Sieburth stared at him. **Who are you kidding, man!**

"But Terry never wrote it," Tyler exclaimed.

"As he would have written it," Mario said. "Don't look at me so, *amici!* My muse is *specialmente* generous today. I will need a possession of Terry's, something he had with him when Donlan came into the kitchen."

Sieburth went to one of the evidence bags. "His wristwatch?"

"Bene. But I do not touch type."

"I do," said Tyler. **That's a surprise,** Sieburth thought. "Learned it for college," the police chief went on. "Seemed more efficient, somehow.

Look, Bear, you go on in back."

"Okay. Pay a visit to the illustrious perp in the tank." He went to the door. "I'll bring up the subject of Rutherford Kendall."

"Good. We already got some of that," Tyler said, "but we can use more."

Should I play it good cop or bad cop, Sieburth was thinking.

Mario said, "Shall he act the kindly policeman or the stern one?"

Sieburth gave a gasp of incredulous laughter. "Mario! Cut it out, will you? Chrissakes, get out of my head!" He looked in the direction of Ruthann's desk and thought, **Swear jar.** As he closed the door behind him, he jangled the change in his pocket.

"We can all play good cop today," Tyler said, "thanks to you, Mario." He put a blank sheet of paper into the typewriter.

Mario held the watch, concentrating. Haltingly, he dictated:

```
- page 2 -
he was not exactly innocent blood. but he was a
human being too. nobody should have to go back
to jail who would choose being dead a thousand
times over.

okay, i write this in case the suicide theory
does not hold water. so nobody else should get
blamed for something i did. i will say my
goodbyes now. mother, please mom, dont take it
too hard. i love you. i do appreciate. i never
gave up on being a christian so remember we will
be together some day in heaven. if jesus for-
gives me for taking that money. i just know he
wont think anything else was a sin. goodbye to
the people who loved me who i couldnt love back,
not in a sexy way, that is, only like a sister.
goodbye to the wonderful guy who took me to bed
in new york, i hope he will understand why i had
to go on saying no after that. goodbye to aunt
eunice, cordene and tonda and odessa and all you
who took care of me and my mother. to mrs.
lisabeth kendall and all my patients, specially
the blue heaven folks, i hope they will get a
```

good nurse now i am gone.

 goodbye to the colors in the sky the way it
looks when the sun comes up, and to the flint
rushing along red in the springtime. the smell of
pine tar, and the smell of you, the fragrance of
your aftershave so subtle it gets into my dreams.

 goodbye to you.

    love to all,
    terry
    terence chatham hapgood, r.n.

They read it through. "Fucking bastard. A.J. Hope he fries," Tyler said. "Pull the switch with my own hands."

And Terry telling lies, even at the point of death, Mario thought, to protect his beloved *assassino*. He said, "The man who would write that, about the sunrise and the river, he was not yet ready to die. *A dispetto di* his despair."

Tyler said, "Got to show this to Fanny somehow. Terry's momma."

The watch lay warm and heavy, folded in Mario's hand. He lied also to me. *"Certo* he never left Lansing's party. Donlan told him..." He heard the doctor's light voice with its touch of Irish, acquired no doubt from his *padre* whom the Pennington clan had despised. Shanty Irish, Reid had called him. "Oh, come on to the party, Terry lad. I'll see to it Royal gets his shot. It's you after all are the true guest of honor."

"You think it was Lansing took Terry to bed in New York?"

"Yes. *Credo di sì."*

"When d'you think Terry twigged? That his big hero was a murderer."

"When he smelled *la fragranza,* the aftershave lotion, in his car."

Tyler said, "Y'see, I knew it couldn't be Terry. I just knew it, spite of the evidence, 'cause you gave us the profile, remember. Said the killer wasn't young, and Terry was young."

"Grazie, Chief Tyler, for believing in me," Mario said humbly. *Lucia, Lucia,* were you there all along? he wondered.

"You told us to look for somebody bent, not sexually normal. And

Donlan. Prettiest wife in the county, and hell, seems like he chose to have no sex life at all."

Mario nodded. "And no sex is surely the most *perversa* of *perversioni,*" he agreed. *I soldi,* the prestige and power, they provided him thrills enough. "His motives are wonderfully clear."

"Tell me about it. Good solid old-fashioned greed. Hundred percent. Plus covering his ass."

Sieburth came back.

"Got real pizzazz, Dr. A.J. Donlan," he said, plumping down on the folding chair, which protested his weight. "He's still full of piss and vinegar. Kendall, now, that one may be a mite tough to prove in a courtroom."

"Dunno," said Tyler. "If the jury's from hereabouts. Lot of folks never swallowed that the old bulldog'd give up 'count of cancer."

Mario said, "And there is the *modus operandi. Certamente* no one will think that a coincidence."

"Yeah, guess you're right," Sieburth said. "'Specially the Bible stuff." **Playful, ain't he. Cold as a Klondike cod. But plenty of flair.**

"Robbing the old folks at Jubilee," Tyler told Sieburth. "Doesn't admit to it yet. Falsified records. Mario'll worm it out of him."

"Listen, Beau, you want me to spell you?" Sieburth asked. "Catch a couple-three hours catnapping?" **Though he looks pretty good, for being up all night.**

"Nah. No way, Bear. I'm not tired."

Hyped on your own adrenalin, hey. "So how'd it go? Kendall's momma cried Thief, so he was sniffing around, investigating?"

Mario nodded, and Tyler said, "Found something, we reckon. Six-seven Jubilee patients. Enough so Donlan had to get rid of him."

"Another aspect," Mario said. "I received an impression he prescribes medicine to make them appear senile."

Let's leave that one lie, Sieburth was thinking. "Lot of those drugs they pump into geriatrics, they affect the mind. And the personality." He took the sheet of paper from the typewriter and read it.

Mario and Tyler pored over the yellow-pad chronology. "We need more on Thursday-Friday," Tyler said. "Like how did A.J. know Earl was in the holding cell?"

Sieburth put down the letter and said feelingly, "Why don't we all three go back there and gouge it out of the murdering sonuvabitch?"

"*Attendente,*" said Mario. "I almost can guess. He would probably insist on confronting the eyewitness. Earl Langford, that is. Randy Funderburk would have set up a rendezvous, no? At the hotel or near the hotel."

"Yeah. Then they saw us," Tyler said, "driving away with Earl in handcuffs."

Sounds right, Sieburth thought. "Funderburk split, you 'magine? But Donlan only pretended to. Then he came here." **Langford and Randy, they were already dead men. Soon as the blackmail began.**

"*Vero,*" said Mario, responding to the thought. "Donlan knew he must kill them. It was only *un problema* of when and how."

"What about Royal Washington?" Sieburth asked.

"Donlan was selling the mill," Tyler said, "not to the Japanese, that was a smokescreen. He was negotiating with Newcastle. Twenty-five, thirty million. Even Jeff didn't know."

Sieburth gave a whistle. "The big boys," he said.

"*Sì,* even I have heard of them," Mario said. "He could not afford even *un vestigio* of labor unrest."

Sieburth thought, **R. Jefferson Pennington, I bet he won't sell. Now that he'll be in the saddle at last.**

"*Vero,*" said Mario again. "He would be nothing without the mill."

"You mean Jeff?" Tyler asked. "I don't reckon he'd sell."

"Let's go on in back anyway," said Sieburth. He got to his feet, stretching his massive bulk. "Dig all we can out of him before his lawyer gets here." He smoothed his beard and hair. **Old Mario working him over, this I gotta see.**

Tyler took up the yellow pad and his tape recorder. "Got the tie?" he asked Mario. "And the statements? His lawyer can't make it here 'fore five-six o'clock."

"*A proposito,* I have been wanting to ask, do you know of an attorney for *Signora* Hicks?" Mario told them what he had learned in the hotel lobby that morning.

"We got a good country lawyer right here in town," Tyler said. He made a note on his desk pad. "I'll see to it."

"Where's Honest Jack?" Sieburth asked.

Mario flipped through the statements in the folder, pausing when he came that of Demetria Owens.

"Sprague's not going anywheres," Tyler was saying. "We don't have a single thing on him, he kept himself clean."

"What of Deacon Howard?" asked Mario. "Was he too at Royal Washington's house Wednesday night?"

Sieburth grinned. **More damn traffic there Wednesday than Highway 301.**

"Demetria told us he tried sneaking out, three in the a.m.," Tyler told Mario. "Sneakin' deacon, Roy called him, remember? I don't reckon he meant Roy any real harm."

"*Probabilmente* simply hoped to dissuade him from disinheriting *Signora* Candace," Mario said.

They went out of the office. Ruthann's sharp brown eyes questioned them, and Duane Potts swiveled round from the switchboard to regard them solemnly. Mario read in their thoughts their urgent need to know, far beyond mere curiosity. **Tell us, how 'bout it, Duane was thinking. What's going on? Ruthann: Let me help, I'll do anything. Please, Chief Tyler. Whatever I can.**

"Ruthann here's got the statement," Tyler was saying. "Demetria Owens?" he asked her.

"*Grazie, Signorina,*" Mario said as she handed it to him. He scanned it, stopping at the penultimate paragraph.

"The deacon was wearing his peejays and slippers," Demetria had stated. "Stepping out quiet-like to the porch. I says, Where you going, Deacon, this hour of the night. And he tells me, Just for a breath of air. Don't know why, but I felt kind of funny about it. So I says, Come on in the kitchen, let's have us a snack. Momma woke up, too. We sat at the table, talking about hellfire and heaven and all till the daybreak. After, when the cops and the ambulance come, when I found out Royal was dead, well. I was mighty glad I'd kept Deacon Howard inside."

Mario passed the statement to Sieburth, who read it, nodded, and returned it to Ruthann. **Wonder whether she was telling the truth.**

"She spoke *la verità,*" Mario assured him. "I read it in her signature."

"How 'bout those gloves," Sieburth asked as they went to the back. "The ones Donlan cut up."

"They're in a red medical waste bin at Warren," Tyler replied. "Mario

337

zeroed in on 'em. Floyd's picking them up."

In the back room, Vernon Bond sat at the middle desk, his plump body ramrod erect in the chair. "I'm watching him," he said without taking his eyes off the cell bars. **Like a hawk.**

Donlan was gracefully ensconced on the bunk. **Welcome once again, O, jailers and inquisitors!** he was thinking. He waved and displayed his perfect white teeth in a smile. **Bloody but unbowed you will find me, a tough nut to crack.**

Sieburth was thinking, **Can we get a confession?**

"In one hour at the most," Mario murmured as they entered the cell.

Alan Jesse Donlan, M.D. concluded his full confession at 4:18 p.m., beating Mario's estimate by several minutes.

Mario and Sieburth followed Tyler to Ruthann's desk. He gave her the tape recorder. "Drop everything else," the police chief told her, "and get this transcribed. I want it signed right away."

"But Chief Tyler," she said tremulously, "that's Dr. Donlan back there." **He taught our Bible class.** "I can't believe he would—"

"Killed five people," Sieburth assured her. "That is, five that we know of."

"It's all here," said Tyler, "victim by victim." He gave her the yellow pad. "Then I want you to type this up neat. Mario'll sit with you, he'll tell you anything more you need to put in."

Mario bowed, and she nodded at him uncertainly. Tyler went into his office and put into a folder the suicide letter and the page Mario had dictated. "I'm gonna drive to Valhalla, and show this to Fanny Hapgood," he said. "I'll be back right away. Bear, you get Duane to call Bonnie's, ask can she send us some dinner. Then give Andrew a buzz, tell him what's happening."

"I can pick up the grub," Sieburth said. "Should I call Reid Taliaferro, too?"

"Yeah, do that. He might want to join us." Tyler went to the door. "You two can get Donlan's john hancock. Mario, you and Ruthann work in here if you want. She seems to have softened up 'bout you considerable." He started out, then turned and came back. He gripped

Mario by the shoulders, his tired face warm with good feeling.

"We did it, hey, Mario," he muttered. "Now how about that."

"We did it," Sieburth echoed. There were fervent handshakes all round.

Once again, Mario tried to enter the police chief's mind and found it as impenetrable as granite. When he noticed Tyler's keen gaze, Mario modestly averted his mind, as another might have averted his eyes. Beneath the tumult and exhilaration, without any psychic powers at all, he discerned a strange guilt, regret for a cunning motive of which he did not think the other capable. Respect and annoyance struggled for supremacy within Mario as understanding flooded him: Tyler had appointed the psychic his assistant for sure, but the employment had also been a lure, to entice the credulous, elusive Claudia back into his own domain. And no doubt the wily young police chief had succeeded.

A wry smile tugged at the corners of Mario's mouth as he confirmed, "We have done it indeed."

XXIV

The walled town of Monte Turchino is ancient and sleepy against the dramatic background of the Brescian Alps. The village overlooks Lombardy's Val Camonica, with its tall poplars and sparkling lakes. On a fine day early in August, Mario arrived by bus from Milan. He stood near the fountain with his suitcases beside him in the little piazza. He had slimmed down during the past year, and in his new tan sports jacket looked trim and handsome, if a trifle travel-stained. Stone fishes poured forth arches of diamonded water under the sightless eyes of a bas relief Triton. The sun was hot and golden, the breeze fresh and pleasantly warm.

Most of the shops were shuttered, and there was no one on the benches. Mario's French watch, long since redeemed from the New York pawnbroker, said 2:05. The hour of siesta. I am very early, he thought. His father was driving here from Perugia with his partner; they had arranged to meet at the albergo restaurant at four o'clock. They planned then to ascend to the dig above the town, where *il professore* was at work.

The church with its stained glass and mellowed stone façade dominated the square. Mario, who had heard of its 17th century wood carvings of the Stations of the Cross, was tempted to enter. But he thought of the unopened bundle of mail he had picked up at the *fermo posta* in Milan, and went instead to the inn.

Il Agnello Turchino, the hanging sign said, with a picture of a gamboling turquoise lamb. The intimate reception lounge was furnished with chess tables and gilt-trimmed red wooden chairs. From the kitchen beyond, where strings of purple onions hung in an arched doorway, came mouthwatering odors of Lombardy cookery. Wide doors at the back of a dining-room gave on to a patio with tables and chairs. An old bronze clapper-bell hung in the entryway. Mario put down one suitcase and swung the bell gently. It gave forth a resonant tone, low in pitch and surprisingly loud.

Il proprietario, aproned, a wooden spoon in his hand, emerged from between the onion strings. "Welcome, Gentleman American," he said, in English, with a bow. He was middle-aged, moustached and red from his culinary labors.

"Io sono Italiano," Mario told him.

"Ah! Lombardo?"

"No, I grew up in Umbria, in Perugia." I vestiti and the luggage, the proprietor was thinking, are not Italian. "But I have lived many years in the United States," Mario added. He inquired about the rooms *il professore* had reserved.

"Two only," the innkeeper said. "We have other guests." For the archeologia, like you. "But the chambers are spacious, and can accommodate more than one."

"That's fine. We will manage very well."

Mario had committed himself to two years of work with the professor, except for a brief visit to Perugia at this summer's end. But Salvatore had been unable to wait that long.

"Would you like to go upstairs now, *Signor?"* the innkeeper asked. I hope he is not wanting *un pasto.* Too early for *pranzo* and too late for lunch.

"Thank you, no. I will wait for my father out there." Mario nodded toward the patio at the back. "I want only a glass of orzata, *per servirla.* We will order dinner later, in the evening." Mario took his bulky parcel of mail from one of the suitcases. "What shall I do with these?"

"Leave them just over there, sir. My son will carry them up when he awakens." Mio figlio l'indolente.

The patio had a sundial, and looked out on a vegetable garden and the flower-filled yards of little tile-roofed houses. Mario, seated comfortably in a ladderback chair with his glass of orzata before him, could see the balustrade of the descending stone staircase at the end of the street. In the distance the snow-topped mountains thrust up against the azure sky.

So here I am, *Lucia mia*. *Inanna*, as they called you in Sumer, *mia dea della fertilità*. I am keeping my promise, a quarter of a century late.

He had never before been this far north in Italy. He found himself comparing the breathtaking view before him, not with the gentler Umbria of his boyhood, but with more muted and melancholy vistas. Floraville, Georgia, where he had spent all of twelve days of his life, was on his mind: shabby clapboard houses, the low line of hills, the red clay of the Piedmont, wornout fields and scrub pines.

His memories were unblurred and undimmed, even after his year of intensive New York activity. The Bible Belt Murders, as the press dubbed them, had received national coverage. Mario's triumphant second performance had drawn an audience from all over the county. When he had bowed at the footlights in the highschool auditorium, the townspeople greeted him with a seven-minute standing ovation.

His role in bringing to justice the eminent doctor, who eventually received a life sentence without possibility of parole, was spectacular enough to reverse the downward trend of Mario's career.

With his penknife he cut the cord of the packet of mail. Last week's *Clarion,* and two back issues, wrapped around a letter from Reid Taliaferro. A postcard from Willie, with a view of the nighttime Los Angeles panorama.

Mario took a sip of orzata, savoring its almond flavor. He slid Willie's card under the newspapers. He may be back in New York by now. I will move out of *dall'appartamento*. He can share with another, or live there on his own. He is not a man to be *solitario*. I will be here there and everywhere with *il professore*.

Something stirred in Mario's chest, poignant and painful. Oriana, he thought. She is *la causa vera*. *Amatissima, mia perduta*. She is everywhere in the apartment, wherever I look, whatever I touch. As long as I remain there, I will live in the past, I will yearn for her.

He made himself turn his attention to a few letters some regarding theatrical opportunities, and an inquiry from a Connecticut commissioner of police. Would Mr. Castigliani be available to assist in an embezzlement case? *"Grazie* but no," Mario said aloud, "Mr. Castigliani will not be available." *Certamente* not this year or next. He found also a tailor's bill for the tan jacket and slacks he was wearing; an unabashed love letter from a wealthy admirer; two appeals from charitable organizations; and a letter from Lauren.

It was handwritten on her expensive stationery with its embossed female symbol. Even before he slit open the envelope, Mario was reassured by the thoughts he received from the neat superscription. Reluctant respect and a grudging affection had been in her mood when she wrote it. *"July 17. Dear Father, Just to say thank you for the money which arrived in good time."* He saw her at the carved, rosewood writing table in her tasteful, professionally decorated, Madison Avenue apartment. She was wearing a simple blue wrapper. Her hair was combed straight back from her forehead, and her broad face was innocent of makeup. This new style becomes her, Mario thought. She has mellowed this past year, my *fanciulletta.* She is more accepting of herself.

"My venture," the letter continued, *"is off to a promising start."* She had accepted a position as Chief Financial Officer for a new publishing house specializing in books giving business advice to women.

Archeology! she had thought. Will he never grow up, my father? Digging up old graves, in dirty work clothes, that's all it amounts to. No money in it. *"Write me when you have a chance."* At least it's not as disreputable as prancing around on a stage. *"Your daughter Lauren."*

Mario held the letter to his cheek for a moment. He laughed silently, ruefully, and put it back in its envelope. Which shall I read now, he asked himself, *i periodici* or Reid's letter. Would there be news of Claudia? He pressed a hand to his throat. He wanted yet feared to learn what had happened to her since their farewell kiss at the top of the studio stairs. He had not seen her again. During his remaining days in Floraville, she had absented herself from the town. Beaufort Tyler told him she had gone to stay a week with her brother, who lived adjacent to his restaurant forty miles away on the interstate highway. She had taken Anne-Marie Donlan with her.

Mario rose, postponing decision, and went to examine the sundial. "TVTTI FERISCONO. L'VLTIMA ASSASSINA," was carved round its rim. "They all wound. The last one kills." A riddle. He found the answer on the base: "LE ORE." "Hours."

He went back to the table and looked through *The Clarion,* thinking, *la lettera* will be for dessert. He read in no particular order, skipping the news of revivals and church socials, going back and forth from one issue to another in search of the items marked with a yellow highlighter.

He had included in the parcel an extra Sports Page, with a story dated December 7, 1990: "WILDCATS CLAW UP KISSIMEE COUGARS" over a photo of the grinning high school football team. "GILMORE DININGROOM TO REOPEN" brought a smile to Mario's lips. Ms. Florence Hicks, who had recently hired a manager, promised that the famous beat biscuit would be featured again.

Mario paused long at the obit page, saddened to read of the death of Elisabeth Kendall. He thought of his promise, never fulfilled, to visit her again. *Cara Signora, mi perdoni.* Mario looked at the sundial, then at his slender costly gold watch. Time, time! *Ah, sì,* Terry! Never enough.

Two issues contained items about A.J. Donlan: the crowds around the courthouse on the day of his sentencing; his transfer to a medium-security prison. The stories were short and did not appear on the front pages. Eh, Reid, even you must bow down to Valhalla!

Mario neatly refolded the newspapers. His eyes sought the mountaintops for a long moment. Then he opened Reid's letter.

```
July 11. Hey there, Mario!
    Don't know how I let near a year get away from
me, and I apologize for putting this letter off
until now. The money you sent for the boys got
here the week after you left. Phil picked out
the camera for Durrell, and yours truly selected
Scott's bicycle. They are both tickled pink.
    Hope the issues I send will be of interest.
Floraville still talks about you, you sure made
an impression. Come back any time, we'll regale
you in style.
    Here's a few more items to bring you up to
date with what goes on here. One of them's
pretty sad: Anne-Marie Donlan is at the Betty
Ford Clinic, undergoing what is politely known as
a nervous breakdown. On the cheerier side,
Lonnie McRae and Christine Collier celebrated
their nuptials last October.
    Beau Tyler just finished building a house on
his farm, and is planting soy beans. The big
```

news is that Andrew Abbot will definitely step into his shoes. Just who pulled what strings to accomplish this I can't say, but I suspect it was Claudia Pennington. She has separated from Jeff, and there's talk of divorce. I guess she twisted his arm one more time. Two more times, maybe: The mill folk got their union at last, and nobody was fired.

Claudia and Beau are seeing a lot of each other. He's an old flame of hers, as you may know, and the whole town knows he's always been crazy about her. Bonnie was pretty woebegone for a while. But she's one great woman, you can't keep her down. I sounded Gwen out about my chances with her momma. She tells me they would be a lot better if I gave up smoking. Funny thing, but that gives me pause. Much as I love and admire her, I know I can live without Bonnie. I've had to, lo, these many years. But can I live without cigars? I'm not sure.

Well, Mario, I'll sign off now. Have a hunch we'll meet again. Could be I'll catch your act in New York one day.

"Reid" was scrawled in green ink across the bottom of the page, giving Mario a glimpse of him, shirt-sleeved, suspendered, sitting at his cluttered desk and taking out a fresh cigar. Reid rolled it, sniffed it, and contemplated it for a moment, then he put it back in the cigar box where it languished for half a minute before he took it out again and lit it.

The shadows had lengthened across the patio. Four-thirty, said Mario's watch, and the sundial agreed. He bundled up his correspondence and went in search of the innkeeper.

"My father and his friend are late," he said, poking his head into the delicious smells of the kitchen. "I must join my colleague. Would you be so kind as to tell my father to await us here? Or, if he wishes to join us..."

Il proprietario sprinkled herbs into a huge casserole, and tasted the sauce. *Ancora un po' di vino.* "Certainly, sir. I will direct him. Would you like my son to drive you to the foot of the path?"

"No, I will enjoy the walk. What are you creating there?"

"Casconcelli alla bergamasca. And for dessert, *un gelato allo zabaglione caldo,* a specialty here."

"Ah! I look forward to dinner."

Spero che your American hamburgers have not ruined *il palato.* "I warn you, Signor, the climb from the road is very steep."

"That is good, it will sharpen the appetite."

Mario went up the worn stone stairs and found the room with his suitcases. It was simple and clean: a wide bed with a down quilt; a free-standing mahogany wardrobe; a small desk and two chairs. The casement was open, overlooking the town and the valley. He put the letters and newspapers into the desk drawer.

"Claudia, Claudia," he murmured aloud as he set out on his walk. Claudia-Oriana. Their images in his memory merged, overlapped. He walked unseeing through the streets of the town, and then along the road, in the grip of relentless nostalgia. When he arrived at the path leading upward, he shook himself, scowling. Stop it, Mario! he scolded. Enough! What am I, a moonstruck *giovane?* Think what awaits you above, think of Her, *la Lucia!*

The climb was indeed challenging. Mario arrived at the narrow cliff shelf panting and sweated. He saw the low cave of the dig, and *il professore* approaching.

They met and embraced. "I would know you anywhere," Mario said. Wiry and limber, the dark eyes eager in the thin weathered face.

"And I would know Mario." **After how many years? Thirty-odd!**

You are balder, *amico,* Mario thought, and *la barba* has gone grey. But outside of that ...

You anche are a bit grizzled. And un poco corpulento, my handsome ragazzo. I should not call you ragazzo.

"You should have seen me last year. I was even fatter."

"But come in the cave," the professor said. "Meet the team, we have three brilliant studenti." **I have so much to show you, Mario mio!**

"It goes well?"

"Meraviglioso. Astonishing." **And if la potenza is with you ...**

"Mio padre may come, I left word at the inn, *Professore.* I will wait out here for him." He made a wide gesture encompassing the magnificence surrounding them, above and below. *"Ecco,* all this! I have to get used to it."

Il professore nodded. **Pero what we are finding is quite as glorious in its way.** *"Bene, ogni cosa a suo tempo.* I will wait a while with you."

"You think he can make it up the path?"

"He was still *molto vigoroso* when I saw him last year."

"Guarda!" Mario pointed to a late model Fiat on the winding road below. "There he is!" The car came to a halt. A white-haired man in a travel-creased suit got out. The driver remained behind the wheel.

"Andiamo, we will go down and meet him," Mario said. His heart was beating fast, and his vision was blurred.

"No, wait." **He can do it.**

Mario's eyes cleared as the sturdy octogenarian made his way upward. Strong as an old tree. The hair *bianchi,* but thick as ever. And he climbs *la montagna* better than I did.

Salvatore achieved the ledge, and caught his breath. His gnarled hands tidied his hair and brushed the dust from his crumpled linen suit. He nodded at the two awaiting him, who regarded him mutely.

"Ah, Professore! A pleasure to see you again." He bowed toward Mario. *"Buongiorno, Signor.* I hope I do not interrupt your work. I am looking for Mario, my son Mario, he said he would meet me here."

"Papà. Sono io. Mario."

Cattivo, disubbediente, you called me that day, Mario thought as he and his father swayed, locked together. *Eh, Papà,* you hit me. Now he read in the old man's mind no hint of reproach for the decades apart, only forgiveness and love unstinting.

The professor had discreetly withdrawn toward the cave when the embrace came to an end. Mario's hands were on his father's shoulders. They were not yet able to meet each other's eyes.

"Eh, Mario! Nice view you got here."

In the valley below a solitary bird soared over the treetops, outlined in the gold of the afternoon sunlight.

"Vedi, Papà," Mario said. "A swallow."

ACKNOWLEDGEMENTS

The authors would like to pay tribute to Clyde Lynwood Sawyer's great grandfather, Robert Ernest Gobel, Police Chief, Kannapolis, North Carolina, 1910.

Bringing this novel to life required the insights of many people. The authors would like to thank the following people (in approximately chronological and geographical order) for their expertise, assistance and especially generous forbearance towards our torrents of questions:

John and Judy Lentini, Marietta, Georgia.

From Charlotte, North Carolina: Beth Ballentine, Joseph Stelluto, Carl Warren, John York and Robert DePiante (the latter two from Sawyer's *Charlotte Observer* days).

From Durham, North Carolina: Drs. Bob Schmitz and Amy Csorba and Dr. John Butts.

From New York, New York: Price Chatham, José Valdez, Horace Thomas, Jennifer Gordon, Richard Sieburth, Bruce Stevens, Stefanie Messina and Alan Arnold.

We'd also like to thank our long-time editor and friend, Michael Simpson, for initial wizardry with his editorial scalpel. And most especially, our companion and mentor, Norman Rosten, the late Poet Laureate of Brooklyn, whose passionate support of the project sustained us from conception to delivery.

Finally, we'd like to express our gratitude to Cynthia Webb and Melanie Kershaw. Their love and dedication to the printed word is unparalleled.

Other Memento Mori Mysteries

MAXIMUM INSECURITY
A Matty Madrid Mystery
by P. J. Grady

DIVE DEEP AND DEADLY
A Luanne Fogarty Mystery
by Glynn Marsh Alam